Rowe is a paranormal star!" ~J.R. Ward

Praise for Darkness Seduced

"[D]ark, edgy, sexy … sizzles on the page…sex with soul shattering connections that leave the reader a little breathless!...Darkness Seduced delivers tight plot lines, well written, witty and lyrical - Rowe lays down some seriously dark and sexy tracks. There is no doubt that this series will have a cult following. " ~ *Guilty Indulgence Book Club*

"I was absolutely enthralled by this book…heart stopping action fueled by dangerous passions and hunky, primal men…If you're looking for a book that will grab hold of you and not let go until it has been totally devoured, look no further than Darkness Seduced."~*When Pen Met Paper Reviews*

🝰🝰🝰

Praise for Darkness Surrendered

"Book three of the Order of the Blades series is…superbly original and excellent, yet the passion, struggle and the depth of emotion that Ana and Elijah face is so brutal, yet is also pretty awe inspiring. I was swept away by Stephanie's depth of character detail and emotion. I absolutely loved the roller-coaster that Stephanie, Ana and Elijah took me on." ~ *Becky Johnson, Bex 'n' Books!*

"Darkness Surrendered drew me so deeply into the story that I felt Ana and Elijah's emotions as if they were my own…they completely engulfed me in their story…Ingenious plot turns and edge of your seat suspense…make Darkness Surrendered one of the best novels I have read in years." ~*Tamara Hoffa, Sizzling Hot Book Reviews*

🝰🝰🝰

Praise for No Knight Needed

"No Knight Needed is m-a-g-i-c-a-l! Hands down, it is one of the best romances I have read. I can't wait till it comes out and I can tell the world about it." ~*Sharon Stogner, Love Romance Passion*

"No Knight Needed is contemporary romance at its best….There was not a moment that I wasn't completely engrossed in the novel, the story, the characters. I very audibly cheered for them and did not shed just one tear, nope, rather bucket fulls. My heart at times broke for them. The narrative and dialogue surrounding these 'tender' moments in particular were so beautifully crafted, poetic even; it was this that had me blubbering. And of course on the flip side of the heart-wrenching events, was the amazing, witty humour….If it's not obvious by now, then just to be clear, I love this book! I would most definitely and happily reread, which is an absolute first for me in this genre." ~*Becky Johnson, Bex 'N' Books*

"No Knight Needed is an amazing story of love and life…I literally laughed out loud, cried and cheered…. No Knight Needed is a must read and must re-read." ~*Jeanne Stone-Hunter, My Book Addiction Reviews*

Acknowledgements

Special thanks to my beta readers, who always work incredibly hard under tight deadlines to get my books read. I appreciate so much your willingness to tell me when something doesn't work! I treasure your help, and I couldn't do this without you. Hugs to you all!

There are so many to thank by name, more than I could count, but here are those who I want to called out specially for all they did to help this book come to life: Alencia Bates, Jean Bowden, Shell Bryce, Kelley Currey, Holly Collins, Ashley Cuesta, Christina Hernandez, Denise Fluhr, Sandi Foss, Valerie Glass, Heidi Hoffman, Jeanne Hunter, Rebecca Johnson, Dottie Jones, Janet Juengling-Snell, Deb Julienne, Bridget Koan, Felicia Low, Phyllis Marshall, D. Alexx Miller, Jodi Moore, Evelyn Newman, Judi Pflughoeft, Emily Recchia, Kasey Richardson, Karen Roma, Caryn Santee, Dana Simmons, Julie Simpson, Summer Steelman, Amanda Tamayo, Nicole Telhiard, Linda Watson, and Denise Whelan. And lastly, thank you to Pete Davis at Los Zombios for another fantastic cover, and for all his hard work on the technical side to make this book come to life, and for the most amazing website. Mom, you're the best. It means so much that you believe in me. I love you. Special thanks also to my amazing, beautiful, special daughter, who I love more than words could ever express. You are my world, sweet girl, in all ways.

▧▨▨▧

Dedication

For my big brother, the very best brother anyone could ever have, on any level, in every single day.

Love you, dude!

Darkness

Unleashed

The Order of the Blade

Book Seven

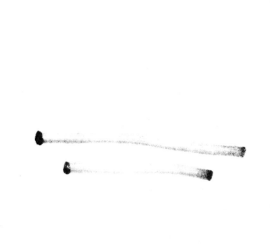

🐾 CHAPTER ONE 🐾

THE AIR WAS RAZOR-THIN. Oxygen was sparse. Vegetation had been cruelly stripped by the harsh winds that raked across the mountain, exposing raw rock, ice so thick it never melted, and earth that could not flourish in such brutal weather. What in hell's name was a woman doing traveling this mountain path alone? And what was her destination?

Grimly, Calydon warrior Ryland Samuels dropped to one knee. He traced his fingertips over the gritty surface of the rock. The cold numbed his fingers instantly, but it wasn't the biting wind that had tried to tear life from his hands. The damage had been caused by the residue of death that was coating the boulder.

The fragments of death indicated he was still on the trail of Catherine Taylor, the angel of death he'd been tracking for almost three weeks. "She's nearby," he said to his two teammates, who had accompanied him on his trek. "The trail is fresh." Staying on one knee, he braced his forearm on his thigh and searched the horizon. The Northern Cascade Mountains of southern Washington stretched far ahead, a seemingly endless maze that could hide—or kill—a woman with ease.

Except she couldn't hide from him.

He wouldn't allow it.

As for the mountains killing her with their brutality? He doubted it would be very easy for a few towering hills of rock, snow, and cold to kill an angel of death. He just didn't see her getting knocked down by freezing temperatures and a little bit of frostbite. It was more likely that the earth itself would kneel to her, cease all adverse weather, and submit to her safe passage.

He grinned. Yeah, angels were powerful shit, and he was about to find the one he'd been hunting for seven hundred years.

"You see her?" Thano Savakis, one of Ryland's Order of the Blade teammates, rode up beside him on his new horse, a massive magical beast he'd named Apollo. His dark hair was even shorter than it used to be, and his heavy black jacket covered his thighs, hiding straps that Ryland knew were there, holding his jean-clad legs to the saddle.

Thano was the only one of the Order less than five hundred years old. Although he hadn't even hit his fortieth birthday yet, he was a kickass warrior, and the one Ryland had specifically chosen to accompany him on this mission. The rest of the team was covering the seaboard of Oregon and Washington, dealing with a sudden increase in rogue Calydons, a proliferation that didn't make sense.

The Order of the Blade was an elite group of Calydon warriors whose mission was to protect innocents when Calydons went rogue, descending irretrievably into the state of violent insanity that would result in a swath of death and destruction that would end only when they were destroyed. The Order members were the only beings powerful enough to cut down a Calydon who had crossed that deadly line. Formed over two thousand years ago, the Order was comprised of the few warriors capable of surviving battles that no one should survive, while plunging their weapons through the hearts of men who had once been their friends, sons, neighbors, or even fathers or other family.

There were nine of them left. Only nine. Not enough. But Ryland was going to make damn sure they didn't lose any more, and that the Order was protected enough that it could begin to grow again and become the force it had once been. With the recent murder of their leader, the team had started to fracture. No leader had stepped up to pull them together. Ryland didn't give a shit about being a leader, but he was damn well going to make sure the Order's protective triumvirate of guardian angels was safe.

Catherine was the only one of the trinity still at large. After the other two had almost been killed, he wasn't taking any chances. The Order had too many enemies, and as one of their guardian angels, Catherine would inherit those enemies.

"No, I can't see her yet," Ryland answered Thano. "But soon." He gestured with his hand to indicate they should continue forward. He began to work his way down the steep slope, to a lower altitude where snow and ice had succumbed to the warmer temperatures. "Let's go."

"Wait." The third member of their party, Zach Roderick, halted them. He was standing on the top of a jagged rock, his face raised to the wind, as if he couldn't feel the cold, which Ryland knew was true. His calf-length leather jacket was flapping around his legs, revealing a white T-shirt and baggy jeans. His only concession to their trek through the mountains was a pair of heavy hiking boots, but Ryland knew those were more for traction than protection from the cold. "There's heat coming from over the northern peaks. Massive amounts of heat."

Ryland turned to look where Zach was pointing. He frowned at the dark storm clouds that seemed to be dumping snow onto the distant mountains. It was summer, but the mountains were still caught in the thrall of winter brutality at their highest altitudes. They were at a lower altitude right now, so they were graced with patches of bare ground instead of snowdrifts, but Zach was pointing toward a higher elevation. Nothing hot should be coming from there. "Heat? You're sure?"

Zach cast him a baleful glare. "You're asking me if I'm sure I feel heat? Really?"

"Shit." Of course Zach knew what he was talking about. The man had an up close and personal relationship with fire that none of them understood. If Zach had the inside scoop on why he could do what he did, he wasn't talking. But the guy could pick up heat from a thousand miles away, and he knew when things were out of balance.

Ryland ground his jaw, knowing that there was only one thing in this region that could generate heat of that nature, but it was buried deep below the earth, never to be exposed to earth's surface. Not *it. She.* "Keep an eye on it," he told Zach.

"As if I wouldn't." His voice edged with tension, Zach kept his attention focused on the distant mountains, on the heat that only he could sense.

Although Ryland had wanted only Thano with him, he'd allowed Zach to come because Thano had requested it. After being incarcerated and tortured by a black magic wizard for several months, Thano had returned with a broken body and the ability to do some weird shit with violet fire. Things were changing every day with him, and no one knew where things were leading. It made sense to bring a fire expert along just in case Thano suddenly went up in flames.

But Ryland and Zach had never been buddies, and he didn't like having someone along who was ready to cut him down at any moment, literally. Although everyone on the team was pretty damned certain that Ryland was on the edge of going rogue at any second, Zach was the one who Ryland sensed was actually looking forward to finally having a reason to take him out, ending the threat that they all felt he posed to the Order. If Ryland so much as drifted near the line of going rogue, Zach would kill him first and check facts later.

Not that Ryland blamed him. As annoying as it was to have to watch his back with Zach all the time, he knew that Zach was the only one who really saw him for what he was.

Not that he had time to spend thinking about Zach. Night would soon be falling and he wanted to have Catherine under his protection.

Yeah, he didn't think the mountains could hurt her, but he wanted her where he could keep her safe anyway. If she was who he thought she was, the safety of the entire Order depended on her survival. "Come on."

He began to jog down the side of the mountain. Behind him was the clatter of Apollo's hooves on the rocks, footsteps that could turn into complete stealth when the horse chose. Zach gave a grunt of irritation, but he leapt off the rock and broke into a steady run to catch up.

As the three warriors continued their slip-sliding descent down the rocky cliff, the sensation of death grew stronger. Ryland's adrenaline began to jack up, and a warning began to prickle at the back of his neck. The black brands on his arms that were in the shape of machetes began to burn, as the weapons strained to be released. Death was near. Was it Catherine?

"Is that her?" Thano was beside him now, Apollo loping with ease as Ryland sprinted along. "Is she the death we're picking up?"

Ryland glanced at Thano in surprise. "You can sense that?" The cold, ominous feeling of death was thick now, cloying to his skin. Prior to now, neither Thano nor Zach had been able to pick up Catherine's trail. He looked over at Zach, who had caught up to them. "What about you?"

Zach shoved a strand of his dark hair out of his face. "In about two seconds, I'm going to call out my weapon and start attacking the air, so yeah, I feel it."

Ryland swore. Up until now, he'd been the only one who could sense Catherine's aura, which meant either she had changed in some way, or else there was something else ahead of them casting the lethal scent into the air. He flexed his hands, readying to call out his weapons, as they continued to sprint down the mountain. Below them was a dark grove of trees that seemed to be defying all odds by surviving in this barren area. He frowned, studying the grove as they neared it. The darkness seemed to undulate between the trunks, as if it were a living creature, taking deep breaths, waiting for them.

Recognition nudged at the back of Ryland's mind, and he instinctively slowed. "Wait a second."

Thano reined in Apollo, and Zach slowed as well. "What's up?"

Ryland stared at the trees, straining to see into the darkness that was too impenetrable given that the sun hadn't set yet. "I don't know." But he'd seen it before. He knew what was hiding. He just couldn't remember. It had been too long.

He came to a complete stop, and his teammates lined up beside him, three warriors abreast.

Apollo lifted his head and flared his nostrils, the great black beast fixated on the grove. For a moment, there was complete silence, a standoff.

Then there was a scrabble of claws from a cliff to their right. Ryland spun that way, searching the rocks, but he saw nothing. Then, from the other direction, another scrape. Then, from behind them, another. "We're being hunted."

"By what?" Zach held out his arms. There was a loud crack, a flash of black light, and then he was holding a three-pronged steel sai in each hand, weapons that matched the black brands etched on his forearms. Every Order of the Blade warrior carried the marks of the weapon that had chosen him when he'd come into his power as a Calydon. Bred for violence, a Calydon warrior could call out his weapons at any moment, a simple mental summoning that made the steel weapons appear in his hands, instruments of death that were an exact match for the symbols etched on his arms.

Thano called out his halberds, the long hooked spears looking deadly as ever, with another crack and a flash of black light. "Maybe it's local wood elves inviting us to a night of drunken debauchery and singing. You know how those guys like to party." Apollo snorted, but didn't move, his gaze still fixed on the woods, as if he knew that's where the threat was coming from.

Ryland's weapons burned to be called out, but he didn't release them. Memories were pounding at his brain, struggling to surface. "I know what's after us."

"Well, then stop messing around and fill us in." Zach turned as there was another scrape, his sai up and ready.

Shit. What was it? Ryland could almost remember, almost connect with the memories from seven hundred years ago. "Give me a second—"

There was a guttural growl from deep in the woods, and suddenly something black streaked out of the woods right toward Zach. It was a misty, shadowy creature with claws and horns that were so faint they were barely visible. Ryland recognized it instantly. "Son of a bitch. It's a talrak!" What was it doing on the earth's surface? They never came out into the light. Ever.

Zach released a battle cry and swung for the beast.

"No!" Ryland shouted. "Don't fight it!"

But Zach jammed his sai into the creature as it lunged for him. His blade disappeared into the shadowed torso, and then the head of the creature became visible, taking shape from the misty outline of its body. Red glowing eyes. A scaled face. A horned nose.

"Zach!" Thano urged Apollo into a gallop as the talrak raked its claws over Zach's chest. He hurled his halberd into the creature, but the moment he did so, its shoulders became solid, taking true form.

"Don't fight it!" Ryland shouted. "You're feeding it!" He whirled around, frantically searching for something he could use against it. A Calydon weapon would never work. The talrak would absorb its violence, using the dark energy to make itself corporeal. If it became fully corporeal, they were in serious trouble. He needed something pure and selfless to kill it. Shit! What the hell would fit that bill up here?

"Catherine!" he shouted, knowing that an angel's touch would blast the creature into oblivion, but there was no answer from the woman he'd been tracking, the one who was supposed to protect them. They were on their own.

"I'm not going to let it kill Zach!" Disregarding Ryland's order not to engage, Thano plunged into the fray. With each blow, the talrak became more solid, and then it split into two creatures.

More shadows moved in the wooded grove, and Ryland realized an army was amassing in the trees...trees! That would do it!

Ryland swore and sprinted toward the grove...and away from the battle. Shutting out the bellows of his teammates and ignoring all his instincts that were screaming at him to rush to their aid and fight, he ruthlessly forced himself not to feel the agony of his teammates as the talraks tore at them, each strike stealing flesh and life force. He reached the trees, and then genuflected before the nearest one. "I thank you for your sacrifice," he said to the tree, forcing his mind to quiet.

He wiped his mind of all thoughts of anger and hatred toward the creatures. "My friends are good, and I take lives only in their defense." Offer made, he lunged to his feet and slammed his machete through the trunk the tree, dropping it in one violent stroke.

Ryland split the trunk lengthwise, three blows splintering it into a dozen wooden spears. He grabbed three of them and spun around. Zach was on his back, a vicious, snarling black wolf the size of an elephant pinning him to the earth. The massive creature bared his teeth, its twelve-inch claws deep in Zach's chest. Thano bellowed with fury and slammed his halberd into its side. The creature immediately swelled to twice its size. It turned its slavering head toward Thano, as the second one leapt on Thano's back. It howled its intent to kill him as Apollo shrieked in outrage, spinning around in a fruitless attempt to bite it and yank it away from his rider.

Ryland fisted one of the spears and took aim at the one on Zach. "I ask only for peace for my friends," he shouted, and then hurled the wooden spear that was still soft and flexible, brimming with the pure life of nature. The splintered sapling hit the talrak cleanly in the shoulder. It barely penetrated, and yet the moment it touched, the talrak let out a howl of agony and dissolved.

Bull's-eye.

Apollo let out a shrill squeal, and Ryland spun toward Thano, unleashing a second sapling at the creature on Thano's back. Again, a clean hit, and the talrak disappeared in a wail of agony. Ryland whirled to face the woods, and then hurled another into the darkness. Again and again, he threw saplings, cutting through the darkness with his crude spears. Each time his wooden spear split the darkness, there was a howl of agonized protest as another talrak fell victim to his blow. Seven times he unleashed his offerings, and with the seventh strike, there was a great, shuddering gasp as if the earth itself had exhaled with relief. The dark shadows in the grove vanished. All that remained were the trees, with the soft rays of the setting sun cutting through the foliage.

They were gone.

Ryland dropped the last of the saplings and whirled around, finally able to go to his team. Zach was on his back, gasping for air, and Thano was hunched over Apollo's neck, gripping his shoulder. "Did you get bitten?" he shouted at Thano as he ran toward Zach.

"No. Just clawed."

Ryland let out his breath in relief, but then swore when he saw the lacerations across Zach's chest. They weren't the six-fingered claw marks. They were the pockmarks of the bite of a thousand teeth, a bite designed to poison him, not tear his flesh apart. "Oh, shit." He crouched beside the fallen warrior. "Zach. Open your eyes."

His face was gray and ashen, his cheeks already sunken, his eyes closed. "What the hell were those things?"

"Talrak. Open your eyes, Zach." Ryland gripped his teammate's arm, dreading what he would see when Zach opened his eyes. *By all that is merciful on this earth, do not let his eyes be orange.* If his eyes were orange, it would be too late. He would have to use the last sapling on his own teammate.

With supreme effort, Zach opened his eyes. They were still brown. Relief shuddered through Ryland, and he grinned. "I knew you were a tough bastard." He looked over at Thano. "If his eyes turn orange, he's in trouble, but they're still brown."

Thano was gripping his shoulder, his face twisted in pain so great that even a Calydon warrior couldn't hide it. "Well, shit, then, let's have a party. I feel like champagne and line-dancing right now, don't you?"

"Yeah, you'd look cute in a denim skirt and cowboy boots," Ryland said as he turned his attention back to Zach. "Can you walk?" Zach might not have crossed over yet, but Ryland knew that they had only a short window to get him treatment. Since Thano had only been clawed, he had a couple days still. The healing sleep of the Calydons would not save either of them from talrak poison. "We gotta get going." There was only one thing that would counteract talrak venom, and he wasn't going to find it out here.

"Yeah, sure." With a force of will that was impressive, Zach hauled himself to his feet. His jaw was gritted, his face pinched, but he was up. "Want to tell me what's going on, Ry? What were those things, and how did you know how to kill them?"

"Talraks. They're vermin from the nether-realm. They never come out into the light, so I don't know why they were here." Ryland used his machete to make a few more spears, then handed a couple to each of his mates. "Anger and violence feed them. The only way to stop them is with purity."

Thano looked down at the supple sapling in his hand. "Nothing is more pure than nature. There is no evil in vegetation."

"Yeah, but you still have to fight the talrak without malice in your heart." Ryland grinned. "It's a good thing I don't like you guys that much, or I would have been too pissed to be able to calm myself enough to defeat them."

Zach frowned at him. "Without malice? Shit, Ry, that's all

you are."

Ryland shook his head as he picked up the last two spears and began heading down the hill. "Malice implies emotion. Violence doesn't. There's a difference." And he knew damn well what that difference was. Emotion was the death knell for a warrior. Cool, calculated violence was the key to victory.

Thano rode up beside him, looking at him thoughtfully, even as he gripped his shoulder. "You feel no humanity toward anyone," he observed. "That's why you could fight them. Because saving us wasn't personal."

"You heartless bastard," Zach said as he limped along beside Ryland, the wound on his chest already beginning to ooze a foul, brown-green viscous substance. "Is that true? You didn't care if we died?"

Ryland looked at him. "I never care, Zach. And I never will."

"You lie," said Thano softly. "You lie like a fucking rug, old man. I heard what you went through to rescue me from the wizard. A man doesn't do that if he doesn't care. You love us. Maybe it's time to admit it. Let's all do a group hug."

"No!" Ryland stopped and faced Thano. The younger warrior's green eyes were glinting with amusement that seemed to ignite a familiar, dark rage inside Ryland "I will never fucking care about anyone again," he snarled. "Not like that. *Not like that.*"

Thano met his gaze in challenge. "Then why did you save me from the wizard? Why do you risk yourself every day for the Order? Why do you mourn Dante every minute of every day? Why have you spent three weeks trekking through the mountains in search of a woman who might or might not be the key to the Order's salvation?"

Ryland stiffened at the mention of their deceased leader, the man who had given him the one thing, the only thing, he'd ever wanted. "I will defend Dante's legacy until the day I die. I owe him. That is all I live for. Dante is the reason for everything I do."

"Dante didn't believe in mindless battle." Zach was breathing heavily now, his lungs straining as the poison flowed through him. "He believed in doing the right thing because he cared about protecting innocents. That was his legacy, not a mindless adherence to the Order and to rules. You don't honor his legacy. You destroy it with words like that, words that support purposeless, mindless violence."

"No," Ryland snapped, unable to keep the anger out of his voice. "I honor it. Dante knows that. He knows."

"He's dead," Zach said. "He doesn't know anything."

Ryland looked toward the sky, and he knew Zach was wrong. Dante had spoken to him after he'd died. He'd been there when Ryland had been hunting for Thano. Somewhere in this existence, his spirit still lived, his eyes still saw, his legend still existed. But it wasn't enough. Without Dante to protect him, Ryland was losing his tenuous grip on the gift Dante had given him. He would fight for Dante's vision until he took his last breath, and that meant protecting his team. The fact it wasn't personal didn't mean he was any less driven. "We must keep moving. Zach doesn't have much time."

He started walking again, picking up the trail Catherine had left behind. They were only an hour or so behind her. They had time to catch up to her and still get Zach the help he needed. Both were critical to Dante's legacy, and Ryland would not rest until they were both accomplished. "Let's go."

There was a pause, and then Thano and Zach began to follow him. For a moment, no one spoke. Then Thano's voice broke the silence. "You said talraks are from the nether-realm."

"They are." Ryland paused to touch the dirt. The faint hint of death was there, and he nodded with satisfaction. Catherine would not escape him tonight.

"The nether-realm is the region between true darkness and earth," Thano observed. "It's pure darkness and evil."

"Sure is." Ryland shaded his eyes and saw they were approaching a valley. At the far end was a faint glow. Light? A village? Faint memories stirred in his mind, and he realized he knew that village. That was where he would find what he needed to heal Zach and Thano.

"So," Thano continued, his voice deceptively casual. "How do you know about a creature that lives in the nether-realm and doesn't ever come to the surface?"

Ryland looked over his shoulder at the warrior he'd spent so long searching for, the one member of his team that somehow seemed to ease the grip of darkness that was always hovering so closely. That's why he'd wanted Thano along. Not for his fighting. For the relief he gave him. "You really want to know?"

Thano grunted in annoyance. "No, it's just that you're so fun to chat with that I like to make up reasons for light-hearted conversation with you." He raised his brows. "Just in case I was unclear, that was a subtle use of sarcasm which actually meant, 'fuck yeah, I want to know.'"

Ryland met his gaze. "Because I was born there."

Thano's eyebrows shot up. "Born where? In the nether-realm?"

"What? You thought I was born in heaven with all the good guys? Easy mistake to make." Ryland kept walking. "And that was sarcasm as well, which meant 'you're annoying as hell with all the damn questions.'"

"But that means you're a demon, or some sort of cursed beast. That's all there is down there."

Ryland looked over his shoulder. "You think I'm a demon?"

Thano's forehead furrowed. "Shit, no, Ry. You're a lot of things, but you're not a demon."

Zach looked over at him. "Are you?"

Ryland didn't answer.

☼ CHAPTER TWO ☼

SHE NEEDED LIGHT. Fast. *Now.*

Her heart pounding, blackness flickering at the edges of her vision, Catherine Taylor clawed her way up the steep cliff, her mind screaming in desperate protest as the shadows of sunset began to lengthen. She lost her grip and slithered down twenty feet, the rock slicing the tips of her fingers as she tried to hang on.

She finally came to a stop on a narrow ledge barely wide enough for her feet. She jammed her hand into a crevice in the cliff and twisted it, locking it in the gap. She rested her cheek against the cold rock, trying to catch her breath. All of her muscles were shaking, her chest was aching, and her head was pounding. As for the cold? It had long ago penetrated all the way to the marrow of her bones, and the shivering had been taking its toll on her for hours.

Maybe she should just wait here and weather the night on the cliff, instead of risking her life for a last gleam of sunlight before the day vanished. Surely on this isolated stretch of the Northern Cascades, there was no one around she could murder during her sleep, right? It would be safe—

A faint roar caught her attention, a shout that sounded almost like her name. Instinctively, she jerked her head around and looked over her shoulder, searching through the fading light to see what had made the noise.

Movement caught her eye on a distant cliff, and agonizing disbelief coursed through her when she saw the three men who'd been following her. They were still on her trail? As much as she wanted to look away and resume her frantic pursuit of sunlight, once again she was mesmerized by the sight of the largest warrior as he stood tall and hurled a spear at the talrak she'd snuck past earlier.

As always, he was shrouded in a black aura that spoke of violence and darkness so thick that she could almost touch it, even from a distance. But there was something in the way he held himself that spoke of more, that reflected honor, courage, and bravery. Things that she had long since given up on. Who was he? Who were they?

She studied them, trying to make them out, but she couldn't discern their faces at all. Just three men and a huge black horse, appearing to regroup following the attack. What did they want from her? Why were they following her? She no longer believed it was a coincidence that the men were traveling the exact path she was. She'd tested it once, taking a nonsensical detour down a dead end.

They'd followed it, turning precisely where she had.

Not only were they clearly pursuing her, but they were also unerring in their ability to track her. She had been careful to leave no footprints, and yet they knew every step she took. How? They would be near by nightfall. Too near. She would hunt them if she slept, and she knew, without a doubt, that the first man she would target would be the tall one, the one who called to her so intensely.

She could not let herself kill him. Them. Anyone. "Dammit!" With a burst of frustrated adrenaline, Catherine dug the toes of her boots into the crevices on the cliff and started to climb again. In order to reach the last vestiges of sunlight drifting across the land, she had to get out of the shadows cast by the mountain she was on, for at least a few minutes. "Come on!" she urged herself, forcing her weary body higher.

Gritting her jaw, she willed herself upward, but when she got to the top, her path was blocked by a smooth ledge projecting out two feet past her head. "Are you kidding?" She stared up at the underside of the ledge, knowing that she didn't have the strength or skill to pull herself over it. The rocky edge was cast in a warm orange glow, a tease from the setting sun that was so close, but so out of reach.

Frantically, Catherine looked around. A small outcropping provided a good handhold, enough to support her. Willing strength into her trembling fingers, she gripped the cliff with one hand, and then leaned out toward the edge of the rock with her other hand, stretching toward the orange glow. A little farther. Almost there—

Finally, her fingers broke the plane of the setting sun. The warm rays kissed her skin and Catherine felt her whole body shudder with relief as the light touched her. Knowing she had only a few minutes until the rays drifted out of reach, she immediately closed her eyes and concentrated on the waning light.

She focused her mind on the brilliant, glowing particles dancing around the tips of her fingers and invited them into her body. The light responded at once to her command, flowing almost violently into her. She drank it in voraciously, spreading the light through her, sucking in every last bit she could. The air nearby began to darken as she pulled the brightness from it, but she didn't stop her harvest. More, more, more. She needed enough to last the night. "Come in, light," she whispered. "Replenish me."

And it came. Fiercely, like a tsunami of glowing beauty bending to her will. The brightness spread through her, gifting her with more time, with reserves that would protect her from the need that burned within her. Her hand began to glow a bright white as the light filled her. It began to creep along her arm, toward her heart—

The sun moved, cutting off the light before the glow had reached her heart. "No!" She stretched farther, trying to touch the rays, but she had no more distance to give. Frustrated, she gave up, swinging back toward the cliff and again grabbing hold, trapping herself once more in her spot in the shade. She closed her eyes, forcing the light toward her heart, her most vulnerable place, trying to shore herself up as much as possible.

It wasn't enough to keep the world safe while she slept, but if she stayed awake, she might make it through the night without doing more damage. It had to be enough. She had no more time to spend in pursuit of light.

She had to keep going.

Time was running out.

☒ ☒ ☒

THE NIGHT WAS DECAYING.

The sudden rush of death nearly knocked Ryland on his ass. He held up his hand, stopping his team as he searched the mountainside for more talraks, but there were no trees and no patches of darkness. Just the beautiful golden rays of a sunset that was too perfect to be wasted on someone as bitter and cynical as him.

Scanning with methodical precision, Ryland surveyed each section of land ahead of them, systematically dissecting the mountains until... "There!" He pointed to a patch of black mist surrounding a distant outcropping. It was at the very top of a wide mountain whose bulk had long since cast it in the afternoon shadows.

The dark cloud around the top of the mountain was unnatural, almost as if it were a void that had been sucked out of the sky. Then, as he watched, a small figure inched its way down from the cloud.

His body went on instant alert, and adrenaline rushed through him. It was Catherine. The woman he'd been tracking. He knew it without a doubt, even though he'd never actually seen her in person. She was miles away, but his preternatural vision easily picked up the curve of her hips, the litheness of her body as she worked her way down the steep decline. She was moving cautiously, a woman who was stretched beyond her limits, not a hardened climber with years of experience.

She slipped, and he instinctively leapt forward, his hands outstretched as if he could catch her even though she was far out of his reach. "No!" he shouted.

She caught herself, and then turned, as if she'd heard his voice. For a long moment, neither of them moved, and he felt himself falling into her stare, as if she could suck him in from miles away. "My angel," he whispered. "I'm coming for you. I will protect you."

The moment the words left his lips, she turned her back on him and double-timed her descent, as if she'd heard him and wanted to get the hell away from him. Ryland scowled as Thano rode up beside him. "That's her?" Thano asked. "The angel of death?"

"Sure is."

Thano was still gripping his injured shoulder. "She looks thrilled to see us tracking her."

Ryland shrugged. "No one is ever happy to see me." But as he watched the small figure reach the bottom of the cliff and start running along the base of the mountain toward the valley, he couldn't help but be a little annoyed by her obvious antipathy. He'd been calling to her for centuries, and yet her only response was to flee? Scowling, he watched as she reached the edge of a wooded area. She looked back at them one more time, then slipped between the trees and was gone.

The moment she disappeared, a fierce protest arose inside him, a need to bring her back, to restore the visual connection between them. Now that he'd seen her, the loss of her from his view roared through him like a great void, and he had to close his eyes to force himself back under control.

He had to stay focused. The Order needed her back, and it was time to retrieve her. "She's following the path we need to take," he said shortly. "We'll pick her up on the way."

He turned back toward his team and saw Zach was sitting

down, his back braced against a rock, his arms draped loosely over his knees. His face was ashen, and his breathing was becoming even more labored. Swearing, Ryland crouched in front of him. "Look at me," he commanded.

His teammate dragged a weary gaze to him. In the corner of his left eye was a dot of orange. Ryland fisted his hand in frustration.

"What is it?" Zach asked, his traditional distrust of Ryland fading under the strain of his battle to survive the poison coursing through him. "It's bad, isn't it?"

"Yeah. You gotta hold it off." Ryland swore under his breath, knowing that they were still a few hours away from the remote village... the village that Dante Sinclair, their deceased leader, had taken him to so long ago. He hadn't been back in this region since that day, and he'd vowed never to return.

To retrieve Catherine, however, he was coming dangerously close to the land that had taken so much from him. Instinctively, he rubbed his hand over his chest, over the binding mark that had held him in its grip so tightly for so long. Provided he didn't go past the village, he should be all right. But as he helped Zach to his feet, he couldn't help the ripple of tension that crept down his spine at the thought of getting that close to the hell that used to bind him.

He slung Zach's arm over his shoulder and supported his weight, well aware that he had no choice about whether to continue forward with the trek. Zach was dying. He was the only one who could save him, and Dante's Order needed Catherine. All he had to do was get Zach and Thano to the village, and then intercept Catherine before she made it past there. Then he could take all three of them back home and leave the land beyond untouched.

Simple. Easy. A done deal.

But when Zach stumbled and let out a curse of pain, Ryland had a grim suspicion that "simple and easy" wasn't the way it was going to go down.

<hr />

IT FELT LIKE HOURS later when Catherine finally reached the bottom of the mountain and slipped into the lush vegetation of the valley. Although the warmer air and rich scent of fertile growth was wonderful, there was no relief for her, not when she saw too many signs that people inhabited the area, people who would tempt her in the darkness. There were well-worn footpaths, a broken tool, and even a basket of fruit, as if someone had run off in the middle of picking apples. To the right was a family graveyard with a dozen or so headstones, including a large tomb in the middle that had been for the matriarch of the family. Fresh flowers sat on the nearest grave, telling her that someone still loved whoever was buried there. Whoever it was had been there recently, and would probably be back.

This was not good. She didn't want to be near people once the sun set, but the night was already taking hold of the land, already gnawing at her.

Her head was pounding again, the brief respite she'd received from the sunlight already fading. It hadn't been enough to sustain her. The physical strain she was putting on her body to traverse the rough terrain was drawing on her resources too much, and the light had served to give her the strength to take another step, climb another hill, not to ease the ominous approach of the danger inside her.

There was a crack, and a man shouted. Catherine froze at the sound. It had come from behind her. The men were closing in that quickly? She had to keep moving. Had to keep her attention on her goal.

An owl hooted, and it was answered by the screech of a bird she didn't recognize. It was a haunting sound, almost like that of a woman screaming. "Okay, stop imagining things." Catherine shifted her backpack and kept walking, even as she scanned the woods for people and kept looking behind her for the men who were following her—

She heard the sound of running water. For an instant she froze, too startled to react. Was it possible? Was the map really right? She closed her eyes and listened more carefully. It sounded like a waterfall. Dear God. *Please let this be the one I'm looking for.*

Adrenaline surged through her. She broke into a run, not even caring when her boots snapped branches or pine needles whipped across her face. She just ran toward the sound of tumbling water, her heart pounding as she prayed this was the waterfall she had been seeking.

She broke through the underbrush, and then stopped in awe when she saw the majestic cascade of water towering above her. The water was tumbling out of the air, as if the heavens themselves were pouring grace and mercy onto the earth. Smooth, white, polished rocks made the water dance as it splashed onto them, forming a pool of crystal clear liquid that seemed to sparkle even in the dim light of the moon.

Catherine quickly shrugged out of her backpack and dropped it on the damp earth. She opened the main compartment, and then unzipped the waterproof, interior pocket. She carefully removed the ancient piece of parchment that she'd sealed in a laminated cover. Her hands were shaking as she turned on her flashlight and set the map on the ground. She'd given all her savings to obtain it from a wizened old man who had sworn to its veracity. Etchings drawn by hand a thousand years ago seemed to shimmer on the paper, and she quickly translated the ancient words for the thousandth time. "Where water comes from heaven," she whispered. She looked up, flashing her light to the top of the waterfall just to be sure.

There were no rocks or earth that the water was coming from. Just air. "This has to be it," she whispered. She was so close! The next words on the map were ingrained in her memory, but she read them again, carefully, just to make sure she wasn't missing anything. "Nature grants a circle of six. Etched in stone, it points the way." Beside the drawing of the waterfall was a sketch of a cluster of six trees in a tight circle, as if they'd been planted that way intentionally.

Catherine quickly stood up and flashed the light around her. Trees were all around, but they all looked the same in the dark. She hurried to the edge of the clearing and began methodically walking the perimeter, searching for a cluster like the one on her map. "Circle of six," she muttered. "Nature grants a circle of six—"

Her skin prickled on the back of her neck, and she spun around, expecting someone to grab her. Nothing was there, but there was violence tainting the air now. Fierce, ruthless violence twisting the particles with deadly intent. She recognized it immediately as belonging to the leader of the men who'd been following her. She'd caught his aura a few times, but never had she been close enough to read him so clearly. He was more than dangerous. More than deadly. More than evil. And he was almost upon her.

Suddenly, she stopped fearing for the lives of the men who were after her, and became afraid for herself. What was he? She didn't have time to find out. She lunged for her backpack, shoved the map inside and threw it over her shoulder. She sprinted for the trees and dove behind a bush for cover. She hunched down, hiding as low as she could as she tried to think of a way to get away from him. How was he finding her so easily? How did he know where she was going? Violence prickled to her right, and she quickly turned her head, trying to peer through the woods in that direction. A thick tree trunk blocked her way, and she leaned forward trying to see around it, only to discover another one was tucked up tight against it, also blocking her view. Weird that two trees would grow so tightly against each other—

Realization rushed through her. It couldn't be a coincidence that two trees were so close together, could it? Catherine crept over to the cluster of trees, and her heart caught when she saw that there was a third tree, and a fourth, and two more, all of them growing in a tight circle. "Oh my God," she whispered. "This is it!" The trees had grown so close together she could barely squeeze between them, and she had to leave her pack behind.

Once inside the circle, she flashed her light, searching for the stone that was the final marker.

But all she saw was a hole in the ground where a stone used to be.

Someone had stolen the marker.

"Oh no." Disbelief plunged through her and she went down to her knees, staring in horror at the empty place that was supposed to tell her how to find her daughter. "How can it be gone?"

But it was. The earth was dried out and cracked, as if the stone had been gone for a very long time. "No!" She plunged her hands into the dirt, trying to drag the earth aside, as if she could force the stone to appear. The earth was so hard there was no way she could shift it. It had been long deprived of the piece that would grant her the path to save her child.

It became too much. Catherine sagged back against a tree and buried her face in her hands as years of toil crushed down on her. Two and a half agonizing years of searching for her daughter. This had been her last chance. The only way to find her. She was out of time to try to uncover and pursue yet another path.

Tears bled from her eyes, anguish poured from her chest. After so many excruciating moments of trying to summon hope, of trying to find the strength to renew her search after another failure, it all felt like too much. What else was there? She had no more ideas. "No!" She screamed her rage and slammed her fist against the tree. Dear God, how could the stone be *gone?*

As overwhelming as the grief and despair was, a familiar urgency was building inside her, warning her that she had to take action. She was out of time to linger here agonizing over the loss of her daughter. There were too many people around. Too many people to tempt her soul. With the men hunting her, and the people who obviously lived nearby, there would be no way to contain herself tonight, not when such hopelessness was bearing down on her so fiercely.

Tonight, if she hunted, she would die, and when that happened, there would be no one left to save her daughter from a hell beyond words. She had to survive. She had to keep herself from hunting. "Dammit, no!" Tears blurring her vision, Catherine lunged to her feet and shoved her way between the trees. She grabbed her backpack, tore open the zipper and plunged her hand into the bottom, into the depths where she had hidden it.

Her fingers brushed against the gray velvet pouch, and she pulled it out. Her hand trembling, she hastily unzipped it and removed the silver locket that she'd kept protected inside her bag. Preserved within was all she had left of her baby girl, the tuft of hair that she'd been holding while she'd been giving Lucy her first haircut, that moment when the man she'd once trusted had charged into her house and stolen her little girl.

No, not a man.

A creature beyond comprehension. A beast from beyond. A demon-wraith who had taken Lucy to the realm between death and life, where evil fermented and torture thrived.

Catherine clutched the locket in her fist, closing her eyes as she reached for the love that had kept her going for so long. Only her love for Lucy seemed to be strong enough to sustain her through dark nights when she'd gone too long without light. "I love you, baby girl," she whispered. "I won't abandon you, I promise. I will find a way."

In her mind, she heard the words that had tormented her for so long. Lucy's frightened cry when her father, Simon, had yanked her away from Catherine. Her innocent entreaty, begging Catherine to save her from this man. Catherine would never forget Lucy's little arms extending back over Simon's shoulder toward Catherine, trying to reach her mama, not understanding why her mother was lying on the ground, her body broken, helpless to do anything but scream in protest and watch that bastard steal her daughter.

Mama. Mama. Mama. The desperate call beat at her, punishing her, begging her to help, and once again, she was consumed with a feeling of helplessness and failure so debilitating it was like a raging void closing down on her, suffocating her, killing her—

A loud crack burst through the memory, jerking Catherine back to the present. Violence leached over her skin, and she knew her pursuers were almost upon her. Her daughter's terrified cry still echoing in her brain, Catherine leapt to her feet. "I will find a way," she promised, as she grabbed her backpack. "I swear it, Lucy."

Frantic, she spun around, trying to figure out where to hide. How had he found her? She could detect his scent now, a rough, rich mix of strength and male. The others faded, until there was only one man assaulting her senses. He smelled of violence and ruthlessness, regret and… death. Death! He was tracking her through *death*! That's how he was finding her!

Catherine whirled around and charged through the trees, circling back the way she'd come. She was crashing loudly through the woods, but she didn't care. She knew he wasn't tracking her by sound.

"Catherine!" he shouted, his voice bursting over her like a thunderstorm on a turbulent August night. It rolled through her, echoing in her chest, making her body vibrate in response. His call was so powerful that she stumbled, consumed by a need to go back to him, to turn herself over to him.

Good God. What was he doing to her? How did he know her name? She shook him off and ran harder. She could feel the thudding of the earth behind her, the wind whizzing past her as she struggled to outrun him. It became a flat out race, like an ancient sprint through coliseums, with death as the only way out. She pushed her weary body harder, knowing she had only one chance to elude him. He was close behind her now, a few yards. She could feel the weight of his presence, his intent, his focus, his all-consuming obsession with *her*.

Then she saw it. Up ahead. The graveyard she'd passed earlier. The spirits would hide her, even from him. She put on another burst of speed. Only a few more feet. She broke the perimeter of the graveyard just as she felt his fingers brush against her backpack. The spirits rose up to meet her, and she welcomed them, sweeping them over her like a great cloak of invisibility. Her identity disappeared, entangled in all the other deaths, spirits woven together in a tapestry of concealment. As a thousand years of death enveloped her, shrouding her from the view of the earth-bound, she looked over her shoulder at him, unable to resist the urge to see who it was that wanted her so badly.

His eyes met hers. Black, deathly turbulent homes of such horror that she almost screamed. For a split second, she forgot to breathe, so overwhelmed by the magnitude of his presence. His dark hair was cropped tight against his head, as if he wanted it out of his way. Blue jeans sat low on his narrow hips, and his heavy leather jacket showed shoulders so wide it was as if he were twice a man. He was sheer, raw power, but it was a dark energy, just like the man who had stolen her child. Dear God, what did he want with her? Fear tore through her and she leapt back as he lunged for where she'd just been standing.

He sailed past her, his hands grasping only air.

He skidded to a stop and spun around, searching the night for her, but she knew he would never find her, not while she was shrouded in all the deaths that masked her trail. She was undetectable to him.

"Catherine," he bellowed in frustration, spinning around as he searched fruitlessly for the woman standing right in front of him.

But it was too late for him.

She'd won this round. But as she fisted the locket with her daughter's hair, she knew the triumph meant nothing if she couldn't find her daughter.

🜲 CHAPTER THREE 🜲

RYLAND SPUN AROUND, engaging all his preternatural senses as he searched the graveyard for Catherine. He knew she had to be close. He'd touched her backpack just before she'd vanished right in front of him.

"Catherine!" he shouted again. He'd been so close. Where the hell was she? All he could sense were the deaths of all the people in the graveyard. Women, children, old men, young men, good people, scum who had taken their demented values to the grave with them. The spirits were thick and heavy in the graveyard, souls that had not moved on to their place of rest.

They circled him, trying to penetrate his barriers, seeking asylum in the creature that would be their doom. "No," he said to them. "I'm not your savior." Not by a long shot. He was about as far from their savior as it was possible to be.

Dismissing them, Ryland focused more directly on Catherine, opening his senses to the night, but as much as he tried to concentrate, he couldn't keep the vision of her out of his head. He'd finally seen her up close. She'd been mere inches away, the angel who had filled his thoughts for so long. Her hair was gold. *Gold.* It must have been tucked up under a hat when he'd seen her before, but now? It was unlike anything he'd ever seen before. He'd been riveted by the sight of it streaming behind her as she ran, the golden highlights glistening in the dark as if she'd been lit from within.

Her gait had been smooth and agile, but he'd sensed the sheer effort she'd had to expend during the run. Another few feet, and he would have caught up to her easily, but she'd sensed him while he'd still been a quarter mile away, giving her a head start that had enabled her to reach the graveyard first.

Shit. He had to focus and find her. Summoning his rigid control to hone in on his task, Ryland crouched down and placed his hand on the dirt path where he'd last seen her. The ground was humming with the energy of death, but again, he couldn't untangle her trail from all the others. He realized that she'd mingled her own scent of death with those of all the other spirits, making it impossible for him to track her. He grinned as he rested his forearm on his quad and surveyed the small cemetery. "I'm impressed," he said aloud. "You're good."

There was no response, but he had the distinct sensation that she was watching him.

Slowly, he rose to his feet. "My name is Ryland Samuels," he said. "I'm a member of the Order of the Blade, the group of warriors that you protect. I'm here to offer you my protection and bring you into our safekeeping."

Again, there was no answer, but suddenly threaded through the tendrils of death was the cold filament of fear. Not just a superficial apprehension, but the kind of deep, penetrating fear that would bring a person to their knees and render them powerless. Fear of him? Or of the fact he said he wanted to take her with him? Swearing, Ryland turned in a slow circle, searching for where she might be. "There's no need to be afraid of me. I would never hurt an angel."

The fear thickened, like the thorns of a dying rose pricking his skin.

Ryland moved slowly toward the far corner, and smiled when he felt the terror grow stronger. She might be able to hide death, but there was no cover for the terror that was hers alone. He was clearly getting closer to her. "Look into my eyes," he said softly. "I don't hurt angels."

There was a whisper of a sound behind him, and he felt the cold drift of fingers across his back. *She was touching him.* He froze, not daring to turn around, even though his heartbeat had suddenly accelerated a thousand-fold. Her touch was so faint, almost as if it were her spirit that was examining him, not her own flesh. Was she merely invisible right now, or had she abandoned her physical existence completely and traveled to some spiritual plane? He had no idea what she was capable of. All he knew was that he felt like he never wanted to move away from this spot, not as long as she was touching him. He wanted to stay right where he was and never break the connection.

He closed his eyes, breathing in the sensation of her touch as her fingers traced down his arm, over his jacket. What was she looking for? Was she reading his aura? Searching for the truth of his claim that he would not hurt her? She would get nowhere trying to get a read on him. He never allowed anyone to see who he truly was, not even an angel of death.

But even as he thought it, he made no move to resist, his pulse quickening in anticipation as her touch trailed toward his bare hand. Would she brush her fingers over his skin? Would he feel the touch of an angel for the first time in a thousand years? He felt his soul begin to strain, reaching for this gift only she could give him.

He tracked every inch of movement as her hand moved lower toward his bare skin. Past his elbow. To the cuff of his sleeve. Then he felt it. Her fingers on the back of his hand. His flesh seemed to ignite under her touch. A wave of angelic serenity and beauty cascaded through his soul, like a deep inhale of intense relief easing a thousand years of tension from his lungs.

At the same time, there was a dangerous undercurrent beneath the beauty, a darkness that he recognized as death. A thousand souls seemed to dance through his mind, spirits lodged in the depths of her existence. Her emotions flooded him. Fear. Regret. Determination. Love. A sense of being trapped.

Trapped? He understood that one well. Far too well. Instinctively, he flipped his hand over, wrapping his fingers around hers, not to trap her, but to offer her his protection from a hell that still drove every choice he made.

He heard her suck in her breath, and she went still, but she didn't pull away from him. Her hand was cold. Her fingers were small and delicate, like fragile blossoms that would disintegrate under a stiff breeze. A hand that needed support and help.

Ryland snapped his eyes open but there was no one standing in front of him. He looked down and could see only his own hand, folded around air. He couldn't see her, but she was there, her hand in his, not pulling away. "Show yourself to me," he said. "I won't hurt you."

Her hand jerked back, and a sense of loss assailed him as he lost his grip on her. "No!" He reached for her, but his hands just drifted through air. "Catherine," he urged, as he strained to get a sense of her. "I—"

"Ry."

Ryland spun around at the sound of Thano's strained voice. His teammate was a hundred yards back, hunched low over Apollo's neck. On his knees beside them was Zach, who was slumped against a tree. "Shit!" He bolted out of the graveyard and sprinted over to the others. He knelt beside Zach. The warrior looked up, and Ryland saw that the edges of both eyes had a faint orange glow. The discoloration was creeping inward, and Ryland knew that when it took over the entire iris, Zach would die and become a talrak.

Quickly he ripped off his heavy jacket and handed it to Zach. "Put this on."

"Fuck that, I don't get cold."

"The talrak venom is poisoning you. You can use all that fire inside you to burn it up and hopefully slow it down, but if you're expending energy toward keeping warm, you'll lose the battle sooner. Wear the damn coat."

Zach met his gaze, then swore and grabbed the coat.

As he wrapped it around him, Ryland looked up at Thano. "Got space on that horse of yours?"

Zach snorted. "I'm not riding that thing—"

Apollo stomped his foot and swished his tail angrily.

"We need to move fast," Ryland said. "Faster than I'm going to let you push yourself." He looked up at Thano. "Yeah?"

Thano looked at the horse, who snorted and bobbed his head. "Yeah, it's cool with Apollo."

Ryland didn't waste time asking Thano why he was asking permission from a horse. He simply picked up the dying warrior while Apollo went down on one knee, lowering his massive body. Knowing he didn't have time to honor Zach's protests to stay on his own feet, Ryland set him astride in front of Thano, ignoring his muttered resistance. The younger warrior locked a weary grip around Zach's waist.

Ryland realized that Thano looked almost as weak as Zach. Adrenaline flooded him, an urgency to get his team to safety. "You think you can hold him in place?"

"Shit, yeah. Youth is a powerful thing, old man. You forget that sometimes."

Ryland laughed grimly as Apollo stood back up, his well-muscled frame towering above Ryland. They had to hurry. But what about Catherine? Without her, the Order was in trouble. Shit! He quickly assessed his options and came up with the only plan he had time for. He reached out with his mind to Thano. *Catherine is hiding in the graveyard. I need to trick her into going to the village so I can grab her there. Follow my lead.*

Thano raised his eyes. *Deception? I love it. Bring it on.*

Ryland nodded, then put on a serious expression. "We have to stay here and find Catherine," he announced, even as his instincts were shouting at him to get his teammates to safety immediately. One minute. That's all it would take to get the ball rolling to make sure Catherine stayed safe while he handled his team. "I know she's in the graveyard." *Tell me that Zach's dying and we need to get the hell out of here. Suggest the village to the north. We need to set her up to go there, so we can deal with her after we get you guys fixed. We need her to think we won't be headed there, so she'll decide that is the only place she can go to escape us.*

Thano winked, then his face darkened. "You want to stay here and search for her? Fuck the girl, asshole. Zach's dying from the talrak bite. He's our priority, not some woman who we don't even know for sure is the one we're looking for." *Is he really dying?*

Not if we can get to the village in time to get the antivenom. "We've been hunting her for three weeks," Ryland snapped, allowing his true frustration to show. "We're so close. Another day—"

Thano called out his halberd and had it at Ryland's throat. Despite the weakness of his body, his grip was firm, his weapon steady. "Shut the fuck up, asshole. This is about Zach. We're going to that village up ahead to the north, and we're going to get help. You can hunt the woman after we save Zach." *Shit man, this is great. I've been wanting to pull a weapon on you for years. Can I stab you, too?* He pushed the tip of the halberd against Ryland's throat, pricking the skin.

You're a pain in the ass. But Ryland was amused by the irony that the most easy-going guy in the Order was playing the asshole. Thano was actually pretty convincing, which was a little weird. Thano wasn't supposed to have that element to him.

Ryland called out his machete, but before he could level it at Thano in what he hoped was a convincing show of men being stupid-ass men, Zach swore.

"No. Thano's wrong. You're both wrong." Zach stirred, and with a flash of black light and a crack that split the night, he called out his sai and leveled it at Ryland's heart. His eyes were still at half-mast, but Ryland felt the press of his mind as he joined their conversation. *I couldn't miss out on the chance to call a weapon on Ryland. Why should Thano get all the fun?* "Fuck the village," he snarled. "Too many people there know Ryland. We can't risk it. We're turning back, and we're doing it now."

Ryland narrowed his eyes, well aware that Zach's hostility was not completely faked, and that both warriors were too damned pleased to be holding him at the end of their blades. But he made a show of lowering his machete, even though his natural reaction was to take their threat and turn it on them. He wasn't a man who stood down for anyone, and that included a couple of arrogant bastards like them. But he wasn't going to let anyone die on his watch, and this was the only way to do it. "You both are complete bastards," he snapped.

"I'll take that as a compliment coming from the king of the bastards." Zach flicked his sai. "Turn around, asshole. We're going home, and since you're the only one who knows about this talrak shit, you're coming with us. I haven't survived five hundred years of battle to die today. Move it."

Thano's eyes glittered with amusement, and he poked his weapon further into Ryland's neck. "Yeah, start skipping along, old guy. Get your saggy old ass back on that trail."

Ryland narrowed his eyes. *You bastards are enjoying this way too much.*

Thano grinned. *Of course we are. The other guys are going to be so jealous when we tell them what we got to do. Come on, finish it out, Ry. Bow to our greatness.*

Zach snorted, and there was no mistaking the pleasure he was getting out of holding a weapon on Ryland.

He glared at them both, and then nodded his acquiescence. "Zach comes first," he agreed, making a show of frustration. "Let's go. I found Catherine once, I'll find her again. We'll circle around. Zach's correct. We have to skip the village."

He gave one last look back at the graveyard, but could not see her, and had no way of knowing if she'd heard the conversation. He needed her to be safe, dammit. He needed her to go to that village where he could protect her. Instinctively, he pushed at her with his mind, even knowing that she wouldn't be able to hear him. Calydons could talk telepathically only with their mates, and with other Calydons. *Go to the village, Catherine. You will be safe there.*

No answer, and he knew he was out of time. Zach truly was dying, and he had maybe a half-hour left to save him. He'd done all he could. It was time to move on and trust that Catherine would take the bait. If not, he would simply have to hunt her later. "Let's do this," he said. "Follow me. I know the shortest way."

Without wasting time with further conversation, Ryland broke into a run, driving all his energy into sprinting toward the one place that could save his teammates. Apollo's hoofbeats thundered behind him as the beast kept pace easily, despite carrying the two massive warriors.

Ryland bent his head against the branches, not slowing to avoid them.

The final bell had begun to toll for Zach. The time was now. But would Catherine still be around when he got back? Or had he lost her? Tension radiated through him as he ran. There were so many critical components of the Order's future dangling so precariously in his hands. Thano. Zach. Catherine. If he lost them all, what would be left of Dante's vision?

Nothing. It would be the final step in the crumbling of what had once been a legend, and it would be his damn fault.

Ryland sheathed his weapon, lowered his head, and ran harder.

He could not afford to fail.

※※※※

HOW STUPID DID THEY THINK SHE WAS?

Of course they were going to the village. And they obviously wanted her to go there as well.

Catherine watched her pursuers disappear into the forest. She'd been riveted by the exchange between the men, by the seething cauldron fermenting inside Ryland, which he'd somehow managed to hold at bay while he'd let the others take control.

She didn't even know him, but it was obvious that Ryland was the man in charge. He exuded a dark power that rolled off him like angry thunderclouds over a vast desert. During the entire discussion about whether to stay or leave, she'd been riveted by Ryland. By the tormented depth of his voice, by the way his hands had twitched with the need to fight back, and by the intense control he'd exhibited to let his men hold weapons on him.

She knew there was no way the others would have pulled weapons on him if he hadn't given them permission. It had been a setup to bait her, clear and simple. Granted, she knew it was true that Zach and Thano were suffering from talrak poison. That much was obvious. And the rest of the exchange? Zach's hostility had been genuine, but she'd sensed a bond between the mounted warrior and Ryland. Something she didn't quite understand, but it had definitely been there.

Ryland was danger and death, but he was also something else, something deeper that had been the bridge that had connected him to the mounted warrior. It wasn't warmth. It wasn't a purity of spirit. But there was something…

No. She couldn't try to find goodness in him. She had to remember that he was the enemy. He was hunting her. He carried death. How, she didn't know. She'd never met anyone like him before. It was fascinating and terrifying at the same time. He'd threatened to take her back to his home, to the Order of the Blade, a thought that made chills of terror race down her spine. If he took her, she would never get to Lucy. She would be trapped, and, dear God, she couldn't be trapped again.

But at the same time, when he'd uttered those words, that promise to keep her safe, she'd felt like her entire world had come crashing to a halt, as if her heart had suddenly begun beating for the first time in her life. He'd sounded so genuine, a man who would lay down his life for her. The promise had been so beautiful, so intense, that she'd wanted to leap out of the shadows and beg for his help.

But she knew too much to fall for that again. She was not the naive fool she had once been. There was no way she was turning herself over to a man who wanted to kidnap her. But even as she thought that, his tormented black eyes drifted through her mind, and her heart ached for the anguish she'd seen in their depths. She wanted to know more about him, and at the same time, she wanted to run away from him as fast as possible.

Her fingers tingled and she rubbed them together, recalling what it had felt like to touch him. Why had she done that? He could so easily have spun around and grabbed her before she could have gotten out of the way. But when she'd seen him standing so close, his shoulders bunched as if he was carrying a thousand burdens in those powerful muscles, she'd been compelled to touch him, to see what she could learn about him.

His coat had been well-worn, laden with stories of the battles he'd been in. So much death surrounded that man. It had caressed her, chasing away her fear and drawing her in. For a brief moment, she'd been lost in his presence, drawn into the aura that was so familiar to her. And when she'd touched his skin…she shivered at the memory. His skin had been so warm, warmer than a man shrouded in death should be. At the same time, it had been velvet soft, as if beneath the rough exterior was a tapestry spun of the softest silk, a thousand colors woven into one rich story of such suffering, torment, and bravery.

When she'd touched him, the gnawing hunger inside her had quieted, almost as if he'd offered her sunlight. She had no idea what had happened, but she now had enough control that she could risk being around people for a little longer, even though it was dark out. Yes, she couldn't take the chance of going to sleep and surrendering herself to the night, but awake would be okay. What had that touch between them done? Would it happen again, or had it been a one-time thing?

Not that she would try. He was too dangerous...and too compelling.

Ryland shouted in the distance, jerking her attention back to the present. Dear God, how had she let herself get distracted by him? She knew better than to think of a man as anything but a threat. God, she knew better.

Wearily, she rubbed her temples, staring in the direction the men had gone. If she had a brain, she'd do as they claimed they were doing, and avoid the village. But how could she do that?

The stone from the map was gone. Her map would be useless if she couldn't find her way to the next mark, a pyre of fire and smoke. Without the stone, she had no idea which way to go.

People who'd lived in the area for generations might know the land well enough to help her. Someone in that town might have the answers she needed. She had no choice.

With a sigh of exhaustion and desperate hope, Catherine slung her backpack over her shoulders and walked out of the graveyard to where Ryland and his team had last been. She closed her eyes and inhaled deeply. Dancing on the air were stories of death. Ryland's stories. His legacy that touched the very core of who she was.

Ryland knew exactly where that village was, and he was going there to save his team. Which meant she had to follow him.

Fisting the straps of her backpack, Catherine began to walk in the direction Ryland had gone, tracking him the same way he'd tracked her: through the fragments of death he left behind. She knew he wouldn't be lying in wait for her. His concern for his team was evident, and he would not stop until he had them safe. But once he did...she shuddered. He would never deviate in his ruthless quest to find her until he had succeeded.

That meant her only option was to get to the village, get answers, and get out before he was free to pursue her.

Sweat trickled down her temple despite the cold air, sweat that had nothing to do with heat and everything to do with her nervousness about putting herself so close to the man who'd been hunting her, the man who seemed to call to her so desperately that she'd almost given up her camouflage because she'd needed to touch him so badly.

She let out a deep breath and touched the silver locket she'd fastened around her throat while she'd been watching the men try to bait her. The cool metal acted as a constant reminder of what was at stake if she lost control or failed in her quest. Ryland might be a threat she didn't fully understand, but by telling her about the village he'd also given her a clue that directed her toward another chance to find her daughter.

For that, she owed him.

Maybe she would send him a thank you note.

Laughing softly, she released the charm and broke into a loping run, knowing that the clock was ticking with each passing moment: the clock that had Ryland distracted by his team, and the clock that gave her daughter life.

"Come on, Catherine. You've got to get this right. Lucy's counting on you." Then there was no time for talking. There was only time for running as if the devil himself was on her tail.

Which, she had a feeling, wasn't that far from the truth.

🐾 Chapter Four 🐾

THE TOWN SMELLED THE SAME as it had a thousand years ago. Ryland was shocked by the scents that assaulted him as he led his team around the outskirts of the village, amazed at how familiar they all were, as if he'd been there yesterday. He'd shut the town from his memory until today, and he couldn't have recalled a single scent of the area even to save his own life. Now that he was here, however, everything seemed to be coming back, flooding his senses. He remembered the hill to the south. The small spring on the north side. The well in the village center.

He inhaled deeply, letting the reminiscent odors of those first memorable breaths drift through him. How could a town smell the same after a thousand years? But it did. It smelled of cow manure and pig slop, of freshly cut hay and day-old fish, of thatched roofs and slow-cooking meat.

The scent was as beautiful as it had been before, maybe even more so. Because it was the scent of freedom.

"Where is everyone?" Thano asked quietly, his voice strained. "It's not that late."

"Most people don't venture out in the darkness," Ryland said. "Not around here."

"Talraks?"

"And others." Ryland reached back into the memories ingrained in his mind, trying to remember which way to go. The roads felt different, beaten down by cars and tainted by exhaust, but the layout was the same. "Right here." He ducked between two buildings and made his way down a narrow passageway, urgency compelling him onward. He slipped between two more slumped wooden buildings, then down a narrow staircase to a door so small that it looked like it was built for a child, not a man.

Adrenaline pushed through him. "It's still here." He knocked on the door as Thano reined in Apollo at the top of the stairs. Two quick knocks, just as Dante had done so many centuries before.

There was no response, and Ryland counted silently. Three. Two. One. Then he knocked again, two quick raps. "By Dante's grace," he said softly, referencing the one who had showed him the way, just as Dante had recited another's name so long ago.

This time, the door swung open with a loud creak, as if the hinges hadn't been asked to twist in a hundred years. Beyond the door was darkness, an impenetrable cavern of mystery. Ryland had no memory of what had happened within those walls, which Dante had said was the way it always was. It was the only way to safeguard whatever it was that lay within. "I have friends," he said into the abyss. "They were attacked by talraks. They're almost out of time. I need you to save them."

There was no response from within the room, no sound except for the swish of Apollo's tail.

Ry? What's up? Thano's voice touched his mind. *We don't have time for this crap.*

Ryland glanced over his shoulder and swore when he saw an orange glow emanating from beneath Zach's eyelashes, his eyes closed now as death began to take him. Adrenaline rushed through him and he whirled back toward the room. "I need help now," he shouted. "These are Dante's men! Help them!"

"Ryland Samuels." The voice was gravelly and rough, just as he remembered it when it had spoken to Dante. The voice was so powerful that Ryland had to fight not to drop to his knees and genuflect. "You were warned not to return, were you not?"

Jesus. Like he had time for that shit. "My friends are dying! Help them!" He turned. "Thano! Get down here!"

Thano immediately spun Apollo to the top of the stairs, and somehow the enormous animal managed to ease down the staircase that was too narrow for him, as if the very building itself had stretched to accommodate him.

Ryland knew he couldn't cross the threshold, but he gestured to Thano. "Go in. He's waiting for you." Dear Jesus, he hoped he was.

Thano peered into the darkness. "You're sure?"

Ryland stayed his hand as Thano began to call out his weapon. "Go unarmed. Just go!"

Zach coughed, a hack that turned into a low groan. Thano met his gaze, and Ryland saw the moment the younger warrior decided to trust him. He urged Apollo forward, and the horse leapt through the doorway that was ten times too small for him and yet had granted him access.

As they disappeared into the darkness, Ryland tensed. His brands burned with the need to arm himself, to leap in there and defend his team. Ten seconds passed and they didn't reappear. Then twenty. Then thirty.

When a full minute had passed, Ryland knew they'd been accepted for treatment. "Jesus." He slumped back against the wall, suddenly drained. Zach had made it there with seconds to spare. Son of a bitch. He'd done it. His team would live. Dante's legacy would live to see another day, at least for now.

For a long moment, he didn't move, recalling too clearly that day when Dante had delivered him to that same door. That day when everything had changed. No way would he betray what Dante had given him. No way would he fail to be the man Dante had believed he could be.

Thano and Zach were safe for now, and they wouldn't be released for a few hours.

Which meant it was time for hunting an angel of death.

Ryland leapt up the stairs and took a deep breath, inhaling the stillness of the night.

He caught Catherine's scent almost immediately and smiled, realizing that she had followed their lead and come to the village.

She'd delivered herself right into his hands. The chase would soon be over. He would have her, and Dante's legacy would be sealed forever.

Brimming with triumph, Ryland began to jog down the silent street, knowing full well that there were no graveyards in this town.

Nowhere to hide. Nowhere to run. He was coming for her.

***

CATHERINE PULLED HER BLACK CAP LOW over her head as she hunched in the shadows of the bar, using the wide brim to hide her face. Men and a few women were moving about, talking in hushed tones. It wasn't the raucous atmosphere of a bar where people were releasing a week's tension and having fun. It was the grim setting of a place on the edge of hell, and her body knew that there were too many vulnerable souls surrounding her. The temptation was great. Sleep gnawed at her weary body, trying to convince her to let her barriers down and fade into the respite of oblivion, as if she would dare let down her guard with so many people around and the thickness of night heavy upon them.

No, not tonight. Tonight there would be no harvesting by her. She rubbed the locket between her thumb and index finger as she took a deep breath, trying to inhale energy into her beleaguered body.

She couldn't afford to waste time. Ryland's trail had deviated to the south when they'd entered the city, but his scent was everywhere, as if he'd been in this room before. Knowing he was near was both terrifying and galvanizing. Even though she knew he was dangerous, every time the door opened, her heart jumped in anticipation of seeing the man who was so compelling.

The walls of the bar were dark wood, and the ceiling was low, as if the room itself was trying to hide from view. The air was thick with a musty scent that wasn't cigarette or cigar smoke. It was something richer and deeper, as if it were emanating from the earth itself. It almost seemed like the soil beneath the building was breathing tainted air and exhaling it into the room.

She leaned forward as she carefully scanned each occupant of the room. She needed someone old, someone grisly, someone who looked like they'd been in this town for five hundred years and seen all there was to see. Someone with one foot in the grave would be ideal, an old-timer who wanted to share their legacy of information before they died. No one else was likely to talk to a stranger drifting through town and asking questions. Not about the kinds of things she needed to know.

She ignored the younger, robust patrons, scanning the room until she found a man sitting at the far end of the bar. His shoulders were hunched, his skin weathered with a thousand years of life, his jeans worn from many experiences. But his eyes were bright, and he watched everyone in the room with avid clarity. He turned his head sharply and looked right at Catherine, as if he'd been aware of her long before she'd noticed him.

Yes, he was a good choice. He would know. She started to stand up, then stopped as fear trickled through her. No, no, no, he wasn't right. She wanted a woman. A woman would help another woman. A man was different. A man would have agendas that could drive him to do things...terrible things.

Catherine jerked her gaze off him and scanned the rest of the room. The only women were young and fresh, women who probably had been born long after the stone had been stolen. Grimacing to herself, she finally decided on a woman sitting alone in the corner. Unlike the others, she wasn't flirting with men or dressed to impress. She was wearing an old denim jacket, and her brown hair was pulled back in a distracted ponytail. There was no beer or wine in front of her, just the remains of a sandwich and an empty bottle of water. She was young, maybe Catherine's age, but there was a grittiness about the set of her jaw that intrigued Catherine.

It was a start. And she had to get going.

Catherine quickly stood up and worked her way past the half-empty tables. As she walked, she caught the faint scent of death, Ryland's scent. She quickly glanced at the door, but no one was there. He was near, though. Very near.

Her heart pounding, Catherine hurried across the well-worn planks to the woman in the corner. The woman looked up as Catherine approached. In her blue eyes, Catherine saw the burdens of a thousand years.

Yes, this was the person she needed. "May I join you?"

The woman's eyebrows went up, but she nodded.

With another glance toward the front door, Catherine slid into one of the empty chairs, facing the room so she could watch it. Her heart was pounding, and her skin was prickling. Ryland was coming for her, and coming fast. "My name is Catherine," she said.

The woman watched her. "Annie."

Catherine tried to manage a smile, but she was too tense. "I need help."

Annie raised her eyebrows. "I can tell."

She leaned forward, unable to keep the urgency out of her voice. "I need to find the pyre of flames. Do you know where it is?" She left the question hanging in the air, praying that Annie would know what she was talking about.

Annie stared at her, then slowly shook her head. "You don't want to find that," she said.

Relief coursed through Catherine. Annie knew what it was. "I do want to find it," she said. "My daughter was kidnapped. I have to find her." It wasn't the pyre of flames that was her ultimate destination. Her ultimate goal was so much worse.

Annie shook her head and leaned forward, her voice urgent. "Listen to me, Catherine. The pyre leads to things, things so horrific they're beyond comprehension. It's the first step into a hell you can't imagine—"

"I *can* imagine. I *do* know." How she wished she didn't, but there was no way to reverse time and choose a life that hadn't taken her where hers had. She simply had to deal with it and move forward.

Annie stared at her for a long moment, then leaned back in her chair. "You'll die if you go."

Catherine shrugged. "Will you tell me how to get there? Please." When Annie began to shake her head, desperation coursed through Catherine. She grabbed Annie's hand. "Think of the person you love most. Imagine them being trapped in that hell you mentioned. What if you were the *only* person in the entire world who could free them?" Her voice burned with tears she couldn't hold back. "What if you lay awake every night, hearing their voice in your head, calling for you, begging you to save them? What if you loved them so much that a piece of your heart broke off with every minute that passed, knowing that they were suffering and waiting for you to help them?"

Empathy flashed in Annie's eyes, and she squeezed Catherine's hand. "I'm so sorry," she whispered. "I'm so very sorry."

"I don't want sorry. I want directions."

Annie almost smiled. "You're a brave woman, Catherine."

"I'm not brave. I'm a mother. Will you help me?" A man would never understand the drive of a mother to save her child, but she saw in Annie's eyes the compassion she needed. Annie got it, on a level so deep Catherine knew it was only because she had personal experience with it. A mother, a child of her own, someone she loved... Annie had lost them, too.

"There's no way to describe the path," Annie finally said. "It changes constantly. I'll have to take you there."

Elation leapt through Catherine. "You will?"

"I'll take you most of the way," she warned. "I won't go all the way to the end. That is up to you. I need to go get some supplies. I'll meet you in the alley behind here in twenty minutes."

"Oh, thank you!" Catherine threw her arms around Annie. The other woman's arms folded around her instantly, hugging her tight. A friend for life...as long as Catherine didn't accidentally kill her first.

※※※

FIFTEEN MINUTES LATER, after having wolfed down a burger and a salad to ease the gnawing hunger in her belly, Catherine was pacing restlessly in the alley behind the bar, waiting for Annie to appear. Not that she could really call it an alley. It was more like a dirt footpath, barely large enough for one small car, and even a compact would probably lose its mirrors on the buildings. It felt cramped and tight, too small, with not enough room to flee if Ryland showed up.

She'd used the time not only to eat, but also to splash her face with water and stand under the light in the bathroom. She'd raised her face to the dingy fluorescent bulb like some downtrodden scavenger, trying to bleed every last bit of energy from it. She'd fed on it until the room had descended into complete darkness, but it still hadn't been enough to make her skin glow even a little bit. Feeling depressingly pathetic, she'd also taken a moment to absorb the emanations from the bulbs in the back hallway, and the spotlight that had illuminated the alley.

The spotlight had been bright enough to take the edge off. She knew she wasn't going to tackle Annie in the next five minutes and drain her soul, but it hadn't gained her enough that she would dare to risk sleep. The relief that Ryland had given her had long worn off. Catherine suspected the respite had been more about her body's intense craving for him as a man, than any actual relief he'd given her, which was just *not* something she wanted to contemplate. She had not fallen for a man since Simon had betrayed her, and she'd thought she was too smart to even notice one now.

But she'd noticed Ryland. She'd almost given away her hiding place because she'd needed to touch him so badly. What was that all about? Nothing good, she knew that much. But even at the mere thought of feeling his skin beneath her fingertips, a deep yearning rolled through her. She wanted more of him.

"God, just stop it," she whispered to herself. "You know better." Feeling exposed, Catherine finally tucked herself into a doorway. She used the building to cover her back while she warily watched the alley for both Annie and Ryland, praying the woman would arrive first.

It was hard to see through the pitch black, an impenetrable shield of darkness that had descended when Catherine had drained the spotlight. The only light that remained was the dull flicker from the spotlight, reaching barely a yard past where she was standing, hiding the rest of the nearby ally in darkness. Farther away, there were lights, but not nearby. Nearby was just darkness. While she waited, every sound was magnified in the looming silence. Catherine couldn't quite suppress the rising fear, wishing she hadn't made it quite so dark. In the dark, things could come and be upon her before she knew they were there—

A cold breeze rippled across her skin, and she froze. It wasn't just the cool night air, it was something else. A threat. Danger. Something beyond the realm of humanity. Something—

"Catherine." Ryland's voice was right beside her, and she screamed, leaping out of the doorway. "Hey, it's me." He stepped in front of her and grabbed both her arms, his massive bulk blocking her path, his hands an iron grip on her upper arms. "I'm not going to hurt you. I would never hurt you."

She froze, almost overwhelmed by the enormity of his presence. When she'd seen him in the graveyard, she hadn't been so close to him, and she hadn't been locked in his grasp. But now, he was in her space, so tall that she had to crane her neck to see him. His jaw was hard and flexed. Several days' worth of whiskers bristled on his face, and his shoulders seemed to stretch a thousand miles. He was a man strong enough to do anything he wanted to her. He was enormous, a specimen of maleness that every young boy—and adult male—would idolize and dream of becoming. But as a woman, she saw him for what he was: terrifying. "Let me go."

Ryland shook his head. "I have to get back to my friends, then we need to get home."

"Home?" She tugged at his grip, but he wasn't foolish enough to release her this time, not that she could disappear without a graveyard to hide in. "I don't have a home."

Something flickered across his face. "You do. With us. With the Order."

Catherine stared at him as he repeated the same bizarre claim as before, linking her with the Order. "What are you talking about? Why are you after me?"

He swore under his breath, and then went down on one knee, in a show of reverence so genuine she took a step backward. Instinctively, her hand covered her heart, trying to shield herself from how beautiful it made her feel to have him offering her such respect. "Why are you kneeling? Get up."

"Catherine Taylor," he said, his black eyes riveted on her. "It is my greatest honor to escort you back to a place of safety. We will fight for you now. I pledge myself to your protection."

Again, something flickered through Catherine, something that made her want to go down on her own knees and turn herself over to him. Instead, she took a step backward, knowing full well that she was too smart to fall for a man again. The fact she was feeling the need to accept his offer meant he was manipulating her somehow to override her reluctance. It was exactly the kind of thing Simon had done to her, and she would not be fooled twice. "How do you know me? Who are you? Why are you after me?" She glanced around, hoping to see Annie, but the woman was nowhere in sight. She couldn't leave until Annie arrived, but she had a desperate feeling that Ryland was going to try to keep her from going.

He didn't rise. "My name is Ryland Samuels. I'm an Order of the Blade member. I was part of the team that invaded Warwick Cardiff's castle." Something glittered in his eyes. "You didn't wait for us."

She stared at him. "You were with Alice?" Her heart tightened at the mention of the woman whom she'd known since she was a child, the one person in the world besides her daughter who brought enough light into her life to stave off the need to feed. Alice was her best friend, the sister she never had. She was the one who had picked Catherine's broken body off the ground after Simon had left and given her the strength to survive. "Is she okay?"

Ryland nodded. "She's fine. She bonded with Ian Fitzgerald, one of my teammates. They seem good."

"She bonded with a man?" Catherine's legs started to shake, and Ryland caught her as she crumpled to the ground. She sat heavily on the dirt, staring at the man still kneeling before her. "Is...is he a good man?" She could barely whisper the question, the thought of Alice being bound to a man was so terrifying. Dear sweet Alice. What had happened to her while Catherine had been locked up by the wizard? "Will he betray her?"

Ryland raised one dark eyebrow. "She is an angel, Catherine. If he wasn't a good man, I would have killed him before I allowed him to bond with her."

The unhesitating violence in his words made her shiver, but at the same time, hope sprang in her chest. She could feel his intense loyalty, his absolute determination to protect Alice. Yet at the same time, the fact he was prepared to kill his own teammate painted a picture of a man who could not be trusted. What if she was the one he decided to sacrifice to save someone else? "Well, thanks for telling me about Alice." She struggled to her feet. "I need to get going—"

"No." He stood up, looming over her again. "You're coming with me."

And just like that, her fear vanished, replaced with a rising anger. No longer would she let a man intimidate her. How dare he try to command her? Catherine set her hands on her hips and glared at him. "I'm not going anywhere with you." But even as she protested, fear ran cold through her veins once again. How could she stop this man from taking her?

Irritation flashed through Ryland's dark eyes. "Warwick was trying to destroy the Order by killing the trinity of guardian angels that protect us. We're bringing them home where we can keep them safe. Alice is our angel of life, and we already have the other. You're the only one left."

She stared at him as she processed his words. "You think I'm one of the Order's trinity of guardian angels?"

"Yes."

She started laughing then, the bitter, ironic laugh of someone who didn't really think things were all that funny. "Well, you're wrong. I'm—"

"You're the angel of death. Our angel of death."

She didn't bother to ask how they knew what she was. If Alice had fallen in love with one of them, she would have told him. Catherine knew what happened to a woman when she fell in love, and she would never blame Alice for spilling her secrets. God, she hoped Alice had been lucky enough to have made a good choice. "I am an angel of death, but trust me when I say I'm not yours."

"Catherine!" Annie came jogging down the alley. She was wearing jeans, hiking boots, and a heavy jacket, a slight hitch in her gait from the heavily loaded backpack over her shoulder. Around her throat was a black cord with a dove on it, carved out of what looked like ivory. "You ready?"

"Yes." Catherine ducked past Ryland and hurried over to her guide, not looking back.

"You need to wear one of these." Annie handed her a necklace like the one she was wearing. "Put this on. It will help protect you from some of the negative energy we'll be encountering."

Catherine took the necklace and started to fasten it behind her neck, only to have Ryland snatch it out of her hands. "Where do you think you're going?" he said, his voice edged with tension.

"Hey!" She whirled on him, furious. How dare he try to stop her from going after her daughter? "Where I go is none of your business. I'm not the Order's guardian angel, so what I do doesn't matter. Leave me alone—"

"No." His voice was soft but lethal. "The other two angels didn't know they were our protectors, either. Just because you don't know that you're ours doesn't mean you're not."

Annie's jaw dropped. "You're an angel?"

"Dammit, Ryland!" Catherine shoved at him. Her identity was not for shouting out to the world. She smiled at Annie, trying to feign innocence when all she wanted to do was scream with frustration at Ryland for interfering when she had things finally worked out. "I wish I was. That would protect us, right?"

Annie nodded, but her eyes were flitting back and forth between them. "It would help," she agreed. "Or damn us forever."

Ryland stepped between her and Annie, cutting off their conversation. "Listen, Catherine, I don't have time for this. I have to get back to my team to protect them. They have no tools against what happens here at night, and neither do you. We're going back—"

"No! I'm not going anywhere with you!" Catherine noticed Annie was starting to ease backwards, and she hurried over to her. "No, wait, please don't go—"

"He brings bad blood," Annie whispered. "Can't you feel it?" She looked at Catherine, her eyes getting wider. "And so do you. I didn't feel it before, but it's stirring now."

"No, wait—" Catherine tried to grab her arm, but Annie ducked out of her grasp.

Annie spat at her. "Get out of this town. Both of you!"

"But my daughter—"

The woman's eyes glittered. "I know what it's like to lose a loved one," she said, "so I'll give you time to run. A concession from one mother to another, but that's all I can do. Twenty minutes is all the head start I can give you, and then they'll come for you. So, *run*."

Then she turned and bolted down the street and around the corner, taking Catherine's last chance of hope with her—

"Oh, shit," Ryland moved closer to her, as if to protect her with his body. "Not now."

"Not now, what?" But even as she asked it, Catherine felt the walls of the building beside her begin to ripple. She whirled around and saw the wood undulating, as if it were steam rising off a hot sidewalk on a blistering summer day. "What—"

"So much for a twenty-minute head start. Come on!" He grabbed her hand, but Catherine twisted out of his reach. "No, I can't leave, I need to find—" A loud shriek tore through the air and a small, black creature leapt off the wall right at her. As it reached for her, its body elongated into a black, sinewy funnel, like a serpent coming to life. She yelped and stumbled back as its mouth opened to reveal six-inch fangs—

"Enough!" There was a crack and a flash of black light, and then Ryland swung his machete, decapitating the creature. "Now, Catherine, *run!*" Even as he commanded her, another serpent leapt off the wall at them. Ryland had just cut it down when another one came, and then another. "Catherine! This way!"

He grabbed her hand and this time, she didn't argue. She just ducked her head, followed his lead, and ran as hard as she could.

❄ CHAPTER FIVE ❄

RYLAND AND CATHERINE SPRINTED down the alley, heading toward where he'd left his team. He knew they had minutes, at best, before every building in the town was alerted to their presence and rose to attack. *Thano!* He thrust the call into his teammate's mind, hoping they were recovered enough to hear him. *Zach! We gotta go! Meet me outside. Now!*

There was a ripple of foggy acknowledgment in his mind. *The pedicure just started. You want to go now? Really?* But even as Thano said the words, Ryland felt the burst of energy from Thano as his teammate sprang to action.

"What is it?" Catherine looked over her shoulder as the alley behind them pulsed with life...or death.

"A protection grid woven into the fabric of the city when it was built. It's designed to ward off any creatures from the nether-realm that escape to the earth's surface. Between the two of us, we set it off." Another serpent came streaming at them from the right, and Ryland hacked it with his machete.

There was a wave of despair from Catherine, an agony so brutal that Ryland almost stumbled. But to her credit, she didn't waver. She just put on a burst of speed, running right down the gauntlet, never hesitating or slowing. Admiration coursed through him as he cut down another serpent going for her head. "Turn left up ahead," he commanded her. "Then take the first right and straight on out of the city." *Thano, meet us at the top of the stairs.*

You got it.

Recognizing a self-preservation instinct when he saw one, Ryland released Catherine's hand so he could fight with both machetes.

He no longer feared that she was going to play any tricks on him or ditch him. She was too intent on getting the hell out of the town alive. "Can you shroud yourself right now?" He wasn't sure if it would work, but if she could cast them all into shadows like she'd done in the graveyard, it might grant them safety.

"No. Not without a graveyard or some sort of burial ground— Ryland!" She skidded to a stop as a great snake sprang up in front of her. It snapped at her hand, but Ryland grabbed her in time and yanked her back. The snake lunged for her, and Ryland killed it, its head dropping to her feet less than an inch from her toe.

"Dear God," she whispered. "What is it?"

"Go!" They were coming out of everywhere now, ghostly serpents with poison more deadly than the talraks. One bite and there was no chance. It cut down on drunken nighttime brawls since the protections would respond to any kind of bad energy, but a tidy late-night bar scene wasn't really a selling point right now. "Come on!"

Catherine started running again. They rounded a corner, and Apollo loomed up ahead of them, his majestic body standing tall in the night. Thano was astride, and Zach was on his feet beside him. Ryland breathed with relief to see the color back in Zach's face, and the determined set to his jaw. Both warriors still looked peaked, but they were going to make it.

Thano's eyebrows went up when he saw Ryland and Catherine charging toward him, an army of predatory ghost-serpents on their tail. "Well, then, top of the day to you both," he said.

Catherine hesitated at the sight of the other men, and Ryland caught her hand again, sensing her sudden fear. She was more afraid of the Order than she was of the snakes chasing them? The woman had her priorities seriously messed up. "To the river," he commanded. "It's northeast about five miles. They won't go in water."

"Five miles?" Catherine looked at him like he'd lost his mind. "I can't run this pace for five miles—"

"I can." Before she could argue, Ryland grabbed her and swung her up onto his back without breaking stride. Catherine let out a yelp of surprise, and for a split second, he felt her debate whether to jump off. Then her body twisted as if she were looking behind them at their pursuers. He felt the moment she committed to accepting his protection, as her arms locked around his neck and her legs went around his hips. Satisfaction pulsed through Ryland. *Yes.* This was how it was supposed to be. The rightness of having Catherine wrapped around him, trusting him with her life, felt more incredible than anything he'd felt before.

By the time he reached the stairs where his team had been waiting for him, Thano, Zach, and Apollo were already on the move. The quintet broke for the woods, barely a yard ahead of a shadowy force that Ryland knew was just the start of what lay beneath the surface in this cursed region.

They had to get out of this area, and fast. It wasn't just the town they needed to vacate. It was the region beyond, the heartless and deadly land they were heading directly towards. The place that had once been his home. His prison. His hell.

※※※

CATHERINE HUNCHED LOW against Ryland's back, the bitter cold aura of their pursuers brushing over her like the teeth of a demon itself. Dear God, what were they? But even as fear clamped around her, there was also a resounding surge of excited anticipation. Creatures like that were the kind she would expect to see in the nether-realm, so she knew she was getting close to her destination. But how could she find it? Annie had known, but Annie would not be giving any more help.

"There it is!" Ryland shouted.

Catherine peered over his shoulder and saw a raging river of white foam and black depths in front of them. It was at least a hundred yards wide, with whitecaps twenty feet high. The mountain river was so deep that not a single boulder protruded from the surface of the rapids. It wasn't a natural river. It was a boiling cauldron of something not from this earth. There was no way they could cross that. Her fingers dug into his shoulder. "Um, Ryland? I don't know about that—"

Ryland increased his speed. "It's the only way," he interrupted, dismissing her concerns. "Thano! We need a ride!"

Catherine felt a rush of cold air on her back. She quickly glanced back, and then screamed as fangs came down toward her head. Ryland whipped around, took out a huge serpent with a single strike, and then was sprinting forward again with hardly a break in his stride. He altered his path, shifting them directly behind Apollo, barely out of the way of the horse's thundering hooves.

"Apollo's on board with it," Thano yelled. "Grab on!"

Not slowing his pace, Ryland sheathed his weapons. "Swing around to my front so I can hold you better," he ordered her even as he pulled her around his body until they were chest to chest. The intimacy of the position startled her, and she instinctively pulled back.

But Ryland gave her no room to retreat, locking his powerful arm around her waist and hauling her so tightly against him that she could feel the beat of his heart and the expansion of his ribs with each breath. "Hang on to me," he shouted. "This is going to get rough!"

She had a feeling that "rough" was a major understatement, but there was no way they could go back. Forcing aside her apprehension about being in such an intimate position with Ryland, she wrapped her arms around his neck and hooked her feet around his waist.

"Tighter," Ryland commanded her as he lunged for Apollo's tail. Zach did the same, each of them grabbing fistfuls of the thick, black strands just as they reached the bank of the river. Ryland's free arm tightened around her, almost crushing her against him. The heat of his body was intense, his raw power terrifying. But even scarier was her body's response to the intimacy, and her need to burrow into his strength and surrender to his power.

"Here we go," Ryland said.

Then, to Catherine's shock, the horse leapt straight off the shore, yanking Zach and Ryland with him, jerking both warriors right off their feet. She had only a second to conclude she was going to die a violent, watery death, when the horse landed on the surface of the water and began to gallop *across the top of it,* dragging Zach and Ryland behind him, through the raging whitecaps.

She and Ryland dipped beneath the surface, and tainted, filthy water flooded her mouth. Then they were jerked free, careening through the air as Apollo leapt over a huge wave. Catherine sucked in her breath desperately, and shook the water out of her eyes. All she could see was spray from the wave crashing over Ryland. He glanced down at her, and for a split second, she thought she saw something soft flash in his eyes. Then it was gone, replaced by the cold, hard visage of a warrior in the midst of battle. A man with the singular objective of survival and protection…which, she had to admit, was exactly the right kind of man to be hanging onto while being dragged through an Otherworld river by a water-walking stallion while being chased by ghostly serpents. She didn't trust men, not ever, but in that moment, she knew she was exactly where she needed to be.

Ryland glanced at her again, and this time he flashed a smile at her. "Glad you can see how great I am," he shouted just before they plunged back into the water when Apollo landed. The current tore at her, trying to jerk her out of Ryland's grasp, but his grip was unyielding, keeping her secure against him even as they were buffeted by the rapids. Then Apollo leapt again, ripping them from the grips of the fuming water. They sailed through the air for a brief reprieve.

"Breathe," shouted Ryland, "while you have the chance!"

Catherine sucked in her breath and then closed her mouth as they crashed down again, plunging into the merciless water that seemed to grab at her limbs. It fought to pry her free of Ryland, as if it were a living creature desperate to feed on her. Then something really did grab her ankle. It jerked her right out of Ryland's grasp and sucked her down straight toward the bottom in a savage, quick move—

A machete whizzed by her head, there was a scream of agony, and then the tentacle released her just as Ryland grabbed her outstretched wrist. She was jerked forward as Apollo's momentum caught her. This time, Ryland's body was not there to absorb the violence of the water, and she was ripped and tossed as they plowed through, her only connection to safety being Ryland's fingers around her arm.

Her shoulder felt like it was getting torn from its socket, and her body burned from getting pummeled by the ruthless current. The pain was too much, way too much.

"Come on," Ryland shouted. With a herculean effort, he dragged her toward him, somehow summoning strength that triumphed over the relentless pull of the water. She slammed into his body, and this time she flung aching limbs around him without hesitation. When he anchored his arm around her waist and pulled her against him, she felt the most incredible sense of relief and hope, as if she now had a chance to make it.

Catherine buried her face against his shoulder, focused on nothing but hanging onto him and catching her breath when they cleared the water. Again and again, they were jerked free of the water and then plunged back into it as Apollo leapt over waves and then landed again. Ryland's grip on her never faltered, even when her arms and legs were screaming with exhaustion and she felt like she couldn't hold on for a second more, he was there for her, keeping her protected and in his grasp.

Finally, she heard the thud of the horse's hooves on solid ground. In disbelief, she raised her head as Ryland landed on the riverbank and released Apollo's tail. He forged onward another twenty yards until they were clear of the water, then he went down to his knees, still gripping her tightly.

She was too exhausted to do anything except sag against him, fighting for breath. They'd made it. *They'd made it.* It was an impossible crossing, but the warriors had found a way.

"Holy crap." Zach was on his hands and knees beside them, his ribs expanding as he sucked in air. His muscles were trembling, and steam was rising from his body. "Remind me never to go swimming in that she-demon of water again."

Even Apollo looked drained. The horse's head was down, his forefeet splayed as his nostrils flared. Only Thano looked fresh atop the horse, his halberd out and ready as he scanned their surroundings, protecting the others while they regrouped. Though battered and drenched, the trio gave off a sense of power and solidarity, a force that seamlessly worked to support each other.

Her throat tightened, overwhelmed by the way the three of them seemed to stand by each other, despite the visible tension that she'd seen by the graveyard. It was amazing, this teamwork, this kind of support...and then she remembered that Ryland had said that he would have cut down Ian if he'd been planning to hurt Alice. Was his bond with Ian the same as it was with Thano and Zach? And if so, how could he be able to destroy it so easily to protect another?

But she knew the answer to that. He was a man who lived by his own rules, and woe to anyone who counted on him for more than that. He wasn't a forever guy. He was "forever until it served his purposes to go in another direction," and she had to remember that, no matter how great he was at saving her from nether-world serpents and rivers.

"You okay?" Ryland eased her down to the ground, his hands moving over her hips in a soft caress too methodical to be a seduction, but more intimate than a simple examination for injuries should be.

"Yes." Her muscles were aching and trembling, and she felt as if every last bit of energy had been sucked from her body by the water. She couldn't keep from gripping his forearms, needing his strength to hold herself up, as if she were some weak female. Which, apparently, she was, at least in this moment. But at the same time, it felt good to have him to lean on. Beautiful even. He'd just saved her life with a show of strength and courage that was incredible. "Thank you," she said quietly.

Ryland cupped her face, and she looked at him. His eyes were black as usual, ruthlessly intent. "I would give my life for yours," he said. "Without hesitation. No matter what."

The raw simplicity of his promise touched her, as did the absolute conviction in his eyes. She knew he spoke the truth, the full truth. For some reason, this man she didn't even know, this man steeped in death and terrible things, had committed his life to her well-being. Tears thickened her throat, but she forced herself to turn away, unwilling to let herself fall for the kind of lines that had stolen so much from her already.

"Catherine," he said softly, for her ears only.

"What?" She didn't look at him, unwilling to let herself get sucked into promises and declarations that were too tempting. She knew her weakness, her need to believe in people no matter what, and she couldn't let him exploit it.

"Look at me."

"I'd rather not."

"I don't care."

Frustrated, she looked at him, then her heart tightened when she saw the raw agony on his chiseled face. It wasn't simply vulnerability, it was humanity that spoke of a soul so tortured that even this great warrior was unable to hide it. "What?"

He took her hand and pressed it against his chest. She could feel the steady, reassuring thud of his heart, the warmth of his flesh through his shirt, and the howling pain in his soul. "I offer you my eternal protection," he said. "I am your servant."

It almost sounded as if he were invoking some ancient ritual binding them together. Terrified, she jerked her hand back. "No, I don't want anything from you."

Something dark and deadly flashed through Ryland's eyes, and she scrambled backward, suddenly scared of what stirred beneath the surface of this man. "Ryland—"

"Damn, man," Thano interrupted. "What happened to the ruthless, selfish bastard on the edge of going completely insane and destroying all that is good in this world? I thought you were pathetic and droopy with the other angels, but you're even worse with this one. You're like a puppy dog in love. What is it with you and angels, dude?"

Ryland ignored Thano and kept his gaze riveted on Catherine, but the truth of Thano's words hung in the air. Catherine could see in Ryland everything Thano had spoken of: the ruthlessness, the selfishness, the insanity, and the destruction of all that was good. It was bleeding through his pores from a source deep inside him.

But that wasn't the scary part of him. The scary thing was that beneath all those things Thano had cited, Catherine sensed a man on the edge of an abyss, someone so loyal and determined that he would indeed give his life for those he had sworn to support. He was born of simple values more pure than the earth itself, when it was swathed in the beauty of a sunrise. The fact that she could see something beautiful in Ryland was terrifying, because it made her vulnerable to him. It made her want to trust him, to put her faith in him, to give the world one more chance to show her she could count on it.

Ryland nodded in apparent agreement. "I'm the right choice," he said quietly. "Believe your gut."

She blinked at the response that seemed to be in direct alignment with what she'd just been thinking. "Can you hear my thoughts?"

"Shit, no." His response was without hesitation. "But you broadcast your emotions with your face. You're easy to read." He grinned. "Sweetheart, I'm one of those ultrasensitive guys who are so tuned into emotions it's like it was born to me. If you cry, I'll hear you. If you decide to trust me, I'll know." Amusement flickered in his eyes. "And if you try to run on me again, I'll find you before you've even figured out where you're going."

She swallowed, his words feeling as comforting as they did scary. What was wrong with her? Those words could only be interpreted as a threat, not as protection. He wanted to take her back with him. She had to go forward. There was no middle ground.

"We camp here tonight," Ryland called out to his team. "We move in the morning. Most things won't go near the river, so we're safest if we stay close to it."

Zach raised his weary head to look at Ryland. "You're sure?"

"Yeah."

Catherine was surprised by the way Zach and Thano didn't question him further. They were in the middle of a strange and hostile territory, and yet his teammates seemed to have complete faith in what Ryland commanded. Zach was already on his feet and gathering wood for a fire, and Thano was unloading Apollo's saddlebags onto a flat, high rock that was level with him from his mounted position. The warriors were quick and efficient, men who had set up camp a thousand times and knew exactly what to do—

"Forgive me, my angel." Ryland interrupted her thoughts, and she looked over at him just as he wrapped a vine around her wrist.

She tensed. "What is that?"

"My protection in case you go invisible again." He looped the other end of the vine around his own wrist, and with a quick flick of the wrist, tied them together.

"What?" She lunged to her feet, fighting at the binding. "What are you doing?"

"As I said, you're easy to read. You're not planning on staying with me. I'm damned good at tracking, Catherine, but when you went invisible, you were completely hidden from me. Impressive as hell, but not something either of us can afford." Ryland caught her arm as she fought, steadying her. "The harder you pull, the more the vine will tighten and dig into your arm. Don't fight it. The vine won't break, and it can't be cut. We're bound together until the sunlight dissolves it."

"Dammit!" She fought to get free. "How could you do this? I have to leave! I can't go with you!"

He lightly gripped her arm. "Hey, hey, hey, Catherine. Calm down—"

"I can't! Let me go!" She tore herself out of his grasp, stumbling backward even as the vine tightened, digging into her wrist and—

"Stop it!" Ryland tackled her and tossed her to the ground, pinning her with his weight to the cold earth. "You're going to hurt yourself."

His weight was so heavy, she couldn't move. She was trapped. *Trapped.* Panic overtook her, her heart hammering frantically. She couldn't breathe. Couldn't get air. "Get off me," she gasped. "Now!"

◆◆◆◆

RYLAND SWORE as panic took over Catherine. She was losing control, driven by a terror far beyond what the situation should have caused. He could feel it reaching up to grab her, to trap her in a spiral of the mindless insanity of fear. Shit! "Catherine! Come back to me." Tying her to him had been a mistake, and he realized it instantly.

Swearing, he called out his machete and tried to cut the vine, but his weapon glanced off it, repelled by a force darker than he could destroy. "Shit!"

She was trembling beneath him, thrashing and fighting, desperate to get free, but he couldn't release her. "Catherine!" What had she responded to before? He thought back to the brief interactions that they'd had, to those moments when she'd gazed at him without fear, to when she'd looked at him as if she wanted to trust him. It had been when he'd been offering her protection and promising he would keep her safe. She'd responded to that, something inside her needing to hear those words and to believe them.

Shit. He had to tap into that again. "Catherine," he said, fending off her blows as gently as he could. "I'm on your side, I swear it."

No response from her. She was in a blind panic, and her heart rate was escalating dangerously.

Crap! Swiftly, he thought back to that moment in the graveyard when she'd touched his hand, to the intensity of his reaction at the feel of her skin on his, at the intimacy of their moment. Everything had stood still in that moment of connection.

That was it. He had to find that again.

Intimacy and protection. Making her understand his commitment to ensure she was safe with him, and only him. He was no tender guy. He knew shit about sweet nothings. So, swearing under his breath, he bent his head and offered her his protection and connection in the only way he could think of, the one thing he didn't offer to anyone, ever: his kiss.

The moment his lips touched hers, Ryland felt the world come to a screeching halt. A thousand years of darkness seemed to fade, replaced by the most incredible sense of rightness. Catherine went still beneath him, sucking in her breath. Her left hand was poised on his shoulder, her right hand above her head, still tied to his left.

Neither of them moved, their breath mingling as their lips froze in an unexpected connection. Need raced through Ryland. It was a raw, untamed craving for this woman, this angel, this being who was so far above him that he could never prove himself worthy of her. He had no right to kiss her, no right to press his body against hers, and no right to notice her breasts crushed against his chest, but he couldn't pull away.

One whisper of a protest from her and he would retreat, but she didn't give him one. She just stayed beneath him, that one hand on his shoulder, not pushing him away, but not pulling him toward her either.

Need strained at him, but Ryland held himself rigid, refusing to take from this angel what she wasn't willing to give.

But then, oh, heavenly, then, her fingers twitched on his shoulder and dug in, an instinctive reaction so subtle that he knew she hadn't done it intentionally. But it was enough. It gave him the permission he needed. With a low growl of intention, he threaded his fingers though her hair, angled his head, and kissed her for real.

※※※

IT WAS THE MOMENT Catherine had been craving her entire life. That moment of beauty and intimacy, that feeling of being cherished and protected, of being wanted with such fierceness that nothing could keep him from her.

Ryland's kiss was electric and intense; flooding her with sensations that seemed to ignite the parts of her that she thought had died so long ago. Desire flooded her, a craving for this man that was so powerful that it terrified her. His lips were demanding and intense, but at the same time, so incredibly soft, as if he would carve out his own heart before hurting her.

His fingers were so gentle in her hair, caressing the strands as if he'd never in his life thought about how easily he could grab a fistful and rip her head back. In his hands, her hair felt like a blessing of seduction and beauty, not a liability that could be used to trap her in a man's fist.

Hopelessly caught in his kisses, she touched his hand, following the path of his fingers as he slid them through the strands, awed by how an action that she'd always felt was so threatening could feel so incredible and seductive.

Her nipples were taut against his chest, her hips were pinned beneath his, and his weight was immobilizing her, but she wasn't afraid. Instead, she felt safe and protected, as if the nightmares in the world could never hurt her, as if this man was the one who could guide her into the place she needed to go—

The realization stunned her. Ryland had led her to the village that was so well-hidden she never would have found it if she hadn't been tracking him. He'd known what was after them in the village, and had been precise and calm in his defense. He'd directed them unerringly to the river, and knew that sleeping next to the river was the safest place for them to be. *He knew the area.* Dear heaven, was he the one she'd been searching for? The one who could take her to her daughter?

He eased off his kiss. "What is it?" His lips brushed against hers, a private whisper just for her, his cheek resting against hers in an intimate position just for lovers. "What are you thinking, my angel?"

There it was again, that sense that he could read her mind, that he knew what thoughts were spinning around in her head. She shivered, but unlike before, fear stayed dormant, eased by the calm he'd given her with his kiss and tender touches. Right now, he didn't feel like a man who would steal from her. He felt like a protector sent to her as a gift to help her on her way. She knew he was dangerous, and tried to remind herself of that. The man could tell what she was thinking. That was not a good thing. It spoke of a power that he had over her, a closeness that gave him access to her very thoughts and soul.

That was bad...no, terrible...no, appalling and terrifying, and she had to remember that.

"I'm not thinking anything," she whispered stiffly, struggling to find the willpower to push him away, but unable to resist basking for one more moment in the feel of his powerful body enveloping her in his protective strength, in the intimacy of his lips against her jaw, and his whiskered cheek against her softer one. "There's nothing to tell."

"You stopped kissing me, but it wasn't fear. Something distracted you," he said, as if explaining the question she'd just posed in her own mind about whether he was reading her thoughts. Again, a chill ran through her. His very explanation about how he knew something was bothering her actually served to reinforce her suspicion that he was reading her mind. He trailed his lips over her jaw. "Talk to me, angel. I'm your servant."

His voice was so urgent, so compelling, and his promise was so achingly appealing. There was no way for her to deny its effect on her, her craving to fall into it and let it envelope her.

Almost against her will, Catherine opened her eyes. She searched the haunted depths of his face, struggling to see the stories and secrets that would reveal him to her. In his eyes, she saw what she had seen before: the danger, the haunted turbulence, the extreme violence, but again, she also saw something else. A humanity. A passion. A connection that seemed to melt into her soul and soften her heart. After being shut down emotionally for so long, it felt so good to encounter a soul that made her want to cry with empathy.

She closed her eyes, trying to break her response to his call, but it didn't help. There was something about this man that seemed to beckon to her. Was it his strength? The suffering she felt in him? Or simply the way he had promised himself to her, sworn to be her right hand, to protect her and serve her? Because what woman wouldn't fall for that, right?

Ryland continued to slide his fingers through her hair, and he bent his head, tucking his face in the crook of her neck. He breathed softly, intentionally, as if basking in her scent in the tender way of a man imprinting his woman on his soul. It was incredible, comforting, and unbelievably seductive.

He pressed his lips to her collarbone, and chills spiraled down her spine. The strangest sense of desire began to build inside her, like distant waves tumbling toward her, growing and building as they roared over the plains. Waves of passion, of need, of sensual awareness. Unable to stop herself, she gripped his hair, her hips shifting beneath his.

"I feel it, too," Ryland whispered, turning his head to kiss his way back up her neck, toward her mouth. "I want to pin you down, tear your clothes off, and make love to you until we both melt into the earth, our very existence burned up in the fire of our lovemaking."

Catherine stiffened as desire pulsed through her belly. "No, no, no," she whispered. "I don't have time. I can't—"

"I can't either." But he kissed her again anyway, the kiss of a man who had every intention of making his vision come true, right then, right there, and to make love to her until they both melted into flames.

And she had no chance of making herself stop him.

✿ CHAPTER SIX ✿

RYLAND WAS STUNNED by his response to Catherine, by the depths of his need to claim her. Her kisses were more than seductive, more than intoxicating. They were an assault on all his defenses, on everything that made him who he was, on everything he believed about angels. She was supposed to be above him, untouchable, a creature from heaven suspended in the air for him to serve. But instead, she was a living, breathing woman with lips like heated silk, a body made of fire, and flesh that he craved beyond words.

With a growl that was more possessive than he'd intended, he tightened his grip on her hair, angling her head for a deeper kiss. He needed more of her. He needed more than a kiss. He needed her spirit entwined in his, entangling in the fire that raged within him all day and all night, every moment of his life.

Her arm tightened around his neck, and he sank deeper into her, awed by the feel of her body beneath his. With the hand that was still bound to hers, Ryland slid his fingers between hers, tangling them together so their palms were against each other, her hand dwarfed by his grasp.

He'd never held a woman's hand before.

He'd never lost himself in a kiss.

He'd never had a moment that he wanted to last forever.

Until now.

Until Catherine Taylor had fallen into his arms, and he'd tasted her mouth.

Until he'd met the angel he'd been searching for his entire life.

So, Ry. Thano's voice breezed through his mind, jerking Ryland back to the present. *Zach thinks if I interrupt you guys, you'll decapitate us both. I think you'll thank me for saving you from the woman who made you forget you're in a battlefield. Which is it? Can we come back to camp, or do we need to spend the night in these trees a half mile away, pretending not to know that you guys are getting it on by the river? 'Cause I forgot my knitting, so I don't have much to keep me occupied if I have to stay here, and Zach's pissed because he left his blankie over there.*

Ryland swore at the interruption and broke the kiss. Shit. What was he doing, losing himself over a damned kiss? *Fuck off, Thano.*

He almost felt the warrior's grin. *So, yeah, okay. We'll head back now. That will give you time to get her clothes back on.*

Her clothes are on, you bastard.

This time, there was no mistaking Thano's laughter. *For now, eh?*

Ryland shut him out, not wanting some arrogant male in his space right now. Or any male at all. The only thing he wanted near him was one particular woman—

"You were talking to Thano in your mind?"

He looked down and saw Catherine watching him. There was no terror in her eyes anymore. Just thoughtfulness and intelligence, which was damned sexy. "Yeah, we can do that." He narrowed his eyes as a sudden thought occurred to him. "Why? Could you hear us?"

He froze as he waited for her answer, shit-ass-terrified that she would say yes. Calydons could speak telepathically only with other Calydons, with one exception: a Calydon could link mentally with his soul mate, the woman who was destined for him. If Catherine had heard his discussion with Thano then that would mean she was his soul mate. His destruction. His fatal destiny. All of which, he had no damned time for—

"No, of course not," she said, her brow wrinkling with a frown that sent gales of relief through him so vast he had to close his eyes for a moment. "But you always get a particular expression on your face when you talk to him, like he's this great gasp of fresh air you need in order to breathe, and you want to strangle him for that fact."

Ryland opened his eyes, scowling down at her "My expression doesn't change when I talk to anyone." He was a warrior for hell's sake. Warriors didn't even have facial expressions.

Catherine laughed softly, her blue eyes almost sparkling with amusement. "Of course it does. You're one of the most expressive people I've ever met." She suddenly reached up and traced her finger between his eyebrows.

Ryland went still, barely able to keep from reacting defensively and blocking her, as if she'd threatened him. No one touched him, ever, and he made sure that no one felt comfortable enough to try. But here was Catherine, actually tracing her fingers over his forehead. He thought he'd hate it, but to his shock, he didn't want to move, he didn't want her to stop. There was something so foreign about being touched like that, but at the same time, it felt fucking incredible.

"Most of the time," she told him, still tracing her fingers over his forehead. "You look like you hate the world, but sometimes little expressions come over your face that are softer, like you really do care beneath that visage you put on."

"As if I care?" That was it. Enough. Ryland clasped her wrist and moved her hand away from his forehead. "Don't mistake what I am, angel. I'm not kind. I'm not caring. I'm not an angel. The only thing that matters to me is honoring my leader and the vision he had for the Order. He's dead, and I will do anything it takes to protect his vision. That's why you're coming home with me, because the Order needs its angels where it can protect them. No more hell like we just went through. Got it?" He was satisfied with his speech: it still held the respect he owed her as an angel, but made it clear that he wasn't some guy she could manipulate with soft words and tender touches.

Because soft words and tender touches were not his thing. He didn't do that shit.

Catherine shifted under him, and Ryland realized he was still on top of her. Swearing, Ryland lifted himself off her, unwilling for his teammates to see an angel in such a compromising position. Shit. What kind of bastard was he to treat her like she was an ordinary woman? He rolled onto his side, propping himself up on his hip as Catherine wriggled free. "Sorry," he grunted. "That was disrespectful of me."

She sat up, rubbing her hand over her lips as if she were wiping him away, which made something dark roll through him "What was disrespectful?" She held up her bound arm. "Tying me up like a prisoner?"

"No, that was for your safety. You seemed inclined to take off by yourself, which is a really bad idea in this area." Despite his words, he regretted his rash decision to tie them together. He'd just had a moment of uncharacteristic panic at the idea of losing her, of her disappearing before his very eyes and vanishing from his life again, forever. He'd lost his shit for a second, something he'd never done before in his life.

How could he have treated her like common chattel? And how could he have made a choice based on some irrational fear? He was a fucking machine when it came to battle. He would have found her again if she'd left him, just like he'd done the first time. And yet, he'd tied them together anyway, choosing the one way to bind them that he'd be unable to break. She'd freaked out, yeah, but at the same time, the knowledge that he was bound to her was equally unsettling to him. He didn't do partnerships, and he didn't like knowing that he had no space, but he'd gone and shackled them together anyway.

Dumbass. That was what he was.

She narrowed her eyes, a slow fire fuming in them. "So, if tying me up was actually a polite and respectful thing to do, then what are you apologizing for?"

That one was an easy answer. "Kissing you like I was some savage beast who wanted to consume you." As he watched, her fingers slowed to a thoughtful caress on those same lips he'd just been kissing, making his loins tighten. Shit, what was she doing to him?

"You've got it wrong." She watched him warily.

"Yeah?" He leaned closer to her, seduced by the temptation of this siren from heaven. "How so?"

She held up her bound hand, making his hand move with hers, controlling him. "This is what you owe me an apology for," she said, indicating the restraint. She lifted her chin, her eyes blazing with accountability. "No apology for the kiss. It wasn't a one-sided thing. I'm as responsible as you are."

He stopped his approach, his gut clenching with raw need. Intense lust began to howl through him at her confession, and he stood up, needing to put some distance between them before he acted even more inappropriately. "Listen," he said, running his free hand restlessly through his hair, while he had to leave his other hand down by his hip, close to hers. The damned two-foot vine was not long enough. Not even close. Jesus. He needed to get away from her, and he couldn't. "We'll camp here, and then break for Dante's mansion at first light. We'll have to travel in a southern arc around the town."

Again, intelligence flickered in Catherine's eyes, an acuity that made him want her even more. "Why can't we go north around the village? Wouldn't that be a more direct route back than the way we came?" Her question seemed casual, but he sensed a purpose behind it, one he couldn't quite decipher.

"Yeah, it would," he acknowledged, "but north has things that you don't want to run into. South is safer—" He paused at the sudden expression on Catherine's face. The fierce determination, the resistance, the clear and focused visage of a warrior. "What?"

She lifted her chin. "I have three things to say."

He almost grinned at her statement. Her determination and feisty spirit were hot shit. She was no delicate angel, that was for sure. "What are they?" If anyone else had given him that look and that attitude, he would have snarled and considered decapitating them. But with Catherine looking at him like that, all he could do was think she was sexy as hell, and damned brilliant.

She held up her index finger, as if she were speaking to a small child with the inability to grasp the most basic concept. "First, I'm not the Order's guardian angel."

He shrugged impatiently, dismissing her statement. "Like I said, the others didn't realize they were either at first. We'll figure it out when you're safe."

Completely ignoring him, she held up two fingers. "Second, I'm not going back with you."

His good humor vanished. "Of course you are."

She met his gaze, and in her eyes he saw a desperation that made his heart twist. "And third," she said. "You will be my guide into the nether-realm."

⚰️⚰️⚰️

RYLAND STARED AT HER for a long moment, so long that her heart started to pound with hope.

She sat up. "I know you're familiar with the area. It's obvious." She grabbed her backpack, which had somehow ended up on the ground beside them after Ryland had tackled her. "See, I have this map, but one of the markers is gone, so—"

"No."

She looked up and her heart sank at the haunted darkness on his face. "You have to—"

"No." His refusal was almost a growl, and his upper lip was curled, as if he were baring fangs at her, not regular human teeth. "We're going home. No arguments. No—"

"Hey!" She jumped to her feet, grabbing his arm as he started to turn away. When she tried to force him back to face her, he spun around so quickly she almost fell over. He grabbed both her upper arms, trapping her. "We're not going to the nether-realm," he snarled. "You're not, and I'm not. End of story."

"No, it's not!" She knew she should be afraid of him, but she was too mad to drum up that kind of emotion. Here was the man who could help her, and not only was he refusing to help her, but he was going to ban her from going herself? "My daughter is trapped in the nether-realm," she snapped. "There's no chance in hell that I'm going to leave her there to suffer for an eternity. She's four years old, for God's sake, Ryland. Four!"

Ryland's eyes closed at her words, and he tipped his face toward the night sky, as if he was trying to make her words go away. "Jesus, Catherine."

Darkness and death were flowing off Ryland, increasing by the moment, but at the same time, she felt a wash of intense emotion from him. She couldn't quite identify it, but it gave her hope. Ryland was not the stoic, harsh man he seemed. Well, he was, but there was something else there. The man had committed his life to protecting innocents. There was no chance he could be immune from the plight of a four-year-old girl. "Ryland," she said urgently. "I have to get there now. I'm almost out of time."

His eyes opened, and darkness glittered in their tormented depths. "Why are you out of time?"

God, the truth was too complicated to explain right now. He'd never help her if he knew what she was dealing with. And why would he help her anyway? She had no leverage to motivate him to help her, nothing except trying to call upon his promises of protection and support, as well as his basic humanity. "Because in three days, there will be no chance to save her." Three days if she was lucky.

Ryland stood for a long moment, and she could feel the battle raging within him. Something was brewing inside him. The aura of death was stronger now, the violence lurking in his eyes. Finally, he met her gaze. "I'm sorry, Catherine, but no."

Then he turned his back on her and ended the conversation.

⌘⌘⌘

RYLAND HAD MADE IT ONLY TWO FEET when he felt the vine around his wrist tighten. Dammit. He'd forgotten about the restraint. Swearing, he turned around. Catherine had folded her arms over her chest and was glaring at him. Not just a glare. The cold, calculated face of a woman who would not give in.

Admiration flickered through him. He understood her need to go after her daughter. He'd had that same need to go after Thano. To preserve Dante's Order. To protect those in his charge. He understood what was driving her. He really did. Not that he would change his mind, but damn if he didn't like her for that loyalty. He walked back over to her, not that he'd been able to get too far with the vine. "Listen, Catherine," he said. "I get it. She's your daughter. I know. But I can't help you. Taking you in there is death to both of us—"

"So what?" she challenged. "Since when does the Order of the Blade fear death?"

"I don't." Jesus. He ran his hand through his hair. Memories of a time long past assaulted him, and that same sick feeling pulsed through him like the rancid stench of a rotting soul. "I can't go back in there."

She pounced on his words. "Back in there? So you've been there before?"

He hesitated, then shrugged. "Yeah, I've been there. I was born there. I lived there for twenty-five years before Dante tore me out of there and gave me another chance."

Intelligence flared in her blue eyes. "So, he rescued you? You couldn't get out on your own? Don't you owe someone that same favor? Where would you be if Dante hadn't rescued you?"

Ryland swore as sweat began to trickle down his spine. He knew damn well where he'd be if Dante hadn't pulled him out of there, and he knew where the rest of the fucking world would be as well. "Listen, Catherine, when Dante pulled me out of there, he gave me a purpose. I will never forget the night at his shack in the woods, the first night away from this cursed region. I was still—" Shit. How could he even explain the darkness that had still gripped him that night? "I almost murdered him that night," he said softly. "Not on purpose, but because I couldn't stop it. If it hadn't been for Dante, all would have been lost, but that night, he saved me from hell. I owe him, Catherine. He was a great man, and his legacy has saved the world in ways you can't imagine. I can't walk away from that, and I can't let you put it in jeopardy. It's so much bigger than you know." He stopped, cutting off the long-winded explanation. What was he doing explaining himself to Catherine? He didn't explain. He didn't engage in discussions. He did what he needed to do. And that was it. "Never mind," he said, turning away to head back to camp. "We're not going."

"Dante? Your former leader was named Dante?" Her voice was a stunned whisper.

He glanced back at her, frowning when he saw her skin had gone ghostly white. "Yeah. Dante Sinclair."

Her face was stark with shock. "He had a shack in the woods? In Oregon?"

Ryland turned back to face her. "I didn't say it was in Oregon," he said softly.

"Did it have a door? Or was it a simple hut about twenty-five yards from a river?"

A cold foreboding began to simmer through Ryland. "No door. Near a river. Why? How do you know that?"

She pressed her hand to her forehead. "Was his weapon a spear?"

Jesus Christ. He grabbed her upper arms and hauled her over to him. "What do you know about Dante?" he demanded. "What do you know?"

She looked up at him. "I took his soul," she whispered. "I took it."

Ryland stared at her in disbelief. "What are you talking about?"

"When he died, I was there to take his soul." She closed her eyes. "I took his soul that night, after those weapons did their job, after those men killed his body."

Ryland went cold, ice cold as his fingers dug into the arms of the woman he'd wanted to make love to only moments ago. He remembered all too well what Ian's *sheva*, Alice Shaw, had told them about Catherine. "No one's soul dies unless you kill them," he echoed. "You are the forever death." His mind shot back to that moment when Dante had visited him after his death, when he'd said he couldn't come back again. Was that the moment Catherine had killed him? The moment when his existence ended forever? Jesus Christ. Was Dante's spirit gone as well?

"I am forever death," Catherine said. "This is true."

"Jesus." His fingers tightened on her arms as he fought to stay in control. He was holding the woman who had killed the man he had dedicated his life to? No, no, no! Furious, he tore his grip off her and turned his back on her, clasping his hands behind his head as he fought to rationalize what was going on. "You're an angel," he said. "Angels aren't evil." He knew they weren't. They were beautiful and amazing, merciful creatures who brought light into darkness.

She laughed softly, a chuckle with no mirth. "No, I'm not evil. But I *am* hell." She touched his arm, and he instinctively stiffened. "I'm sorry, Ryland. I didn't mean to do it, if that is any consolation."

"Didn't mean to?" He spun around to face her, suddenly furious. "How can you kill someone and not mean to? You have to be stronger than that! If you're given the gift of being able to take a life, you have to control it! You can never unleash it by accident!"

Fury blazed in her eyes. "I am strong," she snapped. "I would have killed a lot more if I wasn't! And Dante's not dead forever! They took his soul from me before I could destroy it. So—"

"They took his soul from you? Who? Who has his soul?" Jesus Christ, was Dante's soul still alive somewhere? "Where the fuck is he?"

She met his gaze, and in it he saw the ultimate regret. "He's in the nether-realm," she said.

Ryland stared at her. "What?"

"The nether-realm. They took him."

"They?" But he didn't need to ask who 'they' were. He'd been born in the nether-realm. He knew what it was like there. He knew the creatures who ruled those lands, and he knew what drove them: greed, power, and pure, untainted evil. He knew, because he'd been one of them. "Jesus," he whispered, sinking down onto a damp rock. He bowed his head and ran his hands through his hair, fighting to stay focused. "Dante's soul is trapped in the nether-realm?"

Catherine nodded. "Same as my daughter, except her spirit is still in her body," she said. "I'm going to get her out."

Ryland's fingers dug into his scalp, and he suddenly realized that his fingers were elongating. Silver claws jabbed out of the tips of his fingers. "Jesus Christ." He jerked his hands off his head and fisted his hands, willing the claws to recede. "I can't go back in there," he said. "I fucking can't."

"Why not?"

"Because it will turn me back into this!" Ryland grabbed the collar of his shirt and tore it open with a roar of fury, showing Catherine the secret that he had kept for so long, the secret that only Dante knew.

※※※

EMBLAZONED ON RYLAND'S CHEST was a drawing of a fanged monster with massive wings, blood dripping from its teeth, and claws plunged deep inside the chest of a woman. The creature's eyes raged with violence and death. Its body was covered in spiked scales, its head tipped upward in what could only be a howl of victory. Strewn around the creature were dozens of dismembered people, their faces still etched in the terrified screams of a violent death. It was like an ancient biblical drawing of a horror unleashed upon the earth by the very devil himself.

The image of the creature was a black outline on Ryland's flesh, as though someone had sketched it but never had time to fill it in. As she watched, the eyes of the creature seemed to move, rolling toward her as if targeting her as its next prey. Sucking in her breath, she tried to scramble backwards, stopped only by the vine that bound her to Ryland. "What in God's name is that?" she whispered, too horrified to speak. She could almost see its ribs moving with each breath, its nostrils flaring as it scented her.

"Me." He jerked his shirt closed, and she saw the sharp tips of something silver poking from the ends of his fingers.

Catherine gasped. "How can that be you?"

"It's what I was born to be," he said, his eyes almost boiling over with violence and anger, and death. So much death. "If I go back to the nether-realm, I will become it again." He met her gaze. "And the first thing I'll do is kill you."

She stared at him. "Me? Why me?"

"Because you're good, and I kill good things." He swept his forearm across his chiseled stomach and bowed low. "Say hello to one of the nether-realm's most prized experiments, a slave of the utmost power," he said. Then he raised his eyes to her, even as he maintained his bow. "And your worst nightmare. Everyone's worst nightmare."

"Slave?" she echoed. He couldn't mean *slave*. Ryland was a man of such power, an immortal warrior above and beyond the hold of anything and anyone. Nothing and no one would have the power to force him to submit to their reign. But even as she asked the question, she saw the grim acknowledgment in his eyes. He spoke the truth. *Slave.*

"Yeah." He touched the tail of the creature. "When color begins to fill this in, the power of the nether-realm begins to take me. When the image of the beast is completely filled in, I lose the ability to say no." He looked past her at the mountains behind them. "Every step I take closer to the entrance tightens its grip on me. I can't go there. Dante saved me for a reason, and if I go back there, all he wanted me to become is destroyed forever. And he is who I owe."

She lifted her chin, struggling to recover after his revelation. "Are you so sure about that?" she asked.

He narrowed his eyes. "Sure about which part? Because, yeah, I have a pretty vivid memory of what I used to be and what I had to do."

Empathy flickered through her for what he'd endured, but she fought to suppress it. She had to focus. Her daughter's life depended on it. "I meant the part about how going back there would violate what Dante wanted for you. How do you know what he wanted for you?"

Ryland scowled. "Trust me, I know. I'm not going back there."

She saw in his eyes that he meant it, and she understood it. She really did. She lived every day with being the creature she didn't want to be. She accepted that, and she could not ask him to turn himself back into that which he despised. "Will you at least guide me to the entrance so I can go in and save my daughter? I'll go in by myself."

Ryland laughed softly, bitterly. "If I take you there, how does that protect the Order? You're our angel. I owe you safety, and delivering you to the mouth of hell won't do it."

Catherine gritted her teeth in irritation. "I'm not the Order's guardian angel," she said for what felt like the thousandth time. "I'm an angel of *death*. How would an angel of death protect you?"

Ryland shrugged. "You give our weapons the power to kill."

"Don't you think that goes against what defines an angel? An angel who blesses your weapons with the power to take life isn't really very angelic, is it?"

Ryland narrowed his eyes at her. "I don't give a shit what you think you are," he said. "I know you're our angel, and I'm going to keep you safe. No nether-realm."

She lifted her chin. "Not even to save Dante? You're going to let his soul rot in hell because you don't want to be a demon again, or whatever you are?"

"Hey!" He grabbed her arm, his eyes flashing with fury. "Don't *ever* judge my commitment to Dante. There are not always simple answers."

"So, you'll let him rot there?"

True pain flashed in Ryland's eyes and he swore. Catherine saw the torment in his eyes, the weight of the choice he had to make, and her heart softened. How could she ask this man to break a promise he had made to someone else? There was so little of that kind of loyalty left in this world.

But if she let him be, she would be allowing her daughter to die. And there was no chance of that. Besides, she would never make the mistake of believing in a man again. She could not afford mercy. "If you take me to the nether-realm," she said, offering him what she already could tell he wanted most. "I will be able to find Dante's spirit and free him. You wouldn't have to go in there."

Ryland's eyes flashed with interest, and she knew she had

him. "Take me there," she said. "Let me go get my daughter and Dante. When I come out, I will go with you." And she would. Once her daughter was free, she didn't care where she went. And if Ryland would protect her, then he'd do the same for her daughter.

His jaw flexed, but she saw the yearning in his eyes. "It's too dangerous," he said. "The nether-realm would kill you."

Galvanized by the window of acquiescence she heard in his voice, she stepped forward. "I can't be killed, Ryland. I'm the angel of death." It was a lie, a blatant lie, but she didn't care. So little could kill her, it was almost the truth. Unfortunately, much of what could hurt her was in the nether-realm.

Anger flashed in his eyes. "Don't lie to me, Catherine. Never fucking lie. I hate lies."

She swallowed, again accosted with that creepy sensation that he could see into her soul. "Okay," she said. "There are things in there that can kill me, but I have a lot of control over stuff in the nether-realm. The angel of death has powers down there."

"Do you?" Sudden interest flared in his eyes. "What kind of powers?"

She grimaced. "I don't know exactly. I've never been there. But the nether-realm is about the most heinous kinds of death, and that's my specialty."

"Is it, now?" Ryland met her gaze thoughtfully, then he took her hand and placed it on the creature on his chest. "Tell me, Catherine, could you protect me from this?"

The drawing on Ryland's chest seemed to undulate beneath her hand. She could feel the sharp pricks of scales, the heat of a body hotter than his should be. Was it more than a drawing? Was it actually a part of him, living and breathing on his chest? "Are you a dragon?" she asked.

He shrugged. "Of sorts." He met her gaze. "Can you protect me from it?"

She took a deep breath, and knew it wasn't worth it to lie to this man who seemed to see inside her soul. "I doubt it."

"If you're my guardian angel, you can." He tapped his fingers over his chest. "Because this creature is death, and it's your realm. As you said."

"Well, I don't know exactly what I can do." She shook her head, guilt suffusing her even though she wanted desperately to say all the right words that would make him help her. She might be up close and personal with death, with secrets that were as horrific as his, but at the same time, she *was* an angel. There were limits to what she could live with, and deluding a man into risking his life wasn't one of them. "I can't let you go in there under false pretenses," she admitted. "I'm not your guardian angel, and I can't protect you—"

"I believe you are." His fingers closed around her wrist. "Which means you can protect me from myself. I'll protect us from everything else." His eyes blazed with intention. "We're going in there, Catherine, and we're going to get Dante back."

She stared at him as horror and hope warred within her. "You're going with me?"

"Fuck yeah. We're getting Dante and your daughter, and then we're getting out."

Fear shuddered through her, and she shook her head. She didn't want to stay aligned with him. She needed her space from him, room to find her daughter. "No, I want to go alone. I can't protect you from yourself." She knew better than to trust a man or to align with one. What would he do to her when he realized she really couldn't protect him? She knew too well the power of a man with a vengeance. "Just take me to the entrance—"

"No." He held up his bound arm, dragging hers with it. "We stay together, angel. You help me find Dante, and I swear I will turn over the bowels of hell to find your daughter."

The promise in his eyes struck deep, making Catherine want to cry...at the same time it made her want to flee from him as fast as she could, before he could betray her forever, in the worst way possible. "I can't—"

"You can, and you will. *We* will. There's no other choice." His eyes blazed with adrenaline and purpose, and she knew he was on a mission that would not be denied. "I'm getting Dante back, you're going to help me, and that's the end of it."

"Hey, guys," Thano interrupted, riding up on his horse while Zach strolled up behind, carrying a load of firewood so high it hid his face. "Good to see you all are dressed."

Irritation flashed over Ryland's eyes and he turned quickly toward his team, shrugging his shoulders so his coat fell forward over his chest, sealing the monster from view. "Change of plans," he said. "We're going to the nether-realm to rescue Dante. We leave at first light."

The die had been cast.

The rescue mission was in gear.

But as Catherine listened to Ryland explain to his men about

Dante's soul, and saw their suspicious glances cast her way, the emotion burning deep within her wasn't relief that she'd just found a savior to help her reclaim her daughter. It was the haunting sensation of dark, ominous dread, as if she had just unleashed the darkest shadow over the earth she loved so dearly, and it was too late to lock it back up again.

☉ CHAPTER SEVEN ☉

THE CAMPFIRE FELT GOOD.

Catherine knew she shouldn't relax in the soothing warmth, but she couldn't help it. She'd been so cold for weeks during her trek through the mountains, so worried about her daughter, the map, and the men tailing her. After all that effort, everything was falling into place. She had secured a team to help her breach the nether-realm. She wasn't being hunted. After carrying so much stress for so long, she had no willpower left to resist the temptation of sinking into this brief respite and trying to recharge.

She stretched her hand to the flames, drinking in the warmth and, more importantly, the light from the fire. She felt like a moth, lured to the flame in the dark of night, trying to pry strength from its roaring magic. She called to the brightness, absorbing it into her body. The fire dimmed, fading under her assault.

Zach gave her a strange look and flicked his index finger at the fire. It roared to life again, fed by his energy, while she drained it. Encouraged by the fact that Zach seemed able to replenish what she took from the fire, she harvested more of its energy. The flames dipped into dark shadows as she extracted the light.

Again, Zach flicked his finger at the flames, making them blaze up once more, but this time, he was studying her intently, clearly aware of what she was doing. She managed a smile, trying to look non-threatening, hoping he wouldn't stop feeding her light. She needed it desperately to stave off the decay of her soul long enough to save her daughter.

Plus, in truth, the warmth of the fire felt amazing, even aside from the fact it gave her light. Such a simple pleasure, to be warm, but she would never take it for granted again. Now all that was left was to find a way to sleep, somehow. She was so drained, she knew she needed to rest, but how could she? Since she'd reached the mountains, she hadn't dared slow long enough for more than an occasional brief nap, knowing that Ryland and the others were hunting her. But now that they'd caught up with her, now that they were surrounding her and offering her protection due to her apparent status as an Order of the Blade guardian angel, she felt almost safe.

She would never trust them, not truly, but she was smart enough to realize that Ryland's decision to escort her to the nether-realm was a gift she had to accept. She would take it, she would use his expertise, but she could never dare let down her guard. She would establish a plan to lose him as soon as it was reasonable. As soon as she could actually do it.

Her fingers traced the vine binding her to Ryland. He was several feet away, stretching the two feet of twine to the max. Would he try to put a new one on in the morning, when the sunlight dissolved this restraint? If so, how would she break it? She'd seen him try to cut it, but his blade had bounced off. A plant that an Order of the Blade weapon couldn't sever? What was it? There had to be another way to break it.

Until she figured out what it was, she had to be vigilant to protect herself against these warriors, and the choices they were going to make.

Through her eyelashes, she watched the interaction between Ryland and his teammates, trying to get a sense of who they were, of what the signs would be when they betrayed her. What did they value more than her? What would be the thing each would betray her for? Ryland valued Dante. She knew that. He would choose Dante over her and Lucy in a heartbeat, but that also meant that he would protect her as long as he thought she could help him locate Dante. So, the thing that made him least trustworthy in the end, made him most trustworthy right now. With him, she was safe for the moment.

Zach, she had no sense of. She studied the quiet warrior as he ate his dinner and looked over her map. His tousled hair was ragged, as black as the most barren of nights, a haunting eve when no stars and no moon lit the way. His eyes were a dark brown, not the bottomless black of Ryland's. Down his right temple, almost hidden by his hairline, was a six-inch scar. It was jagged and uneven, a brutal reminder of a battle lost. She knew Calydons rarely scarred, so she couldn't imagine what could have left such a mark on him.

The night was cold, although not as cold as when they'd been up on the mountains, but he was wearing only a T-shirt. His calf-length black leather duster was tossed over a nearby boulder, the metal rivets glistening in the moonlight. He was well-muscled and intense, but he kept his energy tightly wrapped, making it difficult to get a read on him. His loyalty to the Order had been evident in his initial reluctance to endanger her by taking her to the nether-realm, but once he'd understood that Dante's soul hung in the balance, he'd been on board. Loyal to the Order, but it was a different loyalty than Ryland's. Less visible. Less clear. She didn't know what drove him, and that made him dangerous and unpredictable to her.

And Thano. He was irreverent and sarcastic, always moving too quickly on his horse for her to get a sense of him. Her only real impression of him was the way Ryland looked at him, like Thano was the antidote to his hell. But now he was seated on the ground, finally still for the first time since they'd caught up to her, giving her the opportunity to inspect him more carefully. His horse was standing over him, his chin resting on Thano's shoulder as the warrior stroked the animal's face. She'd seen Warwick Cardiff, the black magic wizard who had kidnapped her, riding the beast, but there was no doubt that a bond had already formed between the stallion and his new rider. Was Apollo Thano's driving motivation? The thing that would compel him to betray her?

He turned sharply as she thought of him, his green eyes searching her out as if he, like Ryland, had heard her thoughts. There were hints of violet flecks in them, almost like tiny sparks of... "Oh my God." She sat up abruptly. "It was you." During her time in Warwick's merciless hands, she'd done things that still tormented her, things that had nearly destroyed her soul, things that had stripped her of time to find her daughter. The man sitting before her had haunted her nightmares for days, which could mean only one thing: that she'd visited him in her sleep, and that was never a good thing.

He raised his brows, but there was a sudden lack of mirth in his expression. "You just now recognized me?"

"Yes." She looked down at his legs, suddenly understanding why he was riding Apollo all the time. Thano was stretched out on the ground, leaning against a heavy log, acting like he owned the earth he was reclining on with such presence.

His long legs were stretched out in front of him, crossed at the ankles. His muscles were as thick and cut as Ryland's, teeming with strength, but there was a lack of life in his legs that spoke of damage that ran deep. She had not seen Thano stand up for even a second. When he'd dismounted from Apollo, he'd parked himself right on the ground and hadn't gotten up. Something was wrong with his legs, or his spine, or his body, or something. As the thought drifted through her mind, she suddenly realized what had happened. "Oh, dear God," she whispered. "I did that to you, didn't I?"

He didn't so much as shift in response. "Yeah."

She became gradually aware that Ryland and Zach had stopped talking, and were both looking at her. Her heart aching, she crawled across the dirt toward Thano and reached for his ankle, wanting to see what she'd done—

"No." Ryland caught her wrist, staying her hand just before her fingers brushed his skin. "Don't touch him."

She looked at him, her heart shriveling at the look of accusation on his face, the awareness of what a monster she was. "I'm not going to hurt him."

"You've done enough." He pushed her back from Thano, putting himself between her and his teammate, protecting the warrior from her.

As he did so, her heart sank. Did he really think she had hurt him on purpose? That she would do it to him again, in cold blood? Apparently he did, and the little bit of softness that had opened in her heart for him shriveled back up. If he believed her to be that kind of person, then she could be certain that his loyalty to her would go only so far. So, did he really see her as their protector, or did his instinct tell him the truth, that she was a significant danger to all of them?

"Tell me, Ryland," Zach said as he picked up a stone and held it in his palm. "If Catherine was the one who hurt Thano, why is it that you think she is our guardian angel? Seems to me that a member of the Order's guardian angel trinity wouldn't kick our asses like that."

Ryland glanced at Catherine, and she stiffened at the burning faith in his pitch-black eyes. Despite all the evidence, he still believed she was some great protector of his team. "Explain it to him, angel. Help him understand."

Angel? She realized suddenly that Ryland didn't see her as a woman. He saw her only as an angel, a beacon of beauty and wonder so true that even the broken body of his teammate couldn't dissuade him from believing in her goodness.

God, she wanted to be that woman who Ryland was looking at, the amazing, pure angel he believed in. But she wasn't. She wasn't what he wanted her to be. But in the heat of his gaze, the protest died in her throat. She didn't want that light to stop burning for her. It felt so amazing to have someone believe in her, to look at her with such reverence. It was a lie, an error, a belief based on a misconception, but in that moment, she couldn't bring herself to correct him. Instead, she simply shrugged. "I have no answer," she said softly, leaving her response open to interpretation.

Ryland narrowed his eyes, but Zach scowled and crushed the stone in his fist. "That means she's not our guardian," he said.

"I don't think she is either," Thano agreed, his voice deadly serious. "I'm not even sure she's an angel."

"I am an angel," Catherine said. "That, I can promise."

Thano met her gaze. "Do angels do what you did to me?"

She bit her lip. "Not all angels wear halos and float around in shining white lights," she said.

Ryland leaned forward. "Are you a fallen angel?"

She shook her head. "Fallen angels are those that started off good, who broke the vow they made." She shrugged. "There's no bar that I fell from. An angel of death has her own set of rules." She managed a small smile. "It's always best to stay away from us." She yawned suddenly, and a chill crept down her arms. What if she fell asleep with these men nearby? She looked directly at Ryland. "And never let us fall asleep." It was a request for aid, and when Ryland slowly nodded, she knew he understood.

Relief rushed through her, and she suddenly felt exhausted. Ryland would make sure she didn't kill any of them. She didn't have to fight the battle herself. Wearily, she leaned forward, opening both palms toward the fire. She pulled more light in, and the fire almost died.

Zach flicked it on again, but this time she saw Ryland and Thano watching her as well. She saw from their expressions that they had just realized what was going on between her and Zach.

"You feed on fire?" Ryland asked.

There was no point in lying. "I need light," she said. "Light keeps everything safe from me. Sunlight is best, but the fire helps."

Ryland shot a look at Zach. "Keep the fire going."

"But of course." The fire suddenly blazed in the night, spiraling several yards into the sky. The heat from it was tremendous, almost too much to bear, but she forced herself not to retreat, draining the flames of their light while the men watched. It struck her as unusual that not a single one of them had questioned her need for light, or been surprised by the fact she fed on it. As immortal warriors, perhaps they had seen so much that very little surprised them anymore. Either way, it felt good not to be looked at as if she were insane, and not to be treated as if she were a leper.

She managed a smile at them all. "Thanks."

Ryland nodded, Thano said nothing, and Zach pressed a kiss to the powdered remains of the stone he'd been holding in his hand. It burst into a cascade of yellow and orange flames. He tossed it at Thano.

The warrior snatched it out of the air and closed his fist around the flames. After about three seconds, he dropped it with a curse and shook out his hand. "Shit, that hurt."

Zach ground his jaw. "I guess you didn't get the ability to withstand all fire, then." He looked at Catherine. "What did you do to him? What powers did you give him?"

Catherine blinked. "What powers? I didn't give him any powers."

"No?" Thano held up his hand, and a violet ball of flame appeared on his palm. It was small at first, but as they watched, it slowly grew in size, until it was stretching almost two feet above his palm—

"Put it out," Zach ordered, and Thano instantly obeyed. "Don't push the tests too far," Zach said. "We don't want to wind up blowing up the planet by accident."

Three heads turned toward Catherine. "What did you do to me?" Thano asked. "Where did the purple flame come from, and what happened to my legs?"

Catherine shook her head, guilt surging inside her. "I have no idea," she said. "No one has ever survived what I did to you." She met his gaze, forcing herself to see the damage she'd inflicted, praying that looking him in the eye might finally give her the strength to resist the pull of darkness that held her so ruthlessly and dangerously in its grip. She'd taken his soul, she'd fed upon it, and then regurgitated the remains back into his body. The wizard had forced her to do it with black magic that she couldn't withstand, but she still looked back, wondering if there had been some way to stop herself, if only she'd been stronger. "I'm so sorry. I truly am."

But she could see from Zach and Thano's expressions that she was not forgiven. She looked over at Ryland. He was studying her with the same dark expression he always had, as if he could see into the depths of her soul. There was still reverence emanating from him for the angel he perceived her to be, but at the same time, there were shadows circling his aura, dark shadows that made her shiver. "Are you okay?" she asked softly.

He nodded. "I'm always okay." He flicked a hand at the

others. "You guys get some sleep. I'll take first watch."

Thano and Zach nodded, and within minutes they were stretched out asleep, warriors who clearly knew how to grab every second of shut-eye that they could. But as they went to sleep, their role as chaperones ended, effectively leaving her alone with Ryland, the man who was part nether-world dragon, and part tempter.

She didn't know which was scarier.

⬧⬧⬧⬧

RYLAND STUDIED CATHERINE as she fed upon the fire. The flames danced upon her cheeks, casting orange and red reflections on her skin and swathing her eyes in dark shadows. As the flames darkened, drained of life, Ryland's skin prickled. With her blond hair tangled around her shoulders, the hooded look on her face, and the eerie glow of her hands as the flames bled into them, she looked every bit the destructor. Not an angel of death. More like the grim reaper.

The weapons in his forearms burned, warning him of the threat she posed. At the same time, however, something inside him was edged with interest and intrigue. She practically bled power and darkness, a woman who seemed to mirror all that stalked him. He leaned forward, resting his forearms on his bent knees, watching her intently as she engaged in what almost felt like a ritual feeding. "Why do you need to feed on light?"

Her blue eyes flickered toward him. "My soul needs to summon power from external sources in order to survive," she said. "It feeds upon the light or energy of others. When I take a soul, it nourishes me. Light also feeds me, so if I can fill my soul with light, it helps stave off the need to feed on souls. The thing is that a person's soul is the essence of their life force. It's eternal life, so it's extremely powerful. Sunlight and fire aren't really a close second, you know? I can control it pretty well when I'm awake, but when I sleep, my defenses go down." She managed a smile. "So, don't let me sleep."

He studied her, surprised by her explanation. How was it that an angel fed upon others? It made no sense. "What happens when you feed on a soul?"

She bit her lip, and he felt a wash of guilt from her. "It becomes a part of me," she said. "That means it dies forever, since I'm death." She opened her mouth to say more, then shut it.

Ryland moved closer to her, compelled by this troubled angel, needing to learn more about her. For hundreds of years, he'd survived on the memory of that angel, the ethereal being that Dante had recruited to save him, though Dante had never explained his connection to the angel.

For the centuries since, Ryland had elevated angels to a goddess status. To actually be connecting with a true angel was almost beyond his comprehension. Catherine was nothing like what an angel should be. She was burdened with death, a murderer, and deprived of her own child. It made no sense, and he pulsed with the need to unravel the mystery, to reconcile this woman before him with how angels were supposed to be. "Tell me the rest," he said. "Tell me the things you don't want me to know."

She glanced at him, and he saw incredible agony in her eyes. Burdens so great that her soul was being eaten away by their weight.

He leaned over her and took a lock of her hair between his fingers, needing to reassure himself that she was real, that her hair was the soft, fragile reality of a vulnerable woman. Needing to touch her for his own sanity. "Tell me, Catherine. Tell me." He moved his hand so that his thumb brushed against her jaw. The feel of her skin against his was electrifying, a shock that made them both suck in their breath.

He'd never stroked a woman's skin before. He'd never been so still in a moment that he could actually feel the heartbeat of time as it passed by, but right now, it seemed as if the very earth itself had stopped spinning, as if the wind had stopped moving, as if every one of his senses was attuned to the woman before him. He could hear her breathe. The tempting fragrance of new spring seemed to drift from her skin. The faint pulse of a dark threat seemed to emanate from her through the very earth itself. She was beauty and light, and at the same time, she was an ominous shadow hovering in deadly readiness.

She was pure, elemental beauty and allure, everything that seemed to awaken his very soul.

His angel closed her eyes, her dark lashes resting on her cheeks as if she were a precious innocent. She tilted her head into his touch, as compelled by their physical connection as he was. "Why do I want to trust you so badly?" she whispered.

"Because you know I would protect you with my life," he said, leaning into her space until his lips were so close to hers that he could feel her breath on his mouth. "You're my guardian angel, but I'm your protector." He leaned forward and brushed his lips over hers.

She gasped and jerked backward, a rejection that seemed to knife right across his gut. "No," she said. "Don't."

Ryland ground his jaw, swearing at himself. What was he

thinking? She was an angel. A guy didn't just go around kissing angels. "Sorry." He dropped his hand and pulled back—

"No." This time, as she protested, she reached for his hand. When her fingers wrapped around his wrist, Ryland froze in shock. Her fingers were delicate and feminine, almost fragile in comparison to the thick bones in his wrist. Electricity seemed to sizzle through him as she guided his hand back to her face and pressed it to her cheek. "I need this," she whispered. "Just give it to me for a minute."

Her skin was the softest thing he'd ever touched in his life. Was it like silk? The petal of a new rose? The down on a wolf pup? He didn't have anything to compare it to. He wasn't a touchy guy. He fought. He bled. He killed. He protected. He didn't *touch*.

But as he sat there with his hand on Catherine's cheek, his thumb trailing over the incredibly delicate lines of her jaw, his senses were inundated with everything about her. Her scent, the sound of her voice, the way she seemed to inhale his presence, the warmth of her skin, the mesmerizing shade of her eyes. Everything about her seemed to leap into vivid technicolor so intense that it was almost overwhelming. "I don't understand this." He didn't. He couldn't. The entire experience was so far outside the realm of what he'd lived.

"I don't either." She wrapped her hand around his wrist, as if she were trapping his hand against her face, as if she were as desperate as he to seize this moment and never let it end. "I don't trust you," she whispered. "I know that you'll betray me when the time is right. I know better than to let myself trust anything about you, but your touch feels like a blessing from heaven."

"Betray you?" He could barely voice the words he was so shocked by what she'd said. "*Betray you?*"

She opened her eyes, intense azure depths only inches from his. "Of course you will," she said. "But I know that, so I can protect myself."

"Jesus, Catherine." He slid his hand behind her and cupped her neck as sudden outrage burned through him. "There is no chance on this fucking planet that I would ever betray you." He grabbed her bound hand and pressed it to his chest. "Can't you feel the truth of my words? Lying to make people feel good is a bunch of crap and a waste of time. I have no lies. I fucking mean every word I say." Then he swore again. What the hell was he doing, talking to her like that? "Shit, Catherine, I didn't mean to swear in front of you. You're above that crap." He swore again. "Shit. I didn't mean to do it again. I mean, shit!" He shut his mouth, disgusted by how uncouth he was.

Her fingers dug into his chest, and she smiled, a smile that melted his fucking heart. "Ryland. I'm the angel of death. I'm not fragile, naive, or innocent. I know exactly how rough you are. I can taste the death that bleeds off you. I've seen the darkest side of humanity. I have no faith left in anything. You don't need to worry about swearing in front of me."

"Fuck that." He grimaced, swearing silently to himself. When had he become such a foul-mouthed pig? "No, Catherine, you're wrong. You're an angel, and that won't change no matter how much darkness you've endured." He slid his fingers through her hair, still awed by the softness of the strands, and how unbelievable it felt to have her lean into his touch. "I'm going to clean up my language for you, I promise. But I'm going to warn you, I don't have any practice at that kind of shi—stuff, so yeah. I am what I am."

She laughed then, a magical sound that made his heart stutter. "How an immortal warrior steeped in death and birthed of the nether-realm can be cute, I don't know, but you just managed it."

"Cute?" He stared at her. "You think I'm cute?" He didn't even understand that.

"Yes, cute." Her smile faded into seriousness. "Ryland, you need to understand something. Although I'm an angel, I am not some mythical beauty with a pure and untainted soul, and you need to stop seeing me that way." She lightly clasped his chin. "See me as I truly am, Ryland. I need that."

"I already do." He raised her hand and pressed her palm to his lips. "You're the one who doesn't see you the way you truly are."

She stared at him, and suddenly her eyes filled with tears. "You are a beautiful man," she whispered.

Ryland laughed softly. "Now, who's the one not seeing the truth of the person before them?"

Catherine smiled again, and this time it was a smile of sadness and loss. "Oh, but I do see you." She tapped his chest. "You're a monster, Ryland. You're death. You're mindlessly loyal to Dante at the expense of all else. You don't have empathy for others, and you are bound by the creature you once were. I see it all."

He grinned, relaxing. "Okay, you do see me. Good to know." For some reason, it was important to him that she know who he was and what he was capable of. "As we get closer to the nether-realm, my tattoo may start to fill in," he said. "We need to keep an eye on it. If it happens quickly, I might get caught up in it before I realize what's happening."

Her face grew serious. "What do I do if that happens?"

He thought back to the days long past, trying to remember the stages. He pulled open his shirt and looked down at the creature lying dormant on his chest. "See this band at its neck?" He pointed to what looked like a slave collar around the creature's neck. "That's the critical point. That's when they get control of me. If that starts to fill in, it's too late." He looked at her. "The only chance is death. You guys have to kill me."

She stared at him. "What? No—"

"Yes." He then pointed to the creature's front claws and back legs, to the thick cuffs around those appendages. "It's a five-point indenture," he said. "All five cuffs need to be triggered for them to have full control. Once two of them have filled in, I need to turn back, no matter where I am. By the third and fourth ones, they are gaining control over me. By the fifth—" He touched his own neck, needing to reassure himself that there was no collar there. "I become theirs." Darkness began to swirl through him, and tension radiated off him. "I won't become their slave again," he bit out. "I refuse." He rubbed his neck again, almost able to feel that collar around his neck, the one that had trapped him for so long. His throat became tight, his breath rasping in his throat. He coughed and scratched at his neck again—

"It's okay, Ryland," Catherine said softly, laying her hand over his. "They don't have you. There's no collar there."

Her touch seemed to strip the panic from him, and his hand stilled beneath hers. He didn't move, focusing all his attention onto the gentleness of her touch, stunned by how one simple gesture could take away the memories and bring him back. "How do you do it?"

She raised her eyes to him, eyes full of empathy and sadness. "Do what?"

"I don't know." He gestured to their intertwined hands, to the peace that she'd given him through their touch. "Whatever this is."

"Comfort you?"

"Is that what it is?"

She smiled. "It's called kindness, Ryland. It's what some people in this world do for each other."

"Well, it's good shit."

She laughed, a merry twinkle in her eyes. "As I said, you're very cute." She leaned forward and kissed him lightly, a quick kiss that wasn't about sex and desire. It was playful and intimate, and it seemed to catapult through him like the wind on a mountaintop on a hot summer day.

She paused and pulled back slightly, meeting his gaze. "Cute men are dangerous."

"Immortal warriors from the nether-realm are dangerous," he warned her.

"Put them together, and a girl should run away screaming."

Run away? Sudden tension leapt through Ryland, and he grabbed her wrist. "You're not leaving."

Her eyebrows shot upward. "I'm tied to you. I can't go anywhere."

"Oh, right." Swearing under his breath, Ryland released her. What the hell was wrong with him? What in the name of all that was good in this land had made him react like that at the idea of her bailing on him? Scowling, he shook his head. "I need you to find Dante," he said gruffly. "And to protect the Order."

"I know you do." Something flickered in her eyes. Sadness? Vulnerability? Disappointment? He couldn't tell, and it was gone before he could decipher it. "And I need you to guide me to the nether-realm. We need each other right now."

"Yeah." He shrugged his shoulders, trying to shake out the tension. "So, let's focus on that." He pointed behind her to the mountain range to the north. "It's a half-day hike in that direction."

Catherine sucked in her breath. "We're that close?"

He nodded. "We're just outside the borders of the nether-realm. By mid-morning, we'll be within the surface borders." And then...shit...shit was going to go down. "We'll have to move fast and try to get to the entrance before we're noticed."

Catherine nodded. "Okay. I can move fast."

He raised his brows. "I've been following you for three weeks. I know you can move fast."

She smiled, and there was a hint of pride in her eyes.

"If we follow the river, it will take us a little longer, but the water will protect us from most of the shit...I mean stuff...that guards the entrance." He had a sudden thought. "Can you shroud us the way you hid yourself from me?"

"Only if there are spirits of the dead around."

"We're going into the borderlands of the nether-realm. Almost everyone who ventures across those borders dies within an hour or two. There will be dead bodies the whole way in." As soon as he said the words, he regretted it. Discussing rotting flesh with an angel was not the way to treat her—

But Catherine simply nodded, apparently unaffected by the

crude topic. "Then, yes, I can hide us. It's not infallible if someone is specifically looking for us, but it will help."

Ryland grinned at her response. He'd just announced that they were heading into a land that killed anyone who crossed over, and she'd actually looked pleased. "You're an angel," he said, not able to keep the disbelief out of his voice.

She rolled her eyes at him in a decidedly human reaction. "I think we've established that pretty well by now, but if it makes you feel better to repeat the obvious, then yes, I'm an angel. Surprise, surprise."

He didn't laugh. "So, how can you be like you are? How can an angel be comfortable hiking among the remains of the dead?" He was really struggling to reconcile the woman Catherine was, and the things she was making him feel and sense, with who she was supposed to be as an angel. It was so foreign to the world he'd lived in for so long. He wasn't used to a world where he didn't know all the answers, where he wasn't in control.

She smiled then. "You, my dear man, need to modernize your opinion of angels." She leaned toward him, bracing her hands on her knees so that her jacket fell forward, showing her smooth collarbone and the deep V-neck of her shirt.

Desire shot through him and he swore, shoving his hands in his pockets before he could grab her. "I will not treat you like an ordinary human."

"For heaven's sake, Ryland, stop it! This isn't going to get us anywhere." Frustrated, she shoved at him, and he caught her wrists. Heat leapt through him at the skin-to-skin contact, raging lust that had no place being directed at an angel.

He swore under his breath and tried to release her, but she moved closer, invading his space. No one ever dared encroach upon him, and the fact she was doing it should have pissed him off. But all it did was make the lust thicken in his veins. She wasn't afraid of him. Not at all. And he fucking loved it.

"You need to understand several things about me," she said, leaning even further in, her eyes flashing with frustration as she shoved at his chest. "We're going into a war zone, and if you try to treat me like a delicate flower, we are all going to get killed. I'm an angel of death. I'm almost impossible to kill. I will do anything to save my daughter, and I've seen more horrific things than you can imagine. So, stop treating me like a porcelain doll! You need to realize that you have an asset on your hands, and see me as a woman, a warrior, not some freaking mist of white light. Got it?"

Raw, hot fire of need arose to meet her ire. Her strength and boldness was intoxicating. He was riveted by the way she fought him, completely unafraid of all that he was. "Hell, Catherine, you better hope I don't stop seeing you as an angel. The fact you're an angel is the only thing that's keeping me from throwing you down, pinning you to the earth, and making love to you until my claim on you is burned so deeply into your soul that you can't even take a breath without feeling mine, until your heart can't beat unless it's in rhythm with mine, until your entire body screams for mine every second of every day for the rest of your life."

Her eyes went wide, and she froze, going utterly still except for the pounding of her pulse at the base of her neck. Her cheeks were flushed, and her breath was shallow. "Dear God," she whispered, her fingers digging into his chest. "What was *that* little speech?"

"That, my dear angel, was not kindness." Ryland's hands dug into the dirt, tearing the earth aside in his attempt not to follow through on his threat and grab her. "It's the raw, untamed, burning physical need of a man for a woman." He ripped his hand free of the dirt and locked his hand behind her neck, yanking her down toward him. "It's not pure," he growled against her lips. "It's not ethereal. It's not angelic. It's dirty. It's sweaty. It's the visceral, uncontrollable fire that strips a man and woman of their ability to do anything but consume each other on every level they exist."

Her mouth opened in silent shock. "Really?"

He yanked her closer, until his lips were against hers. Not kissing. Not caressing. Just poised there, like a great predator ready to strike. "I never lie," he growled.

"Lying is a terrible thing," she agreed, her voice so breathy that it went right to his groin.

"Catherine." He gripped her hair, angling her face toward his, his lips moving against hers in seductive temptation as he spoke, whispering the words against her decadently soft lips. "The only thing keeping me from making that our reality is the fact that you're an angel. Don't tell me to see you as a woman, because if you do, my restraint is gone." He bit her lip, and nearly groaned at the taste of her mouth. "Tell me you're an angel," he commanded. "It's your only chance. Remind me that you're an angel. *Now*."

Catherine swallowed. "Ryland."

"Yeah."

"Do you consider Catherine to be a name worthy of an angel?"

He closed his eyes. "Yeah. Yeah, it is."

"Then call me Cat."

◉ CHAPTER EIGHT ◉

"CAT." With a low growl, he kissed her instantly.

It wasn't a kiss like Catherine had ever had before. It wasn't even a kiss. It was a complete possession, an unapologetic taking, a rampant assault on all of her senses. His lips were like the blazing heat of melted rock, burning her mouth even as his kiss drained her of all her senses. He shoved her backwards, and she fell back onto her hands as he took over the kiss. His shoulders loomed over her, massively wide, coursing with strength and muscle. His kiss was ferocious, so desperate and violent she could feel it tear at her shields and strip her bare...and she wanted more.

She didn't even know how to kiss like he was doing. She had no clue how to unleash such emotion and fire into a kiss. But it didn't matter. Her entire soul screamed with the need for more, with a raging desire that seemed to pour through her veins like hot lava, searing her from within.

He locked his arm around her waist and yanked her toward him, her breasts slamming into his chest. Her nipples burned as they rubbed against him. Her thighs seemed to scream with need as he dragged her legs around his waist. His hands clamped on her hips as he lurched to his feet, consuming her with kisses so deep they invaded her soul and ripped it from her grasp.

Heat combusted between them, steaming through the air as his boots thudded across the rocks, as his mouth descended upon her throat, kissing, and biting, and teasing her skin as he carried her. "Where are we going?" she gasped, gripping his hair as his mouth found the swell of her breast.

"I need privacy for what I'm going to do to you." He jerked

her shirt aside and took her nipple in his mouth, sucking so fiercely she almost screamed.

She writhed in his arms, her body restless and aching for more. More of what, she didn't even know. Never had she experienced the intensity of what Ryland was bringing out in her, in them. She felt out of control. Desperate. Frantic. Consumed by how badly she needed him. "It's too much," she gasped, fighting for breath, for control, for sanity.

"I know." He went down on his knees, cradling her in his strong arms as he laid her down.

She had not even a second to register the feel of the soft ground beneath her when he grabbed the front of her jacket and yanked it open, stripping her of her last protections against him. There was no time to get nervous, because he was on her too fast, his body heavy and hard against hers as he pinned her beneath his bulk.

His hips were between hers, moving with tantalizing rhythm. His kisses were penetrating and intense, almost violent with need. It was too much, too rough, too dangerous, and yet it was everything she wanted. She gripped his hair, kissing him back every bit as fiercely. She nipped at his lower lip, she welcomed his invasion, and she screamed for more.

Frantic, she moved her hands between them, wanting to feel his skin. "No more clothes," she whispered urgently. "I have to touch you."

Ryland grabbed her hand and shoved it beneath the hem of his shirt. His stomach quivered as she flattened her palm over it, and electricity seemed to leap between them. At the same time, he jerked her shirt and bra up, exposing her breasts to the cold night air. When the chilly air hit her nipples, reality came crashing back. What was she doing? She couldn't do this. Not with him. Not here. Not now. "Ryland—"

Her protest was swallowed by his kiss, by the desire that plunged through her as he rubbed his thumb over her nipple. Burning need soared through her, tearing her from sanity and plunging her into a world of passion, and desire, and the dark shadows of cravings so intense that nothing mattered but fulfilling them.

He broke the kiss, his mouth moving with heated intention down her body. Over her breasts, over her nipples, down her ribs, over her belly, and then lower.

She twisted in agonized need as he unzipped her jeans. Her hips rose to meet his assault, and then his mouth closed down on her core. The moment he touched her, something seemed to scream to life within her. More than desire, it was like a living thing streaking through her body, tearing her from her own mind and thrusting her into a world of incredible sensation. She twisted beneath his assault, gasping his name as he drew her to the climax—

"Holy shit." Ryland released her almost violently, jerking back from her.

Alarm leapt through Catherine and she jerked upright, yanking her shirt down. "What? What it is? What happened?" As she asked the question, she saw the look of shock in Ryland's eyes. "What?"

"It's started." He gestured to his chest, and she saw that the tip of the creature's tail was a bright turquoise. Just one dot, one brilliant, bright dot where only blackness and his flesh used to be.

"Oh my God." She stared at him in horror. "Why? What happened?"

He gave her a hooded look. "You," he said softly. "I think it was you."

※※※

THE VIOLENCE WAS SEETHING inside him. He could feel it coming alive, almost like a thousand demons awakening in his flesh. He hadn't felt it in hundreds of years, but in an instant, he was back in that moment as a child, when he'd first felt it. The horrific realization that something lived inside him. Something brutal and terrible. And now it was coming back to life.

"Me?" Catherine was staring at him, her blue eyes wide with horror. "How did I do that?"

Ryland yanked his shirt closed and shrugged his jacket back on. Then he crouched in front of her, searching her stricken face for answers that she had hidden from him. "What are you really, Catherine? Besides the angel of death. What's your relationship to the nether-realm?"

Her cheeks paled, and she shook her head. "No, I—"

"I need to know." His hands almost shaking with the urge to call out his weapons and defend himself from a threat he couldn't take down, he clasped the sides of her jacket and pulled it back over her shoulders, needing to hide her tempting body from him. Just the sight of her flesh made him want to finish what he'd started, but he couldn't risk it. Not until he figured out what the hell was going on. "The only thing that controls the beast within me is the nether-realm, but your kisses woke it up. Why?"

She pressed her lips together.

"Dammit, Catherine! Talk to me!"

She finally looked up at him. "I don't know what it is, exactly," she said hesitantly, her face slightly averted, as if expecting him to lash out at her. "When I was a young girl, I murdered an entire community of angels in my sleep. Every last one of them, except for Alice, my best friend."

Ryland swore. "How is that possible?"

"When I sleep, they take me."

"They? Who?"

She shrugged. "I don't know. Demons? Something worse? I hear whispered voices. A man and a woman. I don't know who they are."

A man and a woman? Shit. He knew who it had to be. He fucking knew. An icy, bitter chill seemed to settle in his bones. "How do they take you?"

She sat up, the truth coming more easily now that she'd started talking. "The light keeps me fed, but if I sleep when my soul is too hungry, I become a predator. That day that I killed everyone, when we came back in the morning, the air was thick with demon stench. Somehow, they link through me. I broke away that night with Alice's help. She has such a beautiful light that she sustained me for a long time." She laughed bitterly. "I actually thought I'd defeated them. How stupid is that?"

"You're not stupid," he said softly. "What happened next?"

"They took…" Her voice broke. "Then they took Lucy," she whispered, tears brimming in her eyes. "It broke me, losing her, and the way it happened. I lost all defenses against the darkness, especially when Warwick had me. I was broken, Ryland. And Warwick, he pushed me so far. Too far. So terribly far. He made me do things that—" She looked at him, her face stark with agony. "I have to find her soon, Ryland. I have to."

"We will. We'll get her." Ryland ground his jaw at the tremble in her voice. What had this woman suffered? So much. Too much. Anger rolled through him, outrage on her behalf. He understood too much about what she'd suffered, because it was so similar to what he faced every day.

"They want me to work for them," she said. "They plan for me to kill every Order member so that the earth is no longer protected. I killed Dante. I almost killed Thano. There will be more, Ryland, and

I can't stop it."

Ryland ran his hand through his hair, swearing under his breath at the story that was too much like his. She might not be an actual slave, but she fought the same battle he did, struggling not to become the monster that drove them both. She was trapped, just as he was. "Were you born there? Are you native to that realm?"

"No. My mother was an angel and my father was a human." She closed her eyes. "My parents were killed when I was four. I have this vague memory of something coming during the night, coming for me. My parents protected me, and they died."

Ryland sat down heavily beside her and draped his arms over his knees. "That was the night they got you."

"They," she whispered. "I don't even know who 'they' are."

"I do." He wiped his hand over his brow, surprised to find it slick with cold sweat. "You don't want to know."

"Okay." She didn't argue, and he didn't blame her. He wouldn't want to know either, if he had a choice. "I won't ask. Not tonight."

Ryland was quiet for a moment, digesting her news. It explained much about the dichotomy of who she was. "So, if they're reaching the earth-realm through you, they can use you to bind me." The thought made his skin crawl, and a prickle of foreboding slithered down his spine. He should walk away from her. No, he should run, stripping her of the ability to latch onto him.

But even as he thought it, he knew he couldn't.

She was his key to Dante. And she was the Order's third guardian angel, unable to do her job because the nether-realm held her in its grasp. She needed to be rescued so she could save them all. But he looked down at his chest, as if he could see the dot of turquoise on his flesh through his clothes. "Every minute with you will tie me closer to you, and therefore to them," he said.

"I'm not trying to bind you."

"No. But you are." He looked at the vine stretched between their wrists, at the noose tying him to the person sent to bring him down. What choice did he have? Dante needed him, and the Order needed Catherine. He had to manage the situation and repay his debt. "We'll just have to move fast," he said. "Get in and get out before you can bind me completely to them."

She looked at him, and he thought she was going to ask what would happen after that, when they were free. How would they stop the slide then?

But she didn't ask. She simply nodded. "So, we go in tomorrow."

"No." He stood up, then offered her his hand. "We wake the team and go now. There's no time to waste."

And just as he expected, his fragile, pure, delicate angel took his hand and stood right up, completely ready to go into hell at his side.

⟡⟡⟡⟡

FOUR HOURS LATER, Catherine stopped when Ryland held up his hand in a silent command for them to halt. Thano reined in Apollo. Zach went still, his sai clenched in his right hand as he scanned the sky. The two warriors had not questioned Ryland's decision to move fast when he woke them in the middle of the night, but she noticed that he had not explained about the dragon tattoo on his chest, and had given her a warning look when they'd asked why. Clearly, it was a secret that he wasn't sharing with them. Why had he told her about it? Why wasn't he telling his team? Too many questions, and no opportunity to find answers.

As the party stopped, the dawn was just beginning to break, casting the cold mountains in a swath of gentle light that seemed to bleed hope through the sparse pine trees and rugged shrubs. And with that first breath of sunshine, the vine binding Catherine and Ryland together vanished, freeing them. They looked at each other, and Catherine felt an unexplainable sense of regret, and for a split second, she thought she saw the same on his face.

Then he looked back at his team, taking several steps away from her, putting distance between them the first moment he could. She immediately folded her arms over her chest and raised her chin. How could she feel regret? She needed her space. She needed her freedom. She needed to be liberated to save her daughter when Ryland finally betrayed her, as she knew he would—

Ryland grabbed her arm suddenly and yanked her back over to him. "You will not shut me out," he muttered to her. "Our very survival depends on us being a stronger team than what's threatening us. We stay together. Got it?"

She gazed at him, and felt some of the tension in her chest ease. She nodded.

He flashed her a brief grin, then turned back in the direction he'd been leading them. So far, they'd hugged the river, moving fast, and Catherine had labored to keep up.

Traveling fast solo was one thing, but moving with the Order while they were on a mission was entirely different. They pushed at a relentless pace, with high demands for stealth. She was exhausted and drained, but so happy to see that the sky was cloudless, and they were going to be gifted with a day of bright sunshine.

Ryland went down on one knee and sifted the dirt through his fingers. He then rested his forearm on his knee and looked ahead. After a moment, he called out his machete with a crack and a flash of black light. He wedged the tip in the ground and dragged it through the dirt, making a horizontal line in the earth about six inches in front of him. "This is the border," he said. "This is where the fabric between the nether-realm and the earth begins to thin. Creatures that belong in hell survive in this area, and creatures that belong on earth die."

Apollo stomped his front foot and snorted, while Thano called out both of his halberds. "Excellent," he said. "I love a challenge."

"How do we stop them?" Zach asked. "Saplings again?"

"Depends on what it is," Ryland said. "Some of them, we just have to outrun."

Zach raised an eyebrow. "Outrun to where?"

Ryland flexed his hands, and Catherine could see the tension in his shoulders. "There's a waterfall near the entrance to the nether-realm," he said. "It's a remnant of the purity that once reigned here before the nether-realm leaked out. No harm can befall those who enter it. No harm can be done by those clothed in its purity."

Thano patted his restless mount's neck. "So, that means, once we go in there, we can't defend ourselves against anything until we dry off? Nothing can hurt us, but we can't hurt anything else either?"

Ryland glanced at him. "Yeah."

"So, you're saying that we could dive in there and then all the bad guys will have to skid to a stop at the water's edge. Then they'll sit there doing their nails for the next thousand years, or whenever it is we finally decide to get out of the fountain, at which point they'll kill us, because all we'll be able to do is compliment them on their stylish good looks?"

Ryland nodded. "Pretty much."

"Well, that sounds like a great plan," Thano said. "Let's not even bother to fight. Let's run right there and jump in even if no one is chasing us."

A grin played at the corners of Ryland's mouth, and Catherine saw some of the tension ease from his shoulders. She realized that Thano was good for him, a respite from the darkness, just as Alice had been for her. It was astonishing that the man who carried as much darkness as Ryland had allowed himself to bond with someone else, but it was clear he had. Sort of like a saber-toothed tiger befriending a bunny—

Thano looked over at her. "A bunny? You think I'm like a bunny?"

Catherine's heart dropped. "What?"

"You said I'm like a bunny. I take offense to that, especially when you're comparing Ryland to a saber-toothed tiger."

Ryland stood up sharply. "She didn't say that."

Thano glanced at him. "Of course she did. I'm not deaf."

"She didn't say that," Zach said.

"I heard her," Thano said. He looked over at her. "The old guys are losing their hearing. Tell them you said it, sweetness, before they cart me off to an ENT doc for a look-see."

Her heart was thudding. "I didn't say it," she said. "I *thought* it."

Thano blinked. "What? Are you telepathic?"

"No, of course not—"

"Son of a bitch," Zach whispered in shock. "She's your *sheva*, Thano."

"No!" With a roar of outrage, Ryland leapt in front of Catherine, inserting his body like a shield between her and Thano. "She's not your soul mate," he snarled, holding his machete out, ready to strike. Violence seemed to spew off him, filling the air with the dark taint of death and ruthless hate. "Impossible."

Zach moved just as fast, moving beside Thano with his sai out and ready. "Stand down, Ryland. Don't do it."

Thano held up his hands in surrender leaving his halberds balanced on his thighs. "Dude, I don't want her. She's yours."

"Don't fucking touch her," Ryland snarled. His voice was raspy and rough, nothing like the way it usually sounded. Even as he spoke, he called out his other machete. The moment it appeared in his hand, Zach went into battle position, both of his sai ready.

"Stand down, Ry," he said. "Thano's on your team."

"Ry." Thano's voice was urgent. "You gotta pull it together, man. You're too close to the edge." His gaze flicked to Ryland's hand, and Catherine followed his glance.

Silver scales were glittering on the backs of Ryland's hands, sliding beneath his skin like something was slithering beneath the surface. Oh, God. That wasn't good. "Wait!" She jumped in front of him, blocking his path, then froze when she saw his face. His eyes had changed into bottomless pits of blackness, seething with torment and hell. Dear God. He was starting to go over the edge. "Ryland! Stop it!"

But he didn't even seem to see or hear her. He was fixated on Thano like some ancient predator, ready to destroy.

"Um, yeah, you need to step up here, sweetheart," Thano said. "Tell the old man you love him or something like that."

"Love him? But I don't—"

"Tell him anyway!"

"But—"

"Listen, Catherine," Zach said, his voice low with urgency as he eyed Ryland. "Calydons can speak telepathically only with each other, and the one woman who is his soul mate. Unless you're the first female Calydon in existence, the only explanation for Thano hearing your thoughts is if you're his soul mate."

Catherine stared in shock at the men. "There's no way," she said. There couldn't be. She felt nothing for Thano. There was no spark. No fire. Nothing like what had happened between her and Ryland—

"There's no other explanation," Zach said sharply. "And Ryland apparently isn't so happy about it, which is bizarre as hell because no man ever covets another's *sheva*, but he's a crazy bastard, so I guess the rules don't apply to him." There was no affectionate warmth in Zach's voice like there had been in Thano's, even when he'd been giving Ryland grief.

Ryland was still fixated on Thano, and she could see his muscles straining with the effort of not going after his friend. The turbulence in his eyes was terrifying, and the air was roiling with black taint all around him. Her heart ached suddenly for this man who was suffering, who was being dragged into darkness by the creature he was. Suddenly, she wasn't afraid of him. She understood what he was facing. "Ryland," she whispered, rushing up to him.

"Oh, shit, no, woman, don't do that," Zach said.

She heard Thano's response. "No, let her be. This will work."

Just as Catherine reached Ryland, he let out a furious roar and reared back with his machete— "No!" She threw her arms around him and her body slammed against his so hard that her breath oomphed out of her body. Ryland stiffened, but his left arm locked around her, anchoring her against him.

His muscles were absolutely rigid, and his heart was beating so slowly it was as if he was almost dead. Just the precise, methodical thud of a man so ice cold that his heart barely beat. How human was he? Any at all?

He jerked her behind him, tossing her to the ground and out of his way as he advanced on Thano. "You fucking bastard," he snarled. "You can't have her."

Thano swore under his breath as he held his hands up higher. "I don't want her. I don't have her. She's not mine."

"There's no other explanation," Ryland snapped.

Zach raised his weapons, and Thano's hands twitched as he inched them toward his own weapons. Dear God, they were going to fight him. "Ryland!" she shouted. "Don't do this! I'm not his *sheva*!"

But there was no response from him. Just the intentional, ominous approach toward the men who were his teammates, who were now shouting at him to stand down.

She could see that Thano and Zach weren't going to strike until they had to, but Ryland had no intention of leaving them a choice. Catherine whirled around, struggling to find something to stop him, but there was nothing. *Ryland!* She threw the thought out in her mind, hoping that he would hear her, but he didn't even react. Clearly, she wasn't telepathically connected to him like she was with Thano.

Disappointment rushed through her for a brief moment, but she shoved it aside, galvanized by the danger escalating between Ryland and his men. He was enraged by jealousy so extreme that it made no sense. Dammit. What would reach him? She knew him. *Think, Catherine. Think!* Dante. Dante would reach him. Dante was what mattered. A threat to Dante? He was already dead. A threat to her! She was his link to Dante! But what threat?

She spun around and faced the border. Across that line he'd drawn in the sand lay danger. Danger to her. Danger he could protect her from? *Please let me be right about this.* She'd heard the truth in his repeated promise to protect her, to keep her safe. *I hope you mean it, Ry.* "Ryland," she shouted. "I don't have time for this. I'm going in!" She took a deep breath, and then sprinted over the boundary and into the land of hell.

The moment her feet touched the ground on the other side of Ryland's demarcation, it felt like a deep sludge was coming out of the soil and wrapping around her ankles, as if she had stepped in quicksand. Within a millisecond, she was up to her knees in putrid swirls of gas and goop. She fought to get out, but it sucked her down further, wrapping around her hips, and then her waist. Oh, man. This wasn't good. "Ryland!" she screamed. "Help!"

But he didn't turn around. He kept advancing on Thano, who

was now looking at her with great concern. "Shit, man, we gotta help her!"

Sharp pain hit her ankle, and she yelped. Then the same stabbing jab in the back of her calf. Then her knee. Something was biting her, or cutting her. Eating her alive? True panic began to assault her and she fought harder. "Ryland!" Okay, on her list of great ideas, this wasn't one of them, apparently. "Ryland, stop being a stupid macho male, for God's sake! I can't find Dante if I'm dead!"

And then, with those magic words citing the fate of his mentor, Ryland seemed to break free of the spell he was under. He whirled toward her, then unleashed an animalistic howl of rage. He launched himself at her, sprinting across the ground as the goop sucked her further down, up to her armpits. "Catherine!" he bellowed as he ran toward her. "Get your arms up! Keep them free!"

She dragged her arms up out of the muck, struggling to resist the instinct to fight the goop, to support herself as she sank further. Up to her chin now. Teeth dug into her belly. Her neck. Her breasts. Instinct screamed at her to bat them away, but she knew if she put her arms down, she'd have no way out. So she forced herself to be still, letting herself sink, letting herself be eaten, watching Ryland race toward her, her heart hammering with terror. The muck reached her lower lip and began to ooze into her mouth even as she turned her head, trying to find fresh air to breathe.

He was still fifty yards away. He wasn't going to make it. Dear God. *He wasn't going to make it.*

🐾 CHAPTER NINE 🐾

RYLAND FELT HIS WHOLE WORLD close in as he saw Catherine sinking from sight. Rage consumed him, and terror unlike anything he'd ever felt exploded through him. He ran harder, driving all his strength into his movement, but he knew he wasn't going to get there. He wasn't going to make it.

She met his gaze, and in those blue eyes, he saw fear, real fear, and he felt the sudden press of her energy against him. She was calling to him. Willing him to her. Without him, she would die. "No!" He bellowed his denial, but he knew it was too late. He would never reach her in time.

Unless he became more than a man.

He didn't hesitate, dropping his shields and tapping into the side of him that was brutally dangerous. Fierce pain tore through his body. Scales shredded his skin. Claws burst from his fingers. Fire rolled through his cells, but he fought to control it. Summoning intense willpower honed after centuries of practice, he channeled the energy into his shoulder blades, fighting to direct the emergence of the beast.

With a great howl of agony, he forced the scaled wings to burst free from his shoulders. The massive appendages thrust him forward into the air, the wind rushing past him with violent force just as Catherine's head disappeared beneath the ground. All that were left were her fingers, and then they were gone.

With a ruthless, lethal roar, he reached the pit and dove straight into it. His arms plunged beneath the surface, crashing right into Catherine. His claws locked around her wrists, and then with another burst from his wings, he ripped them both free of the sludge. Catherine dangling from his grasp, he whirled around, driving back toward the safe ground as fast as possible. He had to get back in time. He had to get out of the battle before it was too late to reclaim himself.

He reached the earth outside the border and landed, crashing down as the beast began to rise within him. He released Catherine instantly, screaming in agony as the darkness raged within him. The shrieks of a thousand tortured souls arose in his head, hammering at his consciousness. He gripped his head as he thrashed on the earth, fighting to hold the onslaught back. Pain ripped through him as black slashes tore through his flesh, and his body bowed as his bones fought to transform.

"Ryland," Catherine shouted. "What's happening?"

He couldn't talk. Didn't dare open his mouth and allow the evil to escape. He had to defeat it. Had to bring it back. But it was too much. He'd allowed too much of it out. *Dante! Help me!* But there was no answer from his mentor, no soothing presence to help him.

His body convulsed and his head arched back as a scream tore from his throat. A scream that wasn't his. A scream filled of all the darkness and evil of the beast he once was, the beast that always lived within him. He needed Dante. And he needed him now.

There was no Dante.

There was only the woman who could take his soul.

It would have to be enough.

One of his ribs cracked, and he screamed again as he lurched onto his side. Catherine was only a few yards away, her face white. She was dripping with black mud, and her flesh was ravaged by the mites that had attacked her. Beside her stood Thano and Zach, both of them with expressions of absolute shock. He reached for Catherine, his clawed, deformed hand stretching toward her, asking for help in the only way he could. Her eyes widened as she realized what he wanted.

"Shit no," Zach said, grabbing her arm. "Don't touch him."

"Touch him," Thano urged. "Help him. She can help him. Do it, Catherine! Do it now!" Thano shoved Zach back, freeing Catherine. For a split second, she didn't move, and Ryland knew he had lost—

Then she jumped up and ran toward him, her hand outstretched. Another rib broke, and he screamed in agony as his bones began to crack, preparing to morph—

Then her hand went into his, and he felt the softness of her skin against his hard scales, like a great burst of light. Suddenly, he was back in that moment hundreds of years ago, when Dante had saved him, when he'd brought the angel to him. "Golden light," he gasped. "Give me your golden light."

Her face paled. "I don't have golden light. I'm an angel of death!"

Son of a bitch. No golden light. No easy out. Not this time. "Dante," he rasped out, as his pelvis shattered under the force of the evil breaking free. "Give me Dante. His soul."

Understanding dawned on her face, and she immediately placed his hand on her chest, over her heart. She called him into her, and instantly, he felt like he was tumbling through a miasma of death and suffering. So much death. Shadows. Darkness. Cracks that seemed to be bottomless crevasses of suffering. But woven amongst it all was a spider web of a faint white glow, and he knew instantly it was Catherine's soul. Barely there, torn apart by terrible things, but hanging on. She took him in deeper, and he felt the presence of other spirits, of all those she had taken. There were holes everywhere in her disintegrating soul, and the presence of others lingered at the edge of those gashes, as if their death had taken a part of her with them, leaving behind only the shadows of their existence.

And then he felt it. The faintest, faintest whisper of Dante's presence. He lunged for it, desperate for his mentor's aid. But Dante's presence seemed to slither out of his grasp, an illusion that didn't really exist. *Dante!* But it was no use. There was nothing to hold on to. It wasn't Dante. It was the memory of his existence, nothing but a sliver of time long gone—

Then the white light inside Catherine began to glow brighter. Each white tendril grew thicker and brighter, as if life was returning to her soul. The web of life seemed to wrap around him, binding him in its threads, protecting him as the evil beat at him, trying to take him. But she kept wrapping more and more of her protection around him, thickening the shield around his soul, giving him room to take a breath, to regroup, to find strength.

The monster raged on the outsides of her protections, trying to complete its possession of him, but it was too late. Catherine had given him the space he needed. With a roar of triumph, Ryland shoved the beast back into its cage, tearing himself free of its grasp. With a last scream of frustration, it retreated, locked once again behind his steel will.

Exhausted, he collapsed against her, his body shaking violently with the aftermath. He drew her into his body, needing to feel the softness of her flesh against his, desperate to find solace in her touch. In her kindness. In her world, where things were different.

He needed her desperately.

"It's okay, Ryland," she whispered as she wrapped her arms around him. "You did it."

He still couldn't speak, his throat raw, his mouth burned. His skin stung from the scales, and his fingers bled where the claws had receded. He pulled her closer, and his whole body shuddered in relief as she tucked herself against him. He pressed his face into the crook of her neck, inhaling the scent he'd begun to associate with her: the fresh scent of new spring, of flowers coming to life in the sunshine, of morning dew on the grass. He drank it into his soul, allowing it to flow through him, even as the thousands of tears in his muscles bled the poison that had nearly taken him.

Catherine laid her hand on his back, over the very place where the wings had ripped through his flesh and muscles. Agonizing pain ricocheted through him as she caressed the mutilated skin, but she didn't lift her hand. She sent him no golden healing light, but the mere act of her gentle touch was unlike anything he'd ever felt. It was soft and nourishing. It was that kindness thing she'd mentioned before.

He didn't understand how a simple touch could make a difference, but it did. It wasn't magic or healing or anything, just an ordinary touch, and yet it was so much more. It seemed to ease the pain, and his back shuddered in relief as the tension began to ease from his shredded muscles. He wanted to tell her that it felt good. He wanted to thank her. But his throat was still burning, seared by the fire that had arisen within him. He reached out with his mind, trying to connect with her. *Thank you, Cat.*

She didn't respond, and he knew she hadn't heard him. Frustration roared through him. Why could Thano communicate telepathically with her, but not him? It wasn't really possible that she was Thano's *sheva,* was it? Anger flared inside him, and the beast stirred again, this time, not to save another, but in its true nature, to destroy.

"Hey, Ryland," she said softly as she stroked his back, below the gashes from the wings. "Don't get upset again. You need to be calm."

He buried his face in her shoulder again, surrendering himself to the sensation of her body against his. What was wrong with him? He'd been fine with it when Alice and Sarah had bonded with Ian and Kane. Well, fine with it once he'd realized they weren't going to hurt the angels. It was different with Catherine.

There was no chance in hell he could stand back while she bonded with Thano.

But Thano had heard her thoughts. *He had heard her thoughts.*

"Ryland." She caught his face and lifted his head from her shoulder, forcing him to look at her. Her face was black with mud, and she was still bleeding. Instantly, he forgot about his anger over Thano and swore as he laid his hand over her wounds. "Catherine," he rasped out, wincing as her name ripped his throat.

"No, don't talk." She pressed her finger to his lips. "Just listen to me, okay?"

Her touch was so gentle that he wanted to cradle her hand in his, and protect her from everything, especially himself. He covered her palm with his, and pressed his lips to her fingertips.

She smiled faintly. "Listen to me, okay? Are you listening?"

"Yeah," he rasped.

"I don't know why Thano heard my thoughts, but I am not his soul mate."

He shook his head. "You don't know—"

"I know." She traced her fingers over his forehead, easing the wrinkles from his skin. "I am very good at keeping my distance from men nowadays. I trust no one. Ever." She looked at him then, her blue eyes so genuine and intense as they focused on him. "But you're different. There is something about you that I hear. Something about you that I see. Something about you that touches me. Only you, Ryland. Thano is just a man. You—" She paused. "You burn in my soul, Ryland."

He stared at her, stunned by her words. "What does that mean?" he croaked out.

"I don't know," she said. "It terrifies me, and it endangers me. But at the same time, I—" She hesitated, but her hands were busy, tracing his hairline, stroking his shoulders, touching his jaw, as if she couldn't get enough contact with him. "I've never been able to bring anyone into my spirit like I did with you. I don't know how I did it, but I did. It's only you, Ryland. Whatever it is between us, it's only you. It's not Thano." She gave him a small smile. "So stop being a stupid, jealous male, or you're going to get us all killed."

Ryland grinned, relief cascading through him. "I'm not jealous." His throat hurt like hell, but he wanted to talk to her, and he forced the words out.

"No?"

"No." He leaned his forehead against hers, needing the moment of intimacy. "I just protect my angel."

"That's it? The angel thing? It has nothing to do with how charming and adorable I am as a woman?" Her voice was teasing, but he sensed the honesty of her question, her need to be more to him than an angel.

But what could he tell her? Only the truth. He was no more than he was. He closed his eyes and pressed a kiss to her lips. "I'm not the kind of man who even understands charming and adorable," he said. "I know death. I know protection. I know survival. That's all I know, Catherine. I'm not more than that."

She was quiet for a moment. "You know kindness now," she said softly. "It's a start."

"It's not a start, Cat. There's nowhere for me to go with shit like that." He needed her to understand what he was like. He wouldn't deceive her, or make her think he was some fantastical knight riding to a maiden's rescue. She needed to understand.

"Okay." She wrapped her arms around him, and he rested his head against her shoulder again. He was so drained from fighting the beast. All he wanted was to lie on the damned ground and hold her. "That's a good thing," she whispered. "If you became nice, I would want to like you, and I can't afford that."

He laughed softly. "No one likes me, Cat."

"Lucky man."

"I know." But as he said the words, a strange sense of isolation came over him. A recognition that he had been on the outside his whole life, and that was where he would stay.

"Hey, man," Thano said softly.

Ryland pried his eyes open, not lifting his face from the crevice of Catherine's shoulder. Thano was on the ground beside them, face level with Ryland's. When he saw Ryland look at him, his face broke into a wide grin. "That was some serious shit, Ry."

"Yeah." Ryland couldn't believe Thano had ventured so close to him after what he'd just turned into. Zach was standing back about ten yards, and his weapons were still out. "You're a damn fool. You should have killed me."

"Nah, I had faith." Thano's green eyes were troubled. "What's your deal, Ry?"

He shook his head as he reached for Catherine's hair. He needed to touch her more, to be grounded by her. "Long story, my friend."

"We don't have time for a long story."

"No. We don't."

Thano nodded, accepting the distance Ryland worked so hard to maintain between them. "You gotta heal, Ry. We'll stand guard."

Ryland realized that Thano was referencing the healing sleep of the Calydons. "We don't have time for that—"

"We don't have time not to," Thano said. "Take an hour. It'll be enough to take the edge off."

"No, I'm fine." Ryland tried to move Catherine aside so he could sit up, but his muscles screamed in agony, and he swore, collapsing back against the ground. "Shit."

"Naptime, big guy." Thano glanced at Catherine. "Take her into your healing sleep. She needs help, too."

Ryland swore. "A Calydon can heal only his mate."

Thano raised his eyebrows. "She saved you with her spirit. Seems to me that would be enough of a connection to heal her." His eyes narrowed. "You owe her, Ry. She crossed the border to bring you back from a killing rage. Fix her up. We'll stand guard." Without waiting for Ryland's response, Thano whistled for his mount.

Apollo trotted over and went down to his knees beside Thano. The warrior grabbed the horse's thick mane and swung himself onto the animal's back. He pointed at Ryland as Apollo leapt gracefully to his feet. "One hour, my friend. That's all you've got."

Then he called out his halberds again and spun the horse away, galloping up the top of an embankment so he could survey their surroundings. Ryland looked at Zach, who was still fisting his sai. "Next time, kill me."

Zach narrowed his eyes. "Don't worry. When it's time to kill you, I'll do it. But not before I have to. You're a crazy bastard, but you're damn good at what you do, and we're keeping you alive as long as we can. Sleep. We don't have time for this shit." Then he, too, turned away, heading over to guard the borderline that separated them from hell.

His departure left Ryland alone with the woman who had saved him. The woman he owed his humanity to. The woman who was still bleeding from a thousand cuts to her body, suffered because he'd been too much of a bastard to keep himself under control.

He looked down at her, where she was still tucked beneath him on the ground. She smiled faintly, but he could sense her pain. He knew Thano was right. He had to help her. But hell, inviting her into his healing sleep was an invasion of his space, an opening of himself to her. He didn't do that kind of shit.

"Fifty-nine minutes," Thano yelled. "You look like shit, old man, and we can't afford that if you want to get out of there alive with Dante."

With Dante.

Right.

He had no choice. For Dante, for the Order, he would do it. He needed to be in top shape, and so did Catherine. "Okay," he said, keeping his voice business-like and hard. "I can heal myself in my sleep. Calydons can heal other Calydons, and their own soul mates, but that's it, because it takes an interconnection of the souls to make it happen."

She raised her brows. "It seems that being a *sheva* has a lot of helpful benefits."

Ryland shook his head. "If a Calydon and his mate complete all five of the bonding stages, he'll go insane and destroy everything that matters to him and any innocents who get in the way. The only way to stop him will be for her to kill him. Then she'll kill herself. It's the Calydon destiny."

Catherine blinked. "Well, that's not so helpful."

"Yeah, no shit." He grimaced. "And we both know I'm not cheerful enough to skip the deranged killer aspect of the bonding destiny."

She glanced down at his chest. "How are you?"

Ryland didn't open his jacket, not wanting the others to see. "That little episode had nothing to do with being close to the nether-realm. I called it on purpose."

She met his gaze, so much knowledge in her blue eyes. "You did it to save me—No," she corrected herself. "You did it to save Dante."

An image of Catherine disappearing into the muck flashed through his mind, and Ryland tightened his grip on her. The moment he'd summoned his power, he hadn't been thinking of Dante. It had been all about the woman. Not the angel. It had been about *her*.

Jesus. The idea made a cold sweat break out on his body and he rolled off her, needing to put distance between them.

Catherine sat up. "What's wrong?"

"Nothing." He pressed the heel of his hand to his forehead, fighting off memories of her in the muck, of her slipping out of sight. "Nothing. I'm fine." He turned toward her. "Okay, so I can't bring you into my sleep because you're not my mate, apparently." Which was a good fucking thing right now. "But you brought me into your spirit. So, you're going to do that again, and once we're connected, I'm going to go into the healing sleep. You need to keep us connected and come with me, and then my healing will help you. Got it?"

She nodded. "Okay."

"Okay. Just like that. Okay." He touched her face. "Doesn't anything rattle you, angel?"

"You," she whispered.

He laughed softly, without mirth. "Yeah, well, touché on that one." He stretched out on his back and clasped his hands behind his head. He wanted to wrap his arms around her, but he didn't dare. He was still freaked by the realization that he'd called his beast to save her. "Let's do this."

"Right." She stretched out on her side facing him.

For a brief moment, their eyes met, and he felt something tighten in his chest. Then he shook it off and closed his eyes. "Connect us," he said.

"Okay." She clasped his arm, tugged his wrist from behind his head, and pulled it toward her.

Ryland's pulse began to race in anticipation as Catherine set his hand on her chest. He could feel each beat of her heart beneath his palm, the steady intake of her breath, the softness of her body beneath his touch. She was all woman, a sensual siren calling to him like no woman ever had. No wonder he hadn't been able to handle it when Thano had heard her thoughts. What man could?

Then she set her hand on his chest, sliding it beneath his shirt so her palm was resting on his bare skin. "It will be easier if I have skin-to-skin contact," she said, as if she had to explain why she'd touched him more intimately. "Closer connection."

Without a word, he hooked his thumb over the collar of her muddy shirt and moved it aside so he was palming her bare skin. With his eyes closed, all of his senses were attuned to his sense of touch. Her skin was warm and incredibly soft. Fragile, as if a stiff wind would tear it apart. "Like this?"

"Yes." She snuggled closer to him, so she was pressed against his side. One of her breasts was against his ribs, a mound of temptation that called to him with a force he'd never experienced.

He fought against the desire building in him and quieted his mind, focusing on Catherine, forcing himself not to fight her invasion as she opened herself to him and invited his spirit to mingle with hers.

Unlike before, when it had been a desperate battle to save him, this time the connection was intimate and erotic, as her femininity called to him, seducing him with its warmth and beauty. He wanted to resist it. He wanted to claim his space and retreat into the world he knew, but he didn't. He owed her this much. He had to allow her in so he could heal her.

Her spirit wrapped around his, a tender embrace that reminded him of what it had felt like when she had touched him in comfort. It was beautiful and seductive, an allure that he didn't dare respond to. It was so foreign to him, all this gentleness and softness that was wrapping around him—

A shadow drifted across their connection, a cold mist of darkness and death. He recognized it instantly, and he realized it was coming from Catherine. Death was as much a part of her as the light and beauty. Protectiveness arose instinctively, and he reached out with his spirit, trying to enfold her in his protection, to keep the darkness away from her light. The moment he did, he felt something hum between them, a bond that sizzled and ignited. Suddenly, there were no barriers between them. He could feel every fissure of death that had split her soul, as well as the humanity struggling to survive in the miasma of doom and darkness. He was stunned by how much darkness she carried, by the depths of scarring on her being, by the weight of so many deaths on her existence.

He could feel the labored pain with each breath she took, and he sensed the depth of her physical suffering from all the bites she'd received in the mud. He knew what kind of damage the mites could cause, their poison going deep into the tissue as it ate away at the flesh. Fierce resolution poured through him, and he gathered her against him. *I will heal you,* he promised, offering the thought not through his mind, but through his feelings, through his soul, where they were connected.

You're so handy, came the reply, making him laugh softly. Damn, it felt good to feel her presence within him, to be so connected.

Tucking her more tightly against him and wrapping his spirit around hers, Ryland opened himself to the healing sleep of his kind. As it began to take him, he felt Catherine tighten the bond holding them together, and then he was asleep, and she was with him.

⬙⬙⬙⬙

"CATHERINE."

She awoke to the sound of Ryland's voice by her ear, his warm breath caressing the side of her neck, sending goose bumps down her spine. Her body was warm, nestled against his powerful one. She didn't want to wake up. She wanted to snuggle down against him into the safety net he gave her— "Oh my God!" She bolted upright so fast, her head almost hit him on the chin, but he jerked back just in time. "I fell asleep!" She frantically looked around, but Thano, Zach, and Ryland were all there, completely alive and fine.

She hadn't killed them in her sleep. How was that possible? She'd been so depleted, there was no way that she wouldn't have needed to feed...but there they were. Just as alive as they'd been when she went to sleep.

"Hey, you okay?" Ryland touched her arm, and she looked over at him. His eyes were back to their usual pits of black doom, and his skin was no longer covered in black slashes.

"I didn't try to kill you when I slept? Any of you?" She had to make sure.

His eyebrows went up. "Not me." He looked at his team. "You guys?"

Zach shook his head.

Thano shrugged. "No, but you had some erotic dreams about the big guy there. You gotta learn to shut me out, Catherine, because there are things about Ry that I just don't want to know."

Heat suffused Catherine's cheeks as she recalled some of her dreams. "You saw those?"

"Shit, yeah." Thano gave a visible shudder. "I'm too young to be exposed to that kind of stuff."

She looked at Ryland. "Did you—"

He gave her a hooded, heated look that made a searing heat plunge deep into her belly. "We were fully merged, Cat. There were no secrets during that healing sleep."

"Ohhh..." Complete mortification did not even begin to describe the depths of her embarrassment. She hadn't even thought about sex since the day Simon had betrayed her, but the kiss with Ryland had awoken the part of her that had been long dormant, and it had returned with a vengeance. And they'd all seen it? She could not think of a single response to make it go away. Not one brilliant idea came to her blank mind. "Um…"

"It's okay," Ryland said, looking unmistakably smug. "Thano wasn't in those dreams, just me, so it's all good." He stood up and held out his hand to her. "Let's go. We want to be out of the nether-realm before sundown."

"We do?" Catherine put her hand in his and let him help her to her feet. The sun was so bright it was almost blinding, so strong she didn't even have to try to harvest it. It just filled her with its light all on its own. Was that why she'd been able to sleep without killing them? Because the sun had been streaming over her? She knew that she'd been able to give Ryland the white light of protection earlier because the sun had risen and she'd channeled its energy into him. Had her sleep been innocent for the same reason? Or had it been something else? Had Ryland somehow been able to contain it when she'd been merged with him?

She watched him as he conversed with his teammates, briefing them on the creatures they were going to find. Alice had been helpful for containing Catherine's dark side, but even Alice hadn't been able to help her once Lucy had been kidnapped. She'd lost it, which was why it had been so easy for the wizard to manipulate her. Was Ryland like Alice, only a thousand times more? And if he was, what did that mean?

He looked over at her. "Did you hear that? Are you paying attention?"

"No."

He gave her such an exasperated look that she almost laughed. "Get over here, woman." He grabbed her wrist and tugged her over to them, his gesture almost playful.

As he slung his arm over her shoulders and yanked her against him, Thano raised his brows at them. "You don't look cranky, Ry. You must be poisoned or something. You feel okay?"

"The angel had erotic dreams about me," Ryland said. "What's to be cranky about?" Then he grinned at her and kissed her hard, taking away her embarrassment before it could rise again. It wasn't just a kiss. It was a statement of ownership, claiming her in front of the others, accepting her dreams as her own claim on him.

She didn't want to claim him. And she didn't want him to own her. But what choice did she have? They were going into the nether-realm, and their guide was a volatile warrior on the edge of turning into a murderous beast. The situation was too precarious, their need for Ryland too great.

If letting Ryland go all he-man on her increased the likelihood that she could save Lucy by making him sane, she had to do it. But she had to remember what happened before with Simon. She had to remember who Ryland truly was—a creature from the same place as Simon.

She couldn't make the same mistake she'd made before, and trust the man who had the most power to destroy her.

She could never forget that. Ever. No matter how tantalizing his kisses were.

🐾 Chapter Ten 🐾

THEY TRAVELED IN ABSOLUTE SILENCE once they crossed the border into the outlands of the nether-realm.

Even Apollo's massive hooves made no sound as he cantered across the forest floor.

Ryland was in the lead, moving in a steady lope across the lush terrain. Per his orders, Catherine kept pace on his heels, so close that she could feel the heat from his body as they ran. She carefully placed her feet precisely where he'd stepped, following his instructions exactly, not daring to deviate in this hostile land that only he knew how to traverse.

Right behind her was Zach, mirroring her footsteps with the same precision that she was tracking Ryland's.

In the rear were Apollo and Thano, who traveled so lightly she wasn't sure they were actually touching the ground.

Ryland had guided them around the sinkhole, and then broke into a hard run along the river, telling them to stay in the sunshine for as long as possible, which was fine with her.

But now, almost an hour after they'd crossed the border, the sunlight was beginning to fade, obscured by a layer of a sickly green mist that became more oppressive the farther they progressed. The air became thick and heavy, swirling around her like the steam from a hot spring, coating her skin. The ground was spongy and damp, her feet sinking too far down for comfort with each step. The trees were coated with heavy black moss that seemed to bleed vengeance and anger. Glowing orange eyes tracked them as they walked, visible in the depths of the woods beside them.

Ryland hadn't paused to acknowledge any of them. He just

kept moving swiftly and with deadly certainty. He knew exactly where he was going, and he knew where all the traps were.

She hoped.

He raised his hand and flicked his wrist in a circle to draw their attention. Up ahead was a chasm of black, swirling smoke. The edges of it descended into rocky cliffs that vanished into a bottomless crevasse. Discs of black mist appeared to float across the space, diving and spinning as if they were alive and playing some kind of dodgeball game. Ryland paused at the edge of the chasm, studying the discs. His concentration was so intense that the air was actually vibrating with it. After a moment, he picked up a log that was near him. He hurled it into the air, into the midst of the spinning, misty discs. The air ignited with a violent humming and then thousands of discs converged upon the wood. Within a millisecond, the log had been reduced to sawdust, sliced to pieces by the discs.

Catherine swallowed as the discs dispersed again, resuming their random circling... No, she realized. They weren't flying randomly. They were hunting for prey with precise, strategic stalking. Dear God. What were they?

After a moment, Ryland turned and looked back at her.

Cat?

She was startled by the sound of Thano's voice in her mind. Not Ryland's. Thano's voice, but it was Ryland who was looking at her, as if he had spoken. *What?* She spoke tentatively, unsure how to respond. Could she really speak in her mind and have Thano hear it?

Ry wants to know whether you can shield us from those discs. Can you make us invisible to them? Apparently, we need to get across there.

She looked at Ryland, whose face was shuttered and tense, no doubt because he'd had to feed the question to Thano to ask her. She assumed that it was too risky to speak aloud, and the only way to connect with her was through Thano. It was uncomfortable to feel Thano so intimately connected to her, but she knew she had no choice. They were in a hostile land now, and precautions had to be taken. Telling herself to chill out, she looked past Ryland at the flying discs, trying to get a sense of what they were. Could she really hide them from those things? One mistake and they would all be dinner.

Ryland walked over to her and grabbed her hands. *Cat.*

Again, Thano's voice in her mind, while Ryland was staring at her. Weird. Really weird. *What?*

Ry said to tell you that you can do it. Think of your daughter. You can't fail her.

Resolution surged through her, and Ryland smiled. He touched her face and gave a brief nod.

Good job, Thano said. *He wants you to know that you're hot as hell when you go warrior on him, but I just want to go on the record that giving sex messages between the two of you is off limits. You guys need to develop sign language for that or something.*

Her heart jumped, but Ryland's gaze snapped to Thano, giving him a look designed to kill.

Thano's laughter echoed in her mind. *Okay, he didn't say he thinks you're hot as hell. But it's obviously true.*

Ryland made a slicing motion across the front of his throat, and Thano's laughter faded. *So, let's do this,* Thano said, his voice clipped and precise, a warrior ready for battle.

Ryland took her hand and moved her up beside him to the edge of the cliff. A quick gesture from him told her that he wanted to carry her across the crevasse. She didn't bother to protest, not when he was so much more athletic than she was. If he wanted to leap across a bottomless pit guarded by flesh-eating Frisbees, she was more than happy to rely on his physical capabilities instead of hers. So she let him pick her up. Trying to still her pounding heart at the intimacy of their position, she wrapped her arms and legs around him as their bodies melded together, chest-to-chest. He locked his left arm around her waist and kept his right arm free for fighting, his machete gripped tightly in his fist.

Catherine looked over his shoulder at Thano, Zach, and Apollo. All three of them were watching her, waiting for her to shield them. For a split second, trepidation filled her. What if she failed and these good men died? What if the creatures took her as well? There would be no one left to save her daughter. Tension rippled through her, and Ryland's arm tightened around her waist. He turned his head so his mouth was against her ear. "You can do it," he whispered, his voice nothing more than a breath, hidden from all except her. "I believe in you."

She closed her eyes, realizing he meant it. His commitment to Dante's Order was insurmountable. He would never choose a path that would result in his death. Ever. He would only choose one he was sure would work. So...yeah. She had to go with it, then. He was the one who knew what the creatures were, and he knew how her cloaking worked. If he thought it would suffice, she would have to have faith in him.

She let out her breath, tightened her hold on him, and then

called to the darkness that surrounded them.

Death rose swiftly to meet her, sweeping through her cells like the old friend it was. It mingled with her body, her spirit and her scent until she was simply a miasma of all the creatures and people who had died in this pit. There were so many, a virtual flood, that it was easy for her to harness all the energy and cloak each member of their team.

As she watched, each of them, including the horse, became swathed in death. They appeared to vanish, swallowed up by the energy she'd summoned. Even she couldn't see them.

Damn. Thano's voice was filled with admiration. *That's impressive. Why didn't you give me this skill instead of some lame ass violet fire?*

I didn't give you the fire, Thano. Violet isn't my color. You got that somewhere else. His legs, yes, that was her. The violet flame? Not her.

She felt his surprise, but before he could pursue further questions, she felt Ryland tense his body. Oh, God, he was really going to jump across that thing? He moved backward swiftly to get a running start, and she could only guess that the others were doing the same. Due to her cloaking of them, she couldn't hear or see them, and the only way she knew Ryland was there was because she could feel him against her.

Maybe he'd wanted to carry her so they wouldn't lose each other.

Right now, she felt okay with that. This was not her territory. It was Ryland's. As much as she was all about the independent woman thing, in this moment, she was supremely grateful to have Ryland on her side.

His voice again whispered in her ear. "Hang on, angel. And don't forget to keep us hidden."

Nodding her agreement, she tightened her grip around him, and then he launched himself forward. Every muscle in his body strained as he raced toward the edge of the cliff. Faster and faster. Gaining speed. His arms pumping now as he ran, his body absolutely silent in its approach. She squeezed her eyes shut, focusing all her energy onto the shield she'd called to protect them, swirling it around them all like a living, moving fabric that wove in and out of their existence.

Ryland hit the edge of the cliff and launched them into the air. The wind whipped past them, and she heard a faint, high-pitched wailing as they entered the airspace. A creature slammed into her back, and she almost screamed, then Ryland knocked it away with his machete. The wailing suddenly amped up in intensity, the wind rushing around them as the creatures swarmed, trying to find them. Another hit her back, and then her shoulder, teeth tearing through her flesh.

Around her, she heard the thuds and slashes as Thano and Zach cleared their own path through the creatures. The wailing was frenzied and angry now as the creatures tried to track them, to find the enemies that dared intrude in their space.

"Come on," Ryland shouted. "Keep the shields up!"

Catherine focused harder, but each time something hit her, her concentration wavered. Something latched onto her cheek and she yelped, her eyes jerking open. Then she almost screamed when she saw what was around them. The air was almost impenetrable with discs shooting everywhere, closing down on them, swirling madly as they fought to find them. Dear God, they would eat them alive in a second!

"Focus, Cat! Focus!"

She saw Thano flicker into sight, and the wailing erupted into a crescendo of triumph as they all raced toward him. "Oh, God!" She immediately called more of the spirits to him. At her summons, dozens of shadows of death zoomed out of the depths of the crevasse and wrapped themselves around Thano. He disappeared a split second before the masses descended upon him. There was a roar of frustrated outrage from their pursuers, and a screech of victory as some of them found him anyway.

Apollo squealed in outrage, and she knew she hadn't done enough—

Then they hit the ground on the other side of the crevasse, landing with a faint thud that even Ryland couldn't mask. There were two more impacts as Apollo and Zach landed, and the air filled with the irate screams of the creatures who had been thwarted. They'd done it! Elation leapt through her, and she couldn't keep the grin off her face.

"Keep us shielded," Ryland shouted. "Check in!"

"Good!" Thano reported.

"Here," came Zach's tight reply.

"Then let's go. Straight south. Uncloak my weapon, but that's it," he ordered her as he broke into a run.

Fighting hard to keep her concentration, Catherine did as instructed. Immediately Ryland's machete appeared, and she sensed Thano and Zach lock onto it as their guide, following the steel blade through the woods. Together they all ran, hurling their bodies through what was now thick jungle. Ryland sliced at the underbrush as they sped along, clearing the way for them.

Around them, the forest seemed to erupt in a cacophony of noise, creatures who had been awoken by the screams of the sentries. Wings flapped. Low growls filled the night. The screeches of creatures that she didn't want to meet. Shadows undulated, looming over their pathway like a canopy of doom. Even the earth quivered beneath their feet, dark and threatening. But nothing struck them, nothing found them. Their disguise was still holding.

Onward they ran, not taking the time to fight. Instead, they took advantage of how fast they were moving and the freedom that Catherine had given them to navigate unseen.

Catherine gripped Ryland tightly, struggling to hold onto their camouflage, but the spirits she'd called were waning as they got farther away from the chasm. "I can't hold it much longer," she said.

"Almost there," Ryland said. "Stay with it."

She fought for mental clarity, calling to the part of her that flowed with such relentless force, asking it for help, but her grip on the spirits continued to fade. Ryland's shoulder came into view, and Catherine closed her eyes, concentrating even more fiercely, searching the ground around them for more deaths to utilize. She found one, maybe two, but that was it. Most things that had tried to invade the nether-realm had died in that chasm and never made it this far.

"Through here!" Ryland yelled as he cut hard to the right. Something hard banged into Catherine's shoulder, and she looked up to see they were racing through a narrow crack in a rock cliff. Barely two feet wide, Ryland had turned them at an angle to fit through. The rock stretched for a hundred yards above their head, blocking the sunlight.

Then they burst past the end, skidded down a grassy slope and then came to a stop in a clearing.

Beside them appeared Zach, now fully visible. Lacerations slashed across his face, and his clothes were shredded. Apollo suddenly came into view beside him, with Thano still astride. Astoundingly, the horse was untouched, his sleek black coat glistening even in the murky atmosphere, but, like Zach, Thano was also bleeding from assorted wounds.

She looked at Ryland, and saw minor cuts on his face and neck. But he wasn't looking at her. He was looking past her, his gaze intense.

Catherine whipped around in his arms.

They were at the base of a large, stone pyramid that looked like it had been built thousands of years ago. Moss cascaded down its mottled sides. Pyres of orange flames roared at six precise locations in the rock. The top of the pyramid stretched more than a hundred feet above them, and the base was equally as wide.

At the bottom of the pyramid were two ancient, crumbling pillars framing a doorway that opened into a pitch-black nothingness. Her breath caught in awe at the scene that was so similar to the one sketched on her map. "That's it, isn't it? The entrance to the nether-realm?"

"Yeah." But he didn't move, and she could feel his body trembling. His chest was searing hot against hers, and she suddenly felt something move beneath his skin, where the creature was painted on his chest.

"Is it coming to life?" she whispered.

"Of course it is."

She started to reach for his shirt to check it, but he stayed her hand with two words. "Not yet." His voice was so tense that it sent chills rushing through her.

And then she heard it. The sound of a rock tumbling down the front of the pyramid. She turned to watch as a two-foot wide pure-black stone bounced over the rocky surface, moving slowly, too slowly, as if gravity had no pull on it. The solitary stone bounced past the frame of the doorway and rolled to a stop in the middle of the opening. Purple and black smoke began to leak from it, thicker and thicker as it filled the air.

"What the hell's that?" Zach asked, his sai clenched in his fist. "Do we kill it?"

"I have no idea." Ryland shifted her behind him, setting her down on the dirt. "I've never seen it before." He called out his other machete and stood ready. The three warriors were armed, waiting to see what was coming next to keep them from the goal that was so close.

RYLAND WAS VISCERALLY AWARE of Catherine behind him as the smoke enveloped the opening of the entrance to the nether-realm. He knew that threats could also be coming from behind them at any time. He couldn't protect her from all sides. They had to keep going. They couldn't stand there.

But shit. He had no idea what the hell was in front of them.

His chest was burning, like a hot poker was being dragged across his flesh. It wasn't good. Wasn't good at all, but they couldn't go backwards. There was no safe path—

"Holy crap," Zach breathed. "It's *men*."

As he spoke, the smoke cleared, revealing five massive warriors blocking the entrance. All of them were wearing black cloaks with hoods that covered their faces. Their chests were bare, streaked with intricate black markings Ryland didn't recognize, their legs clad in the black fur of a dreisen tiger, one of the beasts of the underworld. Their calves and feet were bare, as if they were connecting with the very earth itself.

Their arms were folded across their chests, feet braced wide in a battle position. Visible in the dim light filtering from the sun were thick, black brands on their forearms. Brands that looked all too familiar.

"They're Calydons," Catherine whispered in awe.

Yeah, they were Calydons, but they weren't ordinary ones. There was no mistaking the enormity of power emanating from them. It was a deep, penetrating force that, to his knowledge, belonged to only nine warriors.

"Not just Calydons," Zach said. "They're Order of the Blade."

"Impossible," Thano said, while Apollo shifted restlessly. "We're the only ones left."

But apparently, they weren't.

Friend or foe?

As Ryland heard a low rumble behind him, signaling the approach of a nether-realm creature he didn't want to deal with, he knew it was time to find out.

⊠⊠⊠⊠

RYLAND DIDN'T LOWER HIS MACHETES as he spoke aloud to the five warriors guarding the entrance. "We need to access the nether-realm," he announced, not bothering to introduce himself. The warriors before him would recognize his team as Order just as easily as he had identified them.

The warrior in the center took a step forward, distancing himself from the others. His face was shrouded by the hood, but Ryland felt his eyes burning down on them. *You are Order.* The voice was deep and hostile, flooding Ryland's mind without invitation.

As are you, he replied, thrusting his own thoughts with equal force. Even as he spoke, he reached behind him and took Catherine's wrist. He pulled her tight behind him, making it clear to the cloaked men that she was under his protection. Thankfully, she did not resist.

You should not exist, the warrior said.

I was thinking the same thing, Ryland replied. He touched the minds of his teammates, channeling his telepathy away from the cloaked Calydon. *Be ready for them to strike. I don't trust casual conversation.*

Thano and Zach acknowledged his warning, and he felt their readiness. Three against five were usually easy odds for the Order, but the men before them carried the same power they did. *Grant us passage,* Ryland said. *We are not here to harm.*

Because you are Order, we grant you freedom to leave, the cloaked warrior said. *Leave now, warriors.*

Ryland swore under his breath. *Our leader is trapped in the nether-realm. We will not abandon him.* If these men were truly Order, that would be all the explanation they would need to step back and allow Ryland and the others to pass—

There was a boom that shook the very earth, and the night flashed with an explosion so bright that it blinded Ryland for a split second. The power that rushed him was too familiar, and he swore, knowing that the cloaked warriors had just called out their weapons. "They're coming for us!"

Still blinded by the light, Ryland channeled his preternatural senses, focusing on the ripple of energy around him to track his assailants. He swung hard with his machete, and a sword crashed into his blade as his vision returned in time to see two warriors closing in on him. "Shit!" He barely sidestepped another blow, and then they were on them, fighting with brutal force. They were effortless in their movements, so graceful it was as if they weren't even truly human. As they fought, their black cloaks never budged, still hiding their faces, making it feel like he was being attacked by the grim reaper itself.

"Catherine," he yelled. "Get to the entrance!"

"Okay!" She didn't hesitate, and she raced past him, darting across the open area as the warriors engaged his team, clearly trusting him and his team to protect her as she ran. There was a roar of fury as the one Ryland was fighting noticed her. The male broke contact to run her down.

"You guys go in there!" Thano shouted as Apollo charged after the warrior pursuing Catherine, the massive beast gaining on him with surreal ease. "We'll hold them at the entrance!"

I'll get her. Ryland broke from the battle, hauling ass across the field toward Catherine. The warrior was bearing down on her, his weapon raised to strike—

"No!" Ryland hurled his machete, and it slammed into the back of the warrior...*who didn't even flinch.* He just slammed his sword toward Catherine, who looked over her shoulder at him.

Her eyes widened, and she held up her arms to cover her face—and then Thano's halberd appeared in her hand with a crack and a flash of black light. Ryland stumbled in shock, stunned by the fact she'd called Thano's weapon, something only Thano's *sheva* could have done. The look on her face was equally shocked, and he felt Thano's surprise plow through his mind. For a split second, the battle seemed to stand still, and all Ryland could see was the weapon of his teammate in Catherine's hand.

Then, still in full motion and unable to avert himself in time, the warrior impaled himself on the end of it, right in his heart. Gasping, he stumbled, but he was already reaching for the weapon to yank it free.

Get her out of here! Thano shouted. *Now!*

Thano's urgency split through Ryland's shock, and he lunged for Catherine. He grabbed her wrist, and yanked her to the side as the warrior lurched to his feet. "Come on!" he shouted at her as he scooped her up, racing for the entrance, the warrior hot on his tail.

Fifty yards away.

Forty yards.

Wind whistled past his head, and he ducked as a sword side-swiped his shoulder, taking a chunk of flesh with it. Catherine hurled Thano's halberd again, and Ryland heard the thud of it hitting flesh.

Son of a bitch. A Calydon's weapon would respond only to a Calydon and his mate. She'd thrown Thano's twice. *Twice!*

"I got it covered!" Thano yelled. "Go!"

Fighting to keep his focus, Ryland vaulted up the steps of the pyramid. The moment his foot touched the stone, a dark vibration began to hum through him, and his wrists and ankles began to burn, as if the cuffs were already taking form. Sweat poured down his back, and he stumbled to a stop on the threshold, staring into the depths he knew so well. "Jesus," he whispered numbly, as he stared down there. "I can't go in there. I can't do this." Numbly, he released Catherine, unable to even hold her in his arms. Memories assaulted him. The nights. The days. The deaths. The feeling of impotence, of being trapped, of having no control over what he did, over who he hurt—

"Ryland!" Catherine grabbed his arms as she slid down his body, her feet landing on the stone. "Come on!"

But he couldn't move. He couldn't take that step. He couldn't cross over into that hell. He couldn't go back.

"Ryland—"

His legs buckled, and he crashed to his knees, the hard stone smashing into his kneecaps. Bone on stone. Pain. Like before.

"Ryland!" Catherine knelt before him, her face frantic. "We can't stay out here!"

As she urged him to his feet, her voice like an angel's music in the darkness of his mind, he suddenly knew. This angel, this beautiful angel, was his light, and his ultimate, final darkness. "My dear, sweet Catherine." He lifted his hand, tracing it over her soft cheeks. "Your eyes are so blue," he whispered. "Just like hers. So much innocence in you. Just like her."

"Her?" she echoed. "What are you talking about?"

"Her. You. It's happening again." Catherine was the thing that would bring him down, that would return him to the hell he once lived. He understood that now. For hundreds of years, he'd kept himself clean of any emotional entanglements that could be used against him, and now Catherine was kneeling before him, a woman who had broken through his shields. On the threshold to doom, and his tormenters had given him back the one thing that would destroy him. "Run," he whispered. "Away from me. Away from this place. Your daughter isn't here. Dante isn't here. It must be a trick to trap us. It always is." He gripped her hair with sudden fierceness. "Run!" he shouted. "Run!"

Catherine's eyes widened, that azure blue that seemed so out of place in this doomed world. "No," she said. "Never!" Then she surged to her feet, and sprinted over the threshold and into the darkness of hell.

"No!" Ryland lunged for her, his voice an agonizing scream as he leapt to grab her, his fingers reaching for the back of her jacket. They brushed against it, and he seized the slick material triumphantly—

It was too late.

A vortex of wind swept up, jerking him off his feet and hurtling him into the darkness.

They'd crossed the threshold. There was no going back.

🐾 CHAPTER ELEVEN 🐾

THE WIND SPUN CATHERINE RUTHLESSLY, thrusting her into the darkness, tumbling her head-over-heels into a bottomless tunnel of blackness. She couldn't see anything, couldn't feel anything except the ice cold wind slashing at her skin, and the hard grip of Ryland's fist on the back of her jacket. Then even he was yanked away, and she was tumbling wildly, out of control, completely at the mercy of the vortex that had swept her up—

She crashed to the hard ground, as if the cursed maelstrom had spit her out ruthlessly. Pain throbbed through her as she lay on the hard stone, the breath pummeled from her lungs, her body aching from being ruthlessly twisted and yanked.

It was too dark to see anything, and the silence was almost overwhelming, so loud that it seemed to hammer at her eardrums and slam at her head. Where was she? What was coming for her? She struggled to her knees, rebelling against the protests of her body. There was no time to be hurt. No time to cry—

A loud thump echoed beside her, and the ground she was on shuddered from the force of the impact. She jumped, whirling around as she strained to see through the impenetrable darkness. Thano's halberd was no longer in her hand, and she felt naked and vulnerable, completely out of her depth—

There was a loud scrambling, the sound of claws scraping rapidly on stone, and she scurried backwards. Heavy, raspy breathing bounced off the rocks, and then a crash, as if something had run right into a wall. Then more frenetic scrabbling, as if something were hurt and in danger—

"Catherine." Ryland's hoarse voice echoed in the darkness.

"Cat! Where are you? Cat!" His voice became more desperate, and she sat up, trying to pinpoint where he was coming from. "Ryland! I'm here! Where are you?"

"Cat!" He was almost screaming her name, his voice echoing, repeating his desperate call with an eerie frenetic energy.

"Ryland!" She scrambled to her feet and started running blindly in his direction, her hands extended in front her—

Something grabbed her ankle, and she screamed as she was yanked backwards. But it was Ryland's hard body that she landed on, and relief rushed through her. "Ry—"

He crushed her mouth in a kiss, a merciless assault that stripped her words and her breath. He yanked her beneath him, flooding her senses with kisses. His body was shaking violently, and his shirt was drenched with sweat. His breath was harsh, shuddering gasps, as if he couldn't even get oxygen. His lips were cold on hers, his kisses almost clumsy in their desperation. His hands kept slipping over her hips as he tried to hold her still, as if he couldn't even summon enough control over his body to hold her.

"It's okay, Ryland—" Again, she couldn't even finish her words, as he took her with another frantic kiss. His need for her was so frenzied and insane, that her heart broke for this big, strong man who was crumbling in her arms, asking her for strength, for help.

Tears filled her eyes for him, for his suffering. The shields she'd erected around herself seemed to crack in the face of his vulnerability. She wrapped her arms around his neck and pulled him close, kissing him back, offering all she had. *I'm here, Ryland. It's okay. You're safe.*

He didn't respond, but his kisses grew in crazed energy, and she knew he hadn't heard her. Frustration rolled through her. After the intimacy of the telepathic communication with Thano, it felt so right to expect that with Ryland, but there was no connection between them, at least not on a mental level.

But beneath his hands and his kiss, under his body, she felt herself come alive in response to his assault. It was more than desire and lust arising within her. It was the deepest need of her soul coming to life. An awakening for this man.

She knew it was dangerous to let herself succumb to him, but it didn't seem to matter. There was no way to resist how he called to her, how she wanted to respond. When he yanked up her shirt and took her breast in his mouth, she gasped and arched her back, unable to do anything but offer herself to the man falling apart in her arms.

With a low growl, Ryland bit her nipple, and she gasped

as hot waves of desire rushed through her. The same level of urgency that seemed to consume him flared to life inside her, driving her into his embrace and his kiss. The moment transformed instantly, from a one-sided desperate attempt at salvation, to two people burning with need so hot it seared their veins as they surrendered themselves to the passion exploding between them.

His hands were suddenly on her breasts, his mouth on her belly, his body burning with heat. Catherine couldn't get enough of his skin. She kept running her hands repeatedly over his bare chest, his chiseled stomach, and his hips.

"More," Ryland whispered. "More."

"More," she agreed, catching her breath as he tore her jacket off and tossed her shirt aside, along with her bra. Cold air assaulted her as he descended on her, but the heat of his body ignited warmth that chased away the chills and sent intense waves of passion ricocheting through her.

The feel of his bare chest against hers was intoxicating, almost overwhelming her senses. So much flesh, so much life, so much intense connection. She gripped his shoulders, her fingers digging into the muscle as he kissed his way down her body again. Not a kiss of an intentional, planned seduction. It was a wild assault on her senses, a primal claiming of her body.

When he reached her jeans, there was no hesitation as he tore open the button and zipper. His mouth closed on her body even as he yanked her jeans over her hips, and she gasped at the invasion, barely aware of her pants sliding over her calves. Then they were gone, and he pulled back long enough to ditch his clothes. Then he was back between her thighs, kissing and touching, his body gloriously naked between her legs.

It was so dark, she still couldn't see him. All her senses were attuned to his touch, to the heat of his skin as she locked her legs around his shoulders, as his hands dug into her hips, holding her at his mercy while he teased her core with his mouth. He had her trapped, exactly as he had with the vine, but this time it wasn't scary. It was an incredible, indescribable moment of perfection and safety, of passion and fire, of the formation of a bond between a man and a woman that could never be severed.

"I need you," he rasped as he lurched upward and caught her mouth in a kiss so urgent it was almost violent.

He didn't wait for an answer. He simply inserted his knee between hers and moved her thighs apart. Catherine inhaled sharply, knowing what was next. Her body tensed in anticipation, aching for his invasion, desperate for him to finish what he'd begun and to bind them together forever.

"Cat," he whispered as he moved his hips, pressing against her entrance. He slid his hand beneath her head, cradling her from the hard rock beneath them. "Now."

"Now," she whispered.

He thrust deep, so deep that her body seemed to come apart in his arms as it accepted him completely, shifting and morphing to accommodate him. He went still, holding his position deep inside her, his breath coming in violent rasps. His body was still trembling, his back was slick with fresh sweat, but as their bodies adjusted to each other, Catherine felt a tremendous shudder echo through his body.

"My dear angel," he whispered into her mouth. "You're the salvation for my soul."

The depth of his reverence brought tears to her eyes, but a part of her heart ached for what he hadn't said. "I don't want to be your angel right now," she said. "Just your woman."

He kissed her again, so deeply it seemed to go right to her soul that was crying out for more. She needed to hear him say her name, to have him acknowledge that the respite he was seeking from her wasn't simply because he needed an angel, any angel. She wanted to hear *her* name on his lips, to know that he was with *her*, and her alone.

But he said nothing as he began to move his hips, sliding out of her with agonizing denial of what she wanted, and then thrusting deep, stirring her into a frenzy of sensual passion so intense that she stopped caring about him using her name. The name didn't matter, not when the connection between them was so intense that it was imprinting upon her very soul, cutting through the years of scarring and opening her heart in a way that should have terrified her. The strength of his arms, the passion of his kisses, and the electricity of their love-making were so powerful that there was no room for fear. Just complete and utter commitment to the bond between them.

He drove deep again, and suddenly her body exploded in a cascade of fireworks so powerful she felt as if her soul had been ripped from her body and thrust into the whirling firestorm that lived within him. His spirit met hers as his body bowed and a shout tore from his throat. The winds seemed to whip through their very spirits, swirling them into a world of fire and passion and light and hope. It was as if everything she'd never dared reach for had suddenly been thrust into her grasp for the taking.

Ryland's arms tightened around her, holding her close as their bodies bowed under the strength of the climax, as if the only thing holding them together was his physical strength and sheer force of will...which meant that when his will changed, and he was forced to choose between her and Dante, there would be nothing left to hold them together. All this magic, this feeling of safety and belonging...it would all be gone.

Tears fell from her eyes even before the orgasm released him, depositing them back into their bodies, into the reality of their situation and lives.

RYLAND BURIED HIS FACE in Catherine's neck, shocked by the tremors still racking his body, by the intensity of what had happened between them. He couldn't believe he'd taken her like that. That had never been his intention. Ever. Yeah, he craved her body relentlessly, but he never would have caved to such base instinct and had sex with her, an angel of the highest order.

But he had. He'd taken her almost violently, in the entrance of hell, on a bed made of rock, as if he thought she was nothing more than some common woman. But he hadn't been able to stop himself. The need for her had blinded him to everything else, consuming him like a raging inferno that would have destroyed him if he hadn't filled it with her.

Scowling at himself, he rolled onto his side and tucked her closely against him, even now overwhelmed by the feel of her body against his. Her back was pressed against his chest, her hips nestled against his groin, her hair draped over his arm, her head resting on his shoulder. He clasped her wrists to her chest and draped his leg over hers, enfolding her in the shield of his body, needing to offer her protection and safety. "I'm sorry," he whispered as he brushed a kiss over her hair.

Even as he spoke, he reached out with his preternatural senses, trying to figure out where they were in the nether-realm. The vortex could have spit them out anywhere—in one of the few hidden corners, or right in the middle of the worst parts. But when he caught the scent of wild rose, he relaxed, knowing exactly where they were. They were in one of the few pockets of protected area left over from the ancient days, places he'd sought out and found during his tenure there. Relief rushed through him, as he realized that he must have instinctively called upon his old skills of directing their trip through the vortex to land in a safe spot.

It was damn good news for both of them that he still had his instincts, but it was also eerie to realize how close his ties to this realm still were. He was a part of this hell, and that hadn't changed.

"Again with the apology," Catherine said wearily, drawing his attention back to her. "What is it this time? You didn't tie me up, so it can't be that."

Ryland frowned at how shaky and vulnerable her voice sounded, and he turned her toward him, wishing he could see her face in the darkness. He knew how to get them light, but to do so, he'd have to get up, and he didn't want to let go of her, almost afraid that she would somehow disappear on him again. With her in his arms, this hell felt different, like there was a chance that he wasn't the beast he once had been.

So, instead of getting up, he simply brushed a kiss over her forehead, and then her cheek. When he tasted the salt of her tears, he frowned. "What's wrong?"

"You."

He bowed his head, knowing of what she spoke. He was a monster, and she'd been victimized by it firsthand. He'd sullied her with his need and his fury. "Catherine, I should not have—"

"No." Her fingers pressed against his lips, silencing him. "Don't say that. It was beautiful and incredible, and I don't want it soiled with some apology where you say how you didn't want to do it. Just let it be, Ryland."

Shocked by her words, Ryland was speechless for a moment. She didn't regret it? She didn't condemn him for succumbing to the most basic male needs? "You're okay with it?"

"Okay?" She shoved at his chest. "For heaven's sake, Ryland, try to be a little more poetic. We just made love. It was amazing. Dangerous and all sorts of stuff like that, but for what it was—" Her voice softened and she blessed him with a tender stroke across his forehead as she brushed his hair back. "It was life-giving," she whispered.

Warmth swelled through him, and he caught her hand, pressing his lips to each knuckle. "It was," he agreed. "And I did want to do it. I've been burning for you since I first caught your scent." He tucked her more tightly against him, their legs tangled together intimately. He knew they had to get up and get moving, but for a moment, he didn't want to go anywhere. They were safe where they were, hidden in an oasis created by old faerie magic long ago.

Catherine tapped at his arm. "I need my clothes."

"Not yet." He nuzzled her hair, astonished by how soft it was against his face. He'd never experienced anything like this moment, with her soft, curvy body enfolded in his embrace, her scent wrapped around him, her hair tickling his face. If there was truly such a thing as peace in this world, this would be what it was like. "We're in one of the few protected areas of the nether-realm. As long as we stay here, we're hidden."

"Really?"

"Yeah. I hid here many times before—" He stopped as a cold chill rippled across his skin again, as memories long hidden flared to life.

Catherine squeezed his hand. "Before what?" she urged.

He swore and rolled onto his back, resting the back of his wrist across his forehead, fighting against the memories trying to surface. Instead, he focused on Catherine, on her scent, on his mission. He was here to find Dante. He was here to salvage the Order for his leader. He was here to protect the Order's guardian angel. He had no time for shit from his past.

"Ryland. Tell me." She scooted closer and crawled on top of him, stretching out so that her feet were resting on his shins, her elbows braced on his chest. Ryland traced her face, and could tell that she was resting her chin on her palms, comfortably ensconced on top of him.

It was such a casual intimacy. So unfamiliar, but at the same time, there was something so right about it.

"You couldn't even make yourself cross the threshold into the nether-realm," she said. "What happened to you here? Help me understand, so I can help you through it."

Ryland swore and gently set her aside. He sat up and grabbed for his jeans. "We need to focus on now," he said. "We're in the southeast quadrant. Can you sense Dante's spirit from here?"

She didn't move. "Ryland. We need to talk about this."

Scowling he squatted in front of her. "Listen, Cat. I don't do this."

"Do what?"

"This." He gestured at her, at them, even though he knew she couldn't see him. "This...this..." Hell. He didn't even know how to describe what it was. "We're here on a mission. Not to do some therapy shit."

She laughed softly. "You mean, you don't know how to have a

conversation with someone about something that matters to you? You don't make love to a woman, and then hold her in your arms while you share your secrets?"

Horror congealed in his gut, and he recoiled. "Make love? Shit, no. I've never made love in my life to anyone. I've only fu—"

She covered his mouth again. "No, Ryland, I don't need to hear your words for describing what you've done with women in the past. What we just did was making love, so you *have* done it, and that's what it's like."

He had no answer for that. He didn't even know what to say. What did a guy say to that kind of statement? Because that had been some kind of hard-core experience between them, some serious shit far and beyond anything he'd ever experienced. But making love? Jesus. Even the sound of those words sent coils of ice-cold fire through him. "Making love is a trap," he said. "Love is a trap. I don't do that. I'm a warrior, Cat, so don't try to make me into something I'm not." But even as he said the words, he felt an unpleasant ache in his chest, like he didn't want to say something like that to her. Not to Cat. Swearing, he ran his hand through his hair. "I mean, hell, I'm not trying to dishonor what you said. It was definitely...something...unusual that just happened between us. It's never been like that before—"

Shit. He didn't even know what to say.

"Hey." Catherine shoved at him, catching him off balance in his crouched position. He landed on his butt, and she leapt onto him. He caught her, and then she settled herself deeper on top of him, her hips sinking against him in a way that made his body start getting hard again. "We're about to invade the nether-realm, and my guide absolutely freaked out when he got in here. We need to deal with your mental state right now, Ryland."

He scowled at her word choice. "I didn't freak out—"

"Shut up for one second, and let me talk." She shifted against him, grinding her pelvis into his cock, and he began to think she was trying to distract him on purpose.

It was working. Damn her.

"Yeah, okay, go for it. Talk." He set his hands on her hips and adjusted her against him, so that he was in a better spot, her belly right up against his increasingly hard cock. Her teasing him was sheer pleasure, and there was no damn chance he was man enough to walk away from it.

"So, here's the deal," she said. "Every warrior has a weakness. The only way to defeat it is to acknowledge it, and establish a plan to manage it. So, you are going to tell me what happened here before, or else I am going to disappear and go it on my own, because I can't afford to have you lose it again."

Ryland's amusement with their unspoken sensual play dissolved. "You're not leaving me."

"Then talk." She wiggled again, and he sucked in his breath. "You were a slave here," she said. "Tell me what happened, or we're never going to succeed in here. You may be a big, tough, badass warrior, but you've got scars from this place, Ryland, scars that are going to get us killed."

"Fuck that. I'm fine."

"Then why are you clawing at your neck as if there is already a collar around it?"

Ryland realized he was scratching at the front of his throat, dragging his knuckles across his flesh as he had so many nights when he'd lain on that barren rock, trying to get himself free of his shackles. Swearing, he dropped his hand, but even when he did, he could feel the same cold sensation of heavy golden cuffs on his wrists and ankles. He clasped his arm, but it was only flesh. "I can feel them," he said.

Catherine's fingers wrapped around his wrist, sliding beneath his hand. "There's nothing there, Ryland. You're not a slave anymore."

He swore and released his grip on his wrist, but he could still feel the cold metal on his skin, as if it were a heavy weight locking him down. Shit. She was right, wasn't she? He knew she was. He *had* nearly lost his shit on the threshold, and his mind was already playing tricks on him.

She was his guardian angel, right? So her job was to protect him. He was supposed to tell her shit like this, because that was her job. Right?

Damn. It was time. Time to go back to hell. Time to face what he'd thought he'd left behind. But just the thought of revisiting the life he'd once endured sent tension spiraling through him.

"Come closer." He stretched out more comfortably on his back, pulled her high on his chest, and wrapped his arms around her. "Give me peace, my angel," he whispered.

"Always." She tucked her head under his chin and rested her cheek against him. "I'm right here."

"Yeah, okay." Ryland took a deep breath and began his story. "I was told I was created here from the spirits of the dead," he said. "A child of darkness, bred by the female and male who rule here, Desdria, and the Dark Lord."

"Your parents?"

"No. Not my parents." He spat the words, refusing to even catalogue them as parents. "There was a woman who took care of me when I was little. She said...she said she was simply a servant of Desdria, but that's crap. She was my mother. I'm sure of it. I don't know how I was born, or if I was, but she..." He ground his jaw, remembering only bits and pieces of that time, the flashes of safety when she was there.

Catherine stared at him. "Of course you had a mother. Everyone has a mother."

"No, not everyone. Not creatures created by forces beyond life and death."

She raised her brows. "Ryland. You're not a creature. You're a man. You're real. If you think she was your mother, she was. A child always knows."

For a split second, something tightened in his throat at her confirmation of what he had always believed, and he had a sudden urge to wrap a lock of her hair around his fingers, grounding himself in the silkiness of the strands, in something that was pure and good. "A child is always born innocent, but I was a carrier for some unbelievable shit. They wanted to bring it out in me, so they—" He stopped, recalling that first night Desdria had come to him. "She had a burning poker in her hand," he said. "I was maybe a year old, just strong enough to survive their persuasive efforts." His stomach flexed, as if defending against the wounds inflicted so long ago, scars that he would never show to the outside world.

Catherine stiffened. "What about your mother? She let them hurt you?"

"Shit no. She tried to stop them, and they killed her. It was the first time I'd seen blood before. So much fucking blood. I can still hear the screams as she fought them, trying to protect me. She had no chance, but she gave her life trying." He looked at her. "I learned about protecting innocents from her," he said softly. "You give your life, at all costs. It's what you do."

She nodded. "Your mother," she agreed. "She gave her life for you. It's what mothers do." She smiled. "You had a mom, Ryland. You're not a monster."

"Oh, but I am, and Desdria and the Dark Lord figured out how to get it out of me. They had to inject evil into me to unleash the monster they wanted me to become, the one they knew was already inside me."

Catherine rubbed his chest, her touch so fucking surreal he

didn't even understand it. "They wanted you to become a killer, didn't they?"

"An assassin at their command, yeah." Catherine had been inside his soul. He realized that she'd probably seen parts of him he hadn't shown anyone. "They wanted me to kill innocents, to be the enforcer of doom. I wouldn't do it." His mind shifted back to that time. "They would bring me innocents to torture, but I wouldn't do it, so they tortured me instead. They did everything they could to force me, held back only by their need to make sure they didn't actually kill me. They thought that if they hurt me badly enough, I would agree to what they wanted, but I never did. I fucking would never go down that road. I could not attack those people, those creatures. Hurting innocents is bullshit. I never lost my human form. I never became what they wanted me to be. There was no fucking way they could make me cross that line. Until—"

He stopped. Shit. He didn't want to go there. To that night that had made him violate all that he believed in, all that he stood for.

"Until what?" she urged gently, stroking small circles on his chest, as if to remind him that she was still there, still with him, still his guardian angel.

Swearing, he rolled Catherine off him and sat up. He rubbed his neck, needing to feel bare flesh against his hand. There was no slave collar on him. No wrist cuffs. No ankle cuffs. He was still free. It was all simply a memory. "There was a woman," he continued. A woman? No, not just *a* woman. An innocent of the purest spirit. "Marie," he said. "She was one of the faeries of the nether-realm. She was a water faerie, one of the purest kinds of faeries that exists. They live here, but they're good."

"Water faeries? Here? How can they possibly survive in so much darkness?" Catherine sounded surprised, and he didn't blame her.

"Their purity is like water. It flows over everything, and simply washes past the taint. The water faeries are the balance that keeps the nether-realm from destroying itself with its evil. I met her once when I was hiding from the king and queen, and after that, our friendship was sealed. She was so sweet and innocent, this gift of purity in this hell I was living. It was indescribable what she brought to me, showing me things I never knew existed." He smiled, recalling their past. "She was the first person I'd ever heard laugh. I freaked out when she laughed, and tried to kill the berries she was eating because I thought they were creatures that were choking her."

Catherine laughed softly. "Protecting the innocents even when you were a boy."

His smile faded as darkness settled in his bones. "I failed her," he snapped out bitterly. Restless, he stood up, no longer wanting the darkness.

He strode across the floor to the wall and felt around until he found the opening he remembered. He shoved his hand past hundreds of years of dirt and grime, and found the emerald that Marie had showed him. He pulled it out and held it in his palms. It began to glow instantly, filling their cavern with green light. The shadows were cast back, and a beautiful green glow radiated through the area.

He set it back inside the hole, but it continued to glow, and would not fade until they left.

"How did you fail her?" Catherine was on her side, propped up on her elbow, her body gloriously naked and swathed in the faint emerald light. Her breasts were petite perfection, her hips a tantalizing curve, her legs an endless gift of ecstasy. And her eyes...that same incredible blue, so vibrant that they held their color even in the green light. She was watching him intently, no judgment or fear on her beautiful face.

Swearing, Ryland fell to his knees before her, in awe of what she was. "She was like you," he said softly, tracing his fingers along her jaw. "She brought something into my life that I didn't understand, but I knew it was special. It was relief. Hope. Beauty. A glimpse into the truth that all was not the same as what I was living. She was my salvation. She gave me the strength to endure everything the Dark Lord and Desdria did to me. She saw in me things I didn't see and believed I could defeat the two of them and escape from their grasp. She was my mentor, even though she was just a girl my own age."

Catherine smiled, but there was a sadness in her eyes that he didn't understand. "You loved her," she said.

"Love?" The question shocked him. "Why would I love her?"

She blinked. "But you just said—"

"Cat, look at me." He gestured to the beast painted on his chest, to the scars carved into his belly from damage that even an immortal could not heal. "I'm not about love. It's not even a part of who I am."

She frowned. "Of course it is. Love is a part of everyone—"

"Love is a fucking weakness to be exploited. I wouldn't allow it."

Sadness flickered in her eyes, and she touched his cheek. "I know what you mean," she said softly. "I know exactly what you mean."

He took her hand and held it against his cheek. "They found her," he said, his mind held relentlessly in the grip of that night. "They found out who she was, and they brought her to me. The water faeries are critical to the balance of the nether-realm, and they are never touched by the darkness. But Desdria and the Dark Lord broke the rule. They chained me up and—" Sweat broke out on his brow again, and he tightened his grip on Catherine's hand. "They hurt her, Cat. They hurt her in front of me. They tortured her again and again, telling me it was my fault, my fault, my fault for soiling her with my filth."

Suddenly, he was back there again, in that night, the chains digging into his wrists and ankles as he fought to get free to save her. Blood everywhere. "Her screams, those god-awful screams begging for mercy, for me to save her, to make it end. I couldn't break the chains." He could still remember his wrists snapping under the assault, his ankles shattering as he tried to get out of his restraints, fighting so hard his own body gave way. "They carved out her heart, Cat, while she was alive. It broke me. I snapped." Jesus, how he'd snapped. "I called the beast, and I erupted."

Her eyes widened. "You broke the chains?"

"Yeah, yeah, but it was too late. I was too fucking late to save her." He would never forget the roar of anguish as he'd torn himself free of his shackles and fallen to the floor beside her, gathering her fragile body against his. "She died in my arms, her soul bleeding with anguish." He shook his head. "I didn't protect her. I failed her. And when she died, my humanity was gone. She was all that had kept me sane. There was nothing left, and I became the monster they wanted me to be."

"Oh, Ryland." Catherine's blue eyes burned with empathy, not the condemnation he deserved.

"No, no pity for me. I failed her. It's my fault." He dug his fingers into his left wrist, trying to pry off the cuffs he could still feel. "That night, they claimed me. The cuffs went on, symbols of my bondage to them. They owned my soul, they controlled the beast. I no longer existed as an individual."

"What did they make you do?"

His head began to pound, aching with memories that he'd kept hidden for so long. "I killed so many innocents. Again and again. I couldn't keep from doing it. I saw what I was doing, but I couldn't stop. My mind knew what was happening, and there wasn't a fucking thing I could do to stop it."

His body began to shake. Never would the screams of the innocents he'd murdered stop ringing in his ears. Never would his hands be cleansed of their blood. Never would it stop haunting him that he'd failed to protect the innocent. "There's no way to describe what it's like to kill again and again, to be enslaved to monsters like that. I did their bidding, indulging their every whim." He held out his hands. "Do you see the blood on them, Cat? There's so much blood of innocents—"

"No." She took his hands in hers, and folded them against her heart. "The blood is on their hands," she said. "Not yours."

"No," he whispered. "You're wrong. It's mine," he said. "All mine. I was too weak to free myself. That's my fault. My weakness. My failure." He looked down at his chest and saw that the entire tail of the dragon was a purplish-turquoise now, and the cuff on the left ankle of the monster was gold. He swore and pressed his palm to his chest, a sheen of sweat making it shimmer as if it were alive. "They sent me out into the earthly-realm to slaughter Dante, but he called an angel, and he broke their hold on me." He closed her hands in his fists. "He gave me freedom, Cat. The greatest gift a man can have. Do you understand that?"

She nodded, her blue gaze still as fearless as ever. "You're afraid of becoming enslaved again. Of losing your freedom."

"Afraid?" He was a warrior, an immortal warrior assigned to the Order of the Blade. Men like him didn't become afraid. "Not afraid, Cat. Not afraid," he said. "Absolutely, fucking terrified."

Catherine laid her hands on his cheeks. "We won't let that happen," she said. "If you get too close, we'll leave, okay?"

As he stared into her face, into the face of the angel who had been sent into his life, he knew the truth. The deadly, dangerous truth. The horrifically surreal truth. "No, Cat, you don't get it." He pressed a kiss to her forehead. "You're like Marie," he said. "Your innocence, the beauty of your soul, the softness of your touch, the way my body craves you." He slid his hands behind the base of her neck, holding her face before his.

Her eyes stared into his, so wide, so brave, and so pure.

"For you, I would fall once again," he explained. "You are the trap that was sent to reclaim me. You, my angel, are the key to the final destruction of my soul." He touched her face. "To save you, the beast would come, and they will know that, if they don't already. They will hunt you, take you, and then hurt you until I snap. Which I will."

She paled. "Desdria and the Dark Lord are still here?"

"They're immortal. They'll always be here." He looked past her, into the darkness that was so close. Two yards away, and their protection would end. "Do you think it's a fluke that the baby they kidnapped was the daughter of the Order's Guardian angel?"

"What?" She sat up, her eyes widening.

"The whole thing was a setup to bring me back," he said. "They knew that we'd be drawn to each other, that we would find each other, and then the noose would tighten." He looked at her. "We've been manipulated from the start, Catherine, and they're stealing what we both want. Your daughter, and my freedom."

🐯 CHAPTER TWELVE 🐯

A COLD CHILL rushed down Catherine's spine and she scrambled to her feet. "You think they took my daughter to get to you?" At his grim nod, she felt her chest tighten in panic. Lucy had been targeted because they had wanted *Ryland?* He was the one who was the danger to her? How could she have been so blind? She'd been falling right into the hands of the man who would expose her to everything. "I need to get dressed," she mumbled, as she stumbled past him, grabbing for her clothes.

She'd trusted him. Despite all her claims, she'd started to trust him. She'd let him make love to her for heaven's sake. She grabbed her underwear and pulled it on, her hands shaking violently.

"Hey!" Ryland grabbed her arm as she fumbled with her bra strap. "Cat—"

"No!" She slapped his hand away and yanked her bra on. "Don't."

His jaw flexed, and his eyes darkened. "Hey," he said, his voice so low and lethal that she froze. "I am not your fucking enemy," he said. "I didn't steal your daughter—"

"I trusted you!" Her hands shaking, she grabbed for her jeans, needing to be covered up—

"Catherine!" He grabbed her arms and spun her toward him, his eyes fierce. "Don't pull away from me," he growled. "Not right now. I need you—"

"You need me? *You need me?*" How could she have forgotten her goal? Her plan had been to use him to find the entrance, and then continue on her own. And yet she'd screamed at him to come with her. She'd fallen under yet another spell of a man. "You—"

"I did nothing to you," he growled. "I swore I would give my life for you, angel, and I will. I didn't take your daughter. I haven't done a fucking thing but protect you and keep you safe—"

"You made me trust you!" She slammed at his chest, fear hammering at her. "Don't you get it? I trusted him and he betrayed me—"

"Him? Who?" He locked her down against him, trapping her. "Who did you trust? What are you talking about?"

"Simon," she gasped, still fighting to get free of the arms that had held her so tightly while they'd been making love. "I fell in love with him, and we had a baby, and then he stole her and brought her here. He told me I had to work for them to get her back and—"

She couldn't breathe. Panic hammered at her, and she struggled to get free of his embrace, of the arms that she had wanted to stay in so badly just a short time ago. "And now, again, it's happening again, just like before. You led them to me. How could I be so stupid?" She fought to get free. "Let me go!"

"Hey! I'm not Simon!" He swore as he fought to contain her. "Catherine! Look at me! I'm not Simon!"

She squeezed her eyes shut, not daring to look at him. If she did, she knew she would want to trust him, and she knew she couldn't. She had no faith in her ability to know who to trust, to discern who to believe in. She'd trusted Ryland, fallen right into his arms, and yet he was the cause of her losing Lucy? It didn't matter if he was culpable or not. The fact was that he endangered all that mattered to her, and she hadn't seen it. "Let me go," she whispered, finally going still in his arms, too exhausted to fight his superior strength anymore. "Just let me go."

"No."

Fear began to ripple through her, true fear. It started deep inside her, swelling with such fierceness it exploded through her. Her skin turned black, and the light went out in the cave.

Ryland sucked in his breath, and his body flinched. "Jesus, Cat, what are you doing?"

She knew his flesh was burning and decaying everywhere she touched him. Her defenses were taking over, destroying the threat that bound her. "Let me go," she snapped. "You have to!"

He tightened his grip on her. "Fuck that, angel. I'm an immortal warrior and it's not that easy to kill me." His voice was steely with pain, but he didn't release her.

"I'm death, Ryland. Release me!" The fear grew inside her,

attacking Ryland and trying to destroy him before he could hurt her. That fear had come too late with Simon. Her weapons had been stripped from her by her love for him, by her disbelief, by the shattering of her heart. Too late, she'd realized what he was doing. It had been too late to stop him. Not so with Ryland. She was ready this time, protecting herself before all was lost. "Take your hands off me," she repeated, her voice becoming low and haunted, thick with death as her death touch came to life, infecting him, tainting him, *killing him.*

"You forget something, angel." He bent his head so his face was against hers. "I'm death, too. Bring it on, babe. Bring it on." Then he kissed her.

Kissed her!

She was death! She was *killing* him, and he was *kissing* her?

And he didn't stop! He just assaulted her with his kisses, drinking in everything she thrust at him until a slow, horrifying realization came to life within her: she couldn't kill him. She couldn't stop him. He was somehow immune to her touch of death. If he chose to destroy her, she had no way to stop him.

She went cold, the ice cold of death, rigid in his arms.

Ryland broke the kiss right away. "What's wrong?"

"You," she gasped. "I can't stop you." Her legs gave out, and Ryland went down with her as she collapsed on the stone. "I couldn't stop him," she gasped, gripping his arms. "He was my husband, the father of my child. He'd been this great salvation, a white light that kept my dark side at bay. When I slept with him, my mind was quiet, and I didn't kill anyone. I awoke each morning with no new souls in my body."

"Okay," Ryland said. "Tell me more."

She slumped, barely aware of the cold stone beneath her knees, of the chill on her upper body. "He was my salvation, Ryland. Don't you see?"

"He gave you freedom from killing people. Yeah, I get that," he said grimly. "There was a time when that was all I would have wanted for myself."

Catherine closed her eyes. "I was feeding Lucy one morning. Simon came in and asked to hold her, so I let him. Then he walked to the door and looked back at me. His eyes were black, so black, and a horrifically stained aura suddenly flowed from him. I realized in that moment that he was pure evil, pure death, and he'd somehow been hiding it from me. I didn't understand. I didn't believe it. I loved him." She reached out with her hand, just like she had that day so long ago, pleading for him to come back to her. "I didn't understand how dangerous he was to us," she whispered. "Not until he told me that it was time for me to resume what I'd started when I was four."

Ryland's grip tightened on her. "Which was what?"

"Killing souls." She closed her eyes. "After my parents died, some angels found me and brought me to an angel enclave. I was coated in death and evil, but they cleansed me and healed me. I met Alice there, and she was my dear friend. I thought it was all over, that life was good."

Ryland swore under his breath. "That was when you killed everyone?"

She nodded. "They came to me in my sleep. I don't know exactly how it happened, but I somehow flooded the village with death. Everyone died. Demon death, people said, but it wasn't. It was me." She closed her eyes. "Whatever I had unleashed was still there, feeding on everyone. I got Alice out of there, and we ran. God, we ran, even though it was me that we were running from."

"Shit, Catherine—"

"Alice refused to believe it was me, and it was her faith, her misguided naïve faith, that somehow gave me hope. For years, she protected me and kept it at bay, though I was always afraid to sleep unless she was beside me. Then I met Simon, and he was like the gift I'd been searching for my whole life. I felt safe. He gave me a family and a home, and I left Alice to be with him."

"He isolated you," Ryland said grimly. "Took away all your support except him."

Catherine nodded. "The day he snatched my daughter, he said it was time for me to fulfill my legacy, and to destroy the Order. I would get my daughter back only after everyone was dead."

Ryland's grip tightened on her arms. "And that was when you took Dante's soul?"

"No. I refused to sleep again after that, except when Alice was there. She would wake me up after five minutes, before I could fall deeply enough asleep. She and I tracked Simon, because I knew if I could get to him before he made it back to the nether-realm, I could save Lucy. But he was leading us right to Warwick Cardiff. Once *he* found me..." Catherine bit her lip. "I would wake every morning with new taint on my soul. I was taking souls every night, and I didn't remember who or what. I would just feel it in the morning." She realized she was leaning on Ryland, and she instinctively pulled way. "I remember Dante, though," she whispered. "I was awake for him. It was the first time Warwick got me to take a soul when I was awake."

This time, Ryland released her, but she sensed that he was ready to come after her if she tried to bolt. "Why did Alice want to kill you? Why did she say you wanted to die?"

Catherine hugged herself, rocking gently as she fought for control, to regain her strength. "Because every time I take a soul and kill it, a piece of my own soul dies. Eventually, I will kill my own soul, and I will stop existing just like those souls I take."

Ryland swore. "You're the angel of death. You can't just die."

"I can, and I'm very close." Catherine hugged herself, thinking of the sweet face of her baby girl who was in such danger. "I knew that as long as my soul was alive, Lucy would not be alone. I would somehow be able to get to her, even if it was from the afterlife. But if my soul dies, I cease to exist completely. That means I leave my daughter alone and exposed for all eternity." She fisted her hands. "I made Alice promise that if too much of my soul died, that she would take my physical life so that at least my soul would live on for Lucy. Unfortunately, I'm really difficult to kill."

Ryland sat back on his heels. "You would offer your life for your daughter."

"God, yes. Of course I would. What other reason is there to live?" Numbly, she tried to scramble to her feet. "I have to go get her. I have to get her now. I already almost killed you. I've never done that in the daytime when I was awake. I'm falling, and I need—"

"Hey." Ryland caught her arm, stilling her. "You didn't almost kill me. Not by a long shot. You were reacting in fear to protect yourself, because you saw me as Simon."

She stared at him. "I tried to kill you—"

"No. You didn't." Anger was burning in his eyes. "Listen to me, Cat. Simon betrayed you. The bastard lured you in and then betrayed you. He's a scum-sucking pig who should have his balls hacked off and fed to the demons."

Catherine stared at him and had the most inane desire to laugh at the image he presented. "Yes, he's all that, but the truth is that I didn't see him for who he was until it was too late. If I couldn't see that, then how do I trust my judgment with anyone?" She lifted her chin. "I swore to myself I wouldn't make that mistake again, and then I went and did it anyway, throwing my lot in with you."

Ryland's eyes flashed. "I wouldn't betray you."

"That is the same promise Simon made to me every single night for two years." She ground her jaw. "He even gave me a blood promise that he would always be there for me."

Ryland sat up. "A blood promise? What the hell's that?"

"We exchanged blood in a ceremony that binds us forever. It was part of our marriage ceremony. It's a very ancient ritual for angels that isn't done much anymore. But he wanted to do it." She grimaced. "I didn't know that he wanted the bond so that he could manipulate me."

Ryland felt his vision begin to blacken. "You're blood-bonded with another male?"

"Yes." She rubbed her arm, where his knife had carved two lines in her flesh. "I still carry the marks as a reminder every day that I trusted the wrong person. A reminder to stand on my own." She turned her arm over to look at it again and then frowned. "That's weird," she muttered.

Ryland wasn't listening. He had braced his hands on the ground, fighting against the new onslaught. "You called Thano's halberd. You hear his voice. You're blood-bonded with another man—"

Catherine gasped, and he jerked his head up. "What?"

She was looking at her arm. "There's another line here."

"What?" Ryland grabbed her arm and jerked it toward him, sudden adrenaline rushing through him. Making love was one of the stages of the Calydon bond with his soul mate. His mark could be on her—

He went cold when he saw the thin silver lines on her arm. It was a Calydon brand, but it wasn't his machete. It was the handle of *Thano's* weapon on her arm. "Jesus," he whispered, stunned. But there was no doubt. His machete was much wider and plain, but Thano's halberd was long and thin, and the end had a curve on it. She'd called Thano's weapon, which was one of the stages of the *sheva* bond, and now his mark was on her arm. Much of his weapon was showing, more than Ryland would have expected would come from a single stage. How many had they done?

"What is it?" she asked.

"Thano's weapon." Black rage began to course through him, fierce, throbbing rage. "There are five stages to the bond between a Calydon and his mate." He locked his hand around her arm, his body shaking in response to the sight of another man's mark on her skin. "Each time a stage is complete, a part of the Calydon's brand appears on her arm."

She stared at him. "But I'm not his mate."

Ryland's head was pounding so hard he couldn't even think.

Thano's brand. On her arm. Blood-bonded to another male. Catherine. *With another male.*

With a roar of outrage, he tore himself away from her and backed toward the wall. "You're Thano's woman." Jesus. Not his. *Not his.*

Catherine scrambled to her feet. "I'm not Thano's!"

"No, this is good, this is good." He fought against the rage and fury screaming through him. "The *sheva* bond is a trap. It makes me vulnerable to you. You're not mine. You can't trap me." He hit the wall and pressed his back against it. "You can't trap me." But Jesus, he wanted her. He fucking wanted her. This screamed wrongness. She was his. *His.*

"I'm not his!" She walked toward him, and he held up his hand to block her.

"No," he snarled. "Don't come near me. Don't you get it? If we were soul mates, you wouldn't be able to resist me. I could bind you to me, just as you would bind me to you. You want that?"

She stopped, her eyes wide. "No," she whispered. "God, no."

"Yeah, so, yeah, so it's good. We aren't going to trap each other." He closed his eyes, pressing his head back into the cold rock, fighting against the blackness rushing through him. Dark anger. Dark rage. The need to tear himself off that rock, attack Catherine, and make love to her until every inch of her soul was stained with his aura, until she was so much a part of him that no one would ever be able to claim her. *Ever.* "I can't touch you," he whispered. "You belong to another man."

"No." Her voice was so bitter and strident that he opened his eyes. Catherine's hands were fisted by her side, and her jaw was jutted out. "I will *never* belong to another man. Not Simon. Not Thano." Her eyes glittered. "Not you." Then she held out her arm and stared at it.

As Ryland watched, a black shadow crept down her arm from her elbow. It flooded her pale flesh with darkness, obscuring Thano's mark and the scars from Simon, until there was nothing but ash-gray smears on her arms.

Fury continued to vibrate through Ryland, and he wanted to tear the marks from her skin, ripping them out of her very being. Just because she'd hidden them didn't mean they were gone. She dropped her hand and looked at Ryland. "All I want is to save my daughter," she said.

He gritted his jaw. "All I want is to find Dante."

She nodded. "Don't touch me again."

"No chance."

For a long moment, their gazes met, and Ryland felt something inside him crack as he stared into her blue eyes. A longing that was so foreign he didn't even understand what it was he wanted.

"You're my only hope," she said finally.

A need to protect vibrated through Ryland, a sense of purpose. This is what he was born for: protecting the angel meant to save him. He nodded. "I accept the responsibility."

She took a deep breath. "We save my daughter first. Then Dante."

Ryland shook his head. "Dante first."

Catherine blinked. "But once we find Dante, you'll have no reason to help me. You—"

"—were born to protect you," he finished. "I would burn in hell before I abandoned an angel. An angel saved my life, and I transfer that loyalty to every angel I meet. Dante first, then your daughter." His eyes flashed. "You can trust me."

For a long moment, she stared at him, then she shook her head. "No, I can't."

He swore, but he got it. After her story about Simon, he understood. Too many broken promises. The reason he understood was because he'd been equally betrayed by the people who had created him. To be betrayed by someone who you're supposed to be able to trust is the worst fucking hell of all.

He studied her, and then he knew the answer. "You're our guardian angel," he said. "You can't abandon Dante. It's against who you are." Satisfied, he levered himself off the wall. Catherine would not abandon Dante, because she was bound to the Order as their guardian angel, even if she didn't admit it yet. "Lucy first, then Dante." His ribs burned, and Ryland looked down at his chest. The turquoise had taken the beast's lower torso.

Catherine's gaze followed his and she grimaced. "How much time?"

"Plenty." But even as he reached for his boots to finish getting dressed, his heart started pounding. He had no idea how much time he had, but he suspected it wasn't much. Once Desdria and the Dark Lord confirmed his presence in their realm, he would have minutes, maybe seconds, before they would descend.

He shot a glance over at Catherine as she grabbed her shirt and pulled it over her head. As the smooth expanse of her upper body disappeared beneath the fabric, deep regret coursed through him...

immediately followed by the sharp stab of fear. Real fear. The kind of fear that a warrior never, ever wanted to feel.

Because he knew that even though she carried Thano's mark, it didn't matter.

She was his, and that meant that losing her would destroy him...unless he found a way to break them apart. And soon.

❈❈❈

CATHERINE'S FOREARMS WERE BURNING as she pulled on her jeans. It almost felt as if more lines were being drawn on her arms. Another male binding her? First Simon, and now Thano, who she barely even knew? Fear pounded at her as Ryland strode over to the hole in the wall where he'd originally retrieved the glowing rock. The stone that she'd drained was nothing but a faint whisper now, and she could feel the tension rising within her at the lack of light available to sustain her.

He felt his way over the stone wall, his hands broad as he palmed the surface. As he searched, the sheer force of his power seemed to fill their hideaway. His shoulders seemed to be even larger than they had been before, his very breadth seeming to expand. Ryland was such raw potency that it made her heart skip with longing. She wanted to walk over there and offer herself into his safekeeping. Accept his vow that he would keep her safe. Trust that he would be there for her.

And that realization terrified her.

Ryland was everything she shouldn't trust. He was steeped in death and violence, a creature of the nether-realm who was, even now, in the process of falling back under the control of the very creatures who had worked with Simon to steal her child and force her to murder.

But even as she thought it, she found herself craving Ryland's mark on her arms, wanting that silver brand to show a machete, to lock them together for eternity. "Can a Calydon hurt his soul mate?" She blurted the question accidentally, and her cheeks immediately flamed.

Ryland's shoulders stiffened, and he froze for a split second, not turning around. "No," he said. "Don't worry. Thano won't hurt you."

"What about you? What if *you* bonded with a woman?"

Slowly, he turned to face her, his face dark and turbulent. "Why are you asking about me?" he asked softly, dangerously.

Her heart started to pound. Why *was* she asking about him? Because if his answer was yes, if the bond would protect him from hurting her and she was his *sheva,* then she would be able to trust him again. She would be able to trust *someone.* "If you were enslaved again, would your bond with your *sheva* trump anything that Desdria and the Dark Lord wanted you to do?"

For a long moment, Ryland didn't move. Then he rubbed his hand over his wrist, as if he could feel the cuffs on his arms. Finally, he said simply, "I don't know."

"Why don't you know?" She walked over to him, urgency driving her. He was so tall, drawing his shoulders back as she approached, as if he was trying to put up a wall between them. She was so tired of being afraid, of being alone, of not being able to trust. "Haven't Calydons been bonding with their mates for thousands of years? Surely some of them have been pushed to the limit, right? If we completed the bond, then what?"

"*We* will not complete the bond," he said, going utterly still as she neared him. "But when a Calydon completes that bond, he is destined to go rogue and destroy all that they care about, including any innocents who are in the way. No one will be able to stop him, except for his own soul mate. She will kill him, and then kill herself because she is so distraught over killing the one man she loves." The comment ended in silence, and the walls seemed to throb with the doom he had predicted. His story was the same as the last time he'd spoken of it.

"But he won't hurt his *sheva?*" she urged. "He will destroy everything else, but not her?"

Ryland's face suddenly seemed to soften, and he trailed his hand down her jaw, a touch so tender and delicate that it seemed impossible for a man of his size to have done it. "No, Cat. A Calydon will never, ever hurt his mate. Even in the rogue state."

Tears filled her eyes, and she turned away, suddenly overwhelmed by the thought of there being a man she could trust so completely.

Ryland's hands went to her shoulders, and he pulled her against him, so her back was leaning against his chest. "Do not be fooled, angel," he whispered softly. "When a Calydon goes rogue from the *sheva* bond, he will destroy everything either of them care about. For you, that means your daughter. For me, that means Dante. For Thano...hell. I have no idea what it would be for him. He won't kill you, or even harm one hair on your beautiful body, but Thano killing your daughter will eviscerate your heart in a way that your own death could never do. That is what he would do if you completed the bond with him."

Catherine leaned her head back against his chest, feeling the heat of his body thrumming through her. She closed her eyes against the visions trying to swell in her mind. Of Ryland killing her daughter. "I don't believe *you* would hurt her," she said finally. "Even if we bonded, and you went rogue."

"You're terrified I will hurt you, but you're so sure I would protect your daughter?" He put his hands on her upper arms, his grip a seduction that seemed to awaken a deep, pulsing yearning for him.

He was right. That didn't make sense. How could she trust him with her daughter's life, but not hers? But even as she thought it, she simply couldn't see him hurting Lucy. Even rogue. Even with cuffs on.

"I have killed children before." His tone was dead. Bitter. Brutal. "Many children. Children destined for great things. Children destined to be the force that could bring down the nether-realm."

She twisted in his arms, staring into his dark eyes. They were turbulent storms of anguish, haunted by the beings he'd taken. So much death. So much darkness. So much brutality. The creature was stirring within him now. She could sense the power amassing within him. Merciless, ruthless death. "No," she said, laying her hands on either side of his face. "Leave Ryland alone," she said to the beast within him. "Let him be the man he is destined to be."

Ryland locked his hands around her wrists, his grip tight. Too tight. "Don't wake it up," he rasped, but his voice was already rough, a growl that seemed to crawl beneath her skin and claw at her soul.

She couldn't stop. She could feel the tormented souls within him calling to her, death reaching out for a kindred spirit. The creature within seemed to fixate on her. She felt herself falling into its spell, offering it her own power. It reached for her, dark blackness mixing with her aura, with the death eating away at her soul. She saw its eyes in Ryland's, twin spots of glowing crimson light staring at her, beckoning her. Death to death. Two powers. United. So powerful. The connection between them seemed to rise, igniting a need within her. A need to take. A need to consume. A need to harvest more. To thrust death into the world. To inflict the end of life on others. "Yes," she whispered, pressing her body against him. "Yes," she repeated, her voice breathless.

Ryland's mouth was a breath from hers, his breath so hot it felt like fire against her lips. "No," he growled. "Not like this."

Something pricked her hips where Ryland was holding her. She jumped, the pain jerking her back to the present. Ryland swore at the same instant and thrust her back away from him. Less than a yard apart, they both froze, the air thick with the need crawling between them.

"My hands," Ryland said.

She looked down. Silver claws were protruding from his fingertips. Nearly an inch long already, they were sharp and curved, with hooks on the end for tearing out flesh. "Your dragon called to me," she whispered, almost afraid to speak, as if it could hear her. Her skin felt like it was stained, her soul poisoned, from that brush with his monster. She'd never felt anything like that, anything so malevolent. It had been alive, a pulsing, seething malignancy tethering itself to her. It had been trying to poison her mind and corrupt her soul, binding her to it for a destiny so malevolent it sent chills reverberating all the way to her core. "It called to my darkness. It tried to take me." And it almost had.

"It wasn't my beast that was calling you." Ryland's voice was harsh, his breath rasping. "It was Desdria."

🐯 CHAPTER THIRTEEN 🐯

THE MOMENT HE SAID DESDRIA'S NAME, Ryland heard the bone-chilling cackle he'd heard so many times in his life, in his nightmares, in his memories. He went still, frozen by the vileness seething through him, by the low commands whispered in his mind. *Come to my throne, slave. Return to your duty.*

The image of the tall, black throne sprang into his mind. The charred flesh and bones woven together by human hair, the stench of rot, the stain of blood spreading out in a carpet of doom. Sitting on it, ensconced on her podium of power, was the woman, the creature, the she-demon he abhorred. Her black cloak in tatters, her skin a flawless porcelain, her lips deep red like the carpet of blood below her, her eyes hidden behind the shadows that never left her face. His master. His creator. But not his mother. Never his mother.

She turned her head, and he felt her gaze blistering into him. His chest began to burn, his wrists and ankles were on fire. Sharp pains were piercing his head. *Now.* Her command vibrated through him, and he took a step, then another, and then he was sprinting toward her—

"Ryland!" Catherine's voice broke through the spell.

Sudden pain assaulted him, and he went down, gasping in agony as it drilled through his body. The image of Desdria vanished from his mind, his claws retreated, and his body became his own again. He saw Catherine kneeling in front of him. "Cat?" he rasped, reaching out for her. She couldn't be real.

She caught his hands, holding them against her chest. *Real. She was real.*

"Ryland." A smile broke out over her face, a brilliant smile of relief that seemed to reach inside his body and rip him free of the last grasp of Desdria. "I didn't think you were ever going to hear me," she said.

"*Cat.*" He pulled her over to him and buried his face in her hair. He basked in its silkiness, in the warmth of her body, and in the gentleness of her touch as she stroked his head. She was real. She was his angel. Goodness. Not evil. Not death. Not trying to control him. His heart was pounding, sweat streaming down his back, his breath rasping in his chest. He felt like he'd just been in a twelve-hour battle for his own life and had barely survived to fight again.

"It's okay, Ry," she whispered, wrapping her arms around him. "She's not here."

"She *is* here." He pulled back enough to see her face. Her blue eyes were so clear and radiant, her skin pure and soft. He needed her goodness. He needed that gift. He needed her. He needed to make love to her until she wiped out all of that taint. His grip tightened on her hair, and he pulled her closer until her mouth was a fraction of an inch from his. "I need you," he said.

"I know." She framed his face and leaned forward, her lips brushing against his.

For a moment, Ryland could do nothing else but absorb the beauty of her kiss. Her lips were so soft and tender, blessing him with the kindness and light that he needed so badly. His entire soul burned with the need for her, for more, for— "Shit." He broke the kiss, his body trembling with the effort of holding back. "You're Thano's woman. I can't do this."

"I'm not—"

"Look." He gestured to her arm, where more than half of the halberd was now drawn, no longer hidden by the shroud she'd pulled over it before. He stared at it in shock. "I don't understand," he said. "There's so much of the brand already drawn on your arm, that it has to be more than half of the stages already. But you've only done the one stage with him, when you called his weapon." He looked at her. "Unless there are other stages that you did with him? Did you tell each other your darkest secrets? Did you or he risk death to save one another? The blood bond?" No, he knew that. Sex was out. He knew that, too. She'd been with him the whole time.

Catherine shook her head. "No," she whispered. "I've barely spoken to him." She met his gaze. "I feel nothing for him. Not like what you do to me."

He swore, a raw need to claim her pulsing through him. "We had sex," he said. "I shared with you the secrets about my past. You trusted me with the fact you killed Alice's mother and the other angels, and you told me about Simon." He locked his hand around the back of her neck, riveted by the desire crashing through her eyes. "*Those* are bonding stages. Having sex. The trust stage, where we share our deepest secrets or entrust our lives to the other. Those are *my* stages, when I bonded to you. My claim to you. *Mine.*"

This time, neither of them held back when they kissed. He was hit with a crashing need to tear her from Thano's grasp, to bind their souls to each other. The kiss was hot and carnal instantly, two desperate souls fighting to ward off Desdria, the darkness, and the intrusion of another male who didn't belong. Her breasts were hot and full in his hands, her nipples taut and ripe in his mouth, her core achingly wet for him.

Shirts didn't matter. Finesse was lost. Foreplay was gone. All that mattered was that they bind each other. The need surging from Catherine was every bit as fierce as Ryland's, her hands just as frantic as she yanked off her jeans while he ditched his. Then he was on her, thrusting deep, so deep, claiming her, taking her, making her his. She gripped his hair, holding his kisses captive as he thrust, kissing him back desperately, as if she could make everything else disappear.

He felt her soul reach for his, a frantic yearning driven by a need so fierce it made the world spin in frenzied chaos. "Catherine," he growled as he thrust deeper, harder, opening himself to her and drawing her deep within him until there was no way to tell which darkness was hers and which was his. But he knew the light was hers, because there was no light within him. He felt like his soul was alive and glowing, vibrating with freedom and levity, everything he'd never felt before.

He wasn't a fool. He knew it was an illusion. Freedom was not his, not now, not ever, but as God was his witness, in Catherine's arms, he felt like he finally knew what he'd been seeking his whole life—

The orgasm took him with violent intensity, thrusting him into a whirlwind of darkness and light, of good and evil, of lust and desire, of innocence and beauty. Catherine screamed his name, her voice a declaration to the heavens that Ryland was the man in her arms. He joined his voice with hers, bellowing her name, two voices mingling together, denying the existence of anything but each other, their connection and their need for each other…

…until the orgasm let them go, and spit them back out into the reality of their lives.

Into the darkness of the facts.

Into the cold, hard grip of a glittery golden cuff around each of his ankles.

◈◈◈◈

Catherine felt Ryland's body go rigid, and he jerked back so quickly that he almost fell. "Jesus!" He lunged for his ankles, and she saw six-inch golden bands around both of his legs.

"Oh, my God," she whispered in horror, staring at the metal cuffs that were decorated with the same ancient designs as the one on his chest tattoo. Where had they come from? "It can't be—"

With a roar of anguish, Ryland called out his machete with a crack and a flash of black light and slammed it down onto the metal.

Sparks exploded into the darkness, and she ducked her head as they showered down on them, burning her as they landed. They were real. Not their imagination. *Real.*

The cuff didn't move, and Ryland swung again, an unearthly bellow filling their cave. "Get away!" He swung again. And again. And again. Until he was in a frenzy, fighting at them. Sweat was cascading down his body. He was shouting, bellowing, screaming at them, swearing at them, and ordering them off his body. His face was contorted, twisted in fear or hate or terror or something else so overwhelming that it had turned him from a strategic warrior into a beast fighting for its life in a battle that would destroy him.

"Ryland! Stop!" She grabbed for his arms, but he tore out of her grasp and swung again. This time, he missed, and the blade crashed into his ankle, tearing apart flesh and bone. He didn't even react to the blow as he reared back to hit again, this time aiming for the painting on his chest.

Dear God. He was going to try to kill the dragon! "Ryland!" Without thinking, she lunged for him, throwing her body over his chest just as he brought the weapon down. She screamed as it came toward her head, and then at the last second, he pulled the blow, the blade slamming into the stone beside them.

He stared at her, his face ashen. "Catherine," he said hoarsely. His hand was shaking, and his face was stark with horror. "I almost killed you."

"No, you didn't." Gingerly, she sat up, trying not to put pressure on his damaged ankle. "You weren't going to kill me." She managed a shaky smile. "But I'm glad you're back."

He dropped his weapon with a loud clatter on the stone and

grasped her shoulders. His hands were shaking so badly he was making her teeth chatter. "You're okay? I didn't hurt you? Jesus, for a split second, when I saw my blade coming down toward you—"

"It's okay." She cut him off, trying to head off the anguish rising within him. "It's okay, Ryland. You knew I was there. You weren't going to hurt me—" Her arm began to burn intensely, and she instinctively looked down at it, expecting to see that he had actually cut her, but her adrenaline hadn't let her notice it until now.

There was no cut. It was the brand. The tip of the halberd was filling in, as more thin, silver lines appeared on her arm.

Ryland swore and grabbed her arm. "Holy crap," he said. "The death stage."

"The death stage?" she echoed, unable to take her eyes off the marks as they crawled along her arm. Thano's mark. How was this happening? She didn't understand. She wanted to grab Ryland's machete and carve Thano's brand out of her arm. She felt violated with his halberd on her body. The thought of being claimed by a man she didn't want...her stomach roiled and her legs started to tremble.

"Death is one of the bonding stages. Killing to save the other, or offering your life to save them." He looked at her. "You risked your life to save me."

She shook her head. "I didn't—"

"You did. I almost killed you." His eyes were black, raging with emotions so intense she couldn't even read them. "I'd lost my shit. My next blow would have been to my own chest to make it all stop. I would have killed myself, and I almost took you instead." His black eyes were glistening, and there was a rawness to his voice. "You offered yourself to save me." He spoke the words softly, almost as if he were awed by the concept that anyone would make that sacrifice.

She shifted uncomfortably, the magnitude of what she'd done beginning to dawn on her. What if she'd been wrong that he wouldn't hurt her? What if he had struck her? Would he have killed her? And if she'd died, who would have saved Lucy? Had she really just chosen Ryland over her own daughter? No, no, no. She hadn't. She was right. "I knew you weren't going to hurt me. I knew it." She looked into his shocked face as another question dawned. "If what I did just satisfied the death stage for the two of us, or it would have, if I was your *sheva*, then why did it make Thano's mark appear on my arm?"

Ryland said nothing for a long moment, and then recognition dawned in his eyes. "When a warrior blood-bonds with another warrior, it can affect their *shevas*."

Oh…she definitely did not like the sound of that. "How?"

Ryland's face was gaunt and tormented, as if a ghost had just taken him. "I blood-bonded with Thano," he said. "We did it in secrecy not too long ago, so Thano could find me and kill me if I went rogue." He ran his hand over his brow, wiping away the sweat left from his frenzy. "That means that if I do bonding stages with his *sheva*, it is the same as him doing the bonding stages with her. Bonding by proxy."

A cold chill settled in her spine. "You're kidding."

"No." He moved away from her and grabbed his jeans, turning his back on her. "How many stages have we done? Transference, when you called his weapon. Sex, we took care of. Trust, when each side shares their deepest secret or entrusts the other with their life." His gaze was hooded. "Some of our conversations might have covered that."

She stared at him. "But—"

"And the death stage. Killing a direct and certain threat to the other's life, or offering your own life to save theirs. You just satisfied your half of the death stage, but I haven't done mine." His eyes glittered. "The blood-bond is the only other one left. We haven't done that one yet, but—" He looked at the lines on her skin. "It's close."

She covered her arm. "I don't care what's on my arm. I don't belong to Thano."

"Oh, but you do." He scowled, still trying to grasp what had happened. "You really are his *sheva*, and I had sex with you twice. *Shit.*" He yanked his pants on, sucking in his breath when his shattered ankle caught in the fabric. "I don't understand this," he said. "I don't understand how I can crave another man's *sheva*. That never happens. *Never.*"

Catherine felt like she was going to throw up. She was horrified by the idea of belonging to Thano. It was like a noose tightening around her throat. But what other explanation was there? Numbly, she fumbled for her pants and pulled them on. "It can't be," she said. "It just can't. Thano doesn't want me, and I don't want him. Don't we have to want each other?"

"It's because of me." Ryland helped her to her feet, and took over buttoning her jeans, the intimacy of his assistance making tears burn in her eyes. "I overshadowed it. I blocked your connection with him. I interfered with how it is supposed to be."

"How? How could you interfere? You just said that Calydons don't covet the soul mates of other males. So, that's not it. There has to be something else—"

"I'm not a true Calydon." His tone was grim.

"What?" She touched his arms, the brands carved into his flesh. "But you are—"

"No." Ryland retrieved her shoes and handed them to her. "I was born a creature of the nether-realm, but when Dante freed me, it created a bond between us that transferred some of our essences to each other. Dante became...darker...and I acquired some of the traits of being a Calydon. The weapons. The mental telepathy. Enough to blend in and join the Order, but I've never been a part of them. Not really. They have no idea I'm not a full Calydon. Only Dante knows the truth, and when he brought me in, no one questioned it." He looked at her. "I'm not a true Calydon, which means I don't play by all the rules. I can covet you, Catherine, even though my own teammate owns you."

Panic tightened her chest, and she started to have difficulty breathing. "No man owns me."

"The *sheva* bond is a two-way ownership," Ryland said. "He owns you, but you own him."

"Then it's you." She shook him off as he started to argue. "It's you, Ryland. You're the one who is the other half of my soul. Not him."

Regret and yearning burned in his eyes. "The brand doesn't lie."

"Of course it does." She looked down at the cuffs on his ankles, and her heart tightened. "It has to," she said, looking at the already-healing wound on his ankle from when he'd attacked himself to try to escape his bonds. She knelt before him and wrapped her hands around the cuff on his left ankle, looking up at him. "It has to be me, because you need it to be me. You need me to be yours to defeat this."

Darkness flared in Ryland's eyes. "It doesn't matter what I need," he said. "I won't take you from him." Honor was thick and heavy in his words, and he pulled back his shoulders in defiance.

And it was then, in that moment, that she saw the man he truly was. A warrior driven by integrity and loyalty to his team, a man who would give up his life to honor those he had sworn himself to. He might not be a true Calydon, but he was more Order than any other warrior would ever be.

She knew how much he needed her. She'd felt it in the desperation of his kisses every time he'd kissed her, and when they'd made love. Whether or not there had been any risk to her when she'd jumped in front of his machete, there was no doubt in her mind that he would have struck himself in the chest if she had not intervened. He did need her, and they both knew it.

Despite that fact, however, and the grim future that he faced without her help, he was willing to deny his need for her, so he could do what was right. No wonder being enslaved to kill the innocent had nearly destroyed him. He was born to protect, to honor, and to preserve. Somehow, in the midst of this hell, he had been created with more goodness in him than many angels she knew, including herself.

Fierce resolution surged through her, a need to protect him. No way should this man, this beautiful, tormented man, be enslaved and forced to hurt others again.

No way.

Somehow, someway, she had to save him, too, as well as her daughter—

A faint, haunting scream began to echo in the distance, and a thin veil of evil brushed over her skin, the same corrupt essence that had tried to take them both a minute ago. Catherine sucked in her breath and leapt to her feet, her heart pounding. "What's that?"

Ryland turned sharply toward the sound, his muscles tensing. "They're on their way," he said. "They found us."

"Who?"

"Desdria's army. Her connection to me is strong enough now to penetrate this cave. It wasn't when I was a kid, but apparently now things are different. Shit. That's not good." Ryland whirled around and raced toward the wall where he'd retrieved the glowing stone. He passed his hand over the wall, and suddenly a section of the wall seemed to shimmer and vanish, dissolving beneath his hands. "There's no way we can defeat them." He reached inside and pulled out a bag made of a pale silver material. It was glowing slightly, an almost rose-colored blush emanating from it as he shoved it into his pocket. "Our only chance is to outrun them."

"Run?" The area outside the faint glow of their stone was pitch black. What was out there? Tunnels? Caves? Stone? Crevasses? How on earth could they run blindly through there without getting killed?

He grabbed her hand. *"Run."*

※※※

RYLAND LOCKED HIS HAND around Catherine's as he sprinted out of their hideaway into the darkness. The air was thick and suffocating, oozing with noxious bile so impenetrable that it burned his skin. He could feel the hunters descending, closing in from all directions. Their hideaway would do no good if he and Catherine were trapped in it, because the army stalking them could suck all the oxygen out of the area in a split second, rendering their safe spot unviable.

The darkness swallowed the two of them up almost instantly, and he shifted into his preternatural vision, easily seeing the rocky geography that he'd navigated so many times as a child. Catherine tripped, blinded by the darkness, and he caught her. "Come on," he said. "Stay with me." They had to make it to the geyser before the army caught them. That was the only way out of this section of the nether-realm, but it was going to be close.

Catherine tripped again, and Ryland grabbed her. He slung her into his arms and kept running, but his brands burned with warning. There were threats everywhere, and he needed his arms free to fight. But she couldn't see to run. Shit. *Catherine. Can you hear me?*

No response. If she were his *sheva,* he would be able to connect with her and guide her, but of course, she wasn't and he couldn't link to her that way—

Then he had an idea. Since Thano could bond with her through Ryland, then maybe Thano could be a telepathic bridge between them. Since he was blood-bonded with Thano, they could connect across long distances, though he wasn't sure whether the nether-realm would block them. *Thano. You with me?*

No reply. No sense of Thano's presence. Shit!

Something dove at his head, and Ryland stumbled, trying to hold Catherine and free his right arm. He called out his machete with a crack and a flash of black light, and then swung hard. The agonized squeal told him he'd made contact with the bat, but then the whir of wings told him that more were coming. Swearing, he set Catherine down. "Keep running," he ordered her.

She kept going, but fell almost right away, tripping over the crags. "I can't see," she shouted.

Swearing, Ryland opened his mind to Thano again, to the blood of his teammate that burned in his veins. He felt the other warrior's youthful energy, and he honed in on it, searching that vibration for a connection to Catherine, for the warm, beautiful spiritual essence that he knew so well. *Catherine.* He reached out for her through Thano's bond. "Open your mind to Thano, Cat," he commanded. "Try to reach him."

"Okay." With complete trust in his command, Catherine instantly did as he wanted, and he felt her mind instantly. He was shocked by how right it felt to have her mind in his, to sense her spirit, to feel her so intimately connected to him. This was how it should be.

It was perfection.

Success and irritation rushed through him, bitterness that she could bond with Thano so easily, triumph that it had worked. *Catherine.*

Her shock was palpable, a feminine response that jump-started every protective instinct in his body. *Ryland?*

Of course it's me. I connected us through my blood-bond with Thano. He had a weird urge to play with the connection, to wander around in her mind, but he had no time. He went straight to business. *I'm going to show you the layout of the land through my eyes. Trust what I show you, and then run. I'll be right with you, but I need to fight off the visitors we're about to have.* He then offered her his sight, and he felt another ripple of surprise from her as she saw through his eyes.

That's incredible. You're amazing. She broke into a sprint, running effortlessly over the uneven terrain as she utilized the vision he gave her, accepting his gift instantly.

Amazing? She thought he was amazing? And she'd trusted him enough to accept his vision without question? Yeah, he liked that. A bizarre sense of satisfaction whirred through him, pleasure thrumming at her compliment. *Yeah, well, don't spread the word. I'd hate to destroy my reputation—* The first of the bats attacked, and Ryland swung, taking out six of them in one blow.

More and more came, in bloodthirsty waves of poisoned fangs and barbed wings. But he knew their bite and wings weren't the worst of it. They were the eyes of Desdria, spies that would report back to her all that went on in her world.

A group swarmed Catherine, but Ryland couldn't break from his own defense to block them. *Call out Thano's halberd!*

He felt her acquiesce, and then to his shock, his machete disappeared from his hand and appeared in hers. She let out a yelp of surprise, and then swung it, the weapon performing unerringly for her as it would for any male's soul mate. For a split second, disbelieving hope raged through him that she was his—and then he realized that she was simply accessing his weapon through his bond with Thano. He was closer, so she'd called his instead of Thano's.

The level of disappointment that ricocheted through him nearly brought him to his knees, and he was almost too late calling out his second weapon. He barely armed himself in time to behead a tandem of bats gunning for his throat.

Ryland? What's that noise?

The screaming was getting louder, bouncing off the walls as if a million rubber balls were ricocheting off every surface, hammering at their senses and trying to confuse them. "Come on!" He sprinted up to her and grabbed her hand, giving up fighting off the bats.

The bats didn't matter if they couldn't get to the geyser. Who gave a shit about a few hundred venomous bat bites? Child's play compared to what was coming for them.

Catherine sprinted hard beside him, somehow keeping pace with him even though he was running all out. Together they ran, side by side, as the terrain began to angle downward. Their feet pounded on the ground, and he didn't need to look down to know that the rock was turning to charred earth, tainted with blood, bones, and carnage... much of which he was responsible for.

The tunnel began to glow with a faint orange light, indicating that the army was getting close, and Ryland swore. "Faster!" he yelled.

The penetrating din grew louder, and Ryland felt the sharp bite of a cold wind slap at his neck. He didn't waste time turning around. He knew what was behind them. Only yards back. But they were almost there. *Don't look back. Just run right through the geyser.*

Okay.

They skidded around the corner, and in front of them was a monstrous geyser, shooting black steam into the air, a billow almost twenty feet wide. It was in the middle of a round cave with tunnels streaming out on all sides. Glowing orange light filled every tunnel, and shadows danced as the army closed in.

He and Catherine were twenty feet away now.

Ten.

Five.

The walls suddenly erupted. Mutilated creatures that looked like they had once been men burst out of the tunnels. Blackened, distorted faces. Rotting teeth. Skin that oozed brown pus. Fingers that were little more than bone and decayed tendons. Eyes that were bottomless pits of the damned. Clenched in their fists were weapons made of bone forged in the fires of hell.

Catherine gasped as they swarmed the room, but she didn't even slow down. Damn. A guy could seriously fall for a girl who didn't even hesitate when walking into this kind of party.

Ryland tightened his grip on her, and his muscles coiled. *Jump!*

Together they leapt toward the geyser. A split second before they hit the steam, a burst of black and silver flames exploded from it and consumed them. Catherine screamed as her skin ignited, and

Ryland hauled her against him, enfolding her in his body. There was only one way to survive black fire. Only one creature that could defend against it. It was too risky to do with the cuffs already on his ankles and Desdria's grip tightening on him, but if he didn't, Catherine would never survive.

One woman was going to win, and it wasn't going to be Desdria.

Without hesitation, Ryland reinforced the mental connection between himself and Catherine, infusing them as one, and then he called the beast within to life.

🕸 CHAPTER FOURTEEN 🕸

CATHERINE'S SKIN TURNED TO SCALES.

Claws burst out of her fingers.

Her bones screamed and cracked.

A haunting evil tore through her, like acid poured on her soul. The agonizing shrieks of tortured souls erupted in her head, and she screamed, trying to cover her ears against the pain—

And then her scream changed. No longer human. It became the roar of the beast. Ryland's monster. Coming from *her* mouth! Terror ripped through her, and she fought in violent panic against the onslaught of darkness rising from within to consume her. *Ryland!*

I'm holding our form. We needed to shift to survive. His mind was fragmented and broken, his words halting and rough. *I'm going to need help bringing us back when it's time. When I give the word, turn on your angel magic. This shit isn't going to want to let us go.*

He'd done it on purpose? Seriously? The man was insane! She didn't wait to call her light. She knew she couldn't. The darkness inside her was thick and predatory, an evil so dark it made her want to unleash her worst upon every living creature she could find. It was calling to the darkest part of her soul, the part that she worked so hard to control. Was this really what was inside Ryland? How could he live with this every day? How could he resist its call? It was so insidious, so powerful, it seemed to cut off her air and freeze the blood in her veins.

She immediately reached inside her, to her angel's light, to the part of her that Ryland awakened. Not what the beast had brought to life, but the inner part of her that had been touched by Ryland in his true form: the man who kissed her like she was his oxygen, who made love to her like she was his salvation, who protected her as if he was born to be her guardian.

She called it to her, letting its goodness fill her. She bound it within her, not allowing it to leak into Ryland, but holding it in reserve while the creature thrashed and fought inside her. As she summoned the light, the pain leveled out, and her bones stopped shifting, holding her in mid-change. She and Ryland seemed to free-fall through flames and steam so hot she could feel the heat trying to burn her. But it couldn't. The scales protected her, and Ryland's strong body guided their fall.

Then they landed, a jarring impact lessened by Ryland as he took the blow. He grunted with the impact, but his body shielded hers. *Cat! Release it now!*

Catherine instantly unleashed the goodness, sending it through them both with as much force as she could muster. At first, the monster didn't retreat. She felt Ryland's soul scream in anguish, so she reached deeper, to her own reserve of power, the last of what she carried. She asked it for help, and then shared it with Ryland, flooding both of them with the power of her heritage.

The monster finally released its tenacious hold on them both, and they fell to the ground, drained and exhausted. Ryland groaned and rolled to his knees above her, calling out his machete as he covered her with his body, protecting her as he scanned for threats, rapidly assessing their surroundings.

After a moment, he lowered his arm. *We're clear. They didn't follow us.*

Maybe *they* hadn't, but she and Ryland were still in trouble. She had drained the last of her inner light to bring them back. Her soul was empty and starved, needing life-giving force...either through light or the soul of another. She had to rescue Lucy and get them both back to the surface, to light, *now.*

"You okay?" he asked, brushing her hair back from her face in a gesture that was awfully tender for a man who didn't do tender.

"Peachy." Catherine opened her eyes. They were bathed in light, but it wasn't natural. It was a strange, eerie silvery glow that seemed to hum with the faint screams of the dead. They were in the middle of a vast wasteland, a desiccated expanse of burned-out homes, dead trees rotting where they lay, and noxious purple smoke rising from the earth as if a battle had just ended. Strewn across the rutted ground were bodies, stripped of their souls, now just empty husks filled with darkness. Chills raced down her spine and she sat up, staring across the horrific scene. "Dear God," she whispered. Her baby was here somewhere? Pain jabbed her chest, and her throat tightened. Her body started to shake, and for a moment, panic threatened to overtake her.

"Stay with me." Ryland touched her arm. "We'll find Lucy. I promise."

She squeezed her eyes shut against the tears, her heart aching at his response. How good did it feel to have Ryland hearing her thoughts? She wasn't even trying to project to him, and he was still there for her. She needed that connection with him right now. "She's a baby. How can she survive this?"

"Hey, this was my playground growing up, and I turned out okay, right?" His voice was grim, but his words eased the tension in her body.

Ryland had turned out more than okay. He was a heroic protector, a guardian of all that was good. "Yeah, okay." *I'm coming, Lucy.* She reached out with her soul, searching for her daughter, but to her relief, she couldn't sense Lucy at all. She could track only dead people, and if she couldn't sense Lucy, that meant her daughter was still alive. "We have to find her."

"I know. We will." Ryland's voice was rough, and she glanced over at him. His skin still had a silvery tint, and glittering scales were mixed in with his hair. She brushed her hand over his head, and the scales didn't fall out. "You didn't shift all the way back."

"No. Not this time." The grim tone to his voice suggested that it hadn't been voluntary.

She tugged open his shirt. The beast was in vivid color up to its shoulders now. Both front legs were turquoise, and golden cuffs gleamed around its front legs. Quickly, she released the shirt and touched his wrist, but it was still skin. The cuffs hadn't come to life yet, but his flesh was hard and scaly to the touch, even though it looked normal. "Oh, God," she whispered. "We're both almost out of time."

Ry nodded his agreement. "We have to hurry. They'll be on us soon."

Catherine scrambled to her feet and looked around. In each direction, all she could see was the post-apocalyptic graveyard that had once been humanity and life. "What happened here?"

"It's been like this for thousands of years," Ryland said. He turned toward the far side, facing what looked like the glow of a sunset. In the distance, so far away she could barely make it out, there was a structure that looked like a massive, ancient temple made of stone, rising up from the ruins like a skeletal wraith surveying its swath of destruction. "It's like a moat of hell that surrounds the main temple."

"Temple?" She moved up beside him, shivering even though the heat pouring from the earth was brutal. "The one over there?" She pointed to the blackened structure with huge pyres of fire billowing from the top of it.

"Yeah. It's where Desdria and the Dark Lord reside." His jaw flexed. "It's the only place where the air is clean enough to sustain a human child."

"She's not human. She's part angel and part…" What had Simon been? A human servant to Desdria and the Dark Lord? An assassin from the nether-realm?

Ryland's eyes slid over to her. "Or a child that is not born of the nether-realm," he clarified. "Lucy will be in the temple."

Resolution flowed through Catherine, but at the same time, a dark sense of foreboding filled her. "That's where they want us," she said. "They want to claim you, and they want me to destroy the Order. If we go there, they own us."

He cocked an eyebrow at her. "You want to turn around? Maybe hold hands and skip into the sunset?"

She managed a small laugh at the image of Ryland skipping anywhere. "I want to get my daughter first."

He nodded. "And I want Dante."

"So, we'll table the skipping for later?" She didn't know why she made such a light quip. It seemed so out of place for where they were, for what they were facing, but somehow, it gave her comfort to think of something as innocent and pure as skipping into the sunset holding hands. It was a reminder that there was more to life than what they were facing right now.

"Yeah, it's a date…on one condition." He went down on one knee and sifted his fingers through the dirt, testing for…what? She didn't know.

"What condition?"

"You teach me to skip. I never learned that as a kid, and I think that's why I'm such a bitter, fucked-up adult."

She did laugh that time, the laughter of a tension-breaker. "Yes, I can see how that could happen. The first time I met you, I thought, 'this man is not a skipper.' Tough times for you."

"Yeah, tough times." He stood up. "We're going to have to blood-bond."

Catherine's heart stuttered. "What?"

He was still looking into the distance, not letting her see his face. "One of the stages of the *sheva* bond is a blood-bond. It enables a

Calydon to find his mate at all times, no matter how far away they are."

"But I'm not your—"

He turned to face her. "We'll do it through Thano. It will blood-bond you to him, but also to me."

Fear rippled through Catherine, and she stepped back. "No, no, no," she said. "No blood bond. I don't want to be bound to either of you. To anyone." It already made her sick to think that she was forever linked to Simon.

He caught her arm. "You don't have a choice, angel. It's going to be hell in there, and we could easily get separated." His eyes glittered. "Only one thing in this life matters to me, and that is honoring Dante's legacy. His legacy is the Order. You are the Order's guardian angel." His grip tightened. "I will let *nothing* interfere with my ability to protect you."

Catherine swallowed. How on earth could this man possibly still believe that she was a guardian angel for the Order? Guilt ate away at her, and she knew she could not let him risk his life for her under false pretenses. "Ryland," she said quietly. "I was created to destroy the Order. I took Dante's soul. You believe that, right?"

"Yeah, I get that."

"So, how on earth could I be your guardian angel, if I was brought here to kill you and everyone else? I've even begun to do it, when I took Dante's soul."

He stared at her, and suddenly, she saw recognition dawn in his eyes, a truth he'd been unwilling to accept until this moment. For what felt like an eternity, he didn't move, then he dropped her arm and walked away, turning his back on her.

Regret filled her, but at the same time, a sense of liberation, a freedom from being held to the highest standard by this man who honored her only for who he *thought* she was.

After a long moment, he turned back, and his eyes were an even deeper black. "If you aren't our guardian angel, who is?" His voice was bitter and dark, making shivers run down her arms.

"I don't know."

"You didn't run into any of them trying to protect Dante when you went to kill him?"

She shook her head. "No. No one was there from the spirit realm."

"There was an angel," he muttered. "The oracle said the angel of death."

She frowned, trying to follow the change of subject. "What

oracle?"

"When Dante freed me, an angel helped him. She was an oracle, a seer of the future. She read my future and then gave me a golden light while I lay dying from my wounds. She said an angel of death would come to me and bring life." He looked at her. "That's you, Catherine. You. I've been looking for an angel of death ever since. For centuries. You're the first one I've found. It has to be you."

Her heart ached at how badly she wanted to be the woman he saw her as, to be something other than what she was: an angel who killed, a mother who had failed to protect her child. "Then she meant something else, Ryland. I'm not the guardian."

Again, he considered her, then resolution flashed across his feature. "Fuck it." He grabbed her hand again, and turned her palm up. "Maybe you're not the Order's guardian, but you still matter. The oracle said you were coming, and here you are. I don't know what you're going to do, but I've been waiting almost a thousand years for it. I stand by my pledge." Then he jabbed the end of his machete into her palm.

She yelped and tried to jerk her hand backward, but he didn't release her. Instead, he dragged his free hand over the end of the machete, so that both of their palms were bloody. His gaze fixed intently on hers, he slowly raised her palm to his face and pressed his lips to her wound. Electricity hummed through her, and heat crashed around her. "I can't—" she protested.

You can. You wanted the protection of a sheva *bond? This is it. This is your protection. No matter what, I will save you as my mate...my mate by proxy, I mean.*

Her body went cold, her hands started to shake, and sweat trickled down her back. "You don't understand, Ry—"

I do understand. You were betrayed by the man you gave your heart to. I get it. But are you willing to risk your daughter because you're too damn scared to ask one more man for help? A man who owes angels a life debt. A man who has been looking for you for hundreds of years. A man who has the skills to get us all out of here alive. The man who is the only fucking chance your daughter has?

Tears burned in her eyes, fear gripping her so tightly she felt like her entire body would collapse from the strain. *I love her,* she whispered. *I love my daughter with every ounce of my soul. I can't let her be trapped here.*

He held his bloodied palm toward her. *Then be brave enough to help her.*

Catherine ignored the offering and stared at his face, searching for the promise she needed. *Will you make me a pledge? As my soul mate? As a man who treasures angels? As the man I know you are?*

Honesty burned in his eyes. *Depends. I won't promise what I can't deliver.*

She encircled his wrist with trembling fingers. *Will you promise that if I die, if my spirit dies, that you will find Lucy and bring her out of here? The same way Dante did for you?*

He didn't answer.

She closed her eyes as anguish washed over her. Of course he wouldn't promise that. If he had to choose between Dante and Lucy, he would choose Dante.

Simon made you promises, he said. *Do you really put so much faith in words? Words betrayed you already. Why do you ask for more? Why do words mean so much to you?*

"Because it's all I have! I trusted my instincts and I was wrong!"

Were they? Challenge glittered in his intelligent eyes. *Or did instinct give you all the signs you needed, but you were so desperate that you ignored them?*

"What? How can you say that? I'm not that stupid—"

No. Not stupid. He placed his bloodied palm over her heart. *You were broken. Enslaved by your gift. Simon was your chance for freedom. You took it, because you're a survivor, because you chose a path that gave you a chance, despite the risk. I know, because I did the same thing.*

Tears began to roll down her cheeks, and she put her hand over Ryland's where it was resting on her heart. "I was so scared of what I was becoming," she confessed softly. "I was haunted by what I'd done to the angel enclave."

I know, Cat. You chose to survive at that time, and Simon was the answer. The bastard then preyed on your vulnerability, but in return, he gave you the tools you'd been missing. Wisdom. Power. Determination. Focus. You aren't the woman you were back then. You got it all now, sweetheart, and you just have to believe in it. You know whether to trust me. Don't let fear win. Let intelligence and instinct win. He tapped his fingers on her chest, over her heart. *Listen to this. It never lies.*

Catherine felt warmth spread beneath his palm, emanating out through her body. His touch felt like a gift, a great gift from heaven. She stared at him, at this monster with the silvery scales and claw-tipped fingers. What was he? What was he truly?

Honor. Truth. Loyalty. Power. Empathy. Hope.

And the other side of the coin: Death. Destruction. Violence. Murder.

But nowhere in him did she sense deceit, lies, or dishonor. It simply wasn't there…or was it that she couldn't see it? Because all she could see was a man who made her heart sing, a protector her entire soul hungered for, a warrior she wanted with every fiber of her being. The intensity with which she ached for Ryland was far beyond anything she'd ever felt for Simon. What she'd felt for Simon had been enough to obscure her ability to see his true self, which meant that what she felt for Ryland could also be strong enough to keep her from seeing past her own cravings for him. How could she know what was Ryland's truth, when her perception of him was so entangled in a deeper need that could overshadow all else? How could she—

With a low growl, Ryland fisted the front of her shirt and yanked her over to him. He slammed his mouth down over hers, and the kiss erupted within her. Fire. Heat. Desire. She could taste the copper of her own blood in the kiss, still on his lips. Her entire body leapt into awareness, and all her walls fell, crumbling beneath the sensual assault of the man she craved so badly.

You can't think things like that and expect me to behave honorably. I can hear every damn thought in your head about how badly you want me. Ryland's voice was rough and raw in her mind, igniting a cascade of fireworks of desire.

You are *honorable,* she protested.

No, I'm not, and we both know it. If I was, I wouldn't be coveting another man's woman, and I wouldn't be kissing her. He framed her face with his hands, angling her head as he pressed deeper for the kiss, taking more, offering more, giving her everything he had. *I'm the one who's a bastard, Cat, and we both know it.*

No, you're not. Her heart swelled for this man who was so rough and so tormented, who didn't even understand love or kindness, yet made her feel safe and protected even when she shouldn't. He was addictive and dangerous and—

He swept his thumb over her lips, and awareness began to sing through her. Her lips began to tingle, and desire pulsed low in her belly. *Ryland? What did you—*

He captured her thought with another kiss, so deep that it seemed to unfurl something buried inside her. Something more than desire. Something more than lust. Something more than need. Something that ached so badly it seemed to bruise her deep inside—

You are mine. His voice was a feather whisper through her

mind, and then his finger slipped past her lips. More coppery taste. Her blood? Dear God, no. *His.* He'd completed the blood bond?

You bastard! Fear exploded through her, and she started to pull away, but then something changed. The fear, the resistance, the anger…they were all instantly banished by the fierce, uncontrollable need that thrummed through every level of her being. Not just need. That same longing in her soul as she'd felt before, but now it was a thousand times more intense. The ache in her heart was beautiful, as if the bruises were the result of a battle won, of freedom achieved, of life and home finally coming together as one. She turned her head into his touch and accepted the gift of his blood, his soul, and his eternity.

Sweet, Catherine. Ryland's voice was a caress, so beautiful it was as if he were an angel himself, a sound that seemed to lift to the heavens and cascade down upon her in a shower of snowflakes and warmth. *Mine to you. Yours to me. Bonded by blood, by spirit and by soul, we are one. No distance too far, no enemy too powerful, no sacrifice too great. I will always find you. I will always protect you. No matter what the cost. I am yours as you are mine.*

The power of his speech was mesmerizing, and she knew instantly that it was Ryland speaking, not Thano, not as a proxy. His words bled with a thousand years of suffering. They hung with death. They reverberated with a passion born of a heart so powerful it could survive anything. It was Ryland, the truth of who he was, filling her, offering himself to her, swearing his allegiance to her.

The answer rose within her, unbidden, and she welcomed it, offering it with the same purity of truth that Ryland had. *Mine to you. Yours to me. Bonded by blood, by spirit and by soul, we are one. No distance too far, no enemy too powerful, no sacrifice too great. Ryland, I will always find you. I will always keep you safe. No matter what the cost. I am yours as you are mine.*

This time, when she felt the burn on her arm, she knew it was Ryland's mark, Ryland's connection, Ryland's claim. She was Ryland's, and right then, in that moment, in his arms, in his kiss, it was exactly where she wanted to be.

STILL IN THE MIDST OF BATTLE with the cloaked warriors, Thano sensed Catherine behind him. He whirled around toward the entrance of the nether-realm, shocked by the sudden intensity of her presence in his mind, so powerful he was certain she was standing right behind him.

She wasn't.

There was nothing but the vast darkness of the cavernous entrance, and the odious mist drifting from the opening. Urgency pulsed through him, a need to connect with her. To find her. "Catherine!" he shouted.

No answer.

"Hey!" Zach yelled at him, and Thano spun around just as a massive cat-like creature leapt off a nearby rock right at him, massive teeth bared, ready to kill. Its eyes burned red with insanity, and its black and green striped fur undulated with living shadows as it launched itself at them. Apollo sidestepped with incredible speed, and Thano struck the creature as it hurtled past him, its claws trying to gut the horse as it passed.

"Too slow, kitty cat—" Thano taunted, then swore when shadows fell across the clearing. He looked up as dozens of the grotesque cats emerged from the trees, launching themselves at all the warriors at once, not just him and Zach. "Incoming!" he yelled.

The other men looked up, and with a chorus of fearsome shouts, they abandoned their battles and engaged the creatures. The enemy became the ally, loyalty springing up between clashing Order members united against a common goal. The battle launched into a full-scale assault, with Zach and the five mysterious Order members fighting side-by-side, defending against the onslaught, allied by the need to survive. Thano kicked his horse into a gallop, plunging into the fray, when Catherine's presence filled his mind again.

Swearing, he reined Apollo to a stop. What the hell was going on? *Catherine?*

No reply. No connection. But as he opened his mind, he suddenly realized he knew exactly where she was, deep beneath the earth, as if he were linked to her directly. At the same time, he felt Ryland's presence, and he realized what had happened. Ryland had blood-bonded with her. What the hell did that mean?

Weapons were clashing all around him as the others defended against the creatures that had cornered them. "Zach!" Thano shouted. "We need to get into the nether-realm—" Another wildcat landed on Thano's back, ripping open his flesh with such force that he felt the bones in his shoulders shatter. It yanked him off Apollo and dragged him over the rocks. Zach and the others were pinned down against the far side of the cliff, their space being ruthlessly encroached. No chance they could come to his rescue.

Thano jammed his halberd over his shoulder into the creature's head, a last desperate attempt to free himself. The creature howled with agony, and then clamped his mouth down over Thano's neck. The teeth sank deep, tearing flesh—

Apollo reared up over him, his massive hooves flashing as he slammed them down onto the creature, crushing it beneath the sheer force of the blow. The beast died instantly, its teeth still clamped around Thano's throat as it convulsed in the throes of death, deepening the wounds.

"Go party somewhere else, you son of a bitch." Thano pried the creature's jaws free with his halberd, gasping when it was finally off. Blood was cascading down his neck, and he knew that an artery had been torn open. He fell back down, too weak to stand. Apollo positioned himself over Thano, his forefeet on either side of Thano's head, his rear feet braced and ready, protecting his master as more creatures attacked, drawn to the scent of blood and the temptation of death.

Thano stared up at the belly of his horse, and knew that Apollo was his last protection. "Stay with me, buddy," he said, as he closed his eyes and directed all his energy onto his neck. He had to heal now, right now, or he would be dead within a minute. He concentrated on the wound, visualizing the slowing of the blood loss, the sealing of the artery. But even as he did it, his strength began to wane. He was losing too much blood too fast.

He was going to die.

🐼 CHAPTER FIFTEEN 🐼

THANO'S BRAND WAS STILL ON HER ARM.

Ryland's insides turned to a fermenting, dangerous boil when he looked at Cat's arm and saw Thano's halberd sitting smugly on her skin. Son of a bitch. He grabbed her wrist and stared at it. "How the hell is that possible?" How could it be Thano's halberd traveling down her arm, almost finished? The blood bond had been between Catherine and himself. Not Thano. It hadn't been by proxy. There was no way that it would have felt like that. No fucking way.

But there was Thano's weapon, filling in even as he watched.

That fucking halberd was on her arm. Not his machete.

He wasn't going to deny the truth anymore. The sight of Thano's brand on her arm seriously pissed him off.

"What are you talking ab—" Catherine followed his glance, and she paled. "No," she whispered. "That's not right."

Wrath and irretrievable anger began to swarm inside Ryland, emotions that were so dangerous to his self-control. He could not go there. *He would not go there.* "Fuck!" He wrenched his gaze off her arm and searched her face. "Tell me you're mine," he gutted out, not even caring about being honorable enough to respect his teammate's claim on her. Not right now. He couldn't turn Catherine over to Thano. Couldn't even handle the idea. He was too close to the edge, and he needed this to be right. Thano's brand might be on her arm, but she could overrule it. She could deny it. She could fucking take her life for her own, and he needed to hear that her choice was the warrior standing before her. "Tell me that there is no fucking chance on this planet that you belong to Thano."

Catherine's eyes widened, and he saw the deep fear in them.

Fear of being bound to anyone, including him. *Crap.* He realized she wasn't going to be able to say it. That was the one thing Catherine couldn't give him: herself. Stumbling away from her, he tried to pull his shit together. "We need to get to the temple," he rasped out, ruthlessly directing his thoughts to the battle they faced. "Come on. Now." His wrists hurt, and he knew that the cuffs would soon be appearing. He had no time to obsess about Thano stealing his damned woman, or her inability to give him what he wanted. They had to *go!*

He grabbed her hand and started loping relentlessly through the wasteland, knowing exactly which parts were solid, and which places would send them spiraling downward into hell if they stepped on them. Catherine ran beside him, her breath coming in short gasps as she labored to keep up. Against his will, he glanced over at her. She was too damned pale. Where was the woman who had run hard with him through the woods, having no trouble keeping up? "What's wrong?"

"I'm almost out of life force," she gasped. "I need light. Or a soul."

"How can an angel be out of light? That's what you are." He grabbed her around the waist and lifted her over an innocent-looking trickle of water that promised acidic torture.

"I'm an angel of death," she said, limping along beside him. "It's not the same thing. I can't generate my own energy. I'm a parasite."

"Parasite?" Just the idea of her cutting herself down like that pissed him off. "Fuck that, Cat. Come on! You're a powerful being of the Otherworld. You got the tools." He took them to the right, carefully skipping a fermenting pool of odiousness, and sliding between two burned-out homes.

Catherine stumbled beside him. "I know I have tools," she gasped. "But I have them because I steal lives and light." She tripped again, and Ryland picked her up, tucking her against him as he continued to move quickly over the carnage. Ahead, the temple grew larger. The place that had trapped him for so long. The site of his hell.

"You're no different than anyone else," he said, trying to focus on Cat instead of what he was approaching. "Everyone feeds on something. It's how life sustains itself. Cut yourself a break, woman. It's not helping us right now—" Something twisted deep inside his gut, and he lost his footing. He hit the ground hard, and Catherine spilled out of his arms onto the barren dirt.

She groaned softly, bracing her hands on the earth. Her face was pale, her beautiful hair hanging in tangled strands. "Ryland? You don't look good."

"I'm fine." He gritted his teeth as his stomach undulated, as life began to take shape within him. He remembered it all too well from the night they killed his faerie. It was the first stage of complete surrender. He surged to his feet, staggering as his equilibrium failed him. "Come on," he said. "We need to hurry."

Catherine grabbed his hand, and together they pulled her up. This time, they held hands tightly as they resumed their trek across the wasteland. They'd made it only twenty yards when dark shadows began to swirl over the earth. "Oh, crap," he muttered. "Really? Now?"

"What is it?"

Ryland shoved his hand into his back pocket, searching for the bag he'd taken from the crevice in the wall where the green glowstone had been. It contained a vial of a powder created by the water faeries. Marie had always kept a supply there, and they'd saved his ass more than once—until he'd come into his destiny and kicked ass all on his own.

He'd been hoping he wasn't going to have to use the vial. "Get on my back," he ordered Catherine, who immediately jumped on just as the shadows whirled around where her feet had been.

Shit! It wasn't in that pocket! "Climb higher," he commanded as the shadows entwined around his ankles and began to climb his legs, like vines. His legs went instantly numb, and his muscles started to tremble as they fed on his life force. His fingers closed on a small vial, and he jerked it out of his pocket. He tore the stopper out as they reached his hips. His pelvis went numb, and weakness assaulted him.

Swearing, he turned the bottle over, fighting desperately not to collapse. He'd seen too many creatures fall into the mist and be instantly consumed. They had to stay vertical. A silver powder floated out of the bottle, sifting down into the shadows.

The shadows went still, and he gritted his teeth, waiting for that telltale whoosh as they retreated...*but it didn't come.* With a fresh surge, they moved higher, around Catherine's ankles and his torso. Jesus. The powder must have lost its impact over the centuries.

"Ryland!" Catherine's voice was shaky now, and he knew they were closing around her chest, taking away her oxygen.

His legs were shaking violently now, and Ryland stumbled again as weakness invaded his body. Catherine slipped slightly, and he knew she was weakening as well. It was too much. They were so close, and they weren't going to make it—

"Balthazar. You have returned." The voice was ancient and

beautiful, like glass bells tinkling in a light wind as it called the name he hadn't heard for hundreds of years, the name that used to be his.

"Matalan?" he whispered in shock. "Help us—" Then he collapsed.

The shadows swarmed them, and he pulled Catherine into his arms, uselessly trying to shield her with his body. He tucked her head against his chest as weakness consumed him, waiting for the death—

Balthazar. The name whispered again, and he opened his eyes to see a blue-green apparition floating above him. The woman was ethereal and beautiful, an oasis in the hell they were facing. Her skin was as flawless as it had been a thousand years ago, but her eyes were nothing but sadness and pain. She was the mother of Marie, the faerie who had died for him, a woman who had never been able to look at him again after her child had lost her life. And yet, here she was, seeking him out. In her hand was a long, wispy frond and she waved it gently over them, showering them with a sparkling silver powder.

The moment she did, the shadows vanished, seeping back into the parched ground, leaving them behind. Alive.

Ryland sagged to the earth, his body so depleted he could barely hold himself up. "Matalan. Thank you."

"It is you, Balthazar. The boy has returned a man." She smiled sadly. "I never thought I would see you as a man again once the beast took you."

Ryland rubbed his chest, knowing all too well how she had last seen him. "I'm sorry about Marie," he said. He'd never had the chance to apologize. He'd been a monster from that day onward. "I'm so sorry she died for our friendship."

Matalan smiled sadly. "She loved you, Balthazar. She would never have traded what she had with you in exchange for a longer life."

Her words were a shock. Love? Marie had loved him? He didn't understand. How could she have chosen death over life for him? "I didn't ask her for that. I wouldn't have wanted her to do that—"

"No. You do not get to choose how others love you. All you can do is honor their choice if they bless you with their love." She shook her head as she floated down, running her ghostly hands through Catherine's hair. "An angel's hair," she said. "Life-giving. May I take some?"

Catherine sat up, her eyes wide as she stared at Matalan. "Of course."

Matalan nodded, and she swiped the frond through Catherine's locks, taking a handful. She bowed gracefully. "Balthazar," she said. "Time grows fleeting down here. The border grows thin. Desdria is working with dark, dark forces. We are leaving."

Ryland sat up. "What? The water faeries are leaving the nether-realm? But without you, it will fall into darkness."

"We cannot hold it up anymore." She smiled sadly, her fingers drifting over his cheek like a soft breeze. "Less than a hundred of us remain. We are dying, Balthazar, and we must go."

At her words, he suddenly heard the weakness in her voice, and saw the trembling of her hands. Realization surged through him, and he grabbed her hands. "No, Matalan. Not you." She was the only kindness he'd had there. She and Marie.

She touched his face, and tears fell over her misty cheeks that were becoming even more faded. "You have returned to us, Balthazar. You will either bring the final destruction or hope for redemption. May peace be with you." She faded further, her turquoise eyes shifting to a pale gray.

"No!" He lunged for her, but his fingers went right through the apparition.

Tears glittered on her cheeks as the faerie blinked out of existence, the last light in a world of haunting death. The last light he'd ever had. Emptiness roared through him. Isolation. Loss. Such a gaping chasm that hollowed him out, leaving behind only a raw wound of pain. Everything was gone. Marie. Dante. And now Matalan. Darkness seemed to press in around him, obscuring everything—

"Ryland." Catherine's hand touched his arm. "Look at me."

He dragged his gaze up to the angel before him. "Your eyes," he gasped. "They're so blue. How are they so blue?"

She smiled and pressed a kiss to his forehead. It wasn't a chaste kiss. It wasn't lust. It was connection and hope. It was an intimacy shared only between two souls bound together. Ryland sank his hand into her hair, and leaned his forehead against hers. Their noses were pressed against each other, their lips, their cheeks in a moment of silent connection. Of shared grief. Of mutual acknowledgment that the other was all they had to count on.

He'd wanted words from Catherine declaring that she belonged to him, not Thano. He'd wanted her to promise the very connection that they were sharing in this moment, just as she'd wanted words from him that he would save her daughter. But as they shared breaths, he knew that he had the answer he'd sought. She was his, only his, on every level, regardless of the mark she carried on her arm. Words were not necessary. "You're my light," he whispered. "You're my hope.

You're the goodness I've been seeking for so long."

Catherine said nothing, but he felt a surge of warmth from her. The feeling she offered him was so breathtaking and so compassionate that it made him want to lift her in his arms, take her out of the darkness into a field of white flowers, and make love to her while the sun warmed their bodies and brought light into their souls.

Ryland, she breathed. *That's beautiful.*

He grimaced. *You weren't supposed to hear that.*

No, it's lovely. I'm glad I did. She pulled back, her blue eyes so intense. *I know who you are, Ryland. I know that making love in a field of lilies isn't a promise you can keep. But the mere fact you even thought it is one of the most beautiful moments I've ever had. Lightness in darkness. Hope in the face of despair. Beauty in the face of carnage. Thank you.* She smiled. *Maybe you're the angel, not me.*

He laughed softly, tugged at a lock of her chopped-off hair. *You are one crazy broad.*

I know. You're no prize yourself.

This time he laughed aloud. Humor in the midst of such darkness felt cruel, but at the same time, he needed it. "How are you feeling?"

"Terrible."

"Me, too." He looked past her. They were close enough to see the iron gates of the temple, and the fires burning around it. "Let's do this, sweetheart."

She turned around, and she tensed. "My baby is behind those gates."

Ryland climbed to his feet, his entire body still numb with weakness. "We'll get her." He reached for her, only to see the glitter of gold around his wrists. He swore, staring at the thick gold bands around his arms. His wrists were cuffed now. A cold stab of fear knifed through him, and his weapons burned in his arms, desperate to fight against a foe he couldn't even see.

"Oh, no." Catherine grabbed his wrist, her fingers so small against the hard metal band. "Oh, my God, Ryland. They almost have you." She pulled open his shirt and they both saw that the collar around the beast's neck was a faint yellow, and the turquoise was completely filled in all the way to that point. Only the head was still black and white. She looked at him. "You have to go back."

Fear hammered at him, but Ryland ground his jaw. He was so close. So close. The nether-realm was descending into so much darkness. How could he walk away now? From an innocent little girl?

From Dante? "Do you sense Dante?" he asked, ignoring her order.

She stared at him, then closed her eyes. He felt the air thicken as she reached out. She wavered, as if she were going to lose her balance, and he caught her, summoning all his strength to hold her up. Her eyes snapped open, and they were bright with excitement. "I do," she said. "His soul is in the temple." Regret flickered in her eyes. "He's suffering."

Ryland swore and looked past her at the gates that had trapped him for so long. On this side, lay freedom. On the other side, lay slavery. And Dante. And Lucy. How could he possibly turn around and walk away, leaving the innocents behind? Too many had died because he hadn't protected them. It ended now. "We're going in."

"But the cuffs—"

He gripped her hand and started walking toward the temple, a ruthless, determined stride. "I owe Dante. I vowed to protect the Order. I will not walk way."

"And Lucy?" She hurried beside him, her breath coming in weak gasps.

His jaw flexed as he thought of Marie dying, and then Matalan. No more death. *No more.* "We're getting her, too."

But even as he said it, there was a sharp stab of pain in his chest. He didn't look down to see what the picture was doing. "I think we need to run," was all he said.

Catherine glanced at him, her face even paler than it had been. "I agree."

Together, hands clasped, they summoned energy neither of them had, and sprinted across the wasteland toward the iron gates of hell.

※※※

THEY WERE ALMOST TO THE GREAT TEMPLE.

So close that the heat from the pyres singed his skin.

Ryland stopped, his entire body shaking violently as the massive iron gates loomed up in front of him. Beyond those gates lay the hell that he never thought he would escape. The one that had haunted his nightmares for centuries, until he finally believed it could never trap him again. And now he was back.

His breath began to rasp in his chest, and he went down on his knees, fighting for oxygen. He leaned forward, bracing himself on his hands, his chest inches from the black earth. Fear seized him, a fear so deep that even the toughest warrior couldn't will it away. It assaulted him from every direction. Memories knifed at his brain. The same horrific feelings of helplessness came catapulting back to him, and his entire being howled with the anguish of it.

"That's it," he rasped. "That's where it happened. Where they finally enslaved me. In the main room of the temple. Right there."

Catherine knelt beside him, her touch on his back so fucking soft that he almost couldn't even register it. But he did, and he focused all his energy into that touch, using her to ground himself.

"You don't have to go in—"

"Fuck that. Of course I'm going in." His palms still flat on the ground, his elbows bent, he slowly raised his head, staring at the gates. "Today, the nightmare ends," he said softly as new energy and determination began to build inside him. No more fear. No more nightmares. Tonight, he took control. Tonight, it was *his.* "You get a read on Dante yet? Is he definitely in there?"

She turned to look at the crumbling stone temple, and then a chill drifted through his bones, as if he'd sensed what she did. "Yes," she said. "His soul is in there."

"And your daughter?"

She shook her head. "I don't sense her."

Ryland shoved himself to his feet and called out his machetes. "Sweetheart, when we get her back, we need to get that girl in a blood-bond so that we can always find her."

Catherine stared at him. *"We?"*

"You. I meant you." But even as he said the words, he knew it was a lie. He would never walk away from this woman, and that included everything that mattered to her. He was going to make damn sure that little girl was safe for the rest of her life. "Let's go." With Catherine following right behind him, Ryland moved silently up toward the gates. As he approached, they swung open by an invisible force, and the fires flared higher on either side, inviting them in.

Catherine sucked in her breath. "They know we're here."

"Of course they do." Ryland called out his machetes with a crack and a flash of black light as he began to walk toward the gates, forcing his resistant body to take each step. Closer. Closer. "They're banking on the fact that they're still stronger than I am. Than we are."

Catherine moved close to him, but there was no hesitation in her gait. Just firm, unyielding determination. "Well, they've never messed with an angel of death who needs to protect her child," she replied, her voice low and calm. "And you're not the boy they once dominated. You're their nightmare coming back to take them down."

He glanced over at her. Her jaw was jutted out, her hands fisted by her sides, her blue eyes blazing. Yeah, she was pale, and moved as if each step was a tremendous effort, but there was a dark, almost violent energy pouring off her. *The angel of death has come to life,* he said softly, unable to keep the admiration from his voice.

She looked over at him. *I've been fighting my not-so-nice side my whole life. It's time to finally use it.* She gave him a grim smile. *I'm really not that nice, you know.*

He grinned. *I'm not sure they have souls for you to take.*

Everything has a soul...until I come get it. Catherine reached the gates and looked up at them. They stood more than forty feet above their heads. "Mama's here, Lucy," she said into the darkness. "It's almost over."

As Ryland watched Cat make promises to her daughter, a sense of deep longing came over him. The bond between Catherine and her daughter was incredible, evident in the depth of her words, in the emotion pulsing through her, in her absolute lack of fear. He could feel the intensity of her love, the absolute commitment of her entire being to that little girl. It was pure selflessness. Pure...love? Yes, it was. For the first time in his life, he was witnessing—and experiencing—the real thing. He'd never understood the power of it until that moment.

Oh, he knew loyalty, the kind that was so deep that a man would give his life for it.

He knew honor.

But love...that was different...and it was fucking incredible. Without even thinking about it, he locked his hand behind Catherine's neck and kissed her. It wasn't a kiss of passion, lust, or even desire. It was a kiss full of what she'd been putting out into the world. He wasn't a soft guy. He wasn't kind. He wasn't tender. But in that moment, he strove to be all that. For this one instant, he wanted to offer Catherine that which she gave others, including him.

She stiffened, and then kissed him back just as gently and sweetly. It was, he was quite certain, the very best, most hopeful, most beautiful moment he'd ever experienced...which was exactly what he needed before reentering his past.

Catherine pulled back and gifted him with a smile so tender that he felt something tighten in his chest. "See?" she said. "I knew you had that softer side to you. You may not see the beauty of who you are, but it's coming out anyway."

He pulled her tight, anchoring her against him as he buried

his face in her hair. She hugged him back, and for a moment, he felt all her energy surge into him like a coat of protection, warmth, and purity. Together, they wrapped it around him, cloaking him in kindness and warmth, the only kind of protection that would serve him as he entered the domain of his former masters.

Finally, after what felt like an eternity, but was actually only seconds, they released each other. Without another word being necessary, they simply turned and walked over the threshold together.

※※※

THE MOMENT RYLAND AND CATHERINE passed the gates, the wasteland they'd been walking in vanished into impenetrable darkness. In front of them appeared a stone staircase leading up to a massive archway in the center of the temple. Catherine kept close to Ryland as they climbed, reaching out with her mind for Dante. "Dante's spirit is in the building ahead," she told Ryland.

Urgency drove Ryland faster. "How is he?"

"Surviving." She didn't want to tell him that he was tormented and in pain, but from the grim set to Ryland's jaw, it was apparent he already knew what a soul trapped in the nether-realm would suffer.

No sense of Lucy, which scared her, but at the same time, she knew it was right. Heaven help her if she ever sensed Lucy's soul, because that could mean only one thing: that her beautiful, innocent daughter was dead.

The mere notion of Lucy's fate sent a chill of dark, terrifying horror through her, and she quickly shifted her thoughts. Envisioning her daughter dead would paralyze her. Instead, she imagined the look on her daughter's face when her mommy walked in the door. The feel of Lucy in her arms again. The sound of her daughter's voice. "Yes," she whispered, sudden strength rushing through her. "Is Lucy in here?"

"She has to be." Ryland nodded. "The temple is the only place that has enough of a controlled climate to protect a small child. The rest of the nether-realm is too harsh. She's definitely in here."

Anticipation rushed through Catherine as they reached the top of the stairs and two massive doors swung inward to admit them, decorated with bronze carvings of people dying so brutally that Catherine had to avert her gaze. She opened her mind to Ryland's, seeking his reassurance and strength. His energy flowed through her, a warmth that seemed to melt the fear gripping her heart.

Despite her initial bravado about invading the nether-realm

by herself, she had to admit, she was so glad he was here with her. So very glad.

They walked through the doors, and Dante's soul became even stronger, pulsating with energy and pain. She looked around quickly, searching for the telltale haze of his aura, but she couldn't find it. *Dante's in here,* she said. *Somewhere.*

We'll find him. There was no mercy or hesitation in Ryland's voice. Just the sheer, intense focus of a warrior on a mission.

The towering doors swung shut behind them with a crash that made her jump. Ryland didn't move, keeping his gaze fixed ahead of them. Catherine followed his gaze, and then sucked in her breath in surprise.

At the far end of the arched cathedral-like room there were two massive stone thrones on a raised platform. On one of them perched a regal woman clad in an all-black long-sleeved gown that seemed to slither over her as if it were alive. The only bit of color was a scarlet ruby between her breasts. Her hair was raven-black, her face pale as death, her eyes a brilliant jade green. Her aura was thick with black and purple, drenched with horrific things that made Catherine's stomach turn. As the woman rose to her feet, the entire room seemed to shrink away from her in fear, as if the stones themselves were afraid of her. "Balthazar," she said, her voice a throaty rasp of pure menace. "How nice of you to return."

Ryland gripped his machete and said nothing, but Catherine could feel the battle raging within him. Penetrating terror. Vile hatred. Lethal force. An anger so fierce it threatened to burst out and consume them all. There was so much negative energy swirling through him, threatening to devour him. The golden cuffs on his wrists seemed to glow even brighter, as if the beast was gaining strength within him.

Catherine moved closer and put her hand on his back. He jumped in a startled response, but then settled into her touch, never taking his eyes off the woman. "Desdria," he said softly, his voice taut. "Release Dante and the girl, and we will let you live for another day."

Catherine was shocked by Ryland's offer. How was he possibly managing to control himself enough to propose a negotiation, instead of simply going after her? But she knew how he was doing it. Despite all the darkness inside him, there was a stream of decency so powerful that it could trump anything. Dante hadn't rescued him all those years ago. The angel hadn't rescued him. Ryland had rescued himself, with a little bit of help.

Desdria laughed, a cackle that made the hairs on Catherine's arms stand up. "What a charming offer. I reject it."

There was a loud clang, and suddenly Ryland careened backward, as if some giant invisible hand had snatched him by the back of the neck and jerked him off his feet. He slammed into the wall, and then chains exploded out of the stone, slamming into his cuffs with a violent rat-a-tat. Within a split second, thick golden chains were fastened to his wrist and ankle cuffs, binding him to the wall.

With a roar of fury, he lunged forward, trying to free himself. Black smoke began to fill the air around him, and his skin began to glitter. "Ryland! Stop!" Catherine hurried toward him, then gasped as a golden collar appeared around his throat.

"Oh, dear God, *no.*" Catherine's heart stuttered in horror as a chain shot out from the wall, attached to the collar and then jerked him backward.

He slammed into the wall with such force that the entire temple shook.

Ryland. Catherine reached out with her mind, diving past the churning darkness in his mind. *Don't lose control.*

Ryland pressed the back of his head against the rough stone, his eyes shut as he fought for breath. His shirt was hanging open, and Catherine could see that the drawing on his chest was completely filled in, except for the beast's eye. His body shook with the effort of maintaining control, but how could he withstand it? Adrenaline thundered through her as she felt Ryland's mind reach for hers. *Cat. Help me.*

She knew instantly what he wanted. Not physical help. He needed something positive and good to counteract his terror and anger. *I love you.* The words appeared in her mind before she'd even thought them.

Fear slammed through her. Oh, dear God. What had she just said? Horrified, she clapped her hand over her mouth as Ryland's eyes snapped open.

He stared at her, and for a split second, his eyes were a bright blue. Not black. Not black? Then he blinked, and the black had returned. Had she imagined it? *You are a foolish angel, picking me to love.* But he didn't sound mad. His voice was actually reverent, almost disbelieving. Stunned.

I didn't pick you. It just happened. Now that she'd said it, she could feel the emotions burning through her. It was the truth, a terrifying revelation, but at the same time, it felt incredible to put her faith in someone again.

Her words still vibrating between them, she felt a new power rise within Ryland, a calm focus that seemed to be trumping the beast. Had her declaration soothed him? She couldn't help but feel pleased. His response to her was not a lie. If he'd said he loved her back, she knew now that those were just words. Anyone could say them. But for her words to give him the ability to pull himself back from the edge of demonhood? That couldn't be faked. She mattered to him. She didn't know how much or on what level, but she definitely mattered. Relief cascaded through her, and she felt almost giddy with relief. *What now? Can you get free?*

He grimaced. *No. This is what happened last time. I can't get free unless I fully engage the beast.*

Fear began to hammer at her. *No,* she said. *This isn't like before. You're centuries stronger than you were back then. It's not the same. They don't know how powerful you are.* She met his gaze. *I do.*

Ryland stared at her hungrily, and fierce, dark determination began to flow through him. *You are insane, woman.*

She shrugged. *As long as I'm right, I'm okay with that. You can get out, Ryland. There is a way—*

"My dear, sweet, Catherine. How lovely of you to come by."

The voice knifed fear right into her heart. She whirled around, shock numbing her as her former husband, the father of her child, walked into the room from a hidden door at the back. He was far taller than she remembered, almost seven feet. His shoulders were huge, barely covered by the black satin shirt open to his navel. Tight leather pants were caked on his legs, a thick gold chain glittered around his neck, and huge jeweled rings clung to every long finger. Gone was the lean, unsophisticated man who wore jeans and T-shirts, who chopped wood for his family. "Simon?" she gasped.

Simon? Ryland's voice was equally shocked. *That's Simon?*

Fury exploded through her. "You bastard!" She summoned all her death energy, sucking it into her body, amassing it with violent intensity "Where is my daughter?" Her voice was low and haunting, a dangerous, lethal threat that she didn't try to contain, for the first time in her life. She opened herself to it, inviting every last bit of darkness inside her to the surface.

He laughed at her.

Laughed? He *laughed?* She threw out her hands and charged him, thrusting all her death energy into her palms. All she had to do was touch him and he—

No! Ryland shouted. *Don't—*

Simon raised his palm. Silver light shot out of his hand, slammed into her chest and threw her backwards. She screamed as agony consumed her, as her body writhed in pain. She crashed into a stone, and she gasped as it slammed into her back, knocking the breath out of her. What had he done? Where had he gotten that power?

Catherine! Ryland shouted into her mind. *Get up! Get up!*

Driven by the urgency in his voice, Catherine dragged herself to her feet just as the ground where she'd been lying turned black and began to sizzle. She stumbled away from it, not even wanting to imagine what would have happened if she had still been lying there. *What's going on?*

Ryland cursed. *He's the Dark Lord. Desdria's mate.*

Catherine spun toward Ryland. *What? Simon is the Dark Lord?* Dear God. That was impossible.

Get out of here. Just run. You can't save Lucy now. Not from him.

Screw that. Enraged, Catherine whirled to face Simon, the man who had once made her believe in love. "Give me back my daughter," she snapped. "Or I will bring you all down."

Simon smiled, a slithering, disgusting smile that made her stomach turn. "No, my dear Catherine, you don't understand. I'm not finished with what I need from you yet." He nodded at Ryland. "There are still more warriors who need to die, starting with him."

She drew her shoulders back. "Never." She knew he couldn't make her kill Ryland. She loved him, and nothing could break that. Ryland had given her hope and light, and that was enough. She opened her heart to her love for him and for Lucy, thrusting it out into the world as protection for herself and the two people who mattered to her.

"No?" Simon laughed again. "Then there's something that you need to see." He held out his hand to Desdria, who handed him a glass canister with a stopper. "You should have this."

She didn't take it. "Give me back my daughter."

He held it up. "If you want Lucy, you need to look at this."

Don't touch it, Ryland warned, but Catherine was already reaching for it.

He said it had to do with Lucy. I have to see.

Simon brushed his fingers across her palm as she took the bottle from him, and she shuddered. Ryland let out a low growl, and she felt his pain as he struggled against his bonds. He was growing in anger and frustration, but still keeping his energy contained and his strength targeted as he worked against his bonds. *Come on, Ryland,* she said. *You can do it. I need you. Dante needs you. Lucy needs you. Free yourself.*

> *You're so damned bossy.*
>
> *I'm a mom. We're all bossy. Get on it.*

"Open it," Simon commanded, gesturing to the glass bottle she held.

Don't, Ryland warned her.

I have to. Catherine gripped the cork and yanked it while Simon watched her with an expectant gleam in his eye. She bent her head to smell the content, but there was no odor. "I don't smell any—" Suddenly, her mind was filled with her daughter's energy. The beautiful innocence of the young spirit, the suffering, the loneliness...her soul... Catherine went numb with horror. "Lucy's soul was in here." Oh dear God. *No.* Her soul had been in the bottle before Catherine had opened it. There was only one thing that would have allowed that to happen. Lucy was dead. Dead. *Dead.*

Stunned, she dropped the bottle, and the glass shattered all over the floor. Her legs gave out and she fell, her knees crashing onto the floor. "Lucy," she gasped. "Lucy. *Lucy!*" She screamed for her daughter, for the loss, for the child she hadn't been able to protect. The sobs tore from her throat, ripping apart her soul, screams that wouldn't stop. Screams that would never, ever, *ever* stop.

☾ CHAPTER SIXTEEN ☾

CATHERINE'S DEVASTATION TORE through Ryland as if his own heart had been slashed and ripped from his body. Her grief brought him to his knees, and his soul screamed for her pain. He lunged to the end of his chains, trying to reach her, but his hands were stopped several feet away from her by his restraints. *Catherine! Come to me!* He had to touch her. Hold her. Comfort her.

She collapsed to the ground, holding her stomach as the grief poured out of her, moans of agony so chilling it made his chest hurt. The darkness flowed out of her, a thick, tainted mass of death eating through the air. She wasn't holding it in anymore. She wasn't even trying. She was lost, completely inundated by the grief of losing her daughter.

He knew what that was like. He knew it because he'd been through the exact same thing the day that he'd held Marie in his arms as she died, knowing that he hadn't been able to save her. He couldn't let Catherine go through that. He had to help her. Had to execute some miracle that would spare her that hell.

"Catherine!" He shouted for her, his voice raw with emotion as he strained against the chains. Blood ran down his wrists as the cuffs dug into his flesh. His chest burned from lack of oxygen as the neck collar crushed his throat. But still he fought, channeling all his energy into her, into the angel who had come to him, into the suffering consuming her.

Her knees were bloody from where she'd fallen on the broken glass that had cut through her jeans, and her hands were bleeding as well. Her hair hung in tangled mats, and she was bowed over, her body shaking violently. Her mind was a confused miasma of grief, guilt, and loss. Of isolation so intense it was as if her soul had been stripped into a thousand fragments and sunk into a pool of suffering. She was lost to him, unable to hear him or feel his presence. She was spiraling away from him, from herself, from life.

Jesus. He had to get to her. He had to help her. He had to—

A white light flashed from Simon's palm and hit Catherine in the sternum. "No! Fuck! No!" Ryland roared with anguish as Catherine screamed and fell backward, holding her chest.

"She's going to die," Simon taunted. "Unless you save her." He shot another bolt of light at Catherine. Her body jerked as it hit her, and another scream tore from her throat.

"Catherine!" Ryland bucked violently in his restraints. *Fight back, Cat! I know you can!* He thrust his own healing energy at her, trying to offer her his strength and immortality, but she didn't accept it. Her mind was shut down, unable to connect with his.

Panic began to build inside Ryland, and he tried harder, driving all his energy toward her. How many times had she told him how impossible it was to kill her? He knew she could survive this. She had to survive it. She was death herself, the very essence of what Simon was attempting to do to her.

Ryland knew he could help her get through it. He *had* to help her get through it. *Take my strength, Cat. Come on—*

Simon hit her with another blast, and this time, she didn't react. Her body jerked, but no scream came from her mouth. She just lay on the floor, smoke rising from her burned skin.

"Jesus! Cat!" Fighting for sanity, for strategic thought, Ryland jumped backward to give himself slack, then he called out his machetes and hurled them at Simon in a lightning-fast one-two strike.

Simon didn't even bother to look at him. He just held up his hand. White light shot out of his palm and slammed into the blades. They ricocheted off to the side, spinning completely out of control. Ryland tried to call them back, but they were still hurtling violently away from him, his connection to them severed by whatever Simon had done. Shit!

The Dark Lord finally looked at him. "There is only one thing that will work down here, Balthazar. You know what it is."

Ryland's lip curled in a sneer. "You will not get me again, you bastard. I'll save her without going over the edge. Never, *ever,* again."

"Enough of this." Desdria strode across the floor, her body lithe and strong, like a cat stalking its prey.

Ryland's adrenaline surged even further, and he tried to call his machetes back again. They were lying on the floor against the far wall. Again, they didn't respond. He tried to reach out to Catherine. *Come on, Cat. Take my energy. Call my weapons.* He didn't even hesitate with his next command. *Call Thano's.*

There was no response. She just lay on the ground, motionless. *Jesus.*

"I'm tired of this!" Desdria said. "Things need to be done. The queen is growing impatient."

Ryland narrowed his eyes. "Queen? What queen?" Even as he asked the question, he continued to thrust healing energy into Catherine, his mind still racing as he searched for a solution, for a different ending than the one that happened before.

Desdria didn't answer. Instead, she walked over to Catherine, grabbed her shoulder, and rolled her onto her back.

Ryland went cold when he saw the ash-gray color of Cat's skin, the paleness of her lips. She looked like death, real death. *Cat. I'll get you out of this. I promise.* But there was no response, just an echoing hopelessness and an acceptance of death. She'd lost her will to fight now that her daughter was dead? *No, Cat! No! I still need you. The Order needs you! Dante needs you! There's so much for you here! Don't give up!*

Desdria palmed her hand beneath Catherine's shoulder blades, lifting her so that Catherine's head lolled back in a defenseless posture. Then she raised her free hand high to the ceiling in supplication and began to murmur words under her breath.

Panic and terror surged through Ryland as she began to repeat the same process that she'd used to kill Marie so many centuries ago. "No!" The roar exploded from the depths of his being, and he lunged forward with every last bit of strength. He reached the end of his restraints, and there was a brutal cacophony of cracks as the bones in his wrists, ankles, and neck shattered under the force of his lunge. He bellowed with agony as he collapsed to the floor, completely useless, the shackles still locked around him. His eyes rolling in pain, he managed to elbow himself to his stomach, his head hanging uselessly as numbness began to spread through his body. His limbs went still, frozen, *paralyzed.*

He collapsed, his breath shuddering in wheezy rasps as Desdria continued to chant. As she spoke, her fingers lengthened into barbed claws with razor sharp blades at the end. He tried to move, but there was nothing left. His weapons lay inert on the floor. They would disappear within a few seconds if he didn't call them back first. *Catherine!* He fought to keep his focus, to awaken her. *Use your death touch. Kill her now.*

But there was no response. Nothing.

Simon squatted beside Ryland. "So, looks like you have three choices, Balthazar. Hold onto your independence and let this lovely woman have her heart clawed out by Desdria, so that she not only dies, but is held here in tortured suspension for all eternity. Or, you can surrender to your bad side, break the bonds as if they were made of silk and save the girl. Or, you can do the same thing you did before and play the hero just a little too late, so that you lose everything. So many good choices. What will you choose today? Repeat the past, or try something a little different?"

Ryland rolled his eyes so he could look into Simon's smug visage. "Fuck. You."

Simon grinned. "No, it's more like, *you're* fucked, and so is the girl." He stood up. "Kill her, my dear. Do it now." Then he grabbed Ryland's head and twisted it violently around to face Desdria and Catherine.

His body convulsing from the agony of the movement, Ryland had a split second to register Desdria's claws descending toward Catherine's chest, just like before. At the sight, something broke inside him. Desperation, fear, and rage exploded through him, so intense he screamed as it shattered the protections around his mind. He didn't even hesitate. Not even for a split second. He just focused on Catherine and commanded the beast to come.

It erupted through him with a thousand times the magnitude he'd ever experienced before. His bones shattered under the force of his change and reformed as the beast became him. His neck jutted forward, his teeth became fangs, his eyes blood-red beacons in his horned and scaled head, his twenty-foot spiked tail decimating the massive front doors that had locked him in, crushing them with one violent swipe.

"Do it!" Simon shouted, and Desdria shoved the claws into Cat's chest—

With a roar that shook the very earth, Ryland exploded forward. The chains shattered, and Ryland leapt across the room. He raked his claws across Desdria and hurled her into the wall. He whirled around, driving his spiked tail into Simon's chest as he scooped up Catherine's limp body in his massive jaws. He spun around and galloped for the door, unfurling his massive wings as he ran—

"Balthazar, *stop.*" Desdria's voice rang through the air.

Ryland slammed up his mental shields as his muscles started to slow down and obey the command. Clenching Catherine so carefully in his jaws, he kept going, shoving himself forward as if he were slogging through air so thick it was like a swamp.

"Balthazar, I said *stop.*"

The command rippled through his mind, and frustration coursed through him as his wings folded up, and his legs stopped running. *No!* He forced another step. And one more. Toward the door. He had to get out. Had to escape. Had to—

"Drop her!" Simon shouted.

Ryland's mouth opened, and Catherine tumbled from his grasp onto the stone floor. Helplessness flooded him as he stared down at her on the ground. Every instinct screamed at him to gather her to him and fly her to safety, but *he couldn't move.* All he could do was stare at her. His body did not belong to him, just like before.

Then he remembered Catherine's words, that it didn't have to be like before. That there was a way out. That he was different than he had once been. *Come on!* Outrage roared through him, and he fought to pick her up, but instead, he went into a crouch, his tail flicking as Simon walked up, holding his hand to the hole Ryland had put in his chest.

He walked right up until his face was pressed up against Ryland's massive snout. "Piece of shit," Simon snarled. "You think because you got a few extra steps before obeying that it's different this time? Never." He raised his palm and smacked Ryland on the side of his head.

A flash of white light blinded Ryland, and pain shot through him, dropping him to his belly with a guttural groan. He landed beside Catherine, his nose pressed up against her hip. Blood was streaming from a wound in her chest, but Desdria hadn't taken her heart yet. Relief rushed through him, and he tried to nudge her with his nose... but couldn't move. *Catherine. Wake up.* He pushed at her mind, and he thought he caught a faint pulse of energy. *Catherine! I—*

"Look at me." Desdria strode up, limping slightly from his attack, but perfectly sound.

He fought it. He fought obedience with every fucking ounce of strength he had, but it didn't matter. Ryland felt his soul wail in dismay as he obeyed her command, swinging his head around to face her.

Desdria reached up to his neck and grabbed his collar. She yanked on it, the action sending shocks shooting violently through his body. "Never, ever, deny us again," she snarled. "You are ours, Balthazar. You are nothing but a slave, and you will never be anything more."

Bile spilled through him, a dark, seething violence to destroy her...but he didn't move. Couldn't move. Catherine was wrong. It wasn't different this time. Not different at all. But even as he had the thought, he reached out to her with his mind. They could control his body, but not his thoughts. *Catherine. Help me. I need your help.* She was his angel, the angel of death that the oracle had predicted, the Order's guardian angel. This was why she'd been brought into his life: for this moment, for this event, to salvage him from hell so he could finish his job and save Dante and the Order. *Catherine!*

But she didn't respond.

Fear began to hammer through Ryland. Why couldn't he connect with her? She couldn't be dying, could she? *Catherine!*

Simon walked over and slid his arms beneath her. Outrage roared through Ryland as he watched the bastard touch her, easing his palms over her skin before picking her up. Vile disgust spewed through Ryland, and he raised his lips in a deathly snarl.

"Silence," Desdria snapped.

The growl cut off instantly, and helpless frustration roared through Ryland as he watched Simon carry her toward the door, away from him. His woman was in the arms of the man who had used her and betrayed her, and then killed her daughter. Ryland's soul unleashed a battle cry, and he lunged for Simon.

Simon's eyes widened in surprise, then he shouted at Ryland. "Down!"

Ryland dropped to his belly like a fucking lap dog. His heart was racing, his body shaking with the need to attack him, but he was paralyzed, stuck to the floor, unable to do anything but watch as the Dark Lord descended the temple steps and disappeared into the darkness, heading toward his lair with Catherine.

Desdria stepped in front of Ryland, blocking his view of his woman. She crouched in front of him, running her hand over his nose. "Tonight, you will service me, Balthazar. You will show me the man you have become."

Ryland stared at her, disgust boiling through him.

"But first, my dear slave, you will take care of one little matter for the queen."

The queen again? What queen? Desdria was the ruler of the nether-realm, never subordinating herself to anyone. Who the hell was she talking about?

"There is a little matter of some Order of the Blade members causing a ruckus outside." She smiled, an expression of such merciless cruelty that his blood ran cold. "Go to the entrance and kill them all. When you finish, you will return to the dungeons, where you will take your human form, lock yourself in my private set of chains, and then await a visit from your master." She dragged one of her claws down his front, tearing open a chasm leaking with acid and poison. He ground his jaw, not taking his eyes off hers as she opened a path down to way below his waist, to the parts of him that belonged to Catherine, not *her*. He didn't move, refusing to be cowed as she jammed extra deep in his testicles, then pulled her claw out of him, leaving him intact...but barely. It was a bitterly familiar promise of what would be coming later. She was filth and waste, and it filled him with her putrid taint.

No, he snarled silently, conjuring up an image of Catherine's blue eyes in his mind. He locked his mind onto that bright azure, drawing her goodness into him, struggling to hold onto that light in the onslaught of such darkness.

Desdria stepped back, his blood dripping from her claw. "Go," she commanded. "Kill them all, and then return. Now!"

Disgust at his own weakness spewed through him as he obediently stepped past her to the top of the temple steps. His wings unfurled, stretching fifty feet in either direction as he began to flap them, stirring up the ashes of so many long dead.

Desdria did not even have to tell him again. Her control of him was complete as he launched himself into the air, sweeping forward with that same intense speed he'd always had, careening through the nether-realm.

Once again, he was the beast. The hunter. The slaughterer of innocents.

Only this time, he was on his way to kill his own team. Dante's legacy. The very entity he had dedicated his life to protecting.

They would stand no chance against him. He would destroy them all within seconds.

As he hurtled toward his destiny, disbelieving fury roared through Ryland for how badly he'd failed. Catherine was in the hands of the Dark Lord. He was about to murder his team. Dante's soul remained in Simon's hands. Catherine's daughter was dead.

All Ryland needed to do to change things was to resist the compulsion to obey Desdria's command.

That was all.

And he couldn't fucking do it.

He was the same as he'd been hundreds of years ago. The exact same.

As he flew over one of the faerie villages that had sheltered him as a boy, and saw that it was dark and abandoned, Ryland realized finally that Dante, the man he'd revered for so long, had made a mistake, and that mistake had been believing in Ryland.

But as he streaked toward the great entrance, a fierce anger began to build inside him. Maybe he couldn't stop himself from killing his team or letting Simon take Catherine or prostituting himself as Desdria's submissive. But there was one thing that Simon and Desdria could not control, and had never been able to control.

His thoughts, the same ones he'd used to reach out to Catherine.

Even as his wings hurtled him toward his prey, even as his claws elongated in anticipation of ripping apart his team, even as his mouth salivated at the idea of fresh meat, Ryland drew his attention inward, and reached out over his blood bond to the one man who had always stood by him.

Thano. I'm coming out to kill you, and I'm in dragon form. He ground his jaw, then gave them the information that would end all chances of him saving Catherine or Dante, but would give his team a chance to live. *Strike a single blow in the eye of the dragon painted on my chest. It will kill me instantly. Do not hesitate.* He paused, and then added one last request, relinquishing his claim on the one woman who gave his life meaning. *Catherine is your* sheva. *Follow the blood bond to her and rescue her. Please.*

There was no reply from Thano as Ryland continued his ascent toward the entrance. He knew that he hadn't been able to connect with Thano from the depths of the nether-realm, but was he close enough to the surface now for him to hear him? As the light from the outdoors began to illuminate the interior, Ryland could only hope that his teammate had heard him.

If not, carnage would ensue, and there would be no one left alive to save his woman. *Do not hesitate,* he told Thano. *Kill me, immediately.*

He burst out of the nether-realm into the open. The first thing he saw was Thano in the middle of the clearing, stretched out on his back, Apollo standing over him, his body torn and bloody as massive asper cats attacked. The rest of the clearing was pure carnage, as Zach and the hooded Order members were fighting for their lives against a herd of asper cats, one of the most deadly creatures ever to transition from the nether-realm to the earth-realm.

No one was ready for him.

There was no one to strike him down.

It was over.

※※※

"CATHERINE. You will wake up now."

The rough voice pressed at her mind, urging her into consciousness. She recognized the voice of Simon, and bile churned through her. She became aware of his hands stroking her skin, of his fingers on her belly, circling lower and lower. Disgust roiled through her, deepened by intense hatred for the bastard who had killed her daughter...and enslaved Ryland.

Fragmented memories broke through her mind. Ryland being chained to the wall. Shattering his limbs and his neck. The way he'd sprawled there, suffering. Broken. The beast he had summoned... something flickered in her mind, an image of a massive monster delivering her into Simon's hands. She groaned, tears falling for what they both had become.

Ryland was lost to the demon he carried on his chest.

Lucy was dead.

More death. More damage. All because of the man running his hands down her body. Suddenly, staying alive didn't matter. Preserving her soul was pointless. There was nothing to save. Her daughter was gone. Ryland was trapped. The only way to free him was for this bastard to die.

Truly die.

In the way only she could do.

Ignoring Simon's demands that she wake up, Catherine focused her energy inward. She summoned the very darkest part of who she was, calling it from the deepest recesses of her soul. It filled her like a great, lurking shadow swallowing every flicker of light as it swept through her.

Simon swore. "What the fuck are you doing?" He shoved her hard, and she landed on the floor, on her bloodied hands and knees.

She looked up, focusing her gaze on his putrid face. "You aren't a Dark Lord," she said, her voice laced with death. "You're just another pawn who is no match for the angel of death."

His eyes widened, and he raised his palm at her, white sparks flickering off his hand. "Don't fuck with me, angel."

"It's too late for you, Simon." She harnessed all the love she'd once had for him and converted it into hate, the kind of vile hatred that made her kind so deadly.

"Hey!" He hit her with a burst of white light, knocking her backwards. "You listen to me, angel. The well-being of Ryland depends on your obedience. You do what I want, or he suffers. Got it?"

Catherine sat back on her tailbone, brought her knees up toward her chest and crossed her ankles. She braced the tips of her fingers on the ground beside her hips, and lowered her head, studying him through hooded lashes. More death flowed through her, turning her skin into an ominous shade of grayish-blue and purple. "And what is it that you want me to do, *Simon?*" She spat the question, even as she continued to build her energy. She knew it would kill her. Taking another soul would crumble what was left of hers, but it was worth it to free Ryland. To destroy Simon. To end the bastard's existence so that he never hurt anyone again.

Greed lit his eyes. "When Ryland finishes killing the Order that's outside the entrance to the nether-realm, you will kill each of their souls, ending with Dante. You will make it impossible for their immortality to *ever* bring them back. We need them cleared out so that the queen can emerge from where she has been for the last five thousand years. Understand?"

She lowered her head still further. "Oh," she said, her voice throaty. "I understand completely."

Simon grinned. "I knew you would come around." His eyes traveled over her body. "You are still my wife, Catherine. I forgot exactly how hot you are. You've gotten fit after the baby weight."

Dark, dark anger built inside her. "Touch me, Simon," she breathed. "Touch me like you used to." Her skin was burning now, saturated in death. "*Touch me.*"

Anticipation and lust gleamed in his eyes, and he moved toward her. "Yes," he whispered. "*Yes.*"

Nausea churned in her belly as he reached for her, and she immediately turned her thoughts to Ryland, imagining it was his hands reaching for her, that it was his body coming to merge with hers. *Ryland. This is for you. Use freedom well.*

Simon crouched before her and grabbed the front of her shirt. He yanked her to him, and Catherine summoned Ryland to her heart as Simon's mouth closed down on hers.

His lips touched hers. For a split second, he went rigid.

And then he started screaming.

RYLAND BELLOWED HIS TEAMMATE'S NAME as he tucked his wings and dive-bombed toward the clearing, straight at the one man he'd actually almost considered a friend. He was out of the nether-realm now. Could he connect with him?

Desperately, he reached out with his mind and felt a pulse of energy from Thano. Yes! Ryland thrust all of his healing energy into the kid, and felt Thano grasp desperately onto his offering. Hope exploded through him as he opened his mind to Thano's, showing him how to kill him. *Do it, Thano. Don't hesitate. It's the only way to save your woman. You're Catherine's only chance.*

Zach whirled around, shading his eyes to watch Ryland's approach. "Holy shit," he yelled. "What the hell is that?"

The other Order members spun around, and there was a litany of shouted curses as Ryland bore down on them. An asper cat leapt onto the back of one of the cloaked Order members, and then they all spun away, fighting for their lives, with no time to study the mutant beast coming for them. His soul screamed in agony as he watched his team being destroyed. These were his men! They were his charges! He had to protect them! Not kill them!

But he couldn't stop himself, streaking right toward Thano to take him out first. Bile and disgust poured through him, at his pathetic weakness of being unable to stop himself. *Thano!*

Apollo was protecting the younger warrior, keeping the asper cats away from him, but even the horse would be no match for Balthazar.

He was less than a hundred yards away. *Thano! Kill me you stupid bastard. Now!*

Thano's eyes opened, and Ryland met his gaze. Hope leapt through him at the sight of those lucid eyes.

Seventy-five yards.

Dude, she's your woman. Save her yourself. I'm sorta busy here. Thano was still lying on his back, his body bloodied and broken, death circling him in a filthy aura.

Fifty yards away. *You have one shot, Thano. Right in the eye. It is the only way to stop me. Do it.*

In Thano's right hand was his halberd, but his grip was loose and relaxed, not ready for throwing. *Who will piss everyone off if you're dead? No one else is as bitter and miserable as you are. We'd all be too happy and cheerful without you around. Nah, I'm not going to kill you.*

Forty yards.

Ryland's claws elongated and he raised his front legs preparing to tear Thano apart. Panic assaulted him, and he fought to stop, but he just flew harder. Visions thrust through his mind of his team being torn asunder and ripped to shreds, of the Order being decimated. His spirit screamed in outrage, and he tried to divert his flight, but his wings just tucked tighter, increasing his speed. *Catherine will die if you don't stop me. Someone has to save her. I can't do it. You have to do it. Please, Thano, save her. For me. Please.*

Twenty yards until impact. *Shit, Ryland. Since when do you ask so nice? You almost sound like a guy in love.*

Strike me down! Five yards. Swearing, Ryland opened his blood bond with Catherine, summoning her *sheva* connection to Thano, calling Thano's weapons the very way she had done it. Thano's halberd leapt out of his hand and hurled through the air, right at Ryland.

"No!" Thano roared in protest just as Ryland landed on him, his claws primed to tear his friend apart, but instead of the feel of soft flesh giving way, unbelievable pain ricocheted through him as Thano's halberd lanced his chest. A direct hit.

Death was his. *Catherine,* he gasped as he rolled onto his side, his claws still reaching lethally for Thano as he fell beside him. *This is for you.*

✦✦✦✦

RYLAND'S ROAR OF ANGUISH TORE through Catherine, ripping her out of her trance. She screamed as his pain lanced her chest and she hunched over, holding her heart. Simon collapsed beside her, moaning in agony, his skin mottled and gray.

The room began to spin, and heat rose from her body, flooding Simon's dungeon like the fires of hell themselves had been unleashed. Ryland's soul seemed to fly into her body, wrapping itself around her. She could suddenly feel his every breath, his every thought, the beat of his heart, and the anguish of his soul. It was as if he had become a part of her, his spirit so entangled with hers that nothing could ever separate them.

Elation flooded her. A feeling of hope and liberation, as if the great angel of life herself had bathed Catherine in the beauty of her soul. The beautiful symphony of a thousand church bells filled her mind, and a feeling of absolute peace and rightness swelled within her, chasing away all the death, all the darkness, all the damage of her soul, leaving nothing behind but Ryland, the beauty of his soul, and the intensity of her emotions for him.

She gasped as she fought for breath, overwhelmed by the sheer force of the emotions trying to consume her, by the depth of her need for Ryland. Her forearms began to burn with the most intense pain she'd ever experienced, and she yanked her sleeve back in time to see Thano's halberd finish forming on her arm. It flashed once, and then settled.

The bond was complete. She belonged to Ryland. Forever. *Forever.* He'd finished the last stage, his half of the death stage— Oh, no! Catherine lunged to her feet, her heart racing. For him to satisfy the death stage, it meant he had either killed someone to save her life… or that he had offered his own life to save hers. Dear God, please let it be the first one! *Ryland!*

She suddenly became aware of the piercing pain in her chest again. She pressed her hands to her heart, focusing her mind on it. To her horror, she felt Ryland's spirit entangled with the injury. In pain. Grief. Agony. Death was swirling through him, looking for a place to settle. She realized that she was feeling Ryland's pain, Ryland's death... Oh, no. He had taken a death blow!

Ryland! She broke for the door. She just reached the threshold when Simon's hand closed around her ankle. He jerked her hard, and she fell, her head smashing into the wall as she hit. He began to drag her backwards, away from freedom, away from Ryland, and into hell.

Ryland! She screamed his name even as Simon hauled her toward him. *Ryland!*

A faint pulse of energy filled her mind, then a whispered plea from the man she loved. *Cat?*

Don't die! She screamed her command, barely aware of Simon throwing her on the floor and binding her arms and legs. She thrust all her energy into her connection with Ryland. *I need you!*

A myriad of emotions flowed from Ryland, but the most powerful one was a tremendous sense of shame and failure. *Thano will take care of you.*

For God's sake, shut up, you idiot! I want you! You're the only one! She gasped in pain as Simon wrenched her arm behind her back.

It's too late, Cat. I'm dying. It's as it should be. My sacrifice to you— He grunted, and sudden fury exploded from him. *Son of a bitch! They're going down!*

What? Who? Tell me what's happening!

Asper cats. They're killing my team. Shit! Energy flickered through him, and she knew he was trying to get up to help them. The intensity of his need to help his team was so powerful it was almost blinding... No, it *was* blinding. A golden light so bright that it seemed to be setting her on fire. Her breath caught as it filled her, and suddenly she knew. She *knew.* The golden light that Ryland had been seeking from other angels was actually within himself.

He was the one with the angel power.

He was the angel.

And from the intensity of his reaction to the Order being destroyed, she knew that he didn't have to look any further to find the third angel in the Order's trinity. Ryland was their guardian angel. It was him. And it always had been.

Ryland's shock filled her as he read her thoughts. *What the fuck are you talking about? I'm not an angel—*

You don't have time to deny it. Catherine focused on him, offering him all the knowledge she had of what they both were. *Your calling as an angel is stronger than any other force,* she said. *Stronger than mortal death, the call of the beast, or the power of the slave cuffs. You can save them, Ryland. You can rescue your team. It's your job. It's what you were created to do. You're the one they've been waiting for. You!*

🐉 CHAPTER SEVENTEEN 🐉

AN ANGEL? Catherine thought *he* was the angel? Unreal. Un-fucking-real.

He was no angel. He was a monster. Always had been. Always would be.

Denial roared through Ryland as he lay on his side, his life bleeding from his body. His chest was heaving with the effort of breathing, and black blood was oozing from all of his pores, leaking out between his scales. Even in the shadows of death, the form of his beast did not leave him. He'd heard that death always claimed a being in its true form, which meant that he was a monster, not a man.

A beast until the end.

Beside him lay Thano, his body broken and mangled from the cats. The only reason that Thano was alive was because Apollo was still fighting to save him, but Thano couldn't move any more than Ryland could. As they lay there, Ryland swung a weary claw at Thano, trying to fulfill Desdria's orders even as he lay dying. His claw raked across Thano's thigh, and the other warrior flinched. "Shit, Ry. Cut the crap already."

"Can't." His voice was rough and deep, but he managed to form words even though he was in dragon form.

"Fuck that shit. You *won't*, more like it."

Thano's words hit deep, and Ryland flinched. "You believe that?"

"Yeah, 'cause if you wanted to stop, you would." Thano's green gaze met his. "You're more than the rest of us, Ry. You always have been."

"Fuck that. More of a monster."

Thano managed a grin. "Yeah, that too."

Ryland. Catherine's voice was urgent, compelling, and it seemed to fill his entire soul with light and yearning. Sudden realization rushed through him. He didn't want to die. He wanted to be with her. *You need to focus on your team. Accept your mission as their guardian. Don't fight it.*

Again with the angel? Resistance built inside him, raw denial for the lies she was spinning. *I'm not a fucking angel—*

Shut up for one second, she snapped, her voice filling him with urgency. *This is how it works, Ryland. You must accept your true calling, or you can never fully tap into your power. Look at your team, acknowledge your need to save them, and then state that you accept your mission. Do it now!*

"No way." Thano was staring at him in shock. "You're an angel?"

Ryland glared at him. "Get out of my head."

"Dude, you're broadcasting like there's no tomorrow—" There was a loud scream of agony, and both of them turned their heads to see Zach fall as an asper cat leapt on him. One of the other Order members, a stranger they didn't even know, beheaded the cat a split second before it finished off Zach. But even as he did it, another cat attacked, tearing a chunk out of his shoulder.

Outrage roared through Ryland, and the need to save them vibrated through him. But he was too weak to move, his life bleeding away, which was fortunate, because every move he took was designed only for the purpose of killing his own damned team.

Ryland— Catherine's voice was cut off, and he felt a stab of pain from her.

Cat? What's wrong?

Simon. Another burst of pain jerked through her, igniting a lethal anger within him. Possessiveness raged through him, an agony that seemed to rip his heart right out of his body. "Thano! Save her!"

"Really?" Thano shot him a disbelieving look. "You dumbass. Look around. We're all going to die. No one is going to be left to save her, unless our missing third angel shows his pretty little face and helps us out."

Ryland's soul screamed in protest as more pain hit Catherine. Frantic, he looked around the clearing and saw only death. They were all losing. They would all be dead. Thano was right. No one would be left. Not even Catherine. "No!"

Ryland. Help me.

Fierce determination swelled through him, and suddenly Ryland didn't give a shit what he was capable of, what his destiny was, or what anyone thought about him. Only one thing mattered. Saving the people who mattered to him. With a roar of fury, he turned toward his team, following Catherine's orders. He accepted the horror of what he was seeing as the truth. He scented the blood of warriors. He heard their screams of pain. He watched them fall. He let their suffering and torment fill every space in his soul. As their suffering filled him, so did an answering, grim resolve, an unflinching *drive* to protect them, to end their suffering, to make the shit stop. "I need to save them," he growled.

At his confession, something flickered inside him. Strength. Energy.

"I need to save them," he repeated, louder this time. More energy seemed to fill him, flooding his muscles with strength.

"I need to save them!" he shouted. "I accept my mission!" The words seemed to explode from him. Not just from his mouth, but his chest, his heart, from the very depths of all the darkness swirling around inside him. "I am their guardian angel, and I accept my fucking mission now!"

As he bellowed the words, a massive golden light exploded in the sky above them, showering everything with a fiery glow. Life flooded Ryland, and he leapt to his feet with a roar of triumph. He spun around, his massive claws ripping an asper cat off Apollo's back. He hurled it into one of the pyres by the entrance, and it screamed in agony as the fires of hell consumed it.

He tore across the clearing like hell unleashed, his roar flattening the trees for a mile around. He reached Zach first, his massive jaws crushing an asper cat just as it went for Zach's throat. Ripping it apart, he hurled it aside as he smashed his tail into a duo that was ripping the flesh from one of the cloaked Order's body. He was everywhere, moving faster than he'd ever moved before, taking out the beasts as they swarmed him. Hundreds seemed to flood from the woods, summoned to the battle to take out the creature threatening them.

He whirled around, their teeth tearing scales from his body as he attacked them with his claws, his teeth, his tail, everything he had. The air was filled with the tormented cries of the cats, with his howls of victory, in a battle that seemed to stretch on and on and on—

Until suddenly, there were no more left.

Ryland stood on all fours, his massive body heaving as

he stood at the ready in the middle of the clearing, his tail flicking restlessly. Around him, hundreds of asper cats littered the ground. Not a single one breathed. Not a single one had been spared. Creatures that had taken hundreds, thousands of lives, would never hurt another soul.

"What the fuck is that?" Zach shouted.

What? Something else? Ryland spun around, his claws bared, only to discover that Zach and the other five Order members were surrounding *him* in a well-armed circle. Their weapons were out, even as blood streamed from their decimated bodies.

"Don't move," Zach commanded, moving so that he was in front of Thano, blocking Ryland's access to the downed warrior. "Stand down, creature."

Ryland's eyes narrowed at the distrust on Zach's face, at the way everyone's weapons were pointed at him. It was the same as it had always been: his own team looking at him as if he were going to tear them apart, ready to kill him at a moment's notice. Again, he was on the outside.

Which was fine.

He wasn't there to make friends.

He was there to keep the ungrateful bastards alive—

A lone clap made everyone jump.

Then there was another, and Ryland saw Apollo nudge the battered Thano to a sitting position as he clapped again. "Bravo," he said.

"Bravo?" Zach echoed. "What are you talking about?"

Thano continued to clap, harder and harder, and something shifted inside Ryland. He lowered himself into a crouch, his tail flicking as Thano continued to applaud. "It's Ryland," Thano said. "He saved our asses."

Zach spun around to look at Ryland. "That's Ryland?"

Ryland didn't even bother to respond. He just turned to Thano. *I'm going to get Cat—*

"Ryland's our third angel," Thano announced. "He's the Order's guardian angel."

Ryland swore. He did not have time for this shit. He spun around to head back into the nether-realm, then stopped when he found his path blocked by the five hooded Order members. They were standing in a row, feet spread, arms by their sides, swords clenched. A low growl echoed from Ryland. He would not lower himself to speak to them directly. *Tell them to stand aside. I'm going back in—*

The leader of the Order went down on one knee before

Ryland. He bowed his head and laid his swords in a cross at Ryland's feet. "We honor you, angel."

Then, to his shock, the other four did the same, repeating the words. Numbly, he stared in disbelief, stunned by the sight of Order members saluting him. For hundreds of years, no one had ever looked at him as if he had value. He was an outsider, a loner, a ticking bomb that would need to be cut down at any moment.

But here, but now, they were treating him with the reverence reserved for a man as great as Dante. Not for him. Never for him.

He hadn't even figured out how to respond when Apollo trotted up beside them, Thano now on his back. Apollo stood behind the leader of the cloaked warriors and went down on one knee while Thano bowed his head and laid his halberds across Apollo's neck. "You're good shit, Ry. Good shit."

And then, his footsteps uneven and heavy, Zach limped to the front of the line. For a long moment, he stood and faced Ryland, his dark brown eyes hard.

Ryland stiffened, his tail flicking as he waited for the condemnation from the man who had never believed in him.

"You." Zach bit the word out with such hostility that Ryland almost flinched. "You fucking liar."

"Liar?" Ryland repeated, unable to keep the bitterness out of his voice. "I'm a liar? What the fuck is that about?"

"You run around making us think you're going to kick our asses, but all that crap was just a distraction to make us not notice how many times you risked your life to save us, wasn't it? Like when you went into the pit after Thano?" Zach suddenly broke out into a broad grin and slammed his hand down on Ryland's shoulder. "You are one crazy bastard, Ry, and the ugliest angel I've ever seen, but if there is anyone in the entire world I would pick to be my guardian angel, it's you. Shit, yeah." Then he, too, dropped to one knee and crossed his weapons on the ground in a show of the purest deference.

As Ryland stared at the seven men before him, an almost overwhelming sensation of connection and rightness swelled inside him. These were his men. These were his souls. These were his people. These were the reason he was alive. He felt it in the very depths of his soul. This was where he belonged...with them...and with the woman who still needed his help. *Catherine?*

There was no reply, just a wave of darkness and pain. A cold chill settled on him, and his gaze snapped to the dark entrance of the nether-realm.

Thano sucked in his breath. "Son of a bitch. He's hurting her." He urged Apollo to his feet, a dark, lethal expression on his face. "We need to find her."

Ryland's attention jerked to Thano. He'd never seen a look of such lethal fury on the mellow warrior's face. It was the expression of a man on a mission, of a warrior whose mate was being threatened. Son of a bitch. He'd forgotten that it was Thano's brand that was on her arm, that it was Thano who had been bonding with her. But even as he looked at his teammate, he knew he couldn't give her up. She was his.

Thano met his gaze. "The darkness surrounding her is intense. Can you feel it?"

"Of course I can."

"We need to both go in there."

Conflicting emotions warred within Ryland. The need to keep Thano away from Catherine, and a more pressing instinct to do whatever it took to save her. He had no idea what he would become when he returned to the nether-realm, whether he would be enslaved again. The cuffs were still around his ankles and neck. When Dante and the angel had freed him, the cuffs had vanished. This time, they were still there.

He had no choice but to bring Thano. "Okay," he said. "Let's do it—"

Zach stood up. "We're going with you."

"No." Ryland shook his head even as the others stood up. "I won't endanger you—"

"Hey." Zach walked up to him, his eyes dark. "Just because your mission is to save our asses, doesn't mean you coddle us. Nothing has changed, Ryland. We are warriors first. A team. And you don't stand alone. Dante's still in there, and so is Catherine. If you're going in there, we're going in. End of story, so don't bother to argue. Got it?"

A slow, disbelieving grin seemed to spread through Ryland as the others agreed with Zach. "All right then. Get your asses on board."

With a loud battle cry, Zach grabbed one of the spikes on Ryland's neck and hauled himself onto Ryland's scaly back. In less than a second, the other five were also on his back, weapons out and ready. Ryland immediately took off, his wings flapping as he sped toward the opening. Apollo took off after him, keeping up with ease. But as Ryland headed toward the opening, he couldn't quite keep from glancing at Thano, who was hunched low over Apollo's neck. The humorous expression he always wore was gone. Instead, his face was set hard in lethal focus, his hands were fisted around his weapons, and he was urging the stallion on with more intensity than Ryland had ever seen Thano possess.

Apollo was galloping flat out, sweat foaming on his neck as he thundered toward the entrance. Man and beast, on a mission to save a woman. His woman. Ryland's woman.

They were in a race to get to Catherine, and only one man would win.

With a low growl, Ryland stretched his neck out, lowered his head, and tore through the entrance. They swept through the opening side by side, neither of them in the lead. *Catherine.* Ryland reached out to her. *I'm coming.*

At the same moment, he heard Thano echo his statement. *We're coming for you, angel,* Thano said. *The whole damn lot of us.*

Then the vortex caught them, and Ryland focused on controlling their ride, so that he'd come out exactly where they needed to. The man in him half hoped that Apollo and Thano would get tossed in another direction, but even as he thought it, he moved his body over the horse, using his bulk to create a pocket for the duo so they would be able to stay with him, and stay safe.

He was protecting the one man who might be able to take his woman away from him? Really? This angel shit was a pain in the ass. That was all he had to say about it. But when the vortex quieted, preparing to release them, his mind went still with the lethal focus of battle.

It was time to save his woman.

❖❖❖❖

CATHERINE GASPED AS SIMON wrenched her head back and fastened a golden collar around her neck. It clicked shut, and then Simon put his hand on it. It glowed brightly, and seemed to melt into her very flesh. She screamed and tried to claw it off, but her wrists were already bound by the same metal, chained to the wall behind her.

Simon released her, and she fell to the floor, gasping as she landed on hard stone. After using her power to try to bring down Simon, she had nothing left. Her soul was dying. The damage had been done. Simon's skin was mottled and flaking off, and she knew that he was dying as well. They were both going down, but at least Ryland would be free.

"You stupid bitch," he snarled. "How dare you try to steal my soul?"

"I didn't try. I did it."

Simon stumbled toward a cabinet on the wall, his legs barely functioning. "Do you really think it is so easy to bring down the Dark Lord? You're an angel of death. You mean nothing to me." He yanked open the cabinet, and Catherine saw hundreds of stoppered bottles like the one that had held her daughter's spirit.

Tears burned fresh, and grief crashed over her again. Her sweet, baby girl. "How could you have killed her? I don't understand. She's your *daughter*." No. Not his daughter. Simon was a bastard who didn't deserve the title of father. Not ever.

He fell into the cabinet, crashing into the shelves. Dozens of bottles fell and shattered. The air around her filled with souls, the frantic, searching entities looking for their eternity. Lost, and confused. A self-preservation instinct flared through her, a need to feed, to consume the souls and give her enough strength to recover.

She gritted her teeth, digging her fingers into the hard stone, refusing to give in. No more. No more. No more. She would not be that person ever again.

Instead, she waved her hand, offering them her light to guide them on their journey. They passed by her, sailing from the nether-realm, their path illuminated by the angel of death in the role she was supposed to play as a guide for lost souls, instead of being a harbinger of death and destruction.

Simon shoved more bottles off the shelf, his legs giving out as he fell. He lunged for a bottle on the bottom shelf, a pale green bottle that was almost six inches in diameter. A huge soul, one with tremendous power. As he moved it, she caught the faint pulsing of a familiar energy. Dante's? He spun toward her, holding it out. "You will guide this soul into me," he gritted out.

Catherine realized instantly what he wanted to do. He wanted to mingle his life force with another soul and use it to sustain him. He wanted Dante's soul to become his? "No," she said. "Never."

"You don't understand, bitch." He fell to his knees, holding the bottle under her chin. "I am Lucy's only chance to survive."

She stared at him in shock. "What? Lucy's dead."

"She is the daughter of the Dark Lord. She is far too valuable to kill."

Catherine's mind reeled in disbelief. "She's okay?" she whispered, afraid to even say the words.

"Not yet dead." He held up the bottle. "Guide Dante into me, and we will reclaim Lucy together."

Was he telling the truth? Was he lying? She'd sensed Lucy's soul. How could she still be alive?

He leaned forward. "Do you know how long a body can survive without a soul in residence?"

She nodded. "It can't. Not even for a minute. Not if the connection is severed by death."

"Oh, but my dear sweet, Catherine, you are mistaken."

She blinked. "What are you talking about?"

"Under certain conditions, like being killed by the Dark Lord himself on the temple steps, the bond is not completely severed. It takes two hours for that final cord to be cut. Until then, they can be reunited."

She stared at him, inconceivable hope exploding through her. At his grin of triumph, she realized he was toying with her again, just like before. She recoiled from him, shaking her head. "No, you're lying. You're lying! It's impossible!"

"I would think that you, of anyone, would realize that nothing is impossible." He smiled again. "Do you know how long it's been since Lucy has been without her soul?"

Catherine's heart seemed to hover. "How long?" she whispered.

"One hour and fifty-seven minutes." He breathed deeply. "I can smell the body preparing to die, can't you?"

Her heart began to pound. "Put her soul back, then. Put it back!"

"That's your job." He smiled. "You just need to guide her back, like any lost soul. Like you will do for Dante."

For Dante? She suddenly realized what was going on. He was taking advantage of her need to believe the impossible, that her daughter was still alive, to make her work for him. It was all a lie. A stupid lie! Disappointment and weakness shuddered through Catherine. Fleeting hope lost so brutally and quickly. Her arms trembled where they held her up. Death was swirling through her, her soul bleeding out in its final battle. "You lie," she gritted out. "You're lying to me—"

"Am I?" With a roar of fury, he shoved his palm toward the far wall, which was made of stone. White light exploded from his palm, and the barrier disintegrated, revealing an adjoining room. Stretched out on the floor, under a scarlet blanket was Lucy. Tangled blond curls fell about her cheeks, her hands were folded across her stomach, and her skin was so pale it was almost translucent. Her eyes were closed. Her breath silent. Her heart not beating. But there was a faint aura around her still, a body still clinging to life.

"Lucy!" Catherine screamed as she lunged to her feet and ran toward her daughter—

The collar around her neck jerked her back against the wall, and her breath gurgled in her throat, but she still strained toward her child, fighting desperately to find a way to get to her.

Another burst of white light exploded from Simon's palm, and the wall reformed, cutting her off from Lucy. "No!" Catherine screamed. "Lucy—"

Simon grabbed her by the collar and yanked her over to him. "Put Dante Sinclair's spirit into me," he snarled. "Now!"

Catherine grabbed the stopper and yanked it out. The room was immediately filled with the most intense power, a soul so strong it seemed to make the walls bend outward. It was swirling about her, disoriented and confused, just as all the others had been. What did Simon do to the souls to make them unable to find their way?

"Now," Simon snarled.

Catherine immediately closed her eyes and reached out to Dante's soul, but it resisted her, refusing to let her connect with him. It was too strong for her to control. She was too drained to overpower it. *Please,* she whispered desperately, unable to get the sight of Lucy's lifeless form out of her mind. *Please, come to me.* But it didn't. It wouldn't. It strained against the walls, pushing away from her, as if it could sense the threat that Simon posed. Of course it could. It was the leader of the Order. A man who always knew. "Dante, please—"

The door suddenly exploded off its hinges, and a monstrous beast exploded through the front wall. Her heart seemed to leap from her chest. Ryland had returned!

⬤⬤⬤

RYLAND THOUGHT HIS HEART WOULD STOP when he saw Catherine entrapped by the same chains that had bound him for so long. She was slumped on her knees, her skin ashen, her body trembling violently. She was reaching for him, a look of such relief on her face that his chest actually tightened. He was in time. He was there for her. He would save her. "Catherine!" He bounded through the door toward her—

Simon jumped in front of him. "Down, beast, *down!*"

To his horror, Ryland dropped to the ground like a fucking subservient piece of shit. Catherine's face fell. Raw, indescribable self-loathing flooded him. His woman was dying, and he couldn't save her? Unacceptable. This could not happen. He would not allow it. With a low growl, he willed his body to shake off the command, but nothing happened. He didn't move. Fuck!

"You all die!" Simon whirled on the rest of the Order, white light exploding from his palm as the others charged into the massive stone lodging.

"Ryland. Help!" Tears were pouring down her cheeks. Her eyes were haunted, her shirt streaked with blood. On her arms were the completed brands in the shape of Thano's halberds. For a moment, he couldn't take his gaze off them, shocked by the sight. Somehow, *somehow*, he'd thought that at the final stage, when that moment had connected them after he'd offered his life to save her, that his brands would have replaced Thano's. How could they still be on her like that? The connection between them had been about *them*, not Thano. It wasn't Thano!

"Please," she whispered, her voice so full of anguish he felt a fissure crack through him. "Lucy," she managed to say. "She's alive."

"Alive? She's alive?" Son of a bitch. Urgency exploded through him. "Where is she?"

"I have to put her soul back in her body. I—" Her breath stuttered, and her skin grew even paler. "I'm dying," she whispered. "Need light. Nothing left—"

"Catherine!" Her name ripped from his throat, a howl of such longing and need, of a thousand years of suffering finally being released. His life suddenly loomed before him, an empty chasm of isolation and loneliness if she wasn't in it. The magnitude of the loss was debilitating, tearing away at the very fabric of his being, a horror so great he bellowed in agony. "I won't let you die!"

Summoning reserves he'd never before accessed, he lunged for her once again, galvanized by the terror of losing her. For a moment, he was suspended in stillness, frozen in time, but he could feel the invisible bonds holding him begin to weaken. "Now!" he roared, and suddenly an incredible force swelled within him, infusing his body with indescribable strength. To his shock, he broke free of Simon's hold and was suddenly on his feet again! He charged across the room to the only person in the room who mattered to him. "Catherine!" He ripped the chains out of the walls with his claws, then scooped her up, cradling her against his chest.

She was too cold. She was shaking too badly. Her body was limp against his, dying. Losing her soul. Fear was like a cold knife, and he pulled her more tightly against him, as if he could use his body to shield her. *Tell me what you need. How do I help you?*

She closed her eyes. *The east wall. Break it. Get Lucy.*

Ryland didn't even hesitate. He just swung his mighty tail, decimating the wall.

A small child was lying on the floor, shocking him into silence for a split second. Memories assaulted him, images of being on that same slab as a boy. That had been his bed. His home. His hell. And there was another child there, being groomed to replace him? How many other children had suffered his fate? Rage exploded through him, the need to destroy Simon, but he didn't cave to his instinct for revenge. There was no time for that. Time only to save. Time only to steal two precious victims from death before it could win.

Still cradling Catherine, he sprinted for the girl. As he set Catherine down beside Lucy, his insides seemed to congeal in the presence of such innocence. He'd never been near something as pure as this child. Never in his life. His life was death and destruction, and even Catherine was steeped in death. But this child, this little girl... he was overwhelmed by what she represented. "She needs to live," he rasped out, his body vibrating with the intensity of his protective feelings for her, for this child, for her mother.

He lifted the little girl in his bloodied claws, setting her in Catherine's embrace, and then pulled both of them into his arms.

Tears streamed down Catherine's cheeks as she cradled her daughter, pressing her lips to the blond wisps of her hair. Ryland was so connected with Catherine that he felt the swell of her love for Lucy. It filled him with emotions so beautiful, so intense, it unleashed in him things he'd never felt before. Hope. Beauty. Love. In that moment, being part of the circle of love between Catherine, Lucy, and himself, he finally understood love. He wanted to weep for what she was giving him, for what she was showing him.

Then Catherine's arms slid away from the child, falling toward the floor, and her head fell back as Lucy lay inert across her mother's torso. *I'm dying,* she said. *I have nothing left. I can't save her.*

Dark, fierce anger flooded Ryland, the same emotions that had carried and fueled him for so long. *Fuck that, sweetheart. No one dies on my watch.* And with that, he merged with her, sending all his strength and immortality into her. He didn't give a shit that he could feel Thano's energy in the link, still acting as the bridge between them. He tapped into Thano's energy, merged it with his own, and thrust both of their healing energies into Catherine. He wove it through her damaged soul, accepting her encroaching death as his own. With his ties to the nether-realm, death could not hurt him, and he took hers, while he continued to channel his and Thano's Calydon immortality into her.

The depth of their connection was incredible, and he could feel the intricacies of the bond between them as his soul took the scourges of death from her and accepted it into his own body, where it could do no harm. He knew the moment that he'd cleared enough damage from her, and he felt her soul shudder in relief. Sudden light seemed to rush through them, as if the sun itself had broken free of the clouds.

Catherine's arm tightened around Lucy again, and he felt her reaching out with her energy, searching for her daughter's spirit. Although he could not help her on this journey, Ryland mingled his spirit with hers, offering his love and his support as she reached out with her own soul into the tainted air of the nether-realm, calling for her child's lost soul. *Lucy. It's Mama. I'm here to bring you home.*

Her voice was like the purest of angels, so filled with the beauty of a mother's love.

Lucy, it's Mama. Come back to me, baby. Suddenly, fear began to pulse through her. *Ryland, I can't find her. We're running out of time. Her body is dying—*

Ryland focused on the child in his arms, and he instantly sensed that Catherine spoke the truth. The last bits of light were blinking out of her physical being. *I got this one covered, sweetheart.* He'd never heard of anyone doing what he was about to do, but he didn't hesitate, absolutely certain it would work.

He swiftly and precisely tapped into the blood of Catherine that was in her daughter, merging with Lucy through the blood bond he had with her mother. Once he felt Lucy's spirit, he immediately sent his healing strength into her, the same way he'd done with Catherine. His connection to her was thinner, but he held tight to her, balancing her at the very brink of death, keeping her on this side of the Afterlife by the thinnest of threads. *I've got her, love. Go find her soul. But be quick. I don't know how long I can hold her.* Even as he said it, he felt the onset of death, trying to steal her away from the physical world. He sent another pulse of his strength and immortality into her as he felt Catherine direct her energy outward again, sweeping their surroundings for her daughter while she entrusted Ryland with her daughter's life.

There was a loud crash and an explosion of white light, telling him that the battle with Simon was in full force, but he didn't turn around. He kept all his energy focused on the tiny presence in his arms, on nothing else, holding the connection so tightly, knowing that if he faltered at all, he would lose her. The pull of death on her small form was so strong that it was taking all his strength to keep it at bay. Sweat broke out on his brow, and his body started to tremble, but still he held the connection, willing life into the fragile girl in his arms, holding her on this side of life so much longer than she was supposed to be.

He gritted his jaw, tightening his grip on both females, pulling them tighter against his chest as he willed more life into them. But he could feel he was losing Lucy. It wasn't enough. It was as if...as if he was putting death into her himself... Shit! He was! The beast was made of death, and his spirit was tainted by it. For Catherine, she had reveled in it. But Lucy was an innocent. He had to shift back!

Swearing, he gritted his teeth and pictured his human form. He held the image in his head and called it to him, willing the beast to leave. Shifting from full beast to man was impossible, something he'd done only that one time with the help of Dante and the angel, but he didn't give a shit. Tonight, it would work. It had to. There was no other option. He thrust all his force into the request, and then, as if it had simply been waiting for the command, the beast disappeared, leaving him a man.

The feel of Catherine's body against his skin made his heart leap, and he quickly placed his hand over Lucy's heart. Freed from the conscripts of his beast, the purity of his strength and immortality flowed more freely, jerking Lucy back from death just as her body started to quit. He held her there, relentless in his pressure, offering her everything he had, knowing he would hold that child in life even if he drained every last bit of life from himself in the effort.

※※※

SHE COULDN'T FIND LUCY'S SPIRIT. She couldn't find her daughter! Panic raced through Catherine, terror growing thick as time passed, too much time. *Lucy! It's Mama. I love you. I'm here to bring you home.* She sent the call out into the nether-realm, frantically searching past hundreds of other lost souls asking for her help to find their way home. So many had died here, their spirits left to rot until Simon decided to harvest them. She had no time to save them. She could feel the strain on Ryland as he held her daughter alive. *Lucy!*

Suddenly, in the furthest alcove on the far side of the nether-realm, she heard a tiny voice. *Mama?*

Lucy! Catherine sent her soul flying through the darkness, faster and faster, honing in on the presence. She sped around a corner, and then was filled with the beautiful innocence of her daughter, hiding in the very alcove where she and Ryland had taken refuge when they arrived. Catherine reached out with her spirit, through the remnants of her own presence that still lingered there, and realized that her daughter had gone there because she had sensed Catherine's aura lingering. Even after two years apart, Lucy had recognized her and tried to find safety with her. *I'm here, baby.* She reached out with her spirit, and gently enfolded Lucy's soul into her own, cradling the fragile warmth against her. *It's time to go home.*

Holding her daughter tightly, Catherine showed her the path back to where Ryland waited for them, keeping them both safe. Together, mother and daughter sped through the darkness, toward a warmth and a light so powerful that it was calling them back.

Catherine plunged into her own body and gasped awake. At the same moment, she felt Lucy's body jerk in her arms. Catherine opened her eyes to see Lucy staring up at her, those blue eyes full of shock. "Mama? It's really you?"

"It is, baby, it is." Tears streaming down her cheeks, Catherine hugged her daughter to her, holding her so tightly that she felt like she could never let go. Lucy threw one arm around Catherine's neck and then reached up for Ryland, who was still encircling them in his protective embrace. Lucy wrapped her arm around Ryland and smiled up at him with the pure adoration that only a child could have. "Hi," she said. "I know you. You took care of me. My name is Lucy."

The slowest, most tender smile dawned on Ryland's face. "My name is Ryland."

Lucy smiled. "You're an angel, too, aren't you? Like Mama?"

Ryland met Catherine's gaze, and she was shocked to see that his eyes were no longer black. They were a brilliant, azure blue, like she'd seen that one time, for that brief second. He smiled at her and brushed a tender, chaste kiss across her forehead, a kiss that promised so much more when they were alone, but offered only comfort while in the presence of a child. Then he smiled back down at her daughter. "Yes, Lucy. I'm an angel, too."

"I know." Lucy snuggled deeper against his chest, showing no signs of being afraid of the man that so many feared. "We've been waiting for you, haven't we, Mama?"

Catherine smiled through her tears, overwhelmed. "I think we have."

Ryland grinned. *I love you, angel.*

He loved her? Her throat tightened, and her heart seemed to come alive, filling with such love that she felt like she could heal every last hole in her soul, wiping away the damage she'd done to it. *I love you, too—*

She screamed as Thano's halberd plunged right into Ryland's chest, right through the eye of the dragon.

🐾 Chapter Eighteen 🐾

Ryland ripped Thano's halberd out of his chest and shoved Catherine and Lucy behind him, instinctively using his body as a shield to protect them. His torso already going numb from the direct hit, he lunged to his feet, calling out his machetes just as Thano unleashed another halberd at him. He slashed it aside a split second before it plunged into his throat. "Thano!" he yelled. "Stand down!"

The other Order members were still fighting Simon, in a battle of blinding white light. The cloaked Order members were moving so quickly he could barely see them, fading in and out of sight, with blue streaks billowing from their cloaks. Zach was in with them, fighting hard as they moved in perfect synchronicity in their attack on Simon, hammering him ruthlessly.

"You fucking bastard!" Thano screamed as he galloped Apollo across the room toward them, his eyes blood red as he called his weapons back for another blow. "You stole my woman!"

Thano's eyes were *red*? Holy crap. He'd gone rogue. The *sheva* destiny had come for him instead of Ryland, since Thano was her true mate. Jesus. He'd trapped Thano. Condemned him to the *sheva* destiny. Guilt coursed through him, and regret. How could he have done this to his own teammate?

"Oh my God," Catherine whispered from behind him. "He's mad."

"Yeah, he is." *Shit!*

With an inhuman cry of rage, Thano attacked again, spinning Apollo around him in circles.

Ryland swore and blocked another blow, then saw Thano's eyes fixate on Lucy. "It's because of her," he shouted. "That stupid kid stole my woman from me!"

"Oh, no," Catherine gasped, pulling Lucy behind Ryland. "No, Thano! Don't!" she yelled.

Son of a bitch. Just like the legend declared he would, Thano had gone rogue...which meant the next step was for him to destroy that which mattered most to both him and his mate. He'd already delivered a fatal blow to Ryland, and now he was going for Lucy. "Thano! Stop it!" Ryland knew that riding Apollo gave Thano too much of an advantage. He could never defeat him as a man, not with the life already bleeding out of him.

Without hesitation, Ryland called his beast, his bones exploding in pain as he shifted form. He leapt in front of Catherine and Lucy, roaring as Apollo skidded to a stop, barely thwarted in his charge toward Lucy. Weakness thrummed through Ryland as they fought, his energy depleted by the direct blow Thano had gotten to his chest, but the beast gave him additional strength. Even as they battled, however, he couldn't help thinking of the rest of the destiny. That Catherine would have to bring Thano down, and then she would kill herself.

A cold chill slithered down his spine at the thought of Catherine killing herself. No. Never. "Never!" He had to be the one to stop Thano. He couldn't let it be Catherine! With renewed determination, Ryland launched himself at Thano.

The battle crescendoed between rogue and Order member, the same conflict that had been fought for centuries, when an Order member was the only thing that stood between a Calydon and his destiny. How many times had Ryland killed a friend who had gone rogue? How many times had he steeled his emotions while he did what he had to do to protect the innocent? Hundreds of times. Thousands. It was what he did.

But as he fought with Thano, as he saw the red glow in his teammate's eyes, he could not make himself deal the killing blow. Not to Thano. Not to the one man who had stood by him when everyone else had seen him only as a monster. Not to the man who was rogue because Ryland had forced him to bond with Catherine, and then taken her for his own. "I'm sorry," he shouted. "I'm fucking sorry, but I love her, and I can't let her go!"

Thano was far beyond comprehending Ryland's words, and he fought ruthlessly with the strength of a madman. Suddenly, Zach was beside Ryland, fighting side by side to contain Thano. Like Ryland, he was not fighting to kill. He was fighting to contain, which made them vulnerable, because Thano was on a mission to destroy them.

"What do we do now?" Zach yelled.

"Knock him out?"

"You know that's impossible! The only way to stop him is to kill him!"

"Ryland!" Catherine was suddenly on her feet beside him, still holding Lucy in her arms, though she had tucked the child's face into her shoulder so Lucy couldn't see. "Kill him! Then keep him alive while I protect his soul!"

Ryland looked at Zach, who nodded grimly. Together, their blades descending as one, they plunged their weapons into Thano's heart. He gasped, and clutched his chest, and for a moment, Ryland thought they'd succeeded.

Then he seemed to shrug it off, righted himself on Apollo's back and urged Apollo into another charge. "He's too hard to kill," Zach shouted. "We have to behead him!"

Ryland looked over at Catherine, who shook her head. "Beheading is too final, it won't work! I can't bring him back from that!"

"We don't have a choice!" Zach shouted. "He's going to kill us all!"

"Let us help." A new voice joined the discussion. Ryland looked over and saw one of the cloaked Order members looking at him. The man's hood was back slightly, revealing dark eyes, and a strong jaw. A warrior of many centuries, with magic...magic? Ryland definitely sensed something there, a rippling power that was different than what he or his team had. "We can kill him."

But as he spoke, Simon let out a roar of outrage and lunged for Lucy, taking advantage of their distraction. Ryland forgot about everything but the child who had hugged him. He forgot about Thano, he forgot about Zach, he forgot about everything but saving that little girl.

His wings launched him across the room, and he grabbed Simon around the waist, crushing him in his massive teeth. Simon screamed in agony, and held up his palm to send white light into Ryland's head—

Then Zach's weapon crashed down on Simon's neck, severing his head from his body. Instantly, he turned into a black mist, the room echoed with the howls of the eternally damned, and then he vanished.

Into the void came the howl of Thano as he threw his halberd at Catherine and Lucy. With a roar of horror, Ryland exploded across the room, his wings driving him fiercely. He lunged for the halberd, his claws wrapping around it a split second before it made impact as Catherine turned her back, using her own body to shield her daughter. At that same moment, Thano's other halberd appeared in Catherine's hand, and she reared back to throw it.

"No!" If she killed Thano, the next step of destiny was for her to kill herself. He couldn't let it happen! It had to stop now! Ryland dove in front of her, blocking the weapon as she threw it. It hit him in the chest, right in the same spot as Thano's blow. Stunned, he hit the earth. But instead of death gasping through him, energy flooded back into him, restoring life into his body. For a split second, he was so shocked he didn't even believe it. Then he realized what had happened. The only way to kill him was to strike *once*, a single blow, but she'd hit him a second time...nullifying the first. Saving his life. Well, damn, that was a good thing to know!

But even as he lurched to his feet, he saw Thano closing in on them again. There was no way to stop him without completely destroying him...unless the cloaked Order could do it. He had to trust that the men lived by the same code of honor that he did. He looked over at their leader and gave the command that seemed to drive a fissure right through his heart. "Kill him."

All five Order members raced toward Thano, outrunning Apollo. They lined up five abreast as Thano charged toward them. Then, as one, they raised their swords, shouting out a phrase Ryland couldn't decipher.

Their swords ignited in purple sparks and then they threw them. The swords hit in perfect sync in the middle of his chest, making a pentagram, each of the five blades forming one side of the shape.

Thano froze, his eyes widened, and then he collapsed, tumbling right off Apollo onto the ground. Dead. His body flickered and started to fade almost instantly, as the young Calydons always did.

"No!" Ryland was the first to reach him, kneeling beside him and thrusting his healing energy and immortality into him, just barely catching Thano's body hovering in a state so faint he was barely visible. Zach dropped to his knees beside him, and joined his healing energy. Then the five strangers did the same, seven warriors imbuing Thano with their immortality, holding Thano's body alive. "Catherine!" Ryland shouted. "Where's his soul?"

"I've got him."

He looked over at her, and saw her eyes were closed. There was a look of intense focus on her face, but her expression was calm. "I have his soul," she said. "You need to keep him corporeal."

Ryland grimly looked at them all. Seven warriors holding his body alive. One angel of death holding his spirit. One Calydon warrior trying his best to go to the Afterlife. What next? How did they solve this? What in the hell were they supposed to do now—

Then the earth began to rumble and shake. Fissures shot up the stone walls. The ceiling began to crumble. Ryland swore. "Desdria's coming for us," he yelled. "We have to get out of here! Now!"

In a synchronized move honed by what Ryland would guess were hundreds of years of practice, the cloaked Order members picked up Thano and hoisted him onto Ryland's back. Ryland looked over at Catherine. "Come on! Get on!"

She shook her head. "There's no space. Get Thano out of here and then come back for me."

The earth shook again violently, and the ground split open beneath them. Catherine screamed as she and Lucy tumbled off the edge into the sudden crack in the foundation. Ryland dove after them instantly, tucking his wings as he shot straight downward. His riders dug their weapons into his scales to stay on board, but he didn't even feel the pain. All he could see was Lucy and Catherine plummeting away from him.

Below him, Cat's blond hair and Lucy's curls streamed out behind them as they fell into the crevasse. The little girl lifted her head and looked at him, and then she smiled, completely at peace, completely trusting this ugly monster to save her.

No fucking way was he going to let her down.

He put on a burst of speed, caught them gently in his claws, and then swooped through the crevasse. Below him, he could see swirling black clouds, and he thought he could hear the deep, rasping breaths of a monstrous creature. Then he was speeding back toward the top of the chasm. The crevasse was already closing above his head. Apollo was standing on the rim, staring down at them, his tail swishing madly, as if to will them on.

"Faster," Zach yelled. "It's closing!"

"I know!" Tucking Catherine and Lucy against his chest, Ryland summoned all the strength the beast could give him. They shot through the gap just as it closed, the walls brushing the tips of his wings. He burst out of the crevasse and launched himself toward the door, Apollo on his tail. Side by side, they tore through the nether-realm as that same dark smoke seemed to fill it. It was thick and noxious, and spilling right toward the entrance. "She's trying to trap us in here," he yelled. "She's closing off the connection between the earthly realm and the nether-realm." If she managed to shut it down, they would all be trapped for eternity.

"Wait!" Catherine shouted. "It's Dante! He's still lost. I can guide him out! Give me a second, and I can track him!"

For a split second, Ryland's wings slowed. "Dante?" Before he could even look around, an avalanche of rocks tumbled down from near the exit, a deafening roar of the ground capitulating to Desdria. Son of a bitch. He didn't have time to stop. He'd never get them out. Nine lives were counting on him right now. *Nine.* He could not betray them. He looked out across the vast expanse, as if he could see the soul of the man who'd saved him once. He could see nothing, but encroaching darkness. He could not stop for the man who had saved him. He had to make a choice, and he knew what it had to be. *Dante,* he said. *Forgive me.*

Something echoed through his mind, that same voice he'd missed so much. It was one word, one word that spoke so much. *Go.*

Ryland didn't hesitate. He just flew as hard as he could, trusting the team on his back to keep Thano alive. The smoke grew thicker, and thicker, rising fast. A race to freedom. A race to light.

Up ahead, he could see the exit. The light from the sun. Smoke obscuring it. It began to close, filling in from the smoke. "No!" he bellowed, launching himself at the barrier. He broke through it with violent force. Boulders and rocks exploded into the clearing as they burst through. One of them caught him in the side, knocking him off balance. He swore, fighting to stay straight as he crashed to the earth.

He landed hard, but managed to shift his body so that the precious cargo in his arms was protected. The men on his back stayed put, holding on as he skidded across the earth, cleaving a gash through the grassy terrain.

He jammed his claws into the ground, dragging himself to a stop.

The moment his forward movement ceased, the men on his back leapt off, all of them still maintaining contact with Thano. "He needs his soul back," the leader shouted. "Now!"

Catherine handed Lucy to Ryland and rushed off to Thano's side.

Stunned, Ryland looked down at the little girl he was holding in his arms. She smiled up at him, and something seemed to soften inside him. His beastly form melted away, leaving him as a man. Lucy's smile widened. "That's really cool. Will you teach me how to do that?"

He couldn't understand. "Aren't you afraid of me? Everyone

is afraid of me."

Her forehead puckered. "Why would anyone be afraid of you? You're an angel." Then she smiled and snuggled into his arms, as if he was the safest place in the world for her to be.

Which it was. He'd make damn certain of it.

Tucking her against his chest, he turned his attention toward the one other person left that he needed to help. Thano was on his back, his body ashen and gray, barely visible.

"It's too late," Catherine was whispering as she knelt beside him. "His body is too far gone. There's nothing for his soul to attach to."

"Never." With a pulse of focused determination, Ryland raced over to the group, tucking Lucy against his chest while he crouched beside Thano. He placed his hands on his teammate's chest, and instinctively summoned a golden light from the depths of his soul, that same golden light that the angel had used to save him so many centuries ago. An angel's gift that could be summoned once every thousand years and offered only to a worthy soul. Without hesitation, he thrust it into Thano, and the warrior's body jerked and flared into visibility. "Now, Catherine," he said calmly, continuing to hold Thano in the glow of the golden angel light, that same light he'd been seeking from others his whole life.

Catherine placed her hands on his chest and closed her eyes. He touched her mind, and could feel the warmth and love filling her as she guided Thano's soul back into his body. The moment that Thano's soul was restored, his body lurched. Ryland felt the rogue poison swirling inside the warrior, so he poured more golden light into him, trying to wipe away the destiny trying to take him.

Thano shuddered, and then he went still, slipping into a troubled state of unconsciousness, in a suspended state of peace that Ryland knew would not last long. Grimly, he looked up at the team, who were huddled around him. "This is my fault," he said. "I took his woman."

"Did you?" The leader of the cloaked Order met his gaze. "Are you so certain?"

Ryland stared at him, sensing that the man knew something he wasn't sharing. "What are you talking about?"

"You aren't pure Calydon. You couldn't bond with her on your own. You had to do it through him."

Ryland narrowed his eyes. "How do you know all this?"

"I am a seer."

Ryland's heart leapt. He hadn't met an oracle in hundreds of years, not since the one who had told him he would meet an angel of death. "What do you see?"

"You had it backwards, warrior."

"Backwards?" Ryland looked at Catherine, who looked as confused as he did. "What do you mean?"

The warrior stood. "We can heal this warrior, but there isn't much time. With your permission, we will take him with us."

Ryland stiffened. "It's my job to heal him."

"Then you know this is the right choice to entrust him to us."

Ryland studied the dark warrior, opening his mind to the other, who had lowered his own shields to allow Ryland access. Ryland sensed honor, loyalty, and a deep commitment to other Order members, similar to what defined his own team. There was more there too, things he couldn't quite tap into, but the warrior shut him out before he could process them. "What is your name?"

"Rohan." The warrior did not give a last name, and Ryland suspected that he did not have one to give. Not a man, not entirely.

"My name is Ryland Samuels," he said, introducing his team. He nodded at his injured teammate. "This is Thano Savakis. And Zach Roderick."

The cloaked warrior inclined his head once. "We will take Savakis with us."

Ryland gritted his teeth, but his instincts told him that Rohan's team was Thano's only chance. "Fine. Zach, go with him. I'll go back to our team and report in."

Zach stood up. "I'll protect him."

"I know you will." The two men exchanged looks, and then Zach turned away to help with Thano.

Apollo stood restlessly as the men set Thano on top of him, tying him down so he didn't fall off. With a nod that promised they'd be in touch, the group set off toward the woods with Thano. They made it to the edge of the clearing, there was a ripple in the air, and then they were gone, vanishing from sight as if by magic.

Ryland stared after them. So many questions. Who were they? How was there another Order? What did they protect? Why had they been guarding the entrance to the nether-realm?

"It's gone." Catherine's stunned whisper drew his attention back, and he followed her glance.

The entrance to the temple had collapsed. Gone were the archway, the pyres, and even the steps. In its place was simply earth and woods. Even the air was lighter. "She withdrew the nether-realm from this part of the earth." He reached down to sift through the soil. It was clean and pure, no longer tainted.

"Is she gone? Forever?" Catherine's voice was hopeful as she took Lucy back from him, the little girl chattering cheerfully about Thano's horse, showcasing the incredible resilience of children…and of the daughter of an angel.

"No. She'll be back." He couldn't stop thinking of the queen that both Desdria and Simon had mentioned. Who was she? Was there a being more powerful than the two of them that they were answering to? So many questions. "Not to the same place. Maybe not for a while, but she will be back." He sighed. "Somewhere in there is Dante. He's still trapped."

"Maybe."

Ryland looked down at Catherine, who had cocked her head, as if she were listening to secrets in the air. "I showed him the way out, and I felt him respond. I think he might have made it to freedom."

"Really?" Hope churned through him as he reached out with his mind. *Dante?*

There was no answer, but when Catherine slipped her hand in his, the loneliness and grief at Dante's absence didn't hit him as hard or deep anymore. He looked down at the two females, and he felt something in his heart lift. He wasn't alone anymore. "I'm still a monster," he said.

She smiled. "I know. I am too, in a way. I'll always need a steady diet of love, light and souls."

A slow, meaningful grin crept over his face. "I can help with all three." He wrapped his arms around Catherine and Lucy, pulling them against his chest. One tiny set of arms locked around his neck, and a longer, more delicate set joined them. Ryland bent his head, so that his lips were beside both their ears. "I love you," he whispered.

Lucy looked up at him. "Me? Or Mama?"

He grinned. "Both of you."

They weren't empty words. He knew what love was now, and he knew exactly what he was saying. He meant every damn word of it.

🐺 Chapter Nineteen 🐺

A FORTNIGHT LATER, Ryland paused just outside the front door of Dante's mansion. Lucy was asleep in his arms, and Catherine was standing wearily beside him. "This is it," he said. The headquarters of his team. It had been all that mattered to him for so long, but suddenly, he wasn't sure he wanted to go in.

After the last two weeks with Catherine and Lucy, trekking through the woods to head back home, suddenly the idea of reentering a world where he wasn't trusted, where he was almost reviled and barely tolerated seemed to be an empty existence.

He wasn't okay with it anymore.

The door opened, and Gideon Roarke walked out, his blond hair cropped short. He was wearing jeans and boots, his T-shirt actually clean, as it had been ever since he'd found his *sheva* and discovered how much better she liked it when he didn't smell like he'd been on a hunt for weeks and never heard of the concept of a shower. He stopped in surprise. "You're back? You didn't say you were coming."

"I know." Ryland waited, tensing as he prepared for the typical welcome he always received.

Gideon nodded approvingly at Catherine. "You found our angel." Then his brows went up as he registered the child asleep in Ryland's arms. "You found a girl, too."

Ryland tightened his grip on her. "Yeah. She's with me. They're both with me." He couldn't keep the defiance out of his voice. The challenge. He was grimly aware that Catherine still carried Thano's brand.

A slow smile spread over Gideon's face, and he grinned. "Well, damn, Ryland. You went and got yourself a *sheva*, didn't you? How in hell's name did you not go rogue? You, of all people, should have succumbed to that destiny." He turned and shouted over his shoulder. "You guys gotta see this!"

Ryland stiffened as boots thudded inside, and then he felt Catherine's hand slide into his. As she did so, he saw Gideon's eyes lock onto her arm and notice what brand she carried. He jerked his gaze off Catherine and looked past Ryland. "Where's Thano? And Zach?" His voice grew wary and suspicious. "What did you do?"

Quinn Masters appeared behind him, along with Gabe Watson. "You found her," Quinn said, sounding relieved. "Great bring her in—"

Gideon called out his two-sided axe with a crack and flash of black light that made everyone tense. "Where's Thano?"

Ryland stared at the team he'd defended for so long, disgust rolling through him. After dealing with their shit for his whole life, suddenly, he was tired of it. "That's all you see, isn't it? Thano's brand on my woman, and Thano missing? You think I murdered him to get his woman? Well, fuck that. I'm outta here." Keeping a secure hold on Catherine and Lucy, he turned and walked away, heading back down the driveway.

"Ryland?"

He looked over at Catherine, and he was surprised to see tears glistening in her eyes. The steel around his heart melted, and he immediately stopped. He shifted the sleeping child to his other shoulder and pulled Catherine to him. "What, angel? What's wrong?"

"They will never know the truth if you don't tell them. Trust goes both ways."

Ryland shook his head. "No. It doesn't—"

"It does." She stood up on her tiptoes and pressed her lips to his. It was such a beautiful and tender kiss, a treasure he never thought he would deserve. "I love you, Ryland. But the only reason I fell in love with you was because you allowed me to do so. You have to let them in as well."

He ran his fingers through her hair and held her tightly against him. "They're ugly bastards. I don't want *them* to love me."

She laughed, her eyes twinkling with merriment. "Of course you do." She put her hand on his chest, over his heart, over the face of the beast that was still brightly-colored but didn't own him. Both of their cuffs had disappeared when Simon had vanished, and they were free. His beast remained, but he owned it now. "You're so many things, Ryland. You're a warrior. You're brave enough to kill friends when you need to. You protect innocents. You bleed death and so many terrible things." She tapped her fingers on his chest. "But you're also an angel. A beautiful, pure angel who watches over this gang of warriors with all of his heart. You've always done it. Let them see who you really are." She entangled her fingers through his. "I'll be with you. You don't have to be afraid."

He glared at her. "I'm not afraid."

She smiled. "Fear makes us better people. It's okay. I won't tell anyone—"

"What did you do to Thano?" Gideon's low voice broke through their conversation.

Ryland dragged his gaze off Catherine's face to see that Quinn, Gideon, Gabe, and now Elijah had encircled him. Gideon was the only one who was armed, but he could feel the adrenaline humming from the others as they prepared to kill him, to deliver the blows they'd been expecting to have to do for centuries.

Catherine squeezed his hand. "Tell them."

Lucy suddenly lifted her head, her eyes sleepy. She smiled at him and laid her little hand on his whiskered jaw. "Papa? I need some food."

His throat went rigid. He couldn't breathe. He just stared at her. *Papa?* She'd just called him Papa? He looked at Catherine, and there were more tears glistening in her eyes. She nodded, confirming what he'd heard. *Papa?*

Sudden fierceness rushed through him. How could this tiny girl trust him when she had no reason to trust any man? He wasn't going to let her down. He absolutely wasn't. With a low growl, he slung his arm around Catherine and hauled her up against him. He glared at his teammates. "I'm the third fuckin—" He grimaced and covered Lucy's ears. "I'm the third angel of the trinity," he snapped. "I'm the good guy. So back the fu—" Shit. It was going to be really hard to be a good role model. "So, please, back off." Please. Had he really just said please? Yeah, he was pretty sure he had.

The four warriors were staring at him with absolute shock and disbelief on their faces.

It was Gideon who finally spoke. "What?"

"I am the third angel," he repeated, the words coming easier this time. "It's the way it is. Deal with it, or I'm moving on."

Again, just silence.

Catherine sighed. "You really need to work on the touchy-feely stuff, Ry. You're not very good at it."

He glanced at her. "Of course I'm not. I'm always going to be a cranky bastard—" He grimaced. "A cranky jerk. It's the way I am. They can deal with it or not—"

"Papa." Lucy sounded more insistent. "I'm hungry."

Ryland looked down at her and smiled. "Of course, sweet pea. Let's go get something to eat. Do you like donuts? We always have donuts here because these guys are a bunch of useless miscreants who don't even bother to cook decent meals. I bet we have chocolate frosted ones. Does that sound good?"

Lucy squealed and wriggled in his arms. "Yes, yes, yes! Let me go." Ryland set her down, then laughed as she went running fearlessly into the house. He grinned at Catherine. "She's amazing, isn't she?"

Catherine smiled. "She is."

"Let's go feed her." He took her hand and started up the driveway. He paused only long enough to shoot a hostile glare at the other men. "I decided I'm staying. You guys need help." Then without bothering to wait for a response, he took his family into the mansion, leaving his team standing in a shocked circle in the driveway.

✕✕✕✕

CATHERINE SIGHED WITH BOTH HAPPINESS and concern as she watched Ryland say his sixth goodnight to Lucy, tucking her into the king-sized bed that she had claimed for her own in the house made for huge warriors, not small children.

She couldn't believe the sparkle in his blue eyes, the sound of his laughter. It was so beautiful, and so incredible. But at the same time, there was a hollowness in his soul that had been there since they'd left the nether-realm.

"Let her sleep, Ryland," she told him. "She's okay."

"It's a new place," he said as he walked toward the door. Lucy had already rolled over and was breathing deeply, sound asleep. "I don't want her to be scared."

"She's not afraid," Catherine said, her heart warming to him even as she said the words. She knew Lucy had emerged so well from her ordeal because of the bond she had forged with Ryland. It was as if she had instantly realized that he would protect her, and his presence had given her the security she needed. Catherine was sure that once the shock had worn off, Lucy would struggle with what she had endured, but in these first stages of reentry, Ryland's protection had shielded her from the worst of it, and allowed her to reclaim herself.

Ryland's relationship with Lucy was beautiful, yet at the same time, it wasn't enough. Ryland had avoided his team all afternoon, using Lucy as an excuse, but the tension in the house was thick. Word had been sent to Ian and Alice, who would be returning in the morning. They would be bringing Dante's son Drew Cartland, a young, edgy Calydon who was with them doing some training in hopes of becoming an Order member. Catherine was so excited to see her dear friend, and to meet the other women who had bound themselves to the Order members. But first, she had to help the man she loved. "Ry."

He took her hand. "Hey." He kissed her lightly, but his reservation was clear. He hadn't made love to her once since they'd rescued Lucy. He'd said it was because Lucy was too nearby, but she knew it was more than that as well.

He was still laden with guilt over stealing Thano's woman, and absolutely refused to believe Catherine when she categorically denied she had ever felt anything romantic toward Thano, and when she tried to reassure him that she'd never sensed any interest from Thano either, prior to him going rogue. "Make love to me tonight."

He stiffened. "I think I should sleep in Lucy's room. In case she has nightmares."

Catherine sighed. "Ry—"

"We need to talk." Gideon loomed out of the darkness, his muscled bulk casting great shadows in the corridor. "To the living room. Now. Both of you." He didn't leave. He waited for Ryland to follow.

Ryland's face darkened, but he took Catherine's hand and headed down the hall. When they got there, Catherine was surprised to see the living room was full. Gideon, Elijah, Quinn and Gabe were there, plus one other warrior she didn't know. They were all spread out on the massive black leather couches. A glass coffee table was bold enough to stand in front of so many large, powerful warriors, and the muted beige walls were casting a soothing hue onto the room that she suspected might have been wasted on so much testosterone.

Sitting beside each warrior except Gabe was a woman. It was obvious from the intimacy between the couples that they were soul mates. They were all sitting close to their mate, and the men had a protective air about them, as if they were always on guard to make sure the women they loved were safe. It made her smile to see the body language that she'd become so familiar with from Ryland. These were all good men, honorable mates, warriors whose hearts beat with bravery and courage.

Kane Santiago is in the black leather jacket, Ryland explained to her. *His mate is Sarah Burns. They must have just arrived. Elijah is with Ana Mathews. Gideon is with Lily Davenport, and Quinn is next to Grace Mathews, Ana's sister.*

The women all carried brands on their arms that told Catherine exactly who they belonged to. Sudden envy cascaded through Catherine, and she wished it was Ryland's mark on her arm.

"Welcome," said one of the women cheerfully. She had long blond hair and green eyes full of wisdom and experience. Her hand was on Gideon's hip, as if needing to keep a little bit of contact between them. "My name is Lily Davenport. We're thrilled to meet you and have a little bit more estrogen in the house."

Catherine smiled, her heart warming for the genuine welcome she heard in Lily's voice. She hadn't belonged anywhere in so long, not since she'd murdered the angel enclave. But with Ryland by her side, she knew that together they could keep her from doing any harm. It would be safe for her to stay. "Thank you. I'm excited to be here."

"And another child in the house is wonderful." Sarah Burns, Kane's *sheva*, shifted her position, and Catherine saw that she was pregnant. "We're so happy that Ryland found you. I'm one of their angels," she said, her eyes sliding over to Ryland, her voice fading with the question Catherine knew they were all wondering. How was it possible that Ryland was the third part of the trinity?

The man in question stood at the head of the couch, not sitting down. "What do you want?" His voice was hostile and defensive, and immediately, the tension in the room rose.

Catherine put her hand on his arm. *Don't be an instigator, Ryland. They're your team.*

They think I murdered Thano. The bitterness of his tone was evident, his resentment that his team could suspect him of something that was so far from who he was.

It was Gideon who spoke again. "Tell us what happened. Where's Thano? Where's Zach?"

Ryland's eyes glittered. "You don't trust me."

"Come on, Ryland!" Gideon stood up. "What's your problem? Two of our warriors are missing, and you won't talk, except to tell us that you're the third angel in our trinity. What the hell else are we supposed to think? What's going on?"

Ryland's eyes glittered, but they stayed blue. She felt the distrust rolling off his team, the expectation that they would need to strike him down at any second. Ryland was ready for their attack, his fists bunched in preparation for battle. The men were being so stupid! They didn't need a guardian angel. They needed a mediator.

With a sigh of frustration, she stepped forward. "Ryland didn't murder Thano, for heaven's sake. You all know that. Stop being thick-headed cretins and see the man who has been a part of your team for so long! He's rude and cranky, but by God, he's got the biggest heart of any of you! Didn't any of you notice his blue eyes? Even those have changed!"

The room went silent, but Lily raised her eyebrows and gave a silent nod of approval.

For a long moment, no one moved, but she saw the men looking curiously at Ryland's face, their brows furrowing when they noticed that his eyes were no longer black. Honestly, did they have no sense of what was important? How could they not have noticed his eyes were blue?

"They're men," Lily said with a smile. "They don't notice things like that. We love them anyway."

Catherine blinked at Lily's affectionate tone. So tolerant and understanding of how these men were. Slowly, her frustration began to ease just as Kane started to laugh softly.

She looked over at him, and he was shaking his head in amused disbelief. "You think Ryland has a big heart, do you?"

Catherine glared at him. "You know he does—" She stopped suddenly, shocked by the wave of energy coming off Kane. "You're a demon. And an angel. Some of both."

"I am." Kane's smile disappeared and he looked at Ryland. "Like you, mate?"

Ryland met his gaze, and she saw something pass between them. An understanding. She knew in that moment, that the two men had just accepted a similarity between them. Part darkness. Part angel.

Kane nodded slowly, all amusement gone from his face. "Let him talk," Kane said quietly. "I can sense it. The bastard really is an angel."

There was a shift in the room, and then she saw Ryland raise his gaze from Kane's to look around. The men were looking at each other, but she saw their muscles relax. They believed him. Could Ryland feel the difference?

She looked over at him and saw his brow furrowed. Her heart softened, and she took his hand. "Ryland, Thano, and Zach caught up to me just outside the nether-realm," she began, deciding to spare him the need to defend himself. "Ryland wanted to find Dante, and I needed help to retrieve my daughter. We agreed to go in together—"

"No." Ryland interrupted her. "Let me." And then, for what she was sure was the first time in his entire life, Ryland began to explain who he truly was. "I was born...or created...or whatever you want to call it...in the nether-realm," he began slowly, looking warily around the room as if assessing the reaction.

No one moved or tried to stop him, or leapt up with a battle cry and a weapon.

He kept going. "I wasn't a Calydon. I was a monster, and my job was to kill innocents. When Dante freed me, he somehow gave me many of the powers of being a Calydon, but I'm not really one. Not by birth, anyway. I'm not really one of you. Not completely." He paused again, as if giving them a chance to attack him now that they knew the truth.

But they didn't.

Gideon simply sat back down, and everyone in the room leaned forward to listen. Ryland glanced at her, and she smiled. *Go ahead*, she said. *They're ready to hear your story.*

He enfolded her hand in his and walked farther into the room, taking her with him as he finally began to talk, lowering the walls that he'd carried for so long and letting them in. As he spoke, his voice changed from hard and bitter to something more soft and human. More open. More kind. He would never win a prize for being the world's most gentle man, but that was okay. He didn't need to be. He simply needed to be himself, which she suspected he hadn't been since the day Marie had died and he'd become enslaved.

As he sat down on the couch, still talking, answering questions from his team without resentment, Catherine knew she was watching the emergence of the man he truly was, the one he was meant to be. For the first time in his life, Ryland was finally allowing himself to be a part of this group. His teammates were listening with rapt attention, and the discussion was lively as they all discussed the implications of the queen and what Desdria would be up to next. Lily was already on her computer researching information about the cloaked Order members, and Gabe and Elijah had already decided to track them down and find Thano and Zach.

It was pure male bonding. It was obvious that, despite Ryland's edginess and surliness, they had always considered him part of the team, and they still did. The difference was that now, Ryland was seeing it for himself. He was finally becoming the Calydon he had never let himself be. It had taken him realizing he was their guardian angel for him to finally let himself accept how closely he was connected with them, but he had finally done it. She knew she was watching the merging of Ryland with the destiny he was supposed to have. He had never been a true Calydon before, but he was one now.

As she thought the words, she felt her arms begin to burn. She looked down, and to her shock, she saw the brands on her arms shifting, moving. Lines stretched and contracted, straightened and bent. As she watched, Thano's halberds disappeared, and Ryland's machete began to form. "Ryland," she whispered. "Look."

He glanced over at her, then his face went white with shock. He was beside her in an instant, his hand trembling as he clasped her wrist. "I don't understand," he whispered, going down on one knee as his brand took full form on her arm. He looked up at her. "Does that mean Thano's dead?" Guilt tore through him, his eyes haunted.

Catherine shook her head. "I can't sense his soul. He is still alive." Her blood bond with Ryland tied her closely enough with Thano that she knew his soul and could tell it was still with his body. "He's okay."

"Ryland." Elijah spoke from across the room, and they all looked over at him. "Do you remember how Ezekiel was able to bond with Ana through my blood bond with him?"

"Yeah." Ryland's fingers tightened on her arm. "So?"

"So, it was his bond that was happening through me."

"Yeah, like Thano's bond that was happening through me."

"Or maybe it was your bond that was happening through Thano."

The room was silent as Elijah's words settled, and suddenly it all made sense to Catherine. Elation flooding her heart, she knelt in front of Ryland, holding his hands to her chest. "Don't you understand, Ry? You couldn't bond with me yourself because you weren't fully accessing your Calydon side. But you had a blood bond with Thano, so you were able to use his Calydon powers to bond, like that cloaked warrior said." She smiled at his stunned look. "It was always *your* bond with me, but I couldn't carry your mark because you were holding back from who you were. Until now. Until this moment, when you finally claimed your heritage as a Calydon. That's why I can carry your mark now. You've always been the one for me, Ryland. Always."

He looked at her, and her heart seemed to melt at the awe on his face. "You're really mine?"

"Of course I am." She framed his face with her hands and kissed him.

And this time, when he kissed her back, there was nothing between them. Nothing but love. Ryland, the monster, had finally found his peace. She knew he would never be touchy-feely, and he'd always butt heads with his team, but that was okay.

She was an angel of death. It took a certain kind of man to put up with her, and she'd found just the guy.

I love you, Catherine.

She smiled. *I know. It's about time.*

And there's one more thing.

She looked over at him, and her belly tightened at the sudden heat in his eyes. *What's that?*

Now that I know you were never meant to be Thano's, you're not going to escape me anymore. Tonight, when we finally ditch these guys, I'm going to take you upstairs and make love to you until we incinerate the damned mattress. And then I'm going to do it again.

And with those beautiful words, the last of the emptiness finally left her, gone forever, chased away by the man she'd been waiting for. She grinned. *Okay.*

He raised his brows. *Okay? That's all I get? Okay? How about something like 'I've been lusting after you so badly for weeks, I want you to just ditch the meeting, throw me over your shoulder and do it now. If you make me wait one more second to feel your body against mine, I will set fire to your house and punish you for centuries.' That would get my attention. I think you should say that instead of 'Okay.'*

She laughed aloud at his remark, and then leaned forward. *Is that really appropriate to say to an angel?*

His eyes darkened. *Of course not.*

She smiled, unable to keep the wicked gleam out of her eyes. *Then you better call me Cat.*

And with that, Ryland lurched to his feet. "I gotta go, guys. Cat needs me." Then, without even bothering to look back at his team, he scooped her up, tossed her over his shoulder, and headed out of the room.

Heat suffused her cheeks as she braced her hands on his lower back and looked back at the team, unable to hide her giggles. They were all laughing, a knowing and somewhat smug look on all their faces, as if they were thoroughly enjoying the fact that Ryland was whipped. They got it, which was a relief. But at the same time... carting her off in the middle of a meeting? *Put me down, Ryland. This is completely embarrassing.*

You think I care what anyone else thinks? I need you, Cat. Now.

Her heart softened at the desperate edge to his voice. *You're impossible, Ry.*

His arm tightened around her thighs. *You better believe it, baby, and I'm never going to get any easier.*

She grinned. *That's exactly how I like it.*

You mean love it?

Her heart filled. *Yes, I mean love it.* And she did.

SNEAK PEEK: INFERNO OF DARKNESS

THE ORDER OF THE BLADE, BOOK EIGHT (NOVELLA)
AVAILABLE NOVEMBER 2013

In the beginning, many centuries ago…

He wanted her.

There was no way for Dante to deny his response to the whispered warning she had sent dancing along the breeze to him. He had no idea who she was, or what she looked like, but her voice was like the harmony of early morning, the whisper of new leaves brushing against the dew, the delicateness of flower blossoms coming to life. The energy of her words spun through him with restless temptation, prying him from his dark thoughts about Louis and the bloodbath he'd left behind.

In his world, craving a woman this intensely was a very, *very* dangerous thing.

He wanted to race toward her.

He wanted to rip aside the canopy of leaves shielding her from his sight.

He wanted to find her, to claim her, to consume her.

So, instead, he stopped and went completely still. He reached out with his preternatural senses, searching the landscape ahead. The mountain was ominously tall. Turbulent dark clouds coated the sky above him, but it wasn't enough to block her. He caught the faint scent of woman, pure and delicate, and his gut clenched in response. But still, he didn't move. Instead, he carefully located the pulsing energy of the sword she was guarding. She was between him and the sword, an obstacle that he had to pass in order to retrieve the weapon.

Testing her, he turned left, circling around behind her. As he moved, she shifted, keeping herself between him and the sword. She could sense him? Was her awareness of him as intense as his awareness of her?

He looked down at the protective symbols on his arms and saw they were still blazing. As long as they were visible, the *sheva* bond could not affect him. No woman could be his soulmate. He was still safe from that fate...but if that was the case, why was he reacting to her so intensely? He had no time for women. He had no time for seduction. He was never distracted from what he had to do.

So, what the hell was going on with her?

He had no time to play games any longer. He needed that sword, and he needed it now, which meant he had to get past her. He was tempted to call out his spears, but he didn't. Never would there come a day when he approached a woman armed. Ever.

So, instead, he straightened up, fisted his hands, and strode right through the undulating shadows toward her.

His feet were silent on the forest floor, and the leaves moved out of his way as he walked, responding to his silent request for passage, as they always did. Ahead of him, he could see that the trees thinned, and he knew he was approaching a clearing.

His weapons still burning in his arms, responding to the risk she presented, Dante stepped forward through the last of the foliage and into the open, exposed area.

He didn't see her.

Disappointment surged through him as he quickly scanned the vicinity. Trees stood tall above him, their branches long and spindly, tangling into each other, weaving a canopy that protected this area from the rest of the world. Sparse grass clung to barren dirt. Ancient rocks lay battered, half-submerged in the weary ground. He could sense the suffering of this place, of the people who had once lived and died in this clearing. So much to tell him, and yet the one thing he wanted to know more about was hidden. He saw no sign of her, but her presence was strong, a vibrating energy of light and dark. "Show yourself," he commanded.

Again, no response. Not even another whispered reply on the wind.

Awareness still prickling on his neck, he walked further into the clearing, reaching out with his senses, searching for a ripple in the atmosphere that would reveal her location. Out into each direction he sent queries, and then he found her. A block in the transference of energy, a shield of sorts, in the northwest end of the clearing.

He turned toward it, his hands still flexing. Behind her, he could feel the sword's energy calling to him, more intensely than ever before. The urge to respond to its summons was thundering through him, almost impossible to resist, but he refused to acknowledge it. This woman, this mysterious woman who was guarding it, this sensual temptation of danger...she was what he needed to deal with first.

He kept his gaze riveted on the swirl of feminine energy that he'd located. He couldn't see her, but he knew she was there. "I am going to take the sword," he said.

"No." Her voice was clear, a shot to his gut with the raw intensity of it. It wasn't simply feminine, it was powerful and strong, rich with sensuality. "Walk away."

"It's been calling to me." He took a step closer, and felt a sudden burst of wind slam against his chest, as if she'd shoved the air at him as a warning. Could she manipulate air? He'd never heard of that. "The sword wants me to retrieve it."

"Do not touch it." As the words filled the air, a faint mist began to glisten in the location he was watching, like millions of dew droplets in the first rays of morning light.

Adrenaline and anticipation roared through him, and he was riveted by the rainbow-colored prisms as they glittered and sparkled, becoming less transparent. Then he saw her face beginning to take shape. An incredible, vibrant turquoise began to glow as it slid into the shape of her nose, a delicate slope of pure femininity. Smooth cheeks of perfection, the sensual curve of her jaw, parted lips. Her hair began to appear, tumbling down around her in violet and turquoise cascades of thick curls. And then her eyes. Dante stood, transfixed, as her eyes appeared, vibrant blue pools flanked with long, thick lashes, watching him intently.

Her body began to manifest. Long, delicate arms, a mystical dress clinging to her body, showing small breasts of surreal temptation, hips that bled into lean legs, bare feet that seemed to fade right into the grassy tufts by her toes.

"What are you?" he asked, his voice gruffer than he'd intended.

"I don't exist here." There was a sudden shimmer, as if a thousand prisms had shifted position, and then she was standing before him, fully corporeal, with flesh as human as his. Her cascade of colors shifted into a rich, decadent shower of brown curls, and an endless temptation of flesh so pale it looked as though it had never seen the sun. But her eyes were the same, a vibrant, iridescent symphony of violet, rich blue, and enchantment.

Stunned, he closed the distance between them, compelled by

the need to touch her. To see if she was real. She lifted her chin regally as he neared. She did not retreat, but her muscles tensed, and a ripple of fear echoed through the air.

He stopped a mere foot from her and raised his hand. Gently, almost afraid that he would shatter the mirage, he brushed his fingers ever so lightly over the ends of her curls. Silken strands glided through his fingers, the softest sensation he'd ever experienced. She closed her eyes and went utterly still, as if drinking in his touch with every ounce of her being.

"You do exist here," he said softly, forcing himself to drop his hand, trying to shield himself against the depth of his urge to slide his hand down her arm, to feel the warmth of her skin against his. Again, he looked down at his protective markings and saw they were still blazing as black as they had the first time he'd finally succeeded in manifesting them. This wasn't a sheva compulsion. It couldn't be. So what was it?

She opened her eyes, and he saw that they had darkened into deep blue, though they still had the glittery sparkles in them. "You are worthy," she said softly. "I can feel your strength, your capability. The sword has chosen well. Too well," she added, the regret obvious in her voice.

Dante had no idea what the hell was going on, not with the sword that had been summoning him, not with this woman who had manifested from a glittery mist, and not with his own burning desire for her. Swords, he understood. All this? No, but he was going to figure it out, and fast. "My name is Dante Sinclair. I'm the leader of the Order of the Blade." He did not add that he was the only one left of a decimated Order. The last Calydon alive who had a chance to save the earth from the rogues. "Who are you?"

"Dante Sinclair," she repeated, sending warmth spiraling through him as she said his name. She made it sound poetic, like a great gift offered to the very earth upon which they stood. She gave a low curtsy. "My name is Elisha, daughter of the Queen of Darkness. Soon to be consort to the master Adrian."

Dante went cold at her words. "Consort?" That one word had chased every other bit of information she'd offered out of his mind. "What does that mean?"

She rose to her feet, and something flickered in her eyes, something he couldn't decipher, but she definitely had reacted to his fury about her becoming some guy's consort.

She raised her hand and brushed her fingers over his cheek.

"Your anger at my words is beautiful." Her touch was like silk, like the whisper of a new dawn across his skin. Without speaking, he laid his hand over hers, pressing her palm to his face. Her hand was cool, drifting through his body like the cleansing rain of a raging summer storm.

Her gaze went to his. "You have freedom here, in the earth realm. I can sense it about you. Your heart—" She laid her other hand on his chest, moving even closer to him. "—it beats differently than mine. I can feel its freedom. It's like the purest magic, born of innocence and honor." A sense of awe appeared on her face, and Dante felt his world begin to close in on him as he tumbled into her spell.

Unbidden, his hand slid to the back of her neck. He needed to touch her. To kiss her. To claim her. To make her his.

Her eyes widened, and she froze, going utterly still. "No," she whispered. "This cannot be."

"Just like how you don't exist in the earth realm?" He bent his head, his lips hovering a breath from hers. "Because you do exist. And this can be, because it's happening right now."

"No!" A gust of wind suddenly slammed into his chest and thrust him backwards. He landed ten feet away, on his ass, a pawn in the grasp of her power.

Damn. That was impressive. With a groan that he didn't mean to let slip, he vaulted back to his feet, disgusted that he'd let his need for her dictate his actions. Had he really just considered seducing her when his last hope for the rebuilding of the Order lay dead, only half a day's run from here? Shit. He lowered his head, studying her more carefully. The power of a woman. A princess? What in the hell was going on? "Who is the Queen of Darkness? And what realm are you from, if you're not from the earth realm?"

Elisha was facing him, her hands dangling loosely by her sides, her gaze blazing. "You must leave," she said urgently. "You must."

There was no chance of that. "Where is the sword from, Elisha?" He began to walk toward her again, but this time, it wasn't about seduction. It was about his mission, his job, his calling. "How is it calling me?"

"No." Once again, she sent air at him, pushing him backwards, but this time he was ready.

He simply braced himself and shoved forward, cutting through the invisible wall.

Her face tightened with fear. "Halt!" she commanded, with the imperious force of the royalty she'd claimed to be.

He stopped. "Tell me why." She was soon going to be some man's consort? Really? *Shit.* Why was he thinking about *that* when he was facing down an enemy? He schooled his thoughts away from seduction, desire, and temptation, and faced the princess. "Tell me what's going on."

Sneak Peek: DARKNESS AWAKENED

The Order of the Blade, Book One
Available Now

Quinn Masters raced soundlessly through the thick woods, his injuries long forgotten, urgency coursing through him as he neared his house. He covered the last thirty yards, leapt over a fallen tree, then reached the edge of the clearing by his cabin.

There she was.

He stopped dead, fading back into the trees as he stared at the woman he'd scented when he was still two hours away, a lure that had eviscerated all weakness from his body and fueled him into a dead sprint back to his house.

His lungs heaving with the effort of pushing his severely damaged body so hard, Quinn stood rigidly as he studied the woman whose scent had called to him through the dark night. She'd yanked him out of his thoughts about Elijah and galvanized him with energy he hadn't been able to summon on his own.

And now he'd found her.

She'd wedged herself up against the back corner of his porch, barely protected from the cold rain and wet wind. Her knees were pulled up against her chest, her delicate arms wrapped tightly around them as if she could hold onto her body heat by sheer force of will. Her shoulders were hunched, her forehead pressed against her knees while damp tangles of dark brown hair tumbled over her arms.

Her chest moved once. Twice. A trembling, aching breath into lungs that were too cold and too exhausted to work as well as they should.

He took a step toward her, and then another, three more before he realized what he was doing. He froze, suddenly aware of his urgent need to get to her. To help her. To fill her with heat and breathe safety into her trembling body. To whisk her off his porch and into his cabin.

Into his bed.

Quinn stiffened at the thought. Into his bed? Since when? He didn't engage when it came to women. The risk was too high, for him, and for all Calydons. Any woman he met could be his mate, his fate, his doom. His sheva.

He was never tempted.

Until now.

Until this cold, vulnerable stranger had appeared inexplicably on his doorstep. He should be pulling out his sword, not thinking that the fastest way to get her warm would be to run his hands over her bare skin and infuse her whole body with the heat from his.

But his sword remained quiet. His instincts warned him of nothing.

What the hell was going on? She had to be a threat. Nothing else made sense. Women didn't stumble onto his home, and he didn't get a hard-on from simply catching a whiff of one from miles away.

His trembling quads braced against the cold air, he inhaled her scent again, searching for answers to a thousand questions. She smelled delicate, with a hint of something sweet, and a flavoring of the bitterness of true desperation. He could practically taste her anguish, a cold, acrid weight in the air, and he knew she was in trouble.

His hands flexed with the need to close the distance between them, to crouch by her side, to give her his protection. But he didn't move. He didn't dare. He had to figure out why he was so compelled by her, why he was responding like this, especially at a time when he couldn't afford any kind of a distraction.

She moaned softly and curled into an even tighter ball. His muscles tightened, his entire soul burning with the need to help her. Quinn narrowed his eyes and pried his gaze off her to search the woods.

With the life of his blood brother in his hands, with an Order posse soon to be after him, with his own body still recovering from Elijah's assault, it made no sense that Quinn had even noticed the scent of this woman, let alone be consumed by her.

His intense need for her felt too similar to the compulsion that had sent him to the river three nights ago. Another trap? He'd suspected it from the moment he'd first reacted to her scent, but he'd been unable to resist the temptation, and he'd hauled ass to get back to his house. Yeah, true, he'd also needed to get back to his cabin to retrieve his supplies to go after Elijah. The fact she'd imbued him with new strength had been a bonus he wasn't going to deny.

But now he had to be sure. A trap or not? Quinn laughed softly. Shit. He hoped it was. If it wasn't, there was only one other reason he could think of to explain his reaction to her, and that would be if she was his mate. His *sheva*. His ticket to certain destruction.

No chance.

He wouldn't allow it.

He had no time for dealing with that destiny right now. It was time to get in, get out, and go after Elijah. His amusement faded as he took a final survey of the woods. There was no lurking threat he could detect. Maybe he'd made it back before he'd been expected, or maybe an ambush had been aborted.

Either way, he had to get into his house, get his stuff, and move on. His gaze returned to the woman, and he noticed a drop of water sliding down the side of her neck, trickling over her skin like the most seductive of caresses. He swore, realizing she wasn't going to leave. She'd freeze to death before she'd abandon her perch.

He cursed and knew he had to go to her. He couldn't let her die on his front step. Not this woman. Not her.

He would make it fast, he would make it efficient, he would stay on target for his mission, but he would get her safe.

Keeping alert for any indication that this was a setup, Quinn stepped out of the woods and into the clearing. He'd made no sound, not even a whisper of his clothing, and yet she sensed him.

She sat up, her gaze finding him instantly in the dim light, despite his stealthy approach. They made eye contact, and the world seemed to stop for a split second. The moment he saw those silvery eyes, something thumped in his chest. Something visceral and male howled inside him, raging to be set free.

As he strode up, she unfolded herself from her cramped position and pulled herself to her feet, her gaze never leaving his. Her face was wary, her body tense, but she lifted her chin ever so slightly and set her hands on her hips, telling him that she wasn't leaving.

Her courage and determination, held together by that tiny, shivering frame, made satisfaction thud through him. There was a warrior in that slim, exhausted body.

She said nothing as he approached, and neither of them spoke as he came to a stop in front of her.

Up close, he was riveted. Her dark eyelashes were clumped from the rain. Her skin was pale, too pale. Her face was carrying the burden of a thousand weights. But beneath that pain, those nightmares, that hell, lay delicate femininity that called to him. The luminescent glow of her skin, the sensual curve of her mouth, the sheen of rain on her cheekbones, the simple silver hoops in her ears. It awoke in him something so male, so carnal, so primal he wanted to throw her up against the wall and consume her until their bodies were melted together in single, scorching fire.

She searched his face with the same intensity raging through him, and he felt like she was tearing through his shields, cataloguing everything about him, all the way down to his soul.

He studied her carefully, and she let him, not flinching when his gaze traveled down her body. His blood pulsed as he noted the curve of her breasts under her rain-slicked jacket, the sensuous curve of her hips, and even the mud on her jeans and boots. He almost groaned at his need to palm her hips, drag her over to him, and mark her with his kiss. Loose strands of thick dark hair had escaped from her ponytail, curling around her neck and shoulders like it was clinging to her for safety.

Protectiveness surged from deep inside him and he clenched his fists against his urge to sweep her into his arms and carry her inside, away from whatever hardship had brought her to his doorstep.

Double hell. He'd hoped his reaction would lessen when he got close to her, but it had intensified. He'd never felt like this before. Never had this response to a woman.

What the hell was going on? *Sheva.* The word was like a demon, whispering through his mind. He shut it out. He would never allow himself to bond with his mate. If that was what was going on, she was out of there immediately, before they were both destroyed forever.

Intent on sending her away, he looked again at her face, and then realized he was done. Her beautiful silver eyes were aching with a soul-deep pain that shattered what little defenses he had against her. He simply couldn't abandon her.

It didn't matter what she wanted. It didn't matter why she was there. She was coming inside. He would make sure it didn't interfere with his mission. He would make dead sure it turned out right. No matter what.

Without a word, he grabbed her backpack off the floor, surprised at how heavy it was. Either she had tossed her free weights in it, or she had packed her life into it.

He had a bad feeling it wasn't a set of dumb bells.

Quinn walked past her and unlocked his front door. He shoved it open, then stood back. Letting her decide. Hoping she would walk away and spare them both.

She took a deep breath, glanced at his face one more time, then walked into the cabin.

Hell.

He paused to take one more survey of his woods, found nothing amiss, and then he followed her into his home and shut the door behind them.

SNEAK PEEK: ICE

ALASKA HEAT, BOOK ONE
AVAILABLE NOW

Kaylie's hands were shaking as she rifled through her bag, searching for her yoga pants. She needed the low-slung black ones with a light pink stripe down the side. The cuffs were frayed from too many wearings to the grocery store late at night for comfort food, and they were her go-to clothes when she couldn't cope. Like now.

She couldn't find them.

"Come on!" Kaylie grabbed her other suitcase and dug through it, but they weren't there. "Stupid pants! I can't—" A sob caught at her throat and she pressed her palms to her eyes, trying to stifle the swell of grief. "Sara—"

Her voice was a raw moan of pain, and she sank to the thick shag carpet. She bent over as waves of pain, of loneliness, of utter grief shackled her. For her parents, her brother, her family and now Sara—

Dear God, she was all alone.

"Dammit, Kaylie! Get up!" she chided herself. She wrenched herself to her feet. "I can do this." She grabbed a pair of jeans and a silk blouse off the top of her bag and turned toward the bathroom. One step at a time. A shower would make her feel better.

She walked into the tiny bathroom, barely noticing the heavy wood door as she stepped inside and flicked the light switch. Two bare light bulbs flared over her head, showing a rustic bathroom with an ancient footed tub and a raw wood vanity with a battered porcelain sink. A tiny round window was on her right. It was small enough to keep out the worst of the cold, but big enough to let in some light and breeze in the summer.

She was in Alaska, for sure. God, what was she doing here?

Kaylie tossed the clean clothes on the sink and unzipped her jacket, dropping it on the floor. She tugged all her layers off, including the light blue sweater that had felt so safe this morning when she'd put it on. She stared grimly at her black lace bra, so utterly feminine, exactly the kind of bra that her mother had always considered frivolous and completely impractical. Which it was. Which was why that was the only style Kaylie ever wore.

She should never have come to Alaska. She didn't belong here. She couldn't handle this. Kaylie gripped the edge of the sink. Her hands dug into the wood as she fought against the urge to curl into a ball and cry.

After a minute, Kaylie lifted her head and looked at herself in the mirror. Her eyes were wide and scared, with dark circles beneath. Her hair was tangled and flattened from her wool hat. There was dirt caked on her cheeks.

Kaylie rubbed her hand over her chin, and the streaks of mud didn't come off.

She tried again, then realized she had smudges all over her neck. She turned on the water, and wet her hands...and saw her hands were covered as well.

Stunned, Kaylie stared as the water ran over her hands, turning pink as it swirled in the basin.

Not dirt.

Sara's blood.

"Oh, God." Kaylie grabbed a bar of soap and began to scrub her hands. But the blood was dried, stuck to her skin. "Get off!" She rubbed frantically, but the blackened crust wouldn't come off. Her lungs constricted and she couldn't breathe. "I can't—"

The door slammed open, and Cort stood behind her, wearing a T-shirt and jeans.

The tears burst free at the sight of Cort, and Kaylie held up her hands to him. "I can't get it off—"

"I got it." Cort took her hands and held them under the water, his grip warm and strong. "Take a deep breath, Kaylie. It's okay."

"It's not. It won't be." She leaned her head against his shoulder, closing her eyes as he washed her hands roughly and efficiently. His muscles flexed beneath her cheek, his skin hot through his shirt. Warm. Alive. "Sara's dead," she whispered. "My parents. My brother. They're all gone. The blood—" Sobs broke free again, and she couldn't stop the trembling.

"I know. I know, babe." He pulled her hands out from under the water and grabbed a washcloth. He turned her toward him and began to wash her face and neck.

His eyes were troubled, his mouth grim. But his hands were gentle where he touched her, gently holding her face still while he scrubbed. His gaze flicked toward hers, and he held contact for a moment, making her want to fall into those brown depths and forget everything. To simply disappear into the energy that was him. "You have to let them go," he said. "There's nothing you can do to bring them back—"

"No." A deep ache pounded at Kaylie's chest and her legs felt like they were too weak to support her. "I can't. Did you see Sara? And Jackson? His throat—" She bent over, clutching her stomach. "I—"

Cort's arms were suddenly around her, warm and strong, pulling her against his solid body. Kaylie fell into him, the sobs coming hard, the memories—

"I know." Cort's whisper was soft, his hand in her hair, crushing her against him. "It sucks. Goddamn, it sucks."

Kaylie heard his grief in the raw tone of his voice and realized his body was shaking as well. She looked up and saw a rim of red around his eyes, shadows in the hollows of his whiskered cheeks. "You know," she whispered, knowing with absolute certainty that he did. He understood the grief consuming her.

"Yeah." He cupped her face, staring down at her, his grip so tight it was almost as desperate as she felt. She could feel his heart beating against her nearly bare breasts, the rise of his chest as he breathed, the heat of his body warming the deathly chill from hers.

For the first time in forever, she suddenly didn't feel quite as alone.

In her suffering, she had company. Someone who knew. Who understood. Who shared her pain. It had been so long since the dark cavern surrounding her heart had lessened, since she hadn't felt consumed by the loneliness, but with Cort holding her...there was a flicker of light in the darkness trying to take her. "Cort—"

He cleared his throat. "I gotta go check the chili." He dropped his hands from her face and stood up to go, pulling away from her.

Without his touch, the air felt cold and the anguish returned full force. Kaylie caught his arm. "Don't go—" She stopped, not sure what to say, what to ask for. All she knew was that she didn't want him to leave, and she didn't want him to stop holding her.

Cort turned back to her, and a muscle ticked in his cheek.

For a moment, they simply stared at each other. She raised her arms. "Hold me," she whispered. "Please."

He hesitated for a second, and then his hand snaked out and he shackled her wrist. He yanked once, and she tumbled into him. Their bodies smacked hard as he caught her around the waist, his hands hot on her bare back.

She threw her arms around his neck and sagged into him. He wrapped his arms around her, holding her tightly against him. With only her bra and his T-shirt between them, the heat of his body was like a furnace, numbing her pain. His name slipped out in a whisper, and she pressed her cheek against his chest. She focused on his masculine scent. She took solace in the feel of another human's touch, in the safety of being held in arms powerful enough to ward off the grief trying to overtake her.

His hand tunneled in her hair, and he buried his face in the curve of her neck, his body shaking against hers.

"Cort—" She started to lift her head to look at him, to see if he was crying, but he tightened his grip on her head, forcing her face back to his chest, refusing to allow her to look at him.

Keeping her out.

Isolating her.

She realized he wasn't a partner in her grief. She was alone, still alone, always alone.

All the anguish came cascading back. Raw loneliness surged again, and she shoved away from him as sobs tore at her throat. She couldn't deal with being held by him when the sense of intimacy was nothing but an illusion. "Leave me alone."

Kaylie whirled away from him, keeping her head ducked. She didn't want to look at him. She needed space to find her equilibrium again and rebuild her foundation.

"Damn it, Kaylie." Cort grabbed her arm and spun her back toward him.

She held up her hands to block him, her vision blurred by the tears streaming down her face. "Don't—"

His arms snapped around her and he hauled her against him even as she fought his grip. "No! Leave me alone—"

His mouth descended on hers.

Not a gentle kiss.

A kiss of desperation and grief and need. Of the need to control something. Of raw human passion for life, for death, for the touch of another human being.

And it broke her.

Sneak Peek: NO KNIGHT NEEDED

Ever After, Book One
Available Now

Ducking her head against the raging storm, Clare hugged herself while she watched the huge black pickup truck turn its headlights onto the steep hillside. She was freezing, and her muscles wouldn't stop shaking. She was so worried about Katie, she could barely think, and she had no idea what this stranger was going to do. Something. Anything. *Please.*

The truck lurched toward the hill, and she realized suddenly that he was going to drive straight up the embankment in an attempt to go above the roots and around the fallen tree that was blocking the road. But that was crazy! The mountain was way too steep. He was going to flip his truck!

Memories assaulted her, visions of when her husband had died, and she screamed, racing toward him and waving her arms. "No, don't! Stop!"

But the truck plowed up the side of the hill, its wheels spewing mud as it fought for traction in the rain-soaked earth. She stopped, horror recoiling through her as the truck turned and skidded parallel across the hill, the left side of his truck reaching far too high up the slippery slope. Her stomach retched as she saw the truck tip further and further.

The truck was at such an extreme angle, she could see the roof now. A feathered angel was painted beneath the flood lights. An angel? What was a man like him doing with an angel on his truck?

The truck was almost vertical now. There was no way it could stay upright. It was going to flip. Crash into the tree. Careen across the road. Catapult off the cliff. He would die right in front of her. Oh, God, *he would die.*

But somehow, by a miracle that she couldn't comprehend, the truck kept struggling forward, all four wheels still gripping the earth.

The truck was above the roots now. Was he going to make it? *Please let him make it*—

The wheels slipped, and the truck dropped several yards down toward the roots. "No!" She took a useless, powerless step as the tires caught on the roots. The tires spun out in the mud, and the roots ripped across the side of the vehicle with a furious scream.

"Go," she shouted, clenching her firsts. "Go!"

He gunned the engine, and suddenly the tires caught. The truck leapt forward, careening sideways across the hill, skidding back and forth as the mud spewed. He made it past the tree, and then the truck plowed back down toward the road, sliding and rolling as he fought for control.

Clare held her hand over her mouth, terrified that at any moment one of his tires would catch on a root and he'd flip. "Please make it, please make it, please make it," she whispered over and over again.

The truck bounced high over a gully, and she gasped when it flew up so high she could see the undercarriage. Then somehow, someway, he wrested the truck back to four wheels, spun out into the road and stopped, its wipers pounding furiously against the rain as the floodlights poured hope into the night.

Oh, dear God. He'd made it. He hadn't died.

Clare gripped her chest against the tightness in her lungs. Her hands were shaking, her legs were weak. She needed to sit down. To recover.

But there was no time. The driver's door opened and out he stepped. Standing behind the range of his floodlights, he was silhouetted against the darkness, his shoulders so wide and dominating he looked like the dark earth itself had brought him to life.

Something inside her leapt with hope at the sight of him, at the sheer, raw strength of his body as he came toward her. This man, this stranger, he was enough. He could help her. Sudden tears burned in her eyes as she finally realized she didn't have to fight this battle by herself.

He held up his hand to tell her to stay, then he slogged over to the front of his truck. He hooked something to the winch, then headed over to the tree. The trunk came almost to his chest, but he locked his grip around a wet branch for leverage, and then vaulted over with effortless grace, landing in the mud with a splash. "Come here," he shouted over the wind.

Clare ran across the muck toward him, stumbling in the slippery footing. "You're crazy!" she shouted, shielding her eyes against the bright floodlights from his truck. But God, she'd never been so happy to see crazy in her life.

"Probably," he yelled back, flashing her a cheeky grin. His perfect white teeth seemed to light up his face, a cheerful confident smile that felt so incongruous in the raging storm and daunting circumstances.

But his cockiness eased her panic, and that was such a gift. It made her able to at least think rationally. She would take all the positive vibes she could get right now.

He held up a nylon harness that was hooked to the steel cord attached to his truck. "If the tree goes over, this will keep you from going over."

She wiped the rain out of her eyes. "What are you talking about?"

"We still have to get you over the tree, and I don't want you climbing it unprotected. Never thought I'd actually be using this stuff. I had it just out of habit." He dropped the harness over her head and began strapping her in with efficient, confident movements. His hands brushed her breasts as he buckled her in, but he didn't seem to notice.

She sure did.

It was the first time a man's hands had touched her breasts in about fifteen years, and it was an unexpected jolt. Something tightened in her belly. Desire? Attraction? An awareness of the fact she was a woman? Dear God, what was wrong with her? She didn't have time for that. Not tonight, and not in her life. But she couldn't take her gaze off his strong jaw and dark eyes as he focused intently on the harness he was strapping around her.

"I'm taking you across to my truck," he said, "and then we're going to get your daughter and the others."

"We are?" She couldn't stop the sudden flood of tears. "You're going to help me get them?"

He nodded as he snapped the final buckle. "Yeah. I gotta get into heaven somehow, and this might do it."

"Thank you!" She threw herself at him and wrapped her arms around him, clinging to her savior. She had no idea who he was, but he'd just successfully navigated a sheer mud cliff for her and her daughter, and she would so take that gift right now.

For an instant, he froze, and she felt his hard body start to pull away. Then suddenly, in a shift so subtle she didn't even see it happen, his body relaxed and his arms went around her, locking her down in an embrace so powerful she felt like the world had just stopped. She felt like the rain had ceased and the wind had quieted, buffeted aside by the strength and power of his body.

"It's going to be okay." His voice was low and reassuring in her ear, his lips brushing against her as he spoke. "She's going to be fine."

Crushed against this stranger's body, protected by his arms, soothed by the utter confidence in his voice, the terror that had been stalking her finally eased away. "Thank you," she whispered.

"You're welcome."

There was a hint of emotion in his voice, and she pulled back far enough to look at him. His eyes were dark, so dark she couldn't tell if they were brown or black, but she could see the torment in his expression. His jaw was angular, and his face was shadowed by the floodlights. He was a man with weight in his heart. She felt it right away. Instinctively, she laid a hand on his cheek. "You're a gift."

He flashed another smile, and for a split second, he put his hand over hers, holding it to his whiskered cheek as if she were some angel of mercy come to give him relief. Her throat thickened, and for a moment, everything else vanished. It was just them, drenched and cold on a windy mountain road, the only warmth was their hands, clasped together against his cheek.

His eyes darkened, then he cleared his throat suddenly and released her hand, jerking her back to the present. "Wait until you see whether I can pull it off," he said, his voice low and rough, sending chills of awareness rippling down her spine. "Then you can reevaluate that compliment." He tugged on the harness. "Ready?"

She gripped the cold nylon, suddenly nervous. Was she edgy because she was about to climb over a tree that could careen into the gully while she was on it, or was it due to intensity of the sudden heat between them? God, she hoped it was the first one. Being a wimp was so much less dangerous than noticing a man like him. "Aren't you wearing one?"

He quirked a smile at her, a jaunty grin that melted one more piece of her thundering heart. "I only have one, and ladies always get first dibs. Besides, I'm a good climber. If the tree takes me over, I'll find my way back up. Always do." He set his foot on a lower branch and patted his knee. "A one-of-a-kind step ladder. Hop up, Ms.—?" He paused, leaving the question hovering in the storm.

"Clare." She set her muddy boot on his knee, and she grimaced apologetically when the mud glopped all over his jeans. "Clare Gray." She grabbed a branch and looked at him. "And you are?"

"Griffin Friesé." He set his hand on her hip to steady her, his grip strong and solid. "Let's go save some kids, shall we?"

Select List of Other Books by Stephanie Rowe

(For a complete book list, please visit WWW.STEPHANIEROWE.COM)

PARANORMAL ROMANCE

The Order of the Blade Series

Darkness Awakened (Book One)
Darkness Seduced (Book Two)
Darkness Surrendered (Book Three)
Forever in Darkness (Book Four, Novella)
Darkness Reborn (Book Five)
Darkness Arisen (Book Six)
Darkness Unleashed (Book Seven)
Inferno of Darkness (Book Eight, Novella)
Available November 2013
Darkness Possessed (Book Nine)
Available Early 2014

The Ruined Lords Series

Guardian of the Hidden (Book One)
Available 2014
Seeker of the Lost (Book Two)
Release Date TBD

The Soulfire Series

Kiss at Your Own Risk (Book One)
Touch if You Dare (Book Two)
Hold Me if You Can (Book Three)

The Immortally Sexy Series

Date Me Baby, One More Time (Book One)
Must Love Dragons (Book Two)
He Loves Me, He Loves Me Hot (Book Three)
Sex & the Immortal Bad Boy (Book Four)

ROMANTIC SUSPENSE

The Alaska Heat Series

Ice (Book One)
Chill (Book Two)
Ghost (Book Three)
Available Late 2013

CONTEMPORARY ROMANCE

EVER AFTER SERIES

No Knight Needed (Book One)
Fairytale Not Required (Book Two)
Prince Charming Can Wait (Book Three)
Available October 2013
The Knight Who Brought Chocolate (Book Four)
Available 2014

STAND ALONE NOVELS

Jingle This!

NONFICTION

The Feel Good Life

FOR TEENS

A GIRLFRIEND'S GUIDE TO BOYS SERIES

Putting Boys on the Ledge (Book One)
Studying Boys (Book Two)
Who Needs Boys? (Book Three)
Smart Boys & Fast Girls (Book Four)

STAND ALONE NOVELS

The Fake Boyfriend Experiment

FOR PRE-TEENS

THE FORGOTTEN SERIES

Penelope Moonswoggle, The Girl Who Could Not Ride a Dragon
(Book One)
Penelope Moonswoggle & the Accidental Doppelganger (Book Two)
Release Date TBD

STEPHANIE ROWE BIO

Four-time RITA® Award nominee and Golden Heart® Award winner Stephanie Rowe is a nationally bestselling author with more than twenty published books with major New York publishers such as Grand Central, HarperCollins, Harlequin, Dorchester and Sourcebooks.

She has received coveted starred reviews from Booklist and high praise from Publisher's Weekly, calling out her "...snappy patter, goofy good humor and enormous imagination... [a] genre-twister that will make readers...rabid for more." Stephanie's work has been nominated as YALSA Quick Pick for Reluctant Readers.

Stephanie writes romance (paranormal, contemporary and romantic suspense), teen fiction, middle grade fiction and motivational nonfiction.

A former attorney, Stephanie lives in Boston where she plays tennis, works out and is happily writing her next book. Want to learn more? Visit Stephanie online at one of the following hot spots:

WWW.STEPHANIEROWE.COM
HTTP://TWITTER.COM/STEPHANIEROWE2
HTTPS://WWW.FACEBOOK.COM/STEPHANIEROWEAUTHOR

Made in United States
Orlando, FL
02 August 2022

20497432R00154